FALCON

2—

Niki hissed through his teeth. "Bring me what's there."

Harris came back with a needle tab and put it in his hand. Niki slapped the point through his shirt to the vein in his armpit. He was ready for the convulsion, which didn't make it any more bearable. When it was over, he lay flat on the floor, panting.

"You're a junkie," Harris said. His voice was flat on the archaic word.

Niki wanted to raise himself on an elbow. Just now, that was beyond him. "I am a gestalt pilot," he said, with more anger than he could control. "I have a rebuilt nervous system, an unrecognizable metabolism, a connect port on each wrist and a port in the back of my skull, and an addiction to the drug that makes it all work. That's what a gestalt pilot *is*. Don't call me names for being what you've paid me to be."

FALCON

EMMA BULL

ACE BOOKS, NEW YORK

This book is an Ace original edition,
and has never been previously published.

FALCON

An Ace Book / published by arrangement with
the author and the author's agent, Valerie Smith.

PRINTING HISTORY
Ace edition / October 1989

ISBN: 0-441-22569-1

Ace Books are published by The Berkley Publishing Group,
200 Madison Avenue, New York, New York 10016.
The name "Ace" and the "A" logo
are trademarks belonging to Charter Communications, Inc.

PRINTED IN THE UNITED STATES OF AMERICA

10 9 8 7 6 5 4 3 2 1

To Will

For the members of the Interstate
Writers' Workshop . . .

For the alchemists who are Cats
Laughing . . .

For Jane Yolen, who all unwittingly
turned this book on its head . . .

For Jon Singer, who tied off loose
threads at high altitude . . . and Gordon
Garb, who did the same on the
ground . . .

And for Cyn Horton, who knows the
characters herein and some of their
friends . . .

. . . The author is truly grateful.

I❖ EYAS

... That twenty centuries of stony sleep
Were vexed to nightmare by a rocking
    cradle,
And what rough beast, its hour come round
    at last,
Slouches towards Bethlehem to be born?
               —William Butler Yeats,
                  "The Second Coming"

CHAPTER ONE

Some violent bitter man, some powerful man
Called architect and artist in, that they,
Bitter and violent men, might rear in stone
The sweetness that all longed for night and day,
The gentleness none there had ever known;
But when the master's buried mice can play,
And maybe the great-grandson of that house,
For all its bronze and marble, 's but a mouse.
—William Butler Yeats,
"Meditations in Time of Civil War"

The sky was low and gray and looked hard enough to ring if struck. It mocked the blue he meant to remember. The sand he sat on was damp and cold; that was mockery, too. The wind pulled his hair and slapped it against his face. He drew his coat closed over his knees, then wrapped his arms over that, hugging his own warmth. The sound of the sea battered him, the windy rush of the surf and the hoarse whining of gulls.

A voice behind him made him start. "Saying good-bye, Nik?"

Jacob Kelling squatted next to him. Jacob wouldn't sit, unthinking, on the cold sand; he always knew already what Niki found out the hard way. A cap hid most of his ginger hair, and dust-colored thermalskins camouflaged the drawn strength of him, made it look like mere thinness.

"Hullo, Jacob. Storing it up for the winter, I guess."

Jacob squinted into the cast-aluminum sky. "You're storing this? Thanks, I'd rather remember it as it was yesterday. Your Rhiannon's a bit of a bitch."

"No, it's Cerridwen for the seasons. Death and rebirth, remember?"

"So much for my command of classic Celtic poetry."

"Besides, I like it stormy." Niki pulled a strand of his black hair out of his mouth and scowled at it. "I was going to cut this before we left."

"After you spent the summer growing it out?"

"I'll get tired of Uncle Pedr calling me The Artist. Better to cut it straight away and spoil his fun."

Jacob dug a stone out of the sand and threw it left-handed. It marred the glassy hump of a wave. "You let him bully you."

"Not in anything that matters."

"No. Anything that matters, you hide from him."

Niki weighed cool silence and found it wanting. "And because of it, we all live in peace."

"You live like a mouse in the wall in your own home," Jacob said, in the perfectly neutral tone he used for insults. "Don't you want to make yourself a place in the family? It'd please Morwenna."

"Would it?" Niki murmured, distracted. "Mother wants something from me. But I don't think that's it." He was aware, after a moment, of Jacob's sideways look. "And don't I already have a place in the family? I thought I was The Odd One."

Jacob gave a little snort, of amusement or disgust.

"Anyway," Niki went on, "Caernarfon's never seemed much like home."

"You don't like the city?"

"I like it very well. I meant the Castle."

"What, seventy-odd rooms, and none of 'em up to your standards?" said Jacob. Then he asked, "Or do you just want it to yourself?"

"To myself?" Niki echoed blankly.

"History's full of nephews with ambition."

Niki stared, appalled. "You don't mean that."

"Why shouldn't I? Haven't you ever thought you'd do a better job than Pedr, if you had the chance?" Jacob's face under his cap brim was one he used at the chess board: intense and blank.

Then the absurdity of it caught Niki up, and he laughed. "God forbid, Jacob. What the hell kind of prince would I make? No, if Pedr's not enough, then there's Rhys, *and* Kitty's got an heir in the oven. I think I'm safe."

"Don't be crude," Jacob said, but the intensity had left him.

"Kitty wouldn't mind."

"You can bet Pedr would."

"I thought you wanted me to stand up to Pedr?"

"Damned idiot. If Caernarfon's not home, what is, then?"

Niki smiled and waved broadly. "This will do."

Jacob snorted. "You wouldn't say so in winter, with no heat in the beach house."

"Sometimes there's none to be had in Caernarfon."

They watched a redheaded gull plane down and snatch something at the tide line. A wave struck high enough to sting their faces with spray. A salt lizard, like a little ambulatory seaweed bladder, shot out of a pile of rock and scrabbled furiously down the sand and into the sea.

"How's Olwen?" Niki asked.

"Fine."

He didn't know how to ask what he wanted, but he tried. "She hasn't thrown me over, has she?"

"Wouldn't you be the first to know?"

"I haven't sent her word in a while."

"How long a while?"

Niki sighed. He'd brought the subject up himself. "About two months."

"You spend every free minute riding the 'board, and you can't use it to send your lass a note?"

"She'll say that, too."

"Well, you'll have something to patch up, won't you?"

"Is she angry?"

"She wouldn't say so to me."

He'd been prepared to leave a message to her; he'd even opened the 'board to do it more than once. But all the things he'd wanted to share with Olwen had deserted him when the panel lit up. All the words he'd meant to use were thin and banal when they hung at the ends of his fingers. He'd thought of her, instead. He'd imagined her beside him when he swam or ran on the beach, wondered what her pale hair would look like in the moonlight on the beach house deck. He'd let her memory haunt him. After so much time, he hoped he was in love with more than her memory. "Is there any future in this?" Niki said at last.

He thought for a moment that Jacob was upset—but the quirk of features that had made him think so was gone.

"In what?"

"Olwen and me."

"Why shouldn't there be?"

"I'm . . . not sure." Niki shook his head. "It's just the prospect of going back to the Castle, I suppose. It seems as if my life is out of my hands when I'm there.''

Jacob stared at the sky as if reading. "No fault of yours, I'm sure.''

That made him angry, of course. And the heat of it put a glowing edge on the self-pity at the heart of his anger, made it show up clearly. Had he done wrong, in avoiding friction with Pedr? Had he himself given his life into the keeping of others? He shook his head and grinned. "I missed you, too, Jacob.''

Jacob's lips twitched, but he said only, "I should point out that that's your best coat you're mucking up.''

"I'll live without it.''

"And that the damned airship leaves in half an hour, and I've no intention of staying here again tonight.''

Niki rose and brushed sand off the coat. He turned toward the beach house, nestled in the sea-poplars on the slope above him. It seemed too clearly drawn to be real—everything did. He saw in the gray sky uncountable hues, felt the sand in single grains beneath his feet. It was a pain beyond bearing. For one anxious instant he was certain the whole scene would burst apart, rain down in sparkling cinders, and be lost forever. Then the conviction passed, and he could breathe again, and move. He was free to walk up the beach and leave it all.

"You coming?" Jacob said.

Niki bowed his head and followed him.

Restlessness swept the airship's first-class lounge, like sound vibrating an eardrum, well before the captain announced their approach to Caernarfon field. Passengers began to gather scattered belongings, fuss with hair and clothes, chatter to seatmates. Children ran to stare out the windows; their parents, moved by the same nervous energy, snapped at them to sit down.

Niki folded the 'board closed, but left it on his lap. If he put it back in his coat pocket the trip would be over.

Jacob sat across the cabin in a recliner, legs crossed, cap pulled down to the bridge of his bird-of-prey nose. Jacob was immune to unwarranted restlessness. He would fasten his harness at the chime; he would lay hands on his one bag when the time came to carry it off the ship, and not an instant before.

Niki couldn't tell if the mood sweeping the cabin had affected his mother. She always seemed about to do something, never sat quiet. She tossed her head now, making her smooth black hair swing, and rolled her shoulders.

"Stiff?" Niki asked, though he thought not; she'd come back from a walk to the bridge only a minute ago.

She darted a quick, sheepish look at him. "I don't know how you can sit so quiet. I thought you were related to me?"

"I try to live it down," he said, smiling. In fact, they could pass for brother and sister. Morwenna's blue-black hair, so like his own, was barely stranded with white. Her taut, carved features never seemed to age, and those same features in his own face made him look closer to twenty-five than nineteen. He tapped a finger on the folded 'board. "Did you read Damion's article on controlled mutagens?"

She folded her legs under her. "Um. Did you?"

"I got two screens past the summary before he lost me. I should stick to numbers."

"So should he," Morwenna said firmly. "He's an awful writer, anyway."

"Didn't you work with Damion once?"

She almost smiled; he could see it. "Once."

"Another partnership come to a messy end."

That made her break, at last, and she threw back her head and freed the cracking laughter he liked so much. "God, can you tell that from reading a monograph?"

"Well, you're the next thing to an anarchist, in anything to do with research. And he wants a regulatory agency under New Oxford's control. . . ."

"Did you read the rebuttals?"

"Not yet."

"Dr. M. Glyndwr-Jones makes snide remarks about his administrative background."

Niki shook his head. "You know, if you go on like this, no one will so much as share a lab with you."

"It may come to that," his mother said.

"I was joking."

She smiled. "So was I."

And maybe she was. "Anyone meeting us?"

"Your brother, I expect. Maybe we'll stop for dinner in the city."

He wanted to say something about welcoming the delay, but didn't. There was no point in laying the weight of his discontent on her shoulders. And for all he knew, she was no more eager to reach the Castle than he was.

The airship was sinking through the clouds; outside Niki's window, they parted, fragmented, to show him a glimpse of the river delta. River Dyfed into Cystennin Bay into the Meridian Ocean. Who decided which was which, and when the water changed its name? As well name the masses of cloud. As heir to Cymru, should he delight in the cadence of those names? *They give names to craters on barren moons,* he thought. *I suppose I'm a poor excuse for an heir.*

"Niki," she said, and something in Morwenna's voice made him look up. "You're going offworld at the beginning of the year."

A stab of fear—but no, she wouldn't have any part in taking that from him. Pedr might, if he decided that a pilot would be an insufficient ornament to the family dignity. Even Rhys, if Pedr wanted it badly enough, might regretfully suggest to Niki that four years in the College of Navigation on Galatea was an inappropriate use of his time. But his mother would never rob him of his chance to get away. "The enrollment's been confirmed," he said carefully. "They're saving me a place."

"Maybe," she said, and stopped. And said, "Maybe you should think about going early."

Then the warning chime sounded, and the pleasant, artificial voice said things about harnesses, and smoking, and identification. By the time he could speak again, she was staring out the windows on the opposite side of the cabin. Something in the set of her shoulders kept him quiet.

His mother led the way out of the lounge. Jacob rose, hung his overnight bag from his shoulder, and stepped into the aisle. He moved, Niki thought, as if the other passengers were holograms, and he avoided walking through them out of exaggerated courtesy to their designer.

"Don't let me rush you," he said.

Niki shrugged and went before him off the ship and into the mooring tower.

It was late afternoon; sunlight slanted red-gold through the lancet windows, washed the high white vaulted ceiling, and set fire to the red dragon banners that hung from the beams. The dragon was inlaid in tile on the floor as well, but that was lost beneath the feet of arriving and departing passengers and the people meeting or seeing them off. A sound compression system kept noise from bouncing off the hard surfaces, and turned the racket of the crowd into a comfortable hubbub. The Caernarfon mooring towers were some of the most beautiful architecture on Cymru, more lovely than all but the public areas of the Castle—certainly more lovely than the worldport terminal on the other side of the city. Cymru, secure in its isolationism, greeted offworlders with a flat, bland face, and reserved the best of its art for itself.

Niki put his wrist to the scanner at the gate and let it read his embed. Behind him, Jacob did the same. Niki looked over Morwenna's dark head, studying the faces of the people waiting for other disembarking passengers, and saw a white hand wave, caught a glimpse of a rippling cap of golden hair. His heart—cliché-loving organ—leaped.

"Excuse," he said to his mother and Jacob, and slipped deftly out of the queue. "Olwen!" he called. And she was there, elbowing rudely toward him, grinning. For a moment she only stood and looked pleased; then she threw her arms around him, and he lifted her and kissed her on the lips.

"You're not very tan," she said.

"I never am. Where are your freckles?"

"It's been a lousy summer."

"Told you you should have come with me."

"I missed you," she said.

He saw her, by the glamour of four months apart, as a familiar stranger. The enormous eyes and pointed chin were Olwen's, the rose-colored wide mouth, the bone-china skin. But he needed to become accustomed to them again before he could put them comfortably together with the woman he'd left in Caernarfon. "I missed you, too. How'd you know we were coming?"

"Well, certainly not from you," she said, but something in her face held out a hope of forgiveness. "I bullied Rhys into bringing me along."

"Poor Rhys."

" 'Poor Rhys,' indeed," said his older brother, and Niki looked up from Olwen and found Rhys by his side. They shared a rough hug.

"You look good," Niki said. His brother's open, handsome face, the ruddy brown hair and gray eyes, were also made strange with time. Niki felt a pang of belated homesickness.

"So do you," said Rhys. "I like your hair."

"Uncle Pedr won't."

Rhys shrugged. "You go off to Galatea at the new year."

Niki smiled at him, and at Olwen, whose arm was around his waist. "Maybe I'll leave it, then."

"What about your mother?" Morwenna said behind him. "A handshake at least?"

Rhys caught her up in his arms. "Hullo, Mama. Good flight?"

"It drove me crazy, and you knew I'd say so. Hello, Olwen."

"Hello, Lady G. Glad you're back."

Morwenna snorted. "Well, you're glad Niki's back, and I come with the package. Children, if I don't get dinner soon I'll expire at your feet."

By then Jacob had pressed through the crowd. "If she falls down, I'll carry her," he said. "Take your time."

"On second thought," said Morwenna, "I've been hungrier than this and lived."

Everyone laughed, and followed after her toward the down tube. But Niki thought he had heard some constraint in the banter. He knew that for all her quick humor and easy ways, his mother kept her deepest thoughts to herself, her strongest emotions out of the light. She was keeping something from them—even from Jacob, most trustworthy of advisors.

He'd fallen behind the others. After a moment Olwen dropped back, too; came and tucked her arm through his. "Come along, treacle-toes," she said, "you're wasting those long legs."

He looked down into her eyes, and felt lightheaded. He'd kept company with this bright-burning creature; his name and hers had been spoken in the same breath. That was surely the best he could expect out of life, that there should be such a wonderful thing in his past. Too much to ask that it should be in his future, too. "Do you think you can forgive me?" he said. It never hurt to ask, even for too much.

She didn't pretend to misunderstand. "You know, I'm not sure? A week ago, I wouldn't have. Now . . . I'm happy you're here, and I'm still mad at you, too. So what happened?"

"I didn't know what to say," he told her, knowing that however true it was, it was no explanation. "Does it help that I didn't send anything to anybody else, either?"

"Is there something wrong with 'Having a bloody grand time, wish you were here'?"

"Nothing, if you don't mind it."

"Well, I don't," she snapped, and then was silent.

At the down tube access he paused, let her go through first. She stepped into the warm air of the drop field, but laid her palm to the wall to hold herself in place. When Niki crossed the threshold she let go, and they dropped slowly side by side.

"Do you remember the Hans Christian Andersen story, about the girl who used a loaf of bread as a stepping-stone in a swamp, and sank into the mud all the way to hell? These things remind me of it."

"Did you think I'd met someone else?" he asked, and wondered why he was dwelling on it.

Olwen stared up at him. "Yes."

"I hadn't."

She turned to watch the passing walls. "If anyone else said that to me, I'd laugh in his face."

"But not me?"

"No. I don't think you'd be *able* to say it if it wasn't true."

"Ah. Well, do you like me anyway?" That brought her eyes back up to his. "I thought straight-arrow types bored women to death."

"Oh, you stupid, *rotten*—" She put her arms around him and hid her face in his coat.

"That's more like it," Niki said. "Come on, let's get off this thing, or we'll be in hell after all."

The ground floor was nearly as busy as the docking level. Jacob had run their baggage slips through the reader and was waiting at the lift hatch for the results. Morwenna stood a little apart, talking to Rhys, looking alternately distracted and intent.

"Do you know if something's troubling Mother?" Niki asked Jacob.

He raised his eyebrows. "I wouldn't think so."

"Does that mean, 'No,' or 'Mind your own business'?"

Jacob grinned. "It means, 'No, but it's not your business anyway.'"

"Touché. Let me know if there's anything I can do."

"There is," Jacob said. He opened the lift hatch, pulled out a suitcase, and handed it to Niki. "Carry this."

Morwenna loved private cars; she said they were one of the few decent things that came of having too much money. Rhys had brought his bronze-brown Langley Tourer, a sober luxury hover. He drove as he did most things, reliably. His mother sat with Rhys in front. Jacob, Olwen, and Niki had the back, with Olwen in the middle. Niki kept his head a little tilted toward hers. The car roof was higher in the middle, after all. She slipped her hand into his where it rested on the seat cushion and smiled at him, as if those clasped hands were a secret.

"How's Kitty?" said Morwenna.

"Pregnant," chorused Rhys, Olwen, and Jacob.

Olwen added, "Her back aches, her feet hurt, she's gained too much weight, she wants a glass of wine, and she asks all the women she knows when they're going to have babies."

"You're right. She's pregnant."

"Don't tell me you were like that," Niki said.

"Well, I didn't want a glass of wine."

It was difficult to imagine Morwenna consumed by maternity. Not that she wasn't the best of mothers; she simply wasn't maternal. Kitty, however, was probably gloriously, perfectly maternal. And perhaps fatherhood would make Pedr easier to live with. He might stop thinking of Niki as one of his heirs, and stop expecting him to behave like one.

He glanced at Olwen, at her lovely crisp profile, at her gold hair curving around her ear, at the slender column of her neck rising from her collar. Then he turned to stare out the window, glad that he never blushed.

The newest portion of the city, the well-planned part, opened out all around them. Apartments rose up the face of a man-made hill, out of a man-made fairy tale forest. A shopping square surrounded an outdoor theater like a cupped hand. A magnetrain station nestled in a formal garden. The CoOpTech Tower, its indigo glass needle of offices rising from an ornamental lake, glittered ahead of them. Beyond that, the skyline of the Old City—

"Is that smoke?" Niki asked.

Rhys answered him. "Big fire last night on Conwy Street. I expect it's from that."

"Good God. Which end? What burned?"

"Some pub or another. I don't know."

"Was anyone hurt?"

"I couldn't say."

"What do you mean, you couldn't say?"

"Bloody Christ, Nik, if you're that hot to find out, I'll stop and get you a newsfax! How should I know? I don't have time for gossip."

"It's your city," Niki said after a moment.

Rhys spared a glance away from the road to frown at Niki. "Well, it's yours, too, isn't it? I suppose you were reading the news every day, all summer, like a dutiful citizen?"

"No." That was well deserved; he hadn't pulled down a news service since he'd left Caernarfon. "But then, if Pedr drops dead, I don't take over."

"Bloody good thing, too. It's no business of Pedr's, and none of mine, what some damned flamer is up to."

Niki felt dread growing slowly in him, like cold air blowing on his neck. "Flamer?"

"Oh, Nik, leave it be!" Rhys snapped. Peaceful, stolid, good-tempered Rhys.

Rhys's shoulders were stiff and his head a little ducked. Olwen was looking sideways at Niki; there was sympathy, and a little embarrassment, in that look, but nothing else. His mother sat quietly beside Rhys—not normal, that. And Jacob had settled back in his corner of the car, his cap pulled down and the shadow of the brim over his eyes. His mouth was hard as bone.

"Rhys, what's amiss?" Niki said gently.

The Langley slowed, stopped. Before it a high-volt grid, blue with charge, stretched across the road, and a woman in police grays waved them to a halt.

"Ow!" Olwen whispered. "Nik, ease off, that hurts."

It was her hand; he let go of it.

"Ident, please," the policewoman said to Rhys. She had an open holster on her belt. Niki couldn't identify the weapon, couldn't tell if it was lethal or not. There were other people in gray at the barrier. One of them had a military issue stock-mounted rocket, more than enough to pierce vehicle armor.

Rhys held out his wrist, and the policewoman read it with a hand scanner. "Oh, Lord Glyndwr. Sorry for the inconvenience. Do you vouch for your party?"

"Yes, Sergeant. Family and friends."

"Very good." She held up a hand, and the twisted blue pattern ahead of them vanished. Rhys drove on into the city.

"What," Niki said at last, "was that?" Because no one spoke immediately, he added, "And don't anyone say, 'A roadblock.' "

"Pity," Jacob said. "It is, you know." Niki wished he could see his face.

"You haven't read the news, have you?" said Rhys.

"No."

"It's a few damned unemployed malcontents. CoOpTech closed a few plants, and this lot blame the government for it. Summer nonsense—they'll get tired of hanging out in the street when winter comes."

"Rhys, what *kind* of nonsense?"

"Some demonstrations. They've set a couple of fires. Your Conwy Street business might have been one of them."

"And the roadblock?"

"We just want to know where everyone is. Keep this from spreading outside the city, keep agitators out."

Niki stared. When his voice came back, he said, "What's next, Rhys? Curfew? Martial law? Armoreds patrolling the streets?"

From his corner, Jacob laughed.

"Don't blow this out of proportion, Nik," Rhys replied. "It's just what they want."

How had so much changed in four months? Four months of glorious, irresponsible isolation—there wasn't even a vid downlink at the beach house. But had his mother not known?

He turned from the car window and found Morwenna watching him from the front seat. Sorrow and shame; he saw those expressions so rarely on her face that he almost missed them, before she looked away. She'd known.

The rest of the drive stretched Niki's nerves like crepe paper. One more thing and they'd tear, drift out of his hands in a sort of artificial slow motion. Still, he observed the city they passed through with a ruthless disregard for his own feelings. A fury built up in him that was as much despair as it was anger. He thought it would throttle him.

They crossed two more checkpoints. Drifting smoke, smelling of things that shouldn't be burning, dulled the color of the sky. The police traveled in groups of three, and were everywhere—except where the blue jacket and trousers of army uniforms appeared instead. He saw those uniforms, saw the armored troop cars they rode in, and understood why Jacob had laughed.

There were guns. The police had replaced their billy clubs with them, with the oily blue sheen of dark metal and the smooth dull black of cast resin handgrips. Niki imagined them heavier than the target pistols he'd handled, weighted down with their meaning and their intended use.

And he felt every piece of damage, every wound on the city, as if it were in his own body. *So I can think like an heir to Cymru. Damned fine time to discover it.* Then: *How can Rhys bear to see this?* Smoke smeared the heat-warped walls of a burnt-out building, in strokes above the windows like shadowed eyelids. The window eyes looked at him, waiting for a remedy.

Did Rhys understand their message? Had Pedr, who was Prince and caretaker of all this, seen what Niki saw now?

The army stood guard at the hard, polished jewel that was Caernarfon Castle, in dress red-and-blue with scatterguns on their shoulders. A sergeant saluted as the car pulled up in the curving drive, then stepped forward to open the front passenger door for Morwenna. He might have opened doors for everyone, but Niki and Jacob didn't wait to see. As Jacob slung luggage out of the boot, Olwen laughed and said, "Don't I get to carry any?" Niki looked up in wonder at the laugh. The place in himself where laughter came from felt like a lump of chalk.

Jacob headed toward the guard station at the foot of the drive. The rest of them went up the polished green half-circle of stairs, to the double doors of golden glass sunk into the great central tower. The baritone voice of the security system said, "Good afternoon, Lady Glyndwr, Lord Glyndwr, Lord Harlech, Ms. Llangwyn—"

"Has someone been at your programming again?" Morwenna sighed as she let it read her wrist. The security system did not understand, and did not reply. "First name, no honorific."

"Yes, Morwenna."

"Me, too," said Niki, offering his wrist.

"Yes, Dominic."

"Pardon me. Make that Niki."

"You don't have to beg pardon of a computer," Rhys said, a little sharply.

"Better to do it when I don't have to, than forget to when it's important."

Rhys shook his head and walked into the Castle.

The Great Hall was an echoing glass-topped cylinder three stories high. There was a spiral of golden glass balcony that climbed the walls in a glittering helix of stairs and ramps and platforms. The floor of the hall was malachite green, sunk three steps below entry level, and seemed to take years to walk across. Even in summer, the room had the impersonal chill of a morgue table. But it was very grand.

The sound of Kitty preceded her across the room: her footsteps, and her light voice that called to Niki's mind particular sorts of flowers and pleasantly hot afternoons. " 'Wenna! Niki! Welcome home." In spite of her round belly, she scudded across the expanse of green floor like a leaf on the wind. An autumn leaf—she wore a high-necked dress of red-gold, which dropped in a flood of tiny pleats from the yoke to the wide hem, from the shoulders to the long cuffs.

She clasped Morwenna's hands and beamed at her. Then she turned to Niki, stood on tiptoe, and kissed his jaw, which was as high as she could reach.

"Hullo, Kit, old thing," Niki said, hugging her shoulders. "Did you miss me?"

"No, you conceited punk."

"What? You found someone to shoe your pretty little feet?"

"I had to," Kitty said mournfully. "*I* can't see 'em."

"I'd best get back to business," Rhys said. He patted Niki on the shoulder, and Niki felt the apology in it. "See you all at dinner, eh?"

"You work too much!" Kitty shouted after him. The affronted walls echoed her voice. To Niki and Morwenna, she said, "It's awfully good to have you back."

Her skin was clear and pink-tinted; her brown hair gleamed. "You look well," Niki said, feeling as if he ought to say something else.

"Thank you, sir. But do I look good?"

"Oh, always."

"Kitty," said Olwen, "stop flirting with my lad." She wrapped an arm around Niki's waist and grinned up at him.

Morwenna said, "We'll take our bags up, Kitty, and be right back down. Where shall we meet you?"

"I'll take them," Niki offered. "You go chat."

Kitty laughed. "You're just afraid of the girl talk."

He watched them leave the hall, then caught Olwen's hand. "You know, those are the best words in the language?"

"Which ones?"

" 'My lad.' "

"Rubbish. I know lots better ones. And I'd say them for you, but the parents expect me back. Call me later?"

"Mmm." He kissed her. "Need a ride home?"

"I'll walk." She ran up the three steps to the door, turned, and blew him a kiss. "I love you!" she called softly, and bolted out the door.

He stood for a long time staring after her. She was right; she did know some better words. An evening with Olwen might almost drive the city's pain out of him. Almost.

He shouldered the bags and headed for the lift.

CHAPTER TWO

What tumbling cloud did you cleave,
Yellow-eyed hawk of the mind,
Last evening?
                    —W. B. Yeats, "The Hawk"

Niki paused for a moment outside the rooms he thought of as his. He expected anything on the other side of the door—neglect, chaos, decay, destruction. The relief he felt when he opened it was itself a kind of shock. It was only the sitting room, just as it ought to be. The high, milk-white walls and the shining dark floor, the sitting room rug like a pond reflecting an overcast sky. Two dark red softform chairs, a desk with built-in 'board and one locking drawer, a slightly outdated batch of a/v components, and a cupboard full of paper, bound and unbound. On the wall, mounted under a sheet of glass, were the engineering drawings for the pilot's cell of the Aioki C-13 Cheatship. The double doors to the bedroom stood open, and he could see the end of the bed with its red-and-gray coverlet.

He dropped his coat and bag at the edge of the rug and went to the long window. It was flung wide, and the curtains drawn back. After a summer of fending for himself, it seemed odd that someone should have been here before him, airing his room, making up the bed. Did it seem odd to his mother? Was four months enough to make her forget years of being waited on? Or was he the only alien in the whole great pile?

Like any good castle, Caernarfon commanded the high ground of the city, though that was its only fortresslike attribute. From the window Niki could see rooftops dropping away. The near ones were slate and tile and scale-patterned metal in many colors, gorgeous with gables and dormers. Farther down the hill there were roofs of composite shakes and seamed plastic panels. They mixed with commercial structures until by the bottom of the hill Niki could see only the basic geometry of the city, buildings like the etchings of antique circuitry.

He could see the smoke—not a plume, but a sullen smudging of the sky, like a smeary thumbprint. Like someone burning trash. The area was right for Conwy.

There was an all-night tea shop on Conwy Street that smelled of bergamot and bread. Olwen liked to go to it, after a night out, to watch the sun come up and the day people come in for breakfast before work. He'd sit across from her, his eyes burning and his head clogged with a thick residue of pale ale and cigarette smoke, and stare. Her precious-metal hair in the artificial light made him witless; her bright gaze, full of mischief when she'd look over the rim of her cup and see him watching, melted everything beneath his skin.

Conwy Street. There was a dance hall there (where she'd worn black metal sequins and bride-white satin, and a hundred heads had turned to watch them dance) and a gaming palace (he'd won the C-13 drawings from an offworld pilot at the Nightbreaker console, while she'd slouched at his shoulder like a gangster's moll) and a fortune teller (the holo had raised an eyebrow and said, "You've got youth, looks, health, and you're in love. What the hell do you want from *me*?").

Niki wondered what Rhys thought of when Conwy Street came to mind.

The housecom chimed, and Housekeeping said softly, "Lord Harlech?"

"Niki, please," he corrected. His mother was right; someone had been tidying up. He wondered if Pedr had ordered it done as soon as they'd left.

"Niki. His Highness would like to see you as soon as possible."

Not "your uncle," but "His Highness." Had he already set

Pedr's back up? "My compliments to His Highness," Niki said carefully. "I'll come now. Where is he?"

"In his study."

"Thank you." So much for a summer's worth of peace.

Anything called a "study" ought to have been small, unpretentious—even cozy. But Caernarfon Castle defied coziness in its every line. Pedr's study was an echoing tube of a room in one of the towers, with a glass roof that sliced diagonally through the walls like a knife through the stem of a plant. It was decorated in pale turquoise and silver-gray, and would have been a delightful room in the tropics. Niki fought, as always, against the urge to tiptoe across the glossy bare floor.

He'd weighed possible greetings all the way from his rooms. But Pedr looked up from his tabletop display, and Niki felt the meeting slide out of his grasp. Pedr looked—not older, not ill. He showed his thirty-six years, but no more; there was no weakness in his square face, his square hands. His eyes were red-rimmed, but that was nothing strange in a prince with a troubled capital.

It was as if he had been frightened for a long time, or terribly sick, and now felt reassured, or well; but the effects of fear or illness were still with him. Pedr's face was changed in a way that was outside Niki's experience. He was not sure what words would reach a man who wore such a face. Pedr had a prescription inhaler of something in his hands; Niki couldn't read the label. Pedr held it as if he'd forgotten it was there. The gold ring on Pedr's finger, the signet of Cymru, glowed dully in the indirect light.

"Hello, Uncle," Niki said. His bow was uncertain.

"If I hadn't sent for you, would you have bothered to tell me you were back?"

"Yes, of course." When Pedr said nothing, Niki added, "Have you seen Mother already?"

"I don't expect it of your mother. I expect it of you."

Niki wondered if by "it," he meant a prompt appearance in the study. He decided not to ask. "I didn't mean to keep you waiting. We only got in a few minutes ago."

Pedr leaned his elbows on the gray glass of the tabletop and set the inhaler down. "A little over thirty of them, in fact. Who have you spoken to?"

". . . Spoken to?"

"Since you arrived in Caernarfon," he said harshly.

Things were terribly wrong here. His dealings with Pedr had always been flavored with conflict—but this was a different sort. "May I sit down?" Niki asked at last.

"No. Answer me."

"All right. Rhys, who fetched us from the airfield. Olwen, who came with him. And Kitty—she met us in the Great Hall. Oh, and Security and Housekeeping. Now may I sit down?"

"Kitty," Pedr said as if to himself. His jaw worked. "Where did you go this summer?"

"You know perfectly well. To the beach house."

"What did you do?"

Niki clasped his hands behind him as if reciting. "I sat on the beach, I walked on the beach, I rode on the beach, and every now and again I went into the village to do the errands. Pedr, is something wrong?"

Stupid question. His first impression, he realized, had been wide of the mark—Pedr's looks hadn't really changed much since spring. It was the way he moved his face, used his hands, as if he wasn't comfortable with them, as if they hurt him. He twisted the ring round and round on his finger. He didn't seem any more conscious of it than he had of the inhaler. Niki pitied him suddenly. "Can I help?" he asked.

Pedr turned cold, fierce eyes on him, and Niki had time to realize that he'd said the wrong thing. "You'd like that, wouldn't you? You'd fancy seeing everything in shambles around me, so you could ride in, young Viscount Harlech on a white horse, and take credit for setting it to rights."

"Pedr—" said Niki, appalled.

"Well, it's not a shambles yet, my lad. So you can bloody well stand off, and whatever jackals you run with, keep them off as well."

"Pedr, what you're saying—"

"Get out of here."

"—isn't true."

"Out!"

Niki stood his ground. "What am I accused of?"

Pedr breathed deeply, rubbed his temples, and looked almost like the himself-that-was. "I don't know. So damned much going badly, no idea where it's all coming from. . . ." He scowled. "I've fewer people I can trust than I have fingers on one hand. And you're not one of them, boy. So watch how you go."

"Yes, sir," Niki said, since he couldn't think of anything else to say.

"Now get out."

Well, he thought when he was on the other side of the door, *at least he didn't mention my hair.*

He wandered toward the public areas of the Castle with no destination in mind. Which had come first, the turmoil in the principality, or the change in its prince? Niki leaned toward the latter choice, but he knew his biases. Was there anyone in all this who wasn't biased?

No. But the next best thing was at hand: someone whose prejudices ought to run counter to his own.

He turned to the housecom input on the wall. "Housekeeping. Where do I find Kitty?"

"I'm sorry, Niki, I don't know who that is."

"Bloody hell," he muttered. "Where do I find Her Highness?"

Kitty was on the terrace outside the gallery. She still wore the autumn-colored dress, and the fine pleating of the sleeves and body moved in the breeze like foliage, trembling and shining. She looked up from the dappled stars of the tiger lilies as he came through the glass doors. "Niki," she said, sounding pleased.

"No, don't get up," he said quickly when he saw her brace her hands on the marble bench. "Or . . . should you be out here at all? Aren't you cold?"

She cocked her head. "Are you?"

"No."

"Then why do you think I might be? Silly ass. Pregnant women aren't another species."

"Now what do I know about pregnant women?"

"You tell me, bad boy."

Niki laughed, and she patted the stone beside her. "Have a seat."

"Really, though, how are you, Kit?"

"Fine. I'm healthy as the devil himself, and the pregnancy's flat normal. If it weren't mine, I'd say it was bloody boring. It's a boy, by the way."

"That makes Pedr happy, I suppose."

Kitty gave him a long look. "My, but we sound casual. Yes, he's happy. It's Pedr you want to talk about, then?"

Now that the subject was raised, Niki wasn't sure how to

pursue it. He stared blankly at the view over the gardens. "Has he been sick?" he blurted out at last.

"No. Why?"

He sighed, and told her the text, as close as he could remember it, of the scene in Pedr's study. He found some of the things hard to say out loud. Harder, when he saw Kitty's distress.

She folded her hands over her stomach. "He knows it's not true."

"That what's not true?"

"The thing that he's being careful not to say," she replied with considerable asperity. "That you're helping to plot the ruin of his government."

He thought it would sound better if someone else said it. It didn't. "Have I given him any reason to mistrust me?"

She thought for so long that it made Niki nervous. "Probably. But whether anyone else would think he had reason . . ." She shrugged. "It's because you seem so much older than you are, I think. And you're so independent of us all. And so . . ."

"Different," Niki supplied.

Kitty looked apologetic. "Well, yes. He doesn't understand you, you know. His notions of loyalty have to do with family, and tradition, and—oh, God, I suppose a sort of latter-day divine right of kings."

Niki snorted. When she raised her eyebrows, he said, "I'm sorry. It's just hard to conceive of divine right for someone who used to have acne and be afraid to talk to girls."

"That's just what I mean. You're utterly loyal, but your loyalty has nothing to do with *him*. You're loyal to some damned romantic ideal of the Crown."

"Isn't that enough?" Niki asked, stung.

"Yes. But Pedr doesn't know that. So he's afraid."

"He's afraid," said Niki, feeling weighed down by the words as he spoke them, "that I love the Crown enough to want to wear it."

Kitty only pressed her lips together.

"What about Rhys? Do I, perhaps, love the Crown more than my brother? He's next in line, after all. Shall I step over my brother's dead body to get it?"

"Well, don't shout at me over—"

"Speaking of you, what about the junior prince, there? Doesn't he stand in my way, too?" The fire went out of him suddenly, and he pressed his hands over his face. "Hell, Kit, he'd have me wading in blood. No one would believe it. It's madness.''

He felt her hand between his shoulder blades, rubbing his back. "Of course it is. You're a perfect rabbit, and everyone knows it.''

"Oh, thank you," he said, but it made him smile. "Tell me, Kitty, how is it that Pedr doesn't understand me, and you do so well?"

She shrugged. "Maybe you're more like me than like him."

"I'm exactly like my mother. Everyone says so."

"No," she said, smiling. "Only in looks."

The entire episode should have plunged him into despair. Instead he sprawled in a chair in his sitting room, fighting a restless buzz of energy. There was a seductive power in information; he had a little, and craved more. What if he *could* help fix the chaos he'd come home to? Not as Viscount Harlech on a white horse—he'd have to keep his head down, and turn the credit over to Pedr, or Rhys, or Jacob.

He stared out the window. There were ribbons of sunset over the city now—hot orange, red-violet, marine blue streaked with pink. If Caernarfon's troubles were a tangle of string, and Pedr one frayed end, then the other end must lie out there, in the streets, under the rooftops. Why not work from both ends at once?

He bounded out of his chair and dropped into another at his desk. He folded out the 'board and lit it, whistled his passcode. "Call Olwen," he told it.

And in a minute she was there, a hotspot of light at the crown of her hair, a smudge of shadow under her nose. "Long time no see," she said.

"Do you want to keep it that way?"

"Perish the thought."

"Then what do you say to a night on the town?"

Emotions chased across her face: surprise, pleasure, alarm. "I . . . don't know. Since the trouble started . . ."

"Exactly. Let's go find out what the hell the trouble really looks like."

She looked pained. "Mum and Dad'll nail my skin to the wall."

The restlessness churned in him, and he took guilty pleasure in letting it speak. "Then don't tell them."

"Nik? Are you all right?"

"Very. But you have to come out with me tonight. God knows what I'm likely to do without your moderating influence."

"That's blackmail, Dominic Glyndwr." There was a frown still between her brows, but she said, "All right then. Pick me up?"

"Meet you in the lane behind your garden in an hour. Don't wear anything too up-the-hill. Do you know that I adore you beyond telling?"

"If you can't tell it, I don't know how I should be expected to know about it," she grumbled. The display went flat.

He dropped off the communications level and plunged into the news services, spinning keywords and dates, then more keywords as information fell into his hands. He was used to working fast, perceiving only the surface of the packets he snagged and stored, reading them later. But these surfaces were barbed like fishhooks. *Demonstration. Rioting. Arson.* And *Native Materials Quota*, and *Information Control Act*? By the time he'd pulled down a reasonable outline of the summer's events, he was a little sick. This was not the city he'd meant to come back to; only an image of it in a rippling mirror.

The Native Materials Quota had been passed by Parliament, largely because the issue had all the parties in disarray. Co-OpTech, unable to meet the quotas, closed four plants and almost all their platform drilling and refinery operations and sea-cracking stations. The indigo needle of offices was half empty. Cymru's largest employer was leaving.

The Native Materials Quota had been sponsored by Lord Glyndwr. *Rhys, what were you thinking of?*

After that the protests, the demonstrations, the heavy-handed reactions to them. The news files were full of "The Prince refused . . ." and "Lord Glyndwr declined . . ." and "The Prince ordered . . ." *And have you always been unable to admit to a mistake?*

It was all surface, all official. Each layer of words showed him the mist that hid the facts, and not the facts themselves.

He blacked the 'board as the dinner bell rang. *That* was a complication. He thought about telling someone where he was going. No, not even his mother would approve; and though she might not stop him, he couldn't ask her to keep quiet about it. So when the housecom connected him with Morwenna's room, he only said he was tired, and would skip dinner. If she knew

about his meeting with Pedr, and chose to lay his disinclination
for company at that door—so much the better.

He went to the bedroom, and his closet. For his purposes,
looking four months out of date was an advantage. Who could
meet fashion head-on in a depressed economy? High-collared
white shirt; dark blue waistcoat and trousers; dark blue coat that
nearly reached his ankles, its hem weighted for swing. All his
jewelry was too obviously expensive—he settled for a silver ring,
and tied a square scarf around his throat.

He considered taking a weapon. No. There were enough guns
out there.

He took a service lift down, dodged the clatter and warmth
of the kitchen, and loped through the tunnel to the garage.
"Message to Morwenna," he told the housecom there, "her
room only, private. I've gone into town for the evening." He
thought about saying more—a time to expect him back, an apology—but gave up and ended the instruction. When he turned
back to the garage, Jacob was sitting on the nearest fender.

"Where'd you come from?" Niki said, his heart pounding in
his throat.

"The garden. About two minutes ago. What do you think
you're doing?"

Niki looked at his set, hard face and closed his eyes. "I don't
really know. But I'm going to go do it, whether you approve or
not."

"Nowadays rich boys who go downtown for a lark can get in
trouble."

"We've always been able to do that. This isn't a lark."

"That makes it worse."

"Probably." Jacob would keep him here, safe, caged. Innocent of knowledge or guilt, he would go to Galatea at the new
year, where the study of piloting and Cheatspace mathematics
would give him the tools to make the separation permanent.
Whatever Cymru's problems, he, at least, could escape them.
He could say for the rest of his life, in perfect truth, that there
was nothing he could have done. And that truth would poison
him.

"You were at the beach for twenty-four hours," Niki said.
"Wasn't that time enough to tell me about this?" He gestured
toward the city.

"I thought you already knew."

Of course he thought so. Rhys and Pedr might believe that

Niki couldn't be bothered with the state of the world, but Jacob knew better. His level look hurt Niki worse than Rhys's sharp words. "If I stay home tonight, will you tell me everything you know about it?"

Jacob looked away, into a distance the garage wasn't big enough to hold. "No."

"No?"

"I'm the Prince's advisor," replied Jacob, after a moment.

Niki stared at his profile, and was afraid. The Prince's advisor, privy to secrets and truths, mistaken orders, irrational acts. Jacob could never discuss the matter with Niki. They were friends, but this was more than friendship could excuse, or bear.

"Then I have to go," Niki said. He stepped over Jacob's feet and headed for the cars. If Jacob wanted to stop him, it would have to be the hard way.

"Niki."

He turned. Jacob's back was to him; he couldn't see the other man's face.

"Take my car," Jacob said. "The code's three-five-seven-eleven."

"If I press nine instead, does it blow up?"

"Try it and see, if you're feeling lucky."

"Thank you, Jacob," Niki said.

Olwen was wearing something skinny and red. Her hair was silver under the rising moon. "You're late," she told him.

"Almost wasn't here at all. Come on."

When she saw the Jaguar, she said, "Isn't that Jacob's?"

"Mmm. Don't spill beer on the upholstery."

"Nik, you asked him first, didn't you?"

"Actually, no. He volunteered." He twisted the car around the residential square at a tilt that threatened to slip the air cushion. "When did things go bad around here?"

She gave him a long look, but let it drop. "A month and a half ago, maybe two. At least, that's when it got really vile. There are neighborhoods now that the police won't go into, and the army thinks twice about it."

"What do you think touched it all off?"

"Unemployment. CoOpTech."

"And what started that?"

Olwen frowned at him. "Dad voted for Native Materials."

"Good," Niki said. "Tell me why."

"Nik . . ." she said ominously. But he smiled, and she sighed, and continued. "Dependence on offworld materials and technology makes us dependent on offworld governments," she rattled off. "Leaves us open to pressure or even control from—well, particularly the Concorde. Makes it worthwhile for them to manipulate our economy."

"Specious, but seductive."

"Nik! It was Rhys's bill."

"Yes, it was, wasn't it? Why, do you suppose?"

"I *suppose* because he thought it was a good thing."

"And you grew up in a political household. For shame."

"Niki," she said sharply, then broke off, her fingers twisting in her lap. "You sound like the flamers," she said in a small voice. "I don't want you in trouble."

He spared a hand from his driving to lay over one of hers. "No one takes me seriously, Olwen. It's my best defense."

"I take you seriously."

"Yes," he said happily. "You do."

They left the Jaguar in an underground car park a block from Conwy. It was half empty; was there no one downtown, or just no one with a car? He set the Jag's alarms and hoped that Jacob hadn't installed anything more serious.

There were people downtown. They passed a gas club that spilled noise and music and customers into the street, and a dance hall and a game palace, both the same. The entryway of a restaurant, closed, its windows plastifoamed over, offered a roost to three women and a man drinking Munroe's and sharing a smoke. Half a dozen teenage boys shouted at each other over the ringing clatter of a hop-box played by a yellow-haired kid. Olwen dropped a pound chip into the can at the kid's feet, but he was too absorbed in the panels to notice.

The burned building on Conwy Street was a gamers' pub, a favorite of Niki's. The destruction was thorough; only the back wall of the three-story building still stood. The rest was smoking rubble with the rotting-vegetation stink of anoxidant foam. The entire width of Conwy was blocked off by fire barricades. "Explosion," Niki said.

"How do you know?"

"Look—the buildings across the street. The windows are all broken."

Olwen shook her head. "How do you learn these things?"

"A misspent youth, I suppose. Let's go ask nosy questions of someone."

The Thornhill was at the other end of the block; its windows, if it had any, would be intact. Its facade was buried in ivy. The bands of red and green light that framed the entrance were not so much to ornament the door as to make it possible to find it. Niki ducked through that tunnel of rustling leaves and colored light into the action of a projected vid, one of four playing in the gas club's crowded public room. He walked unconcerned through the front end of a glimmering horned horse, and blew a two-handed kiss to the illusion of the vid star, dancing past in ragged white. Someone near the bar hooted and clapped. Olwen stepped through and made a rude gesture at the horse, which got more applause. The noise in the club had a half-wild edge, honed by disaster. Niki could feel it like something sharp pressed against his skin.

He bought a large-denomination chit from the gasman at the counter, poked it into the nearest slot, and handed the hose and mask to Olwen. She took her breath and handed it back. He cupped the mask over his face, inhaled, and held the lungful down as he ejected the chit. The gas coursed his reflexes like a current spike, slammed into his brain. A sense of endless vertical, of motion so swift it was a kind of stillness . . . The room took on a vividness just short of lit-from-within.

"Rich boy," came a quiet voice at his back. "Fall off your hill?"

"Maybe I jumped." Gas breathed out with the words. "Hello, Fisher."

Fisher came around on Niki's left, and Niki handed him the mask. Fisher pressed it to his face and closed his eyes. "Not something I'd do," he said on the exhale. Olwen took the mask. Fisher's hair was thick and khaki-colored, and needed cutting. He swatted it out of his eyes with one hand.

"Why not?"

"You've been away for a bit, haven't you?"

"I'm trying to catch up," Niki said dryly.

Fisher's gaze was steady. "Then there's no place like home."

"What if I want a little perspective?"

"You won't find it here, laddie. Not downtown. I could do you a bad turn just calling you by your name here."

The gas was gone out of him, and with it, the brilliance of the room. Even Olwen seemed dimmed. Her eyes moved from

Fisher to Niki, alarmed and wary. Niki took the mask from her, filled his nerves with lightning.

"What about me, Andrew?" Olwen asked Fisher.

Fisher shrugged one-sided. "Just a rich girl. So mind where you go. And who you go with."

She ducked her head.

"Fisher, Fisher," Niki said, and almost laughed. "Are you trying to get her to let you take her home?"

Fisher swung his hair back again. "You take her home. And once you do, stay there. I'm warning you, Nik, you're not safe here."

"What would it take to turn that around?"

That made Fisher laugh, a bitter snap of sound that was unlike him. "I've no idea. The army's doing a bloody bad job of it."

"The army's business is fighting. I had something else in mind."

"What, then?"

"Let's see justice done," Niki said. He felt like a conspirator, as if he'd said instead, "Let's rob a bank."

Fisher behaved as if he had. He turned his face away. "I've been talking too bloody long. I could take some grief for it."

"From whom?"

"None of your business. Christ, Nik, what do you care about troubles on the street?"

He could never explain what he'd felt that afternoon, that every wrong done to the city was done to him. "I live here. And besides, 'I Serve,' remember?"

"Yeah, your uncle's been servin' us all lately."

"Fisher, I can't dicker with the opposition *if I don't know who they are*."

"Sod off," Fisher said, and turned to go.

Niki caught his shoulder, half afraid that Fisher would come back around swinging. He didn't. Niki spoke first. "You owe me one, I think."

"Do you, now?"

Niki held his ground. "Last year at school. The gymnasium."

Fisher's eyes went to the floor, came back to his. "I'm not calling out your name, am I?"

Olwen shot a quick, curious look at both of them.

"You used to trust me," Niki said.

"This is bigger than that."

"Ah. When did we institute the system of weights and measures?"

"Nik, I don't fancy having bits of me broken."

"All right, all right." Niki rubbed the space between his eyebrows, as if to massage his thoughts. "Let's do this. I'm going to take one more knock off this hose. When I'm done, you'll be gone. If, before that, you happen to drop the name of someone who can help me, then I'll be in *your* debt." He met Fisher's agonized face and said, "All I want is to keep it all from getting bigger yet. So big that it'll cancel all our debts. Please, Andrew. I need this."

He pressed the mask to his face and closed his eyes. The sound of his indrawn breath was harsh in his head, and the rushing of the gas from the valve was loud. His pulse thumped above his right ear, pitched just below hearing. "Jane Wells. At the Lady de Winter," said Fisher.

When Niki opened his eyes, the room glittered. Fisher was gone.

CHAPTER THREE

Hurrah for revolution and cannon come again!
The beggars have changed places, but the lash goes on.
                              —W. B. Yeats, "The Great Day"

The Lady de Winter was, as if to spite its name, a working-class pub. It sat in a neighborhood of small factories, of businesses with flats above them, of narrow streets with narrow sidewalks. It had a sub-office of the government news service as its Siamese twin, joined to it at its plastic-clapboard flank. The wave scoop on the news service roof cast a long shadow over both.

The pub showed signs of recent hard use: one window was foamed over; the others had cheap security grilles over them, the red lacquer still raw and bright. Olwen stood in the shadow of a door across the street, her bright hair like a patch of mist, and looked thoughtfully at the front windows. "What was that 'last year at school' that you said Andrew owed you for?"

"The sort of thing that he wouldn't owe me for any longer if I told it to you," Niki said.

"The girls used to say he 'wasn't one of us,' that he was a charity case, things like that."

"Mmm. Sometimes he may even have regretted it."

"Were you good friends?" she asked.

The past tense seemed appropriate, though he knew some of his melancholy came in the wake of the gas. "As good as we could be, I suppose. Given that he 'wasn't one of us.' "

"Heavens, we're informative," Olwen grumbled. "Do we have to go in?"

"Would you rather I sent you home?"

"Not if you think I can help."

"I could stand to have someone watching over me. Do you mind?"

"Keen on it, actually," she replied with a toss of her head.

When Niki pushed the heavy door open, the place exhaled the sweet-and-sour smell of beer, the layered smell of old and new smoke. The public room might not have changed since it was built, perhaps twenty years after the Removal, except for the game consoles sparkling against the back wall. The bar was a block of white Marblene, irregularly yellowed with age and smoke. The old taps, tubes of pitted chrome and clouded clear plastic, still descended from the ceiling, unused. Behind the bar was a long mosaic of mirror bits. It might have been meant as a joke about bar mirrors; it gave back an image of the room fragmented, in ruins. Some of the pieces had fallen out, showing dabs of adhesive where they'd been. The furniture was a jumble of periods and styles, none of them new—tables, chairs, easy chairs, couches. There were half a dozen people of various ages drinking at the tables. Two women were playing a desultory game of Klepto, and their faces changed color as the display zoomed in and out—fingers, pocket, shop counter, back to fingers. No one sat at the bar.

A woman stood behind it staring off into the middle of the room, waiting, perhaps, for the glass washer to finish its business. She was Celtistani, with cream-and-coffee skin over angular Welsh bones, black eyes, and black hair salted with white. She wore it chin-length, with a straight, thick fringe that hid her eyebrows. Niki put her age at anywhere between thirty and forty.

He leaned on the bar in front of her, and she looked him up and down, then did the same to Olwen, who stood beside him. It was hard to read her expression without the eyebrows.

"Help you?" she said. She had the hoarse voice of someone who smoked, or drank, or shouted at people, or all three.

"Bitter, please. Two." Niki slid three large coins toward her; they lay untouched on the bar, their 'grams flickering rust-red in the validating light.

"Run a tab?" the bartender asked.

"No, thank you."

She drew their beers and set them down. "I'm looking for Jane Wells," he said, before she could walk away. He spoke as he'd begun: just loud enough to reach across the bar.

"Look all you like."

"I was told she was here."

"Who by?"

"Why should you want to know, if he was wrong? I need," he added quickly, "to talk to someone who's up on current events."

"I'll lend you a couple p, and you can buy a fax next door."

"Is that what *you* do, when you want to know what's going on?"

The bartender laughed and began unloading the washer.

"I didn't think so. Anyway, I've read the fax. I'm looking for the other half of the story."

"Pity you've got the wrong place, then. Have a nice day."

She turned her back on him. Olwen shifted from one foot to the other, and frowned at Niki. He shook his head, just a little, and drank his beer, and kept his eyes on the shattered bits of mirror beyond the bartender's head.

Because she was watching him in them, he was sure. Out of malice, to see how he'd take defeat? Out of curiosity? Or to see, perhaps, if he had a last card to play?

He had nothing he could barter for her trust. No—he had one thing. A dreadful mistake, perhaps even a deadly one, if Fisher had chosen to send him into a trap. But that, after all, was what gave the currency value.

"My name is Dominic Glyndwr," he said.

His overstretched nerves waited for an artificial silence to fall on the room. It didn't. Two old men by the door talked about smokes; the sound system played a five-year-old pop song; sirens in the distance wailed like a pack of soprano wolves; glasses clanked as the woman behind the bar finished unloading the washer. "I'm a fool for novelty," she said. "And fools. Ginger!"

A bony woman with orange curls looked out of a doorway at one end of the bar. "What?"

"Take over for me."

"The hell I will, it's my break!"

"You can have all of my next one. C'mon, Ging, don't be a bitch."

Ginger took her place behind the bar, and scowled at Niki and Olwen. Niki smiled at her, and the scowl sagged. "Could I have another?" Niki asked. Ginger filled his glass and handed it back with both hands, as if it were something more than beer.

"Charmer," Olwen grumbled at him as they left the bar.

The Celtistani woman led him through the door Ginger had come in by. The room behind it was more or less an office, with stairs to the second floor at the back. The woman flung herself into a softform chair that didn't seem to be working. "Have a seat, do," she said, and gestured at the hard desk chair. "So glad you could come. Can we expect to be all the crack with the posh set, now?"

Niki forestalled an outburst from Olwen by pulling out the desk chair and propelling her into it. He settled himself on a corner of the desk and sipped at his beer. "No. No one knows we've come here, and we don't propose to tell anyone. This is Olwen Llangwyn, by the way."

"Jolly. I'm Jane Wells."

"I'd sort of thought as much," Niki said apologetically.

Jane Wells might have raised her eyebrows. "You did, did you?"

"When you were trying to chase me off, you never said she wasn't here."

She snorted. "Next time I'll lie. So, here I am, taking my tea break with the Little Viscount himself."

Niki looked down at his own long legs. "They call me that?"

"Not for your size." She pushed herself out of the chair and went to a counter across the room, trailing contempt like a perfume. She took a mug off the rack, flipped the switch on the flash boiler. "I suppose you want tea?"

"Tea is for guests," Niki said. "I'm an intruder. Why do they call me little, then?"

She didn't hesitate. "Well, you're kid brother to all of Cymru, aren't you? According to the news, we're proud of your horsemanship, your shooting, your wits, your fine way with the bottom of a bottle. And one day you might be grown enough to be worth thinking twice about." She let the steaming water hiss into her cup.

Niki laughed and ignored, for the moment, the pinching at

his heart. "Thus showing me my place and my proper ambition, all in one speech."

"Oh, stop it!" Olwen cried, and sprang out of the desk chair. "Are you just going to *take* this?" She stalked over to Jane Wells. "He could get in trouble for coming down here, and now that he's here, there are people who would hurt him just because of who he is. And all he gets out of it is a lot of crap from a barmaid. Just shut up and answer his questions, won't you? He won't leave until you do." Her voice cracked on the last word, and she turned her back on both of them. Her shoulders were very straight.

Wells gave Niki a long, evaluating look. He opened his hands, palm-up—a silent apology. Wells nodded once and took her mug back to the softform chair.

"Am I grown enough," Niki said to her, "to get involved in the business out there?" He nodded toward the door.

Wells studied her tea. "We'll see, won't we?"

Niki wished there was room to pace. He looked at his hands, lying one inside the other on his knees. Long-fingered, big-knuckled, good at lots of things. Useless, just now. And his tongue not much better—he couldn't think of anything to do with it. "I want to know what happened," he said at last. "I didn't think it mattered to me—I thought the welfare of Cymru was my uncle's business, and my brother's.

"Then I came back from . . . from screwing around all summer. The city had gone mad. Or something had. And I couldn't shrug it off anymore, and say it was up to Pedr to fix, or Rhys. Because they'd been here all summer; they must have watched it break down. So how could I trust them to mend it?"

There. It was said. All the things that had gnawed at him since he'd come back, condensed into one damning statement. Olwen stood clutching the back of the desk chair; her face was such an incongruous mix of fear and outrage that he would have laughed, if the expression hadn't been meant for him.

Because what he'd just said was treason. Pedr would be quick to say so, anyway. Did he really blame Pedr for his country's disarray? Did he blame Rhys, his own brother?

Jane Wells was watching him warily from under her fringe. Niki couldn't blame her. She shrugged. "Who can tell how these things start, or where, or when?"

"That," he said, watching her, "is one of my questions. Who *can* tell?"

Silence grew long and fat over the room. "And what'll you do with the answer, if I give you one?" said Wells.

"That depends on the answer. But someone should put things right."

"Someone should put things right," she said, looking at the ceiling. "As if we'd lost a button off our waistcoat. How will you put it right, Little Viscount? Pour money over it? Write a letter?"

She set her mug on the floor and leaned forward, glaring at him from under her hair. "You think we're all carrying on as if we've gone crazy. Well, thank you very much. I suppose it would be sane and well-behaved to sit on our thumbs while our jobs dry up, while we wonder how we'll feed our kids, while they tell us we can't complain, can't assemble, can't speak ill of the govie, can't even go out on the bloody street after dark. Do they teach you history, in your damned expensive universities? Did you learn what the Separation of Subjugated Nations was all about, back on Terra? Were *they* all crazy? If that's so, then Christ save us from sane people."

She picked up her tea mug, carried it to the counter, and drank from it, as if her inconvenient visitors had disappeared.

"That's still not my answer," Niki said, letting the words fall light and quiet.

"Sometimes a single question has a lot of answers. That's one. It's the one you'd get from anyone on the street, if they said more than three words to you at all. Do what you like with it."

He wanted very much to lose his temper. Some of that showed when he spoke, in spite of his efforts. "Whatever you may think of me, I *am* Dominic Glyndwr, Viscount Harlech. It counts for a little something. And I'm willing to help."

Jane Wells looked as if she'd like to lose her temper, too. Or as if she'd like to cry, and would willingly lose her temper to avoid it. "You can't," she said, her voice flat and clogged.

"No, I can't, can't I, *if nobody will give me a bloody straight answer to save her life*?" He clenched his teeth on the rest of what would have been an excellent tirade.

Olwen slammed her hand down on the back of the desk chair and whirled toward the door. Niki reached for her arm just as Ginger stepped into the room, her face pinched white under her orange hair.

"Jane," she said, a little shrill. "Reg Tamsin's out front with a couple of his mates. Wants to see you."

Wells looked up from the counter, from under her fringe. "That happens. Tell him I'm on break."

The door opened again, hitting Ginger in the backside. She shrieked, and a man stepped into the room. He was probably Niki's age, though he dressed and walked as if he'd like to be taken for older. His long brown hair was clubbed at the back of his neck and tied with a ribbon the color of old blood, to match his coat. He was nearly as tall as Niki, perhaps a little wider through the shoulders, and his face was fine-boned and handsome. His gaze moved across all of them, cool and still, like a good gamer at play. Of course—Niki had seen him at Nicholson's, at the Steel Hare, at Little Wheels. Away from the consoles, he was cocky and sullen by turns. At the games, he played, Niki had heard, with ferocity and genius.

"Hullo, Jane," Reg said. "Glad I'm not taking you from your work, eh?" His accent was too carefully upper class.

"Take a flight, Reg," she said. She stood very still at the counter.

"Got company, I see. Anyone I know?"

"I said walk. It's none of your business. They're friends."

Reg stepped forward (Ginger scuttled aside, then out the door behind him) until he was quite close to Niki. "What an elevated lot of friends you've acquired, Jane," he said, smiling. He took Niki's chin gently between his thumb and forefinger, moved Niki's face a little to one side, then the other. "I'd swear this lad's the little Glyndwr. Aren't you?"

Niki met his eyes, saw himself reflected in them as if at the bottom of a well. Reg was even closer to his own height than he'd thought. "Yes," Niki said, since there seemed to be no point in doing otherwise.

"Thought you'd come down for a brew and a nice little chat with the lower orders?"

There wasn't a sensible answer to that, so Niki didn't hunt for one.

"What did you find to talk about, Jane?" There was a sudden edge to Reg's words. Out of the corner of his eye, Niki saw Jane Wells's hand move toward her mouth, then stop.

"Nothing."

"Long time, to talk about nothing."

"How would you know."

"Tommy came to fetch me as soon as you went in here."

"Give Tommy a big sloppy kiss for me. The little butt-sucker."

Reg smiled, as if in spite of himself. "If you say so. I never let him suck mine."

"Excuse me," Niki said softly. "Don't, Olwen. Ginger said something about a couple of friends with him."

Olwen took her hand off the door latch, her face pink with frustration.

Reg let go of him and stepped back, until he could watch Olwen as well. "He's right. You'd be in worse trouble out there than you are in here. Go stand by your boyfriend. Now come on, Jane. Just tell me what you've been saying to these nice people, and we can be done with this."

"Nothing! All right? He wanted to know about the action. And I told him to piss off. Are you happy?"

Reg rubbed his forehead. "Jane, Jane, you could have done that at the bar. I'd hate to have to let on to any of my clients you're unreliable."

"Clients!" Wells spat. "You're a jumped-up little gutter punk, Reg Tamsin, and your 'clients' are a pack of second-rate touts who toss you pennies to do their legwork for 'em!"

Reg took a long hissing breath through his teeth. "Was it second-rate touts kept the Grays off you last month?"

"No. It was a bloody political protection racket. And if that's your idea of the Revolution, I'd rather let the likes of him stand on my neck." Wells jerked her head at Niki. He lifted an inquiring eyebrow, but no one noticed.

"We start wherever we have to start."

"Bollocks. You're thugs trying to pass yourselves off as players."

Reg, Niki decided, had no compunction about losing his temper. From the look on his face, it appeared to be an unpleasant one. "Then I'm a thug. And you're a lily-white revolutionary angel. But I'm still going to send word to my thug mates about you and the aristocracy here. And if they decide to come all over nasty, you know how they'll do it."

Understanding rolled over Jane Wells's face. She clutched the counter and bent over it a little, as if she'd been hit in the stomach.

"She did, in fact, tell me to piss off," Niki said. "Or words to that effect. What are you threatening her with?"

Reg looked at him for a long moment, as if he'd forgotten Niki was a living thing. "Tell him, Jane."

"I live upstairs," Jane Wells said, in a thin voice, her back to the room. "With my kids."

"Christ," Olwen muttered, but Niki wasn't sure what she meant by it.

The look on Reg's face was haughty and frightened at once, like a swimmer too far from shore, too tired to get back, too proud to shout for help. It disturbed Niki as nothing else had.

Niki closed his eyes. "You *idiot*," he sighed. When he opened them again, Reg was watching him, narrow-eyed. "You're making a ghastly mess."

"Shut up, Glyndwr."

Niki stuck his hands in his coat pockets, where no one would see them shaking. "You figured you'd do your bit to usher in the new order. And if it meant you could swagger around and tell people what to do, so much the better. But you're in over your head now." *And so am I.*

"You'd know about swaggering and telling people what to do, wouldn't you?"

Niki's mouth was so dry he could have lit kindling on the back of his tongue. He hooked one foot around the desk chair, pulled it to him, and sat in it backwards, crossing his arms over the backrest. Looking, he hoped, insolently casual. "Yes. And when I tell people what to do, they don't ask questions. Can you say the same?"

"Bloody right I—"

"Careful, your accent's slipping. No, you can't. Do you lead the arm-breakers you left out in the public room?"

"They're not arm-breakers—"

"Whatever they are. Do you lead them?"

Reg, too angry to speak, nodded sharply.

"Ah. But if you let us walk, you'd have explain it to them, wouldn't you? Funny. I don't have to explain anything to people I lead." Niki was careful not to look at Olwen, who knew that he led nothing, had no authority, and never explained himself because no one would bother to ask. He had more in common with Reg than with his own brother, but there was no time to prove it. Only enough time, if he was lucky, to turn Reg away from Olwen and Wells. *Hate me, God damn it. Let's get personal.*

"Shut *up*—"

"I don't think you're a leader at all. I think you're just another arm-breaker."

Reg backhanded him. Niki was ready for it, and turned with the blow; still, his thoughts went gray for a moment with the force of it. Olwen, he realized belatedly, had cried out. She stood, indignant, in the middle of the room, restrained by Wells's hands on her shoulders. Niki tried to reach her with as much message as a look could carry, but she only scowled at him, and at Reg. It was Jane Wells who received his glance with a narrowing of her lips and a movement that might have been a nod.

When he could trust his voice, he said, "How are you going to explain this little action to them? Jane Wells is suspected of saying something you don't want said, but you're not sure what? Or is carrying out sentence before the trial something you don't have to talk them into?"

"It's called security," Reg snarled.

Niki shook his head, as much to clear it as anything. "If someone suggested that my side do that, I'd call it tyranny, and fire the bastard."

Reg, to Niki's acute discomfort, smiled slowly, bitterly, and leaned against the desk. "Would you? That's funny."

"Why?"

"Because when your side does it, we *do* call it tyranny."

It was like stepping into a malfunctioning drop field. "They haven't suspended due process," Niki said. Even as the words formed, he knew they were irrelevant.

Reg nodded. "That's right. But without an arrest, there isn't any 'due process.' Couple of Gray Dogs show up in the middle of the night, want to take you off and ask you questions. Maybe there's something in the way of their badge numbers. Maybe those numbers are off duty, and there's logs to prove it. Sometimes the questions sort of break the skin. When they bring you back, you can never figure out where it was they took you.

"And sometimes," he finished, smiling broadly, "they don't bring you back. Ask Jane, there. She'd like to know where her old man is right now."

Jane Wells, her hands slack at her sides, closed her eyes, as if to keep some shred of privacy. With that she told him, louder than words, that what Reg said was true.

This was why she hadn't wanted to talk to them in the public room. Because there was one coin for which she would give up what she knew, and she needed to find out if Niki and Olwen had her price. But no—they were only nosy, rich children. He felt sick and dizzy, and helpless, and almost too angry with himself to think.

He had to think. His duel of words with Reg had been wrenched away from him, knocked out of his hands by a merciless truth wielded like a cudgel. *Oh, Pedr, did you know about this? Was it you who let the leash slip?*

Reg. Think of Reg. Who might be brought to trade the cool and distant passion of his new cause for a tempered, familiar resentment, for a personal hatred for a rich, well-born, haughty bastard.

Niki unfolded smoothly from the desk chair and advanced on Reg, who, to his credit, didn't retreat. "Have you learned a lesson from that?" Niki asked. "Is that what you've got planned for me? Or do you think you can go the police one better?"

"I haven't got any plans for you. But I know some people who will, once I deliver you."

Niki shook his head and smiled, and was grateful for his high shirt collar that hid the movement of his throat. "There's many a slip, as the saying goes. I'm a pretty big parcel to carry unrecognized through a city full of patrols."

"That's true." Reg's chin was up, and a bleak, panicky determination looked out of his eyes. "So if I have to take you off line instead, I will."

"If you have the stomach for it."

"This is war. On the hill, you don't know that yet. But down here we're prepared to do things that have to be done, and take the consequences."

You don't sound prepared, Niki thought. "Oh, I forgot. You've got the staff out front to do it for you. Careful of that, m'boy. Never ask the underlings to do what you aren't prepared to do yourself."

Olwen gazed horrified at them. "I don't believe this," she said. "You'd think you were both in a bad goddamn vid."

For the second time, Reg shook off the blinding emotion Niki had wrapped him in. He stared at Olwen for a moment, as if adjusting his anger to include her, too. Then he moved toward the door. In another moment, he would open it, call his companions in. Whatever he said or did in front of them could never be taken back.

Niki's hands were empty; he flung words at Reg instead. "If

you made a bargain with me, would the pair out front let you stand by it?''

"I don't need to make bargains," Reg said stiffly over his shoulder.

"Perhaps not. Perhaps you look forward to 'taking me off line.' "

A muscle leaped into sharp relief on Reg's jaw.

"That was it, wasn't it, if I didn't go quietly? For the price of a sporting chance, I agree to go quietly."

Reg had stopped, his palm flat against the door.

"You know me by my reputation," Niki continued, and tried not to sound desperate. "I know yours. When you play for a forfeit, you honor it. So do I. If you agree to this, I'll abide by the results."

"You know there's no reason for me to muck about with this."

"Except that it might make life a bit easier. And keep my blood off your hands, if that matters to you." Niki smiled a little. "I'll point out that, aside from the blot on your conscience, whoever puts a period to me is going to get a hell of a lot of unpleasant attention from the hill."

Niki had watched Reg in the gamers' pubs—at ease in the embrace of his chair, wrapped in other players' nervous smoke, his hands steady and light at the tap plates and balls and mocking fields. The body language was familiar—Niki had seen himself, reflected in glass or plastic or chrome, sitting just that way, working the console with an economy of motion that seemed languid.

Reg turned at last, his shoulders against the door in a defiant parody of relaxation, and said, "And what kind of sporting chance are you after?"

Niki's heart bounded into his throat and hammered there. He realized, when he felt his own surprise and fresh-made hope, that he hadn't expected Reg to agree. "What we do best. I'll play you a game."

Olwen took a step toward them, eyes wide, mouth slack. It was Wells, again, who stopped her.

"Which one?"

"Anything out there." Niki nodded at the door.

"I suppose if you win, I let you all off?" Reg's crack of laughter had no amusement in it.

Niki shook his head. "Only Jane Wells and my friend. If I win, they walk."

Reg's eyes widened a little—not in surprise, but like a sight-hunting animal that sees movement in the grass. "And you?"

"A separate issue."

Reg grinned. "Lord of Annwn, I'll send you a boy hero."

It was gamer usage—victory was sending your opponent down to the land of the dead, to hell. It was gamer's posing and posturing and jockeying for psychological advantage. Harder to do, Niki found, when it might be made literal. But he said, "He must be getting tired of boy heroes. Maybe he'd rather have a stray dog like you."

Reg turned to the Celtistani woman. "What do you think of that, Jane? His Lordship wagering you like a ring off his bloody finger?"

She thrust her jaw out. "It's a sporting chance, like he said. What would I get from your lot?"

"You're all crazy," Olwen said, but not loudly.

Reg asked Niki, "What happens if *I* win?"

"I assume you get it all." At the edge of his vision, Niki saw Olwen flinch.

Reg considered, and smiled again. "No, that's hardly even, is it? Tell you what: If I win, I get the ladies, but you go free. Neat, eh?"

Niki studied Reg's handsome face. This, it told him, was the harvest from all the hatred he'd sown in the other man, all his manipulations. This was the illogical, angry decision he'd driven Reg to make. "You," Niki said bitterly, "have a damned creative mind."

Reg laughed. "Let's get to it."

Olwen stood by the door, arms folded tightly, eyes on the floor. She didn't look up when Niki stopped in front of her, so he put a finger under her chin and lifted. Even her lips were white. He kissed her forehead. "Believe in me," he whispered, and followed quickly after Reg, because he was afraid to hear her answer.

Intolerable, to gamble with other people's lives. Immoral. It was something he should have thought of before he left the Castle—because in everything he'd done since then, he'd hazarded lives. Reg had hammered that home to him with his forfeit. But surely it was better to gamble with lives than to consign them to hell unfought for? So he fed the adrenaline that coasted on his nerves, and strode unhurried across the pub.

Some whiff of events in motion must have escaped the back

room; the patrons at the tables were silent, and their eyes fastened on him, darted away, and came back only when he might not notice. Ginger, at the bar, made no such pretense. Her stare was fixed and blank, as if he were a character on a serial.

Reg stood by the consoles, with his companions. One was a small young man in a two-piece coverall, darkly iridescent like black feathers. The loose, lumpy fabric could have hidden a multitude of wicked things. The other was a large woman who had a strip of green Optiflex tied over her eyes like a blindfold. She would be seeing him as a thermal map: cold spots that might be weapons, the hot surge of nerve impulses and blood that might signal sudden moves. Good for brawling. Good, perhaps, for whatever might happen when the game was over, depending on which of them won.

They were clearly not pleased with Reg's deal. As Niki came close, the man in the coverall was saying, "—goin' t'hang a sure thing out in the wind, just so you can fuckin' strut about!"

"That's enough," said Reg, not loud. "You won't lose by it."

Niki felt a little guilty, to find that his needling had come so close to the mark. *Not in control. But if he had been, he wouldn't have agreed to something as crazy as this.*

Reg propped his elbow on the shining glass globe of the Force Majeur unit. Lightning leaped along its inside surface like hairline cracks, bridged the space between the glass and the simulation of a dark steel sphere inside the globe. The lightning, too, was simulated; it was there to make the console look interesting, and to distract the players. "This all right?" Reg asked.

"Your choice," Niki replied. He slipped out of his coat and dropped it on a chair, untied the scarf at his neck, unfastened his collar.

"Want a pin?"

"Yes, please. Blue Cat, if they've got 'em." And thought, *we're observing the forms, then.*

Jane Wells brought the box, an unopened twelver, from behind the bar. The cat logo glimmered around the edges with bristling holo hackles. Reg took a pin from its nest in the box and flicked the cap off the needle with a thumbnail. Then he handed it to Niki and laid his hand, palm up, on the table. He was smiling, his eyes still wide, and his face didn't change when Niki pressed the point through the fine skin of his wrist. Niki selected his pin, and offered it and his wrist. Reg took it in a hand that was dry and steady, as Niki's had been, centered it over one long blue vein, and waited an instant before he squeezed it home. The wait made the needle's bite a surprise, and Niki blinked. One corner of his mouth lifted in an involuntary salute to Reg.

He felt the Cat as a slow folding-up of his peripheral vision, heat in his face, the taste of pine resin at the back of his mouth. It clutched at his stomach, too, as it hadn't in a long time. Nerves—the kind that could turn to panic and shut down thought. He nodded to Reg, and knew that for him, too, the world was narrowing to a single brilliantly lit point. No bar, no patrons, and no concern but theirs. If it hadn't been for Reg's arm-breakers, Olwen and Jane Wells might have walked out unnoticed.

They sat across from each other at the console. Reg dropped a coin down the hatch; Niki supplied the other. Which could be likened, he thought, to paying one's own hangman. No, the game wasn't life or death to him. Paying Olwen's hangman, then. Clever, clever Reg. For a moment, his reflection in the glass globe caught his honed attention. It was a puzzle pattern of dark and light, without color: white shirt, open at the throat; dark waistcoat; dark hair; eyes unnaturally bright in a white hollow face. They all fit neatly over Reg's image, which he could see through the glass, past the steel sphere. The composite face bore a likeness to both of them, and to neither.

Then he blinked, and let his eyes unfocus. Reflections, steel sphere, and the electrical storm in the globe around it all became part of the background noise. Amateurs played Force Majeur with their eyes.

His hands went under the concealing hood and into the mocking field. It would translate the language of his fingers, movement and tension, into force on the sphere. It would start the game—he had only to touch the back surface of the hood. The second player's touch would start the game, but he couldn't know he was the second until the game began, until the ball began to move. The game could be won in that moment. Niki laid a finger against the back of the hood.

Reg made him wait for the start, but it was a trick too much like the one with the pin, and Niki was ready for it. They met full strength against strength on each side of the ball, and it quivered at the center as they tested each other. Shifting pressure around the steel surface—Niki thought he could feel the simulation under his fingers, cold smooth curving metal. He swapped his grip, shoved upward with both palms. Reg slowed the ball millimeters away from the glass and dissolution, drove it straight at Niki's face beyond the glass. Niki caught the sphere on his thumbs, cursed silently, and sent the thing inching sideways, rocking it back and forth against Reg's answering pressure.

After a while, he no longer thought of his hands. He could feel the simulation as a solid thing, in his head—feel the mass of the ball, the distance from its surface to the inside of the sphere, the force necessary to overcome its inertia. He could feel Reg's pressure, his presence, behind and around it. It was a rich, hallucinatory web of geometry, illuminated by the Blue Cat and by the nearness of life and death. He felt mass and distance outside the game sphere, too. It seemed as if he'd closed his eyes; but he could almost see Reg's face close to the glass, teeth bared, brown hair damp at the roots with sweat.

They were locked in another test of brute power, and Niki was going to lose. He was tired, distracted. He would falter or fade or fail to concentrate for an instant, and Reg would fling him backward into the glass and destroy him. No, not him. Olwen. And Jane Wells, who would be in no danger now if some damned rich boy hadn't come down from the Castle to ruin her life. Viscount Harlech on a white horse.

It was self-disgust that gave him the strength to act on the information from that web of geometry. He shifted his grip. The ball sailed free for an instant, in defiance of all the accepted strategy. Then Niki caught it with a fingertip and flicked it high, back toward himself. In the glass sphere, the vector that was Reg lashed out on an intercept course. Niki felt one lurching beat of his heart, and had the wild, Cat-enhanced certainty that by the time he felt the next beat, the game would be done, one way or the other.

Force Majeur was unsatisfying to watch; there was no way for a spectator to tell who controlled the sphere until the game ended and the console lit up to indicate the winner. The sphere struck the side of the glass globe in a blaze of lightnings and imploded, and in its light Niki saw the faces around the table, suspended in that last instant of hope and fear. He dropped his head forward onto the globe as his side of the console lit up.

He was barely aware of the sound of Reg's chair falling over, of Reg staggering to his feet. He brought his head back up with an effort, and saw that Reg looked as wrung as Niki felt. Reg turned and made for the door. The arm-breakers followed him. Niki settled his forehead on the globe again, and watched a rivulet of sweat mar the polished surface before his eyes.

"Are you all right?" Olwen said next to his ear.

"I don't know. The results aren't in. But you are." He stood with an effort and scraped his hands over his face and hair.

"Go get the Jag," he told her, and gave her the security code. "You remember where it is?"

"I won't leave you here."

"Yes, you will—for just as long as it takes to bring the Jag back. When you turn the corner out there, I want you to be going like a getaway car driver. Which is no idle simile. If I'm not there, or not able to get to the car, keep going, get home, and send help." She looked stubborn, but he thought she'd do it, anyway. He turned to Jane Wells.

"Can you go with her? The car's just off Conwy and Independence."

Wells's face was stiff. "I think I've done enough tonight, thank you."

Niki rubbed his fingers over his face again. "You're right. I'm sorry. But Reg isn't the only dangerous soul on the streets tonight. I'd rather she wasn't alone."

Wells lowered her gaze. "I'll get someone. I'd . . . I don't want to leave the kids."

He nodded. "Thank you." She turned to go. "Jane—Ms. Wells," he said suddenly, and she looked back at him. "Assuming nothing goes wrong once I leave here . . . if there's anything I can do, will you leave word for me on the 'board? It's a secured account, no one will eavesdrop."

She blinked. "How would I find you?"

"I'm in the public listing." He grinned, with an effort. "I'm Cymru's kid brother, remember?"

He wasn't in bad shape, if he discounted the awful wired exhaustion the game and the Cat had left behind. Reg was probably just the same. The two with him, on the other hand . . . He drew Olwen to him, and she pulled his head down and kissed him fiercely. She was frowning. Her mouth felt wonderful.

"Don't fail me, love," he said. He let her go and went out the door.

They were waiting in the street, Reg and his two friends, in a fine rain that was barely more than mist. The woman in the Optiflex blindfold punched for his chin, but he dodged, and the blow glanced off his cheek. Still, it drove him back into the grip of the small man in the coverall, who proved to be unpleasantly strong. This would end much too quickly, if he didn't do something.

"Reg, Reg—are you going to let them fight your battles for you?" The hands around his biceps were cutting off his circulation. "Will they respect you in the morning?"

"Why the hell shouldn't they?" Reg snapped. He looked terrible.

"If I were them, I'd think you were afraid to take the chance. You lost once to me, and you're scared it will happen again."

"We're gamed out, boy hero."

"This is a grudge match, and we all know it. You want to see me bleed. Why don't you do the job yourself?"

Reg had been turning color, red to white to red, as Niki talked. "Let him go," he said at last.

"The hell," said the small man from over Niki's shoulder. "He's better off—"

"Don't you follow orders at all now?" Reg asked, a world of ice in his voice.

After a long, breathless moment, the hands dropped from Niki's arms. "You better take the bastard, then," the small man said. "I'm not goin' empty-handed on account of your toff airs and graces."

Reg pulled off his wine-colored coat and circled in on Niki. Grudgingly, the arm-breakers moved well back.

It was a little like the game all over again, except that the game stayed clear in his memory. The fight was blurred and full of blank spots, and even with the catalog of his bruises and broken skin to work from later, Niki couldn't reconstruct the whole of it. But the style of attack and counterattack, feint and rush, was like the game, so that Niki moved in something that, as he did it, felt like a pattern. Here, too, there were mass and force and distance, mapped and whispering from the back of his head. Pain was part of the pattern, from blows taken and given, pain like bursts and tendrils of lightning on glass.

Then Reg was lying on his back on the wet pavement, with his wrists pinned under Niki's knees, and Niki's thumbs at his windpipe. They looked at each other as if neither of them had expected to reach this point, or thought about what ought to happen after it.

"This," Niki panted, "is a rotten medium for political action."

Reg stared up at him; then he closed his eyes and began to laugh weakly, as much as Niki's thumbs would allow. "Christ," he croaked. "This what you have to do to get an audience for your fucking jokes? Get off my neck."

"If you'll get off my back." He heard the liquid growl of a well-tuned hover, coming in fast. The man in the coverall put his hand inside his jacket. "Don't do it," Niki ordered, "it's my ride." He wondered why he thought that would stop the man, but the words or the voice at least made him pause.

"Okay," said Reg.

"Okay, what?"

"I'll get off your back."

Niki rolled away from him, and the Jag came to a grating stop almost at his shoulder. The door popped up, and Olwen's fingers twisted into the fabric of his waistcoat and hauled. He caught the doorframe with both hands. "I'm serious," he said to Reg. "We wasted a lot of time tonight."

Reg, on his hands and knees in the street, blood dripping from his nose, long hair half unbound, looked up at him and said nothing. His face was empty of hate or fear or anything else Niki could identify.

Niki folded himself into the Jag, and the door hissed shut. As the car leaped forward, pale light coated the windshield like a splash of liquid. Then it was gone, and Niki could see the polarization shift back to normal. The man in iridescent black had the weapon out of his jacket, still aimed at them. "Armourglas," Niki murmured as they rounded the corner. "So that's why Jacob wanted me to take his car."

He stayed curled up in the half-reclined passenger seat, wrapping himself around his bruised ribs and chest. He couldn't seem to stop shaking. His shirt was cold and damp and clinging.

"Don't bleed on the upholstery," Olwen said, somewhere on his right.

"If I do, Jacob will understand."

What she called Reg was both imaginative and genetically unlikely.

"But an honorable one," he pointed out.

He wondered where, exactly, he might be bleeding from. Such a lot of places hurt. He'd forgotten how much fun the aftermath of a hand-to-hand was. And Reg had been rather good at it.

After a bit, the Jag stopped moving, which made him aware that it had been moving for longer than he'd noticed.

"Where are we?"

"Just sit there. I'll be right back."

He opened his eyes as she disappeared out the driver's side door. They were parked in shining darkness. At the end of it, glimmering through the rain like a beacon, was an all-night coffee bar. They seemed to have reached the far edge of town. *Good God,* he thought, dazed. *You miss a lot around here if you blink.*

In a few minutes Olwen came back with rain sparkling in her hair and a throw-away hot cup in each hand. "Drink this," she said, handing him one. It was coffee, it was restorative, and it made him realize he had a cut lip.

"Ouch," he told her.

She took the cup out of his hands, dipped her handkerchief in the other one—it was full of warm water—and began to clean his face.

"I didn't know you carried a handkerchief," Niki said.

"*Do* shut up." Then he realized she was crying.

He cradled her face in his hands, wiped tears away with his thumbs. "Olwen, don't cry. We're all right."

"You're the stupidest man I ever met!" she shouted. "You're the stupidest man in the world! Who do you think you're sticking your idiot neck out for, anyway? You? Me? Them? Why can't you just mind your own business?"

"Ah," he said sadly, and freed her face. But she set the water down and kissed him, carefully, and he tried to take her in his arms. Neither of them was properly positioned for it.

Olwen said something unladylike, and added, "Squeeze over."

He pressed himself closer to the door, and Olwen slid onto the passenger seat. It was wider than the driver's; if they put their arms around each other, they just fit. The comfort of her body against his outweighed all his aches. Her face pressed into the junction of his neck and shoulder, and the warm smell of her hair, and the rain in it, filled his nose. He rubbed her back, and she relaxed slowly, as if each muscle was a lighted room, and someone was walking through the house touching switches. Suddenly she lifted her face and kissed him, a little too hard.

"Mmm. Careful." Her lips brushed across his jaw to his ear, and he caught his breath.

It occurred to him to protest, but he didn't—at least, not when it was appropriate, and when he thought of it again, the notion was tumbled away in a flood of irrationality and sensation. He could smell Olwen's perfume and the skin scent that was hers; he could taste the recent tears in her mouth, and on her face. Her hands moved over him, over places that hurt and places that didn't, and the two blurred together disconcertingly. His hands moved, too, over the long muscles and smooth skin of her thighs, her breasts, firm and small under the soft fabric of her dress.

It was not entirely satisfying lovemaking. They were too hurried, and the car was too small, too full of things with hard edges. Afterward, he stroked Olwen's hair and said, "I suppose that wasn't all it could have been, love. I'm sorry."

"I'm not. And it was my idea."

"After a whole summer—"

"You can stop being an ass now."

He smiled up at the dark. "If you're sure."

Her fingertips moved lightly over his face. "I felt . . . oh, damn, I don't know. I was scared, I suppose."

He knew what she meant to say. "It *was* the sort of evening that makes one aware of one's mortality."

"No," Olwen said after a moment. "Only mine. I was convinced this was the last night of my life. But you never were, were you?"

Niki had no answer for her. The truth, which she had already said aloud, seemed, for no good reason, shameful.

"We'd better start for home," Olwen said, and slipped away from him.

She drove, quickly and well, through the thickening rain. The streets were nearly empty. Niki wondered what time it was, but not enough to break the silence. He stared at the window, at his reflection in the armored glass.

They were almost to the lane and her house when she said, "I can't take that again." Stray light ran over and into the car, and showed her knuckles white on the steering. He studied her profile, and waited. "I can't go along and watch while you throw yourself into trouble. And it's real trouble, Nik, not just another scrape. I can't stand by and hear people insult you. And I can't listen to the kind of thing you were saying tonight."

Ah—his vote of no confidence in Pedr. He looked down at his hands. "I won't stop, you know."

Her chin came up a little sharply. She stopped the car at the end of the lane. "I do know." Her fingers slid away from the controls. "Hell, no, I don't. Or I didn't. I hoped you'd say—Never mind. I guess I didn't expect it." She popped the driver's side door and scrambled gracelessly out.

Niki caught up with her in a few meters. He put his hands on her shoulders, and she stopped. "Will I see you again?"

She made a choking sound that might have been a laugh, or a sob, and turned her face into his wet waistcoat. "One of the things I love about you. You never take anything for granted."

"Except my immortality."

She only shook her head at that. Finally she pulled back, looked up into his eyes. "You won't be seeing as much of me, is all. Not if you'll be spending a lot of time in town."

He tried to grin, and only half succeeded. "I'll write."

"Yeah, I've heard that before." But she was smiling now. "You look like the bloody romantic hero at the end of a vid, do you know that?"

Niki made a rude noise. "What, bruised and wringing wet?"

"With your hair dripping rain on your nose." She brushed the offending stuff back from his forehead. "And very handsome." She kissed the tips of her fingers, pressed them to his lips, and darted through her gate. He listened as it hissed shut, as the automatic lock thudded home, as her footsteps pattered away up the walk. Then he went back to the car.

He'd come in at dawn before; he knew how to do it quietly, how to avoid the Castle systems' tendency to fuss. Jacob was not prowling cat-footed through the garage, waiting for him. Rhys was not guarding the foot of the stairs. His mother was not lying in wait on the landing. He was quite safe. He unlatched the door to his rooms and slipped through.

Kitty was asleep in one of the chairs in his sitting room. He swore, silently and with his whole heart. The curtains were open; dawn was still only a watery lifting of the darkness, but it was enough for him to see her tumbled hair, her feet propped on the seat of the other chair, her parted lips, her hands folded over the mound of her stomach. He sighed, rubbed his eyes, and went to kneel at her side.

"Kitty. I'm home, I'm safe. You can go to bed now."

Her eyes fluttered open. For a moment, he saw, she didn't remember where she was. Then she focused on his face.

"Dominic! Dear heaven, what have you been up to?" She touched his cheek, cautiously.

"The usual. What are you doing in my sitting room?"

"Sitting," she replied firmly.

"Go sit in your own room. You're making me feel guilty."

"Well, I accomplished that much, anyway. Have you, as I suspected, spent the night doing things that could get you killed?"

There was something about Kitty that made it hard for him to lie to her. "Yes," he said, after a moment.

She turned a little away, and he heard her sigh. "Whatever totty-headed opinions you may have to the contrary, you're not expendable. Your mother would be horrified if she knew."

"Who says she doesn't? Morwenna always seems to know what goes on. She doesn't always act on it, that's all."

Kitty gave him a searching look; even in the dim light, he recognized that angle of the head, the quality of her silence. "And that's something I'll never understand. If you were *my* son . . ."

"You'd have to be at least fifteen years older. You wouldn't like it." He helped her out of the chair.

"Oh, my back," she groaned.

"Coals of fire. Go to sleep, Kitty. I'll be fine."

He opened the door for her. She stopped in it, her hair rumpled, her eyelids drooping, her curving brows drawn down. "If there's anything I can do . . ."

And he knew that she wasn't talking about his bruises. He felt, suddenly, an overwhelming gratitude. He lightly kissed her cheek. "Good night, Kit."

He shut the door, set the lock and the housecom for Emergency Only, and realized, at last, that he was ready to drop. Before he did so, he managed to reach the bedroom and get his clothes off. The bed came up to meet him, and he was too tired to be happy about it.

Later, when he woke up, there was a message waiting for him on the 'board.

You left your coat. Come by for it this evening. This time you can have tea.

He removed the note promptly and sat staring at the blank display. Then he stood up, went to the window, and looked out over the rooftops. Maybe it was a trap. Or maybe, just maybe, he was at last grown enough to be worth thinking twice about.

CHAPTER FOUR

I think it better that in times like these
A poet's mouth be silent, for in truth
We have no gift to set a statesman right. . . .
—W. B. Yeats, "On Being Asked for a War Poem"

At noon on the day after his first visit to the Lady de Winter, he wore his bruises out into the hall, and met his mother there. Morwenna lifted her eyebrows, pursed her lips, and said, as if it were something she'd deliberated over, "Good morning."

Niki replied in kind and ambled downstairs. He hadn't really expected her to say anything. If he was disappointed, it must have been because he'd been robbed of the chance to think up a convincing explanation.

His brother Rhys, after a perfect comic double-take in the entrance to the solarium, sat across the table from Niki, ate lunch, and chatted stiffly about inconsequentials. Sun fell over Rhys's broad, straight shoulders like a benediction, or a cloak of office, turned his reddish-brown hair bright as carnelian. The same sun shone in Niki's eyes and made his head ache. *Rhys, he imagined asking, do I embarrass you?* He didn't ask, for fear the answer would be yes.

But once, pouring milk in his tea, Niki looked up to find Rhys watching him. Those gray eyes that followed the trajectory of Niki's hands, his bruised and bloodied knuckles, were full of concern and confusion. Niki almost spoke then, to explain, perhaps even to apologize, though he wasn't sure for what. Then Rhys looked up, every disturbing emotion fallen from his face, and asked for the milk as soon as Niki was done with it. Niki passed it to him. After all, there was nothing to tell yet.

Pedr was nowhere to be seen.

Jacob, not being a member of the family, was not bound by the convolutions of Glyndwr etiquette. Niki was in the stables, saddling his bay gelding, when Jacob led a sweating horse through the double doors. Niki pretended to examine the bay's stirrup leathers.

"You could get someone to do that for you," Jacob said, behind him.

Niki shook his head. "He bites."

"When cross-tied? Do the teeth fly out of his head? No, don't check his hooves. I've seen black eyes before this, I think I can stand to see yours."

Niki stopped with his hand halfway down the gelding's flank, and smiled, and turned finally. "Who told you?"

"Kitty. Who suggested that I talk good sense where you could hear it."

"You always do."

"Also, there's a little ionizing in the finish on the car. Right up around the windscreen."

"I'm very sorry."

Jacob shrugged. "It'll correct itself in a few days."

One of the stablehands took the reins Jacob offered and led the horse away. "Thank you for the car," Niki said. "It saved our lives, I think."

"Then I suppose you want it tonight, too?"

The bay sidled and snorted, and Niki turned to quiet him. "He's getting restless. I should go."

"You are heading into the city again tonight?"

"If you'd rather," said Niki lightly, "I won't take the car."

After a moment, Jacob said, "That was childish."

"No, it wasn't. Or rather, the way I meant it, it wasn't. What I'm doing is my affair, and probably ought to stay that way. Then, if something goes wrong, no one else is implicated."

"Implicated," Jacob repeated, as if the word were new to him. "What about Olwen?"

"She's out of it." Niki unclipped the cross-ties. "Which is as it should be."

He gathered the bay's reins. Jacob stepped forward, laced his fingers together, and held the cup of his hands ready to give Niki a leg up. It was not a peace offering, since neither of them had said anything to require it. Niki set his knee in the cradle of Jacob's fingers, looked down at the bent sandy-red head, and said, "Thank you. Would it help, if I promise to tell you anything useful that I find out?" Jacob lifted, and Niki settled lightly into the saddle.

"Maybe. A little." Jacob moved back as the bay began to fret against the pressure of Niki's hands. "You know, don't you, that you're meddling in something too big for you."

"Yes, I do," Niki said.

"If I told you to leave it alone, would you?"

Niki looked down at him from the gelding's great height. Jacob's shoulders were squared and stiff, his hands closed at his sides, his face so empty that Niki knew how many thoughts must be hidden behind it. "Jacob," he said gently, "you've known me since I was—what, fourteen? What do you think?"

"It'll eat you alive, Niki," Jacob said, and turned abruptly and left the stable.

He *did* know that he'd involved himself in something too big for him. Which was why he returned to the Lady de Winter that night, where Jane Wells tended bar, and a man and a woman asked difficult questions for a long time. And why, on the following night, he traveled, blindfolded, in the back of a stranger's truck, to listen to a man who'd been a CoOpTech rig foreman and a union officer. It was certainly why, when he met Reg again, he spoke to him pleasantly and for a long time. And why, when Andrew Fisher found him at the Thornhill and asked his help in a personal matter, he gave it so quickly.

Alone, he was no match for the forces that gnawed at Cymru. So he would see to it that he wasn't alone.

It was, as it turned out, a fortnight before anyone in the family besides Kitty commented on his habits. The Glyndwrs were accustomed to power; they liked to keep their thoughts and observations to themselves until they decided how to use them, and on whom. Niki decided, after two weeks of having it exercised on him, that it was an unsavory family trait.

On the morning after his favor to Andrew, a voice disturbed his sleep, and he suspected, somewhere in his subconscious, that his period of family grace was over. It was Rhys's voice; it grew slowly, gathering words and volume as it came closer. The bedclothes, which were over Niki's head, muffled it. "Come on, then, get up," it said. "I know what time you came in this morning, but if I wait until you've had your eight hours, I stop 'round and find you've already gone."

"Nnhn," said Niki thoughtfully, but Rhys didn't seem to hear him.

"I want to ask you about something, Nik my lad." Even mostly asleep, Niki recognized the tone, and struggled toward alertness. "Last night, someone crossed the Landfall Bridge checkpoint who identified himself as a courier. His order of passage was a Do Not Hinder, fully charged, with the royal sealcode on it. Now why, you ask, would I wake you up to talk about an accredited courier?"

"Mm-mm." *Oh*, thought Niki, and wished for some more useful thought.

"Every morning, I give a look at the authorizations recorded for the night's traffic. Just routine. This morning there were two royal codes in the list. One I gave out yesterday afternoon. The other one I don't recall. Nor do I recall Pedr issuing it—are you listening?"

"Yes. Go away, Rhys."

That, unfortunately, Rhys heard. The covers were suddenly pulled from Niki's grip. "You stupid bastard—"

Niki groaned and tugged a pillow over his head. "If you won't go away, you can at least talk softly."

"I've no sympathy for your bloody hangover," Rhys said, loud enough to resonate under the pillow.

"Ow. It's not a hangover. Damn." Niki pushed the pillow away and cautiously felt his scalp.

Rhys was beside him on the bed then, parting Niki's hair, peering, his fingers light and competent. They were, Niki recalled uncomfortably, the same fingers that had done just that sort of thing when he was six, or eight, or twelve, or fourteen. This was his brother, the guardian of his rights, the keeper of his secrets. But not this secret. Not yet.

"Christ," Rhys said, "you've the devil's own lump back here!"

"I got coshed with a bottle."

The fingers stopped, drew back, as if Rhys's anger and the reason for it had only now reached the nerves that worked his hands. "Did you deserve it?" he asked, without emphasis.

"Someone thought so."

"I almost wish I'd done it myself."

Niki turned his head. Rhys sat on the edge of the bed, back straight, hands light on his knees—one of the stable postures in which Rhys contained his temper. Rhys was a calm and moderate man. Everyone knew it. "I'm glad you didn't. You probably would have killed me with it."

With a lurch, Rhys was on his feet. He went to the double doors and stood looking into the sitting room. "What were you doing last night?"

"Getting a friend's brother out of town."

"For God's sake, why?"

"I owed the friend a favor."

"I am neither slow nor stupid. If that was all it was, you could have come to me for the order of passage. Who is the friend, and who is the brother? And what did he do to require him to leave town?"

Niki raised himself on one elbow. "I don't interrogate well on—five?—five hours' sleep."

"Tell me who you gave the pass to, and I'll stop."

"There was a name on his orders."

"I repeat. I am neither slow nor stupid." The anger in Rhys's voice was like an undertow, deep, cold, and strong.

"If I name names now, innocent people will catch hell. Rhys, I'm authorized to use that code. The fact that I haven't, previously, doesn't change that. But one two-line entry on AdOp will, and if you don't trust my judgment, feel free to make it."

Rhys turned suddenly, and for that moment Niki thought he had made a mistake, had pushed Rhys into the undertow and would suffer for it. But at last Rhys said, "How did you get hit with the bottle?"

"A disagreement with one of the reasons why the brother had to leave," Niki said, and smiled. "A reflection on my judgment, if you like."

"Was it the police?"

"Do the police hit people with bottles now? No, it wasn't."

"I thought . . . I thought it might not have been a bottle after all."

Niki sank back on his pillow and sighed. "If I lied about that, I could have lied about it not being the police."

Rhys came back to the bedside and looked down at Niki. "What I don't trust is your understanding. There are factions out there that would bring the government down. If you stumble into playing figurehead for the likes of them, even Pedr can't keep your neck out of the noose. If your *friends* don't get you first.''

"You'd disown me?"

"I'd execute you for treason."

"Ah. Then I'll try not to commit any. Rhys, I will tell you all about it, but I can't now. So could you go away and let me nurse my hangover?"

"You said you didn't—"

"Well, after the bridge and the bottle, we thought we ought to get a little drunk."

"You do inspire confidence, don't you?" Rhys said pleasantly. He headed for the sitting room, stopped in the doorway, and turned. The timing of it was a little contrived, a little too much like a good actor's movements. "And Nik—I wouldn't try the trick with the sealcode again."

"You're right. I'll find something else."

"If you can find it," Rhys said, with a smile that was neither contrived nor pleasant, "so can I."

He slammed the door before Niki could pull the pillow back over his head.

"Mary Mother of Christ," Reg whispered, and there was more than ordinary irritation in his voice. Niki peered over his shoulder, around the angle of the construction yard fence, and saw the cause of it. Across West Oswallt Street, in front of the sober green-stone rooming house, were two men in police gray. The streetlamps struck light from their badges, the butts of their weapons, the visors of their helmets.

"Somebody called out the fucking Dogs," hissed Reg, and flung himself backward against the fence. "Damn, damn, damn."

Andrew, sitting on his heels in the shadows farther along the lane, said, "They may not have anything to do with us." His khaki-colored hair was a dusty-pale mass in the dark; a shaft from the nearest streetlight fell across his nose, mouth, and chin, and his hands lying loosely over his knees. He looked like some urban translation of a wicked elf-creature.

Reg gave a spitting, almost silent laugh, but said nothing.

"Or," Niki offered, leaning against the fence next to Reg, "they may be suspicious, but not certain."

"If that makes a difference, you will explain it to me, won't you?" Reg snapped.

This was Reg's operation. Reg had made the contacts, found out about the thing they'd come for, worked to get it into the hands of the woman who was waiting for them in the rooming house across the street. All of it neatly, quietly, without violence. Now the only obstruction was the width of the pavement, and two living men.

The secret of leadership, Niki reflected sourly, was to know how little control one had over others, and to keep them from knowing it, too. He kept his voice low and level, as if he were talking to a nervous horse.

"If they're certain, then they know who, and what, is in that building. And they know who got it there, and who's likely to show up to carry it away. In that case, we're all wanted men, and if we step out of this lane, they'll shoot us and try us for crimes against the state, in that order."

Reg glared at him.

"But if it's suspicion, if Martha Hoddard is under surveillance and nothing more—"

"And nothing more?"

Niki ignored the sarcasm. "If you got her out of there, is there somewhere you could take her?"

Reg tipped his head. "There's a safe house, at the end of—"

"Don't tell me, I shouldn't know." Niki pulled off the deep-brimmed hat he wore and shied it at Andrew, who caught it. Then he untied his neckcloth. "Either of you carry a flask?"

Reg held out a pocket flask, dark enamel and silver. Niki opened it and sniffed. "Peat bog extract. Perfect." He took a mouthful, rinsed it across his teeth, and let it fall in a vaporous, flammable mass down his throat. "Whooo. Llyn Ieuan?"

"Why do I forgive you for insulting my malt just because you call it by name?" Reg asked plaintively. "Peat bog extract, my ass."

"Then I hope you'll forgive me this, too," Niki said, poured some into his cupped palm, and used it for cologne. He shoved his fingers into his hair and made a mess of it. Reg stared, outraged beyond speech.

"I promise to give it back full," Niki told him.

"Of what?"

"Nik, don't do it," Andrew said. "The cops are all on edge.

They might pop a couple holes in you before they've looked to see who you are.''

"I'll let them know I'm coming. All right then—I'll be at the Lady de Winter in an hour, stay until closing, and go home. So if something goes wrong, and I'm asked about it—"

"—You don't know where we are, and you aren't expecting to see us," Reg finished. "You, mate, are the product of generations of bloody-minded politicians."

"It's what made this country great. Is this lane open at the other end?"

Andrew nodded. One corner of his mouth came up in a grin; the harsh half-light made a friendly snarl of it. "You smell like the bottom of a barrel. Good luck."

Niki ran up the lane and stopped at the far end, where it opened onto a cross street. The street was empty. He stepped out and began to walk unsteadily toward the intersection of West Oswallt Street, clutching Reg's flask. A careful distance before he turned the corner, he let the policemen know he was coming. He burst into "All Things Are Quite Silent," with a comprehensive disregard for key.

As it happened, Niki did not reach the Lady de Winter until shortly after closing. After making a great deal of benign trouble and luring the policemen half a block away from where they'd meant to be, he had received a stern and probably sobering lecture about curfews, and an escort home. He'd managed to convince the officer who drove the van that he could find his own way into the Castle. But it was a long walk from the hill back to the Old City.

He rattled his knuckles against the Lady de Winter's heavy door, and the eye in the security plate turned, whining, on him. He grinned at it and held his hands palm-up. The bolt clunked back, and he went in.

Reg and Andrew were leaning on the bar, and seemed to be working out an attack of nervous hilarity. Jane Wells stood behind the counter, drawing their beer. When Niki stepped through the door she frowned at him and thumped the glasses down.

"What if you'd walked in and found the cops, instead of us?" she snapped. "How would you have explained what you're doing here after closing?"

He stopped halfway to the bar and raised his eyebrows. Reg and Andrew had fallen silent and startled; that was some comfort. "I'd have done the rich drunk ass again. I'm in practice, after all."

Jane dropped her eyes, as if to conserve her anger.

"I'm sorry, Jane," Niki added gently. "Were you very worried about us?"

"Me? I can't afford the time."

"C'mon, Jane," Andrew said. "He did a damn good job of it. Give him your blessing and a drink, won't you?"

Jane looked resigned. "What'll you have?"

"Coffee," Niki said. "The smell of burning peat has put me off honest drink altogether."

"The hell!" Reg roared, as he was meant to, and they relaxed into a mood of modest celebration.

Before he left, Reg tossed a little plastic box at Niki. He caught it and looked at the label. "Am I going to catch a cold?" he asked Reg.

"If you do, don't put one of those on your tongue without giving it a look first."

Niki snapped the lid up. The package was almost full, seven blue EfferGest in three neat rows. He upended the box on his palm. On the bottom of one of the tablets, sunk into it like inlay, was the shining rainbowed surface of a romdot. Niki laughed. "God—like a vid full of intergalactic spies." He shook the tablets back into the box. "Why give it to me? It's your trophy."

Reg almost made one of his rude comments—Niki saw him master the impulse and bite down on the words. Instead he said, "You'll know what to do with it. I don't."

"You know what's on this, then?"

"I know what might be on it." He shoved his hands in his pockets and turned away. "Check the street for me, will you, Jane?"

The driver for the door eye grated. "All clear."

"Right, then." And he was gone.

Andrew sighed. "Don't trouble at it. He wouldn't tell me, either."

"Well, it's security," Niki said, and shrugged. "I'll know soon enough." He looked hopefully from his empty cup to Jane, and she refilled it.

"Coffee," Andrew said, on a little laugh. "Isn't that bad for your reputation? Or was the rep unearned?"

Niki looked into the cup, at his reflection in the dark surface. It was true, he hadn't had much to drink lately. He'd lied to Rhys about the hangover. And he hadn't had a pin-scratch, or even gas, since—he wasn't sure. Looking back, there hadn't seemed time for it. "The source of the drug problem among the lower classes," he said, "is too much leisure."

"And the nobs?"

"*Infinitely* too much leisure."

Andrew nodded. "It's poetic justice, then. I'm all comforted." He picked up his jacket. "Reg ought to be good and clear. I need to go home and sleep, or I'll drive a loader into someone's nice starship tomorrow."

"No drug problem for you. What's it like, working at the port?"

"Like work," Andrew said firmly. "Talk of leisure, when shall we three meet again?"

"I'll take a look at Reg's little present and let you know."

Jane checked the street again, and Andrew let himself out. As he did, he looked at Jane. "Don't leave any bruises," he said, and closed the door behind him.

"What, still mad at me?" Niki asked her.

"Don't ask me," she said, stung. "I don't know what he's talking about."

The sound of the floor scrubber was not quite loud enough to prevent conversation. Though it wasn't silence Niki found himself sitting in, it was just as uncomfortable. He drank coffee and resolved to give Andrew fifteen minutes' lead.

"You've got a new nickname," Jane said, and shut off the scrubber.

"I what?"

"Yeah. They call you the Long Beau."

Niki laughed and choked on his coffee. "God, not really?"

Jane looked prickly. "It's better than the Little Viscount."

"Yes, but—well, why?"

Jane drew herself half a glass of stout and leaned at the bar. "Some of them recognize you," she said at last. "Not all of them, but enough. They know who's helping 'em. But it might not be good if they put your name to you."

"But why a name at all? I don't . . . I don't get it."

She looked up. There was something, almost a smile, pulling at her mouth. "They tell stories about you, you ass. They'll be talking about this one tomorrow, about you playing the fool to save some lass from the Grays."

"That's not exactly—"

"And in a week there'll be six versions, every one telling it better than the last." Now she was grinning outright. "How do you feel about that?"

Niki covered his eyes. "Oh, Christ. Embarrassed. Silly. I'm not cut out for this." *Viscount Harlech on a white horse. Pedr would think he'd been right.*

"Reg'd love to be a legend."

"By all means, give him mine. I don't want it."

Jane put her elbows on the bar, one on either side of his coffee cup, and stared at him. "What *do* you want, Dominic Glyndwr?"

He drew back, startled.

"What are you in this for?"

"I want to do what's right."

"There are lots of 'rights.' Every minute of the day there's another flock of right things to do—depending on what you *want*."

"You don't believe in absolute right?"

"No. And neither will you, if you live long enough." She finished her stout in one long swallow. "In the meantime, maybe that's why you get to be a legend and Reg doesn't."

Niki laced his fingers over the top of his cup. It didn't warm them; the coffee was cold. "I've been looking for your husband—for some record of where they might have taken him. But there's a lot of places to look." He wasn't certain why he'd said that; he glanced up quickly, to see if he'd hurt her. "Careful—you're going to break that glass."

"He's dead."

"How do you know?"

"Because unlike some people, I don't believe in fairies. If he's been gone this long, he's not coming back."

"But you can't be sure—"

She was holding her empty glass over the edge of the bar, her face impassive. As he watched, she let the glass go. It smashed on the floor she'd just cleaned. Then she turned the same face to him. "So now you're a prophet."

His nerves rattled and rang like a string of bells in the wind. "What do *you* want?"

She was very still, looking at nothing. Niki studied her profile, severe and interrupted by the fringe over her eyes. It seemed too calm to belong to a woman who'd just broken a glass. "I'll tell you what I want," she said in a steady, distant voice. "I want to quit thinking about death. Dead people, dead things, dead God-damned ideals. Just once, I want to spend maybe a whole half hour on something that only has to do with life.'' Then she looked at him.

He had to drop his gaze. Perhaps, he thought, he'd spent all his courage on her list of dead things, and had none left over for her. Whatever it was, she saw it. She came out from behind the bar and crouched over the bits of broken glass, picking them up and setting them carefully in her palm.

''I didn't mean to—''

''Go home, Niki,'' she said.

He'd hurt her; or he'd come close enough to it that she had to send him away. In shame and sorrow and helpless anger, he left the pub. A sudden cold had come down from the hills and turned the night clear, filled with little noises that didn't carry in thicker air. He could hear the grit under his boot soles as he walked. *I want to go away and be a pilot,* he thought, *that's what I want. No legends, heroes, martyrs, or broken hearts.*

He was ten blocks from the Lady de Winter before it occurred to him that he'd never before heard her call him ''Niki.''

He cracked the blue tablet in half to free the romdot, and blew the dust off it. Then he dropped it into his desktop 'board and snapped the bin closed. He didn't turn the thing on.

Instead he wiped his palms on his thighs and thought about Reg. ''You'll know what to do with it,'' he'd said, and, ''I know what might be on it.'' With none of his usual alkaline manner. Looking at the dead, black panel of the 'board, Niki discovered a thing he wouldn't have believed a month before: that there could be facts he did not want to know. *You don't believe in absolute right?* ''Yes,'' he said to the desktop, ''I do.'' And lit the 'board.

At first, he couldn't read the dot at all. Every format he tried to fit to it produced nonsense. If it had been some other medium, he would have thought it had passed through a security egg-beater. But romdots were burned; they couldn't be rewritten or scrambled in a field. Had Reg been sold an empty egg?

He ran a pattern analysis on the dot's only document, and the panel shone with color and geometry: neat blue uprights with red fretwork leaping from one to another, green-gold joints at all the angles, steel gray spheres like beads threaded evenly throughout. Not nonsense, then—this was the made-shape of code. It was stiff and overly regular, which meant either it was machine-written, or he probably wouldn't have liked the writer.

He turned the pattern into its component parts, into the raw numbers, and let them stream by under his eyes. He could sort the whole business by frequency, as if he were cracking text code. . . . Then he saw a bit string he recognized, and saw it again, and again. Go To, encrypted for—

"AdOp?" He hadn't meant to say it aloud, but he was surprised. This was government-originated, then. He hadn't expected Reg's chain of hands to start in the government. He swung back up to command level, and offered it his own passkey to AdOp. He had a guess, now, that he could test.

Entering Administrative Operations was like looking into a castle through an arrow-slit. It was axiomatic among users that one could only find something in AdOp if one already knew it was there. There were few easy, visible branches, few connections to parallel topics, few hints for the floundering novice. It was a terrible government database—but it was an excellent locked file cabinet. There were guides on-line to finding information, if it was information anyone might have. But sensitive material could be hidden by the simple act of placing it in the system. According to folklore, there was a great sprawling path of classified data in AdOp that no one could find, because some highly placed cabinet member had been hit by a hover and died before he could tell his successor how to get at it.

Niki arrived at the first branch prompt and waited, staring at the panel for a suffocating length of time. He was wrong. The dot was not what he'd thought it might be. He would have to crack the secrets out of the thing the hard way, and if it involved AdOp, he might never crack them. He had, perhaps, several seconds in which to despair. Then the prompt disappeared, and was replaced with another. Niki grinned and thumped the table lightly in delight. The dot contained an AdOp procedure map. And it was running.

Another prompt, and another. The procedure moved in a blind path, which suppressed display of the responses to the prompts. If he needed to know them, he could decode them from the raw numbers. But a blind path was an uncommon precaution. What sort of information would be kept at the end of it?

The file on the romdot was the output of a procedure recorder. Use of a procedure recorder on an AdOp link was a Crown offense. But someone had risked it, in order to steal a record of the sequence of commands used to reach a document in AdOp. Another prompt appeared and disappeared.

He wanted to call it back. He wanted to shut the 'board down; he would have, if the toxins distilled from fear hadn't gotten into his muscles and frozen them. Because Absolute Right, in its Fury guise, was rushing down on him. He could hear its wings.

The 'board went blank for an instant. Then the panel began to fill with words. They appeared at someone else's reading speed, slower than Niki's. But then, he was so very good, so very quick, at working the 'board.

It was a prescription for an analgesic. Nothing more.

Then why was it at the end of a blind path? Why had someone risked life in prison to steal a map of that path? Why had that map been given to Reg?

The first possibility that occurred to him sent his hand flying for the 'board's kill switch. It could be poison bait. It could be setting off alarms somewhere in AdOp even now, identifying the endpoint of a treasonous leak of information. He stopped with the 'board still on. If it was bait, then he was too late already. And it might not be bait at all.

The prescribing physician's name was Arcault. He didn't recognize it, or the name of the analgesic, but the instruction was, "To be taken as needed for headaches. Do not exceed 8 measured applications in any 24 hr. period." There was no refill limit. At the bottom were two validating tags. The first would be the ID of the patient. The second would be the pharmacist's ID, with the date and time the prescription went on file.

Niki stared at the panel, frowning, for a long minute. Then he backed out of AdOp and began to comb his way through a series of other net services. When he was done, he had a new panel full of information.

The drug was a legitimate prescription painkiller. It was packaged in inhaler form. The prescription had been issued two and a half months ago. The pharmacist's ID was not legitimate, not now or, as far as he could determine, ever. No such file. Arcault was real. He had practiced medicine for two years—until a little over a month ago, when he had drowned while swimming.

The patient was Pedr.

The sitting room seemed cold and too big, full of the entombing silence of the Castle at night. Until morning, he was alone with his questions. They were lively company. He got no sleep at all.

CHAPTER FIVE

> He, too, has resigned his part
> In the casual comedy;
> He, too, has been changed in his turn,
> Transformed utterly:
> A terrible beauty is born.
>   —W. B. Yeats, "Easter 1916"

When Niki left his room he was washed, neatly dressed, and half convinced that someone had vacuumed his tongue. He wished desperately that he had a pin of almost anything; even Poison, the purchased suffering of weekend poets, would run like gas-blue fire through his veins and clear his mind with pain. Sleep would have been nice.

It was barely breakfast time; there might not be anyone in the solarium yet. But he was too restless to stay in his rooms. After a moment, he followed the corridor away from the family quarters, toward the public areas. He paused for a minute in the bubble of a dome window, looking out at the hills behind the Castle. The sun was barely high enough to cast light over the shoulders of the slopes, and it was still dawn in the woods there. Niki saw flecks of yellow and red among the greens. That made him anxious, like a general dreading a winter campaign. His campaign couldn't be stopped by snow—but the feeling of running out of time wouldn't quite leave him.

Of course—the new year. Offworld waited, Galatea and a place in the College of Navigation. It was his chance to live at last in the wide world his mother inhabited—wider even than hers, in the borderless country between the stars. He'd wanted to be free of Cymru, its isolationism and its windowbox politics. He'd been afraid that Pedr might take his chance from him. But some time in the past few weeks, he'd been robbed of it more completely than Pedr could ever have done. His country had some use for him, and he would stay and nurse it as if it were a dying relative. He turned away from the window and its glowing view.

He came out into the Great Hall, on the second-floor gallery. The glassy golden balustrade was cold under his hands. Above him was the underside of the third-floor gallery, ornamented with constellations that glimmered as if through atmosphere. It showed the early autumn sky to match the season, with the Flock of Geese low in the west and the Dolphin straight up. High above that, when he leaned out over the railing, he could see the hall's glass roof, milky with filtered morning sun. The glass was fretted with gold in a pattern of overlapping ovals; it looked now like a white peony blossom. Below was the shining deep green disk of the floor.

He wondered how much Reg knew about what he'd handed over. Enough to know that what seemed to be an ordinary prescription had to be more, and that how much more could be best learned from inside the Castle. He would certainly have guessed how uncomfortable the whole problem would make Niki. Probably gloated over it—no, that wasn't fair. Reg hadn't been particularly smug last night at the pub. Niki drummed his fingers on the top rail of the balustrade and watched the Dolphin wink over his head. All his future from that moment looked like swirling water; once he moved into the whirlpool's edge, he would spin down it whether he was ready or not. He wished he had a clearer head for the plunge.

The shining, hard surfaces of the Great Hall carried heat badly, and sound with such caprice that dampers had to be turned on during any public function to make the speeches intelligible. The voices that Niki heard had been reflected so many times before they'd reached him that he couldn't identify the speakers or the words. Then two figures came into view on the first floor, in the archway that led to the state chambers. Neither of them looked up. Even so, Niki stepped back promptly. When he realized he'd done it, he was embarrassed; but he didn't move forward again.

It was Pedr and Rhys. They were walking slowly, making time for their conversation. Both of them were dressed for a stiff, working daytime in long, high-collared jackets; on the breast of Rhys's coat the badge of Cymru caught the light. Rhys was speaking. His hands moved in sharp, angular shapes, as if to package the air between them. His brown hair shone with red lights, vivid against the green floor. From above, his shoulders seemed even wider than they were, and his dark red coat fit smoothly over them, shifted with their movement, spoke the silent language of expensive tailoring. Even from such a distance, his hands looked manicured, and his face was smooth and tanned and handsome even when it frowned. *My brother*, Niki thought, feeling suddenly like a changeling.

But Pedr, his uncle, his prince . . . From this odd vantage point, Niki could see Pedr almost as a stranger, almost as if for the first time. He was struck again by something new in the way he moved. Once, Niki was sure, his uncle had walked and gestured as Rhys did, full of unexamined confidence and the grace that money bought even when it was spent on something else. Now he walked as if he expected the air to block his way, and was prepared to break barriers with every step. As if he hurt, had been hurt, and was ready to hurt back.

Nor did he share Rhys's sleek good health. His skin was sallow and dull. As Niki watched, he pinched the bridge of his nose, rubbed between and over his eyebrows. *Headache*, Niki thought; and Pedr's hand went into his coat pocket and came out with an inhaler. Two long pulls from it—Niki remembered the prescription form. *Do not exceed 8 measured applications.* That was two, and it wasn't even breakfast yet. It was not a dangerous painkiller, but it was a fairly strong one. What would too much of it do?

Niki had been able to understand perhaps one word out of twenty of the conversation below him, and none of them had been significant. He damned all architects as Pedr and Rhys passed through the arch on the other side of the hall, toward the family's rooms and, probably, breakfast. It was time to follow them. He was about to head for the corridor, to retrace his steps, when movement at the corner of his vision made him turn.

In the archway where Pedr and Rhys had first appeared, the one that led to the state chambers, Jacob now leaned. He was watching Niki. Jacob had taught Niki to play chess; he would look at Niki the way he was looking now, when he had moved a piece and wanted to see if Niki understood why. He seemed about as well rested as Niki himself. *They've been working him hard.* Niki shrugged, a broad gesture intended to reach the first floor, and headed for breakfast.

When he opened the solarium doors, sunlight poured out like thick white dust, warm and blinding. He blinked in it, feeling foolish and defenseless.

Amazing, the things one could tell without sight. Grilled salmon, potato pancakes, sour cream. Muffins. Pineapples? Oh, yes. Tea, that had already steeped black and would take the saliva out of the tongue. And the smell of coffee—

Which meant Kitty was there, too.

Shit, he thought. *I wish I were in bed. Asleep. On another planet.*

"*Good* morning," he said, and squinted his way to a chair. It was next to Rhys, as it turned out, across from Kitty, and down the table from Pedr. The hotpot full of coffee was in front of him, so he poured some into a cup and drank it. It stirred the fog in his brain like a great brown-black hand. He nerved himself to look straight at Kitty. And to not think, *Your husband may be in trouble.* After all, if Pedr was in trouble, Niki wasn't sure what kind. It was as good a rationalization as any.

He could have spared himself the effort; Kitty wasn't looking at him. She seemed to be using civility as a cork for some other attitude, and was buttering a muffin as if it required all her attention.

Rhys was casting sidelong glances at Kitty. Pedr, at the head of the table, was eating salmon, scowling, and not looking at anyone. *Lovers' quarrel?* Niki thought.

"Well, I think it's a good morning," he said. "Pass me the fish, will you, someone?"

It was in front of Pedr, but Rhys passed it. "What the devil are you doing up at this hour?"

"You don't sound happy to see me."

"And why should I be?" said Rhys. "You look terrible. Have you been out all night?"

Kitty set her knife down on the side of her plate with a subdued clang. "This family has the worst notions of what constitutes decent breakfast table conversation." She still paid no attention to Niki; her words were for Rhys. "Could you harass your brother later, and let us all digest in peace?"

Pedr broke his silence at last. "What business is it of yours what Rhys says to his brother?"

"None. I'm talking about *my* breakfast, and *my* digestion. And you're all enough to make a recycler sick."

"All of us?" Niki asked.

"Behave," Kitty told him.

"Good advice," Pedr said, "if he'll take it." His voice, the flexible, forceful tool of a politician, was mild. "Perhaps being taken up for public drunkenness and violation of curfew has reformed his character." He raised his eyes from his plate and stared blandly down the table at Niki.

Niki was still wearing some of the smile he'd given Kitty. It froze on his face, along with anything else that was there, when he met Pedr's stare. With an effort, he said pleasantly, "There were no charges."

"I am the Crown," said Pedr. "There are if I want them."

"Wouldn't that violate my civil rights?" *Rhys*, he begged silently, *help me!* But Rhys said nothing, and his fork moved steadily over his plate.

"We're under martial law. You have no civil rights. Breaking curfew would place an ordinary citizen under suspicion of actions against the Crown. Should I treat you differently?"

Niki couldn't look away from Pedr, couldn't tell if anyone else at the table was seeing what he saw. Pedr's square, genial face was full of something that made him think the hounds were at his throat.

"That's enough," said Kitty. Pedr turned his head, and Niki felt as if he'd been yanked bodily out of a nightmare. He looked quickly at Kitty. She was pale and angry and unlike herself. *But then, we all are, aren't we?*

"I beg your pardon?" Pedr said, still mild.

Kitty matched his tone. "I've never seen you use the power of the state as if it were a snapknife."

Pedr seemed taken aback. "I've never had to ask my nephew if he was guilty of treason."

"Heavens, did you ask him that?" Kitty pressed a hand to her breast. "*I* thought you were threatening him with unnamed torments for an undefined crime. Silly me."

Pedr pushed his chair back with a scrape.

"No, don't get up," Kitty said. "I'll save you the trouble." She rose, her dignity not at all impaired by her pregnancy. "Thank you all, it's been a lovely meal. I'm sure I'll see you later." She turned her back on Pedr, her face to the solarium doors. As she did, her gaze fell hard on Niki. It was vivid and urgent and, to him, unreadable. He felt too battered to give her more than a blink in answer.

Her exit was a little marred; she had to wait for Morwenna to come through the door before she could leave. Morwenna watched her go, raised her eyebrows, and looked at Pedr, Rhys, and Niki. "Something I said?" she asked brightly. Niki relaxed a little into his chair. If anyone was capable of playing brittler-than-thou with Pedr, it was Morwenna. She sat at the other end of the table from Pedr, next to Niki.

There might never have been a brother and sister less alike than Morwenna and Pedr. Pedr had never been overweight, but he was a sturdy-built man, rosy-faced when he was healthy, brown-haired, remarkable in his power if not his person. He was ten years younger than his sister, and looked ten years older. Morwenna was small and slender, and a study in black and white—pale skin, smooth black hair. Her eyes were round and gray and brilliant, her face was lean and high-boned, and her features were sharply defined, as if the world were a video image, and she had better resolution than anything around her. Niki knew that the illusion of her agelessness was due in part to cellular rebuilding. But Pedr had taken rebuild therapy, too.

A stranger would never identify Rhys and Niki as Morwenna's children, either. No, he would think Rhys and Pedr were brothers, and that Niki and Morwenna were brother and sister. And he would think that the two families were not getting along.

Morwenna had a pile of printout with her; she dropped it on the table with a bang that made the silverware and Pedr jump. Rhys cast a look, mournful and resigned, at his mother. "So sorry, dears," she said. "Pedr, don't sulk, you'll curdle the milk. Tea, please?"

Niki looked down the table in surprise. Pedr *was* sulking, in an adult fashion. He was so unlike the hunting animal Niki had been facing only minutes ago that it made him doubt his wits. It was as if someone had replaced one Pedr with another when he turned away, and neither was the Pedr he'd thought he knew.

Morwenna stared at Niki as if she'd just noticed him. "What are you doing up at this hour?"

"You'd think I'd never seen the left side of noon before," Niki said. He was careful not to let his gaze wander to Rhys, who had asked that question first. "Having breakfast."

Now it was time for Pedr to renew his accusations, to tell Morwenna that Niki had run afoul of the Dogs last night. Instead, Pedr got up from the table. "There's work waiting," he said. "Bloody finance minister comes 'round in half an hour. Rhys, find out how Deauville's doing on that study, will you?" He frowned at Niki, but absently, as if he was reminded of some irksome, unfinished task. Then he left.

"That," Niki murmured, after staring at the empty doorway for a moment, "is not a well man."

"Nonsense," said Rhys calmly. "There's nothing wrong with Pedr—"

"The hell there isn't. You saw—"

"—and there's nothing to be gained by saying otherwise."

Is that a threat? Niki wanted to ask. It was Morwenna's presence that stopped him. Acting out the whole wretched business in front of her—she would hate it, and it would involve her in it. She had never been touched with this inconvenient sense of allegiance to Cymru. When she came of age, she'd petitioned Parliament to remove her from the succession in favor of her younger brother. The resulting uproar must have been hard to live through; but Morwenna knew even then what she wanted, and it was research, not government. She'd gotten her way in the end. Niki sometimes wondered if she'd had children only to make sure she would never be called on to rule.

So Niki said to Rhys only, "You seemed willing to let him speak his piece to the end."

"He's entitled."

"You didn't disagree?"

Rhys gave him a long, steady, unfathomable look. "We'll never know, will we?" He pushed his chair back and stood. "I won't tell you to stay out of trouble. Mother," he said to Morwenna, inclining his head in farewell.

"You may be excused," she said, wickedly grave.

Rhys sighed. "Yes, I know where he gets his attitudes."

When Rhys was gone, Niki put his elbows on the table and rested his chin on his laced fingers. "Every family needs a black sheep. I think I'm in training to be ours."

"You can't have the job," Morwenna said, grinning. "It's mine."

"Hah. No, we're both wrong. There are no sheep in this family. And you're the alpha wolf."

Her smile disappeared in a headshake. "It's Pedr that leads the pack."

"Mmm. Then who—or what, now that I think on it—is leading Pedr?"

Her hands clasped suddenly on each other, showing white at the joints. "Careful," she said, almost whispering.

"What is it?" Niki asked, covering her hands with his.

He watched her draw control over herself like a veil. She leaned back in her chair, apparently calm, and her fingers slipped away from him. "Pour me some tea, will you?" she said, and her voice was normal.

By the time he handed her the cup, she seemed again like a woman immune to nerves. Then, with Olympian calm, she declared, "I want you to leave for Galatea as soon as you can be ready."

He never spilled things; but there was coffee in his plate. "Why?"

One corner of her mouth lifted. "I thought you wanted to go."

"I did."

She sipped her tea. "Don't fence with me, Nik. You won't win."

She was right, of course. "Smart or stupid," he said, "I am involved in whatever is happening to Cymru. I've involved myself in it. There are people who count on me. For things that may be trivial and pointless, but they still count on me. And they may not be pointless."

"And if you die at it?"

The bald expression of it shook him, but he said, "Then I do."

"Then you will have thrown a valuable life away on a worthless cause."

Her words, and the contained anger with which she said them, drove him to say, "Maybe you've never believed in anything enough to die for it."

"You are a God-damned adolescent, and your understanding of death is that it's the ultimate expression of love." Her eyes were narrowed, as if she were trying to bottle up the fury there. "The squabble for possession of Cymru will kill you. And then you will not be a lover, or a martyr, or a hero. You will be a piece of rotting meat. And everything that has gone into you will be like a glass of water poured into the sea."

"A few glasses have already been poured out, out there," Niki said, jerking his head in the direction of the city.

"I'm not talking about food and sixteen bloody years of

schooling at public expense! I'm talking—'' She brought both hands to her face.

"About what?" he asked, but gently.

She dropped her hands. "Nothing, it seems." There was no catch or roughness in her voice. "And a fine way to lead up to asking a favor." She whisked four sheets off her pile of printout. "Would you work these buggers over for me?"

Niki raised his eyebrows. "What do I know about sticking proteins together?"

"Absolutely nothing, goddess bless you. I want a pattern/frequency analysis on the numbers, and you have a nodding acquaintance with that sort of thing."

"A passing familiarity." He always followed her emotional lead; he did so now, trying not to mind the fragility of the footing. "Do you need them soon?"

"Don't I always?"

He took the pages and stood up. An urge that he was helpless either to ignore or improve on made him rest his hand lightly on Morwenna's shoulder. He couldn't see her face, but this time there *was* a catch in her voice as she said, "Will you think about going, at least? Please?"

"I do," he answered her. "But it's too late now."

She neither moved nor spoke, and he left the solarium not sure that she believed him.

He went first to the terrace overlooking the garden. But the sun hadn't reached it yet, and the damp chill of morning clung there still. Autumn's flowers glowed in the shadows under the topiary: spiral lilies, asters, chrysanthemums, cat's-tongue. The library was empty. The gallery, filled with light and heat like warm honey from its wall of sunshifter windows, was empty, too. The synthichord at one end was a silent wedge of shining, red-veined wood, and no one sat at it. Finally he jabbed a housecom port to life and asked it, "Where's Her Highness right now?"

"In her rooms, Niki."

He was about to buzz her; then he thought of something else. "And His Highness?"

"Meeting with the finance minister in the Hall of Earth."

"Thank you. Call Her Highness's room for me."

There was a delay before Kitty answered, and when she did, it was voice-only.

"It's Niki," he said. "Can I come up?"

"Oh." Then she said, "Well, no one's stopping you."

"Does that mean I ought not to come up?"

"Oh, God—stop being polite. Yes, come up."

He took the lift tube. When he knocked at her door, the latch clacked open, but she didn't call. It was in keeping with her sentiments over the housecom, so he stepped in.

She was stretched out on a softform lounge, turned to look out the tall bay windows at the hills. The room was as light-washed as the solarium, from the windows and from the white and yellow and pale rusty rose the room was done in. There was a holoprint on one creamy wall, of a woman in a yellow dress sleeping among flowers. It was exquisite, evocative; he felt, for a dizzying instant, as if he'd lain next to that woman, felt the breath from her lips, seen the breeze catch and flutter her yellow skirt. The patterned carpet under his feet was thick. The furniture was low, the ceiling high, and the combination settled his mind and lifted his heart, like a clearing amid tall trees. Music played, spatters of notes and sweeps of chords that seemed to sway and nod.

"My feet hurt," Kitty said mournfully, so he knew she'd heard him come in.

"I know. They always do." He crossed the floor silently, and, seized again by the impulse that had placed his hand on Morwenna's shoulder, he kissed the top of Kitty's head.

She drew a short breath, and he came around to the side of the lounge where he could see her face. "Head hurt, too?"

"No."

When she didn't say anything else, he ventured, "Maybe I ought to go away, after all."

She looked startled. "I wish you wouldn't. I'm sorry if I'm bad company."

"You aren't. Not yet, anyway. I like the music."

"Stenshoel's *Daffodil*. The 'Calyx' movement."

A set of related thoughts found each other in his head, and he laughed. "You're always surrounded by flowers. Or images of flowers. You always turn toward the light. I hadn't seen it before."

She flushed. "Is that supposed to mean anything?"

"Maybe we should call you Blodeuwedd."

He'd meant it as a joke, an offering to drive away her sharp mood. But she bit her lip, and said, "Let's not," and he knew it had gone wide.

He sat on the carpet next to the lounge. In the new-made light, her skin was like—no, not like flower petals, she hadn't wanted that. The hair around her face, soft and lifting with static, was fired from brown to amber. She looked nothing like Olwen, but for a moment, he was reminded of her. "Did you know that you saved my skin, back in the solarium?"

She spread her hands.

"It was a nice side effect, even if that wasn't why you told him off."

"That was why."

Her responses weren't, exactly; so he wrapped his arms around his knees, and waited for her to speak, hoping she'd come at last to what he wanted to know. He studied the holoprint, and listened to the music, and by the time she began to talk, he felt almost relaxed.

"I defended him to you, when you came home at the end of the summer. Now I wonder if I should have. You wanted to know why he didn't trust you, and I thought I understood why. Since then . . . things have happened, that I can't understand at all. And I'm beginning to think that what I told you was rational behavior might not have been."

In other words, Niki wanted to say, *Pedr's orbit is decaying.* He didn't say it. He knew how hard it was for Kitty to admit what she had, even in such equivocal terms. He nodded, and kept his eyes on the holoprint.

"Pedr's always been sure of himself. I suppose he's even been obnoxious about it, on occasion. Now—well, he's not anymore. Sometimes he wants to make sure everyone concurs with what he's doing. Other times he refuses to listen to anyone else, as if he's afraid of being questioned. He gets suspicious, even of me. He has moods—one moment he's so jolly you can hardly stand him, and the next, he's throwing a tantrum."

"At you?" It seemed inconceivable.

"Oh, yes. Oh, he hasn't hit me," she said quickly, probably in answer to something in his face. "You don't think I'd stand for that? No, he yells. And I yell back. Like at breakfast. And then he turns into an overgrown grumpy schoolboy, which I think disturbs me more than all the rest of it."

"He did that at breakfast, too," Niki said absently. "How long has he had the headaches?"

"You know about those? Months. They started early in the summer."

"Has he been examined for . . . anything?"

"Tumors, you mean?" she said sharply. "Yes, of course. Nothing abnormal."

"Was the scan done by the same doctor who prescribed his painkiller?"

"No, the scan was earlier. Rhys recommended Arcault after that."

Niki looked up, startled. "Rhys did? Huh. Did you know Arcault was dead?"

It was her turn to start. "No. We *have* been busy, haven't we?"

"Someone has," he muttered. "Someone. Kitty, I'm going to ask you to do me a favor. If you can't, in good conscience, then tell me to get my ass out of your sitting room. But I want you to know that, no matter how bad it looks, I'm doing it for the right reasons."

With a ghost of her old smile, she said, "If I sit here long enough, you'll get to the favor."

He dug his fingers into the carpet. "I want you to get me that inhaler."

She drew a long, shocked breath. "Christ. You think he wouldn't notice?"

"Kitty, I've got to find out what's in it."

"Can't I just copy off the label for you?"

"I know what's on the label. I've been busy, remember?"

She folded her hands over her stomach and stared at them. "You don't ask for easy ones, do you?" she said bitterly.

"Tell me to bugger off. I can try to get hold of it myself."

"You couldn't. He doesn't trust you enough to let you near his pockets."

"And if you get it for me, and he finds out," Niki said, "he won't trust you, either."

She laughed, a short, hollow noise, and bent her head. Her hair fell in a shining curtain and hid her face. He reached out quickly and touched her arm. "I'm sorry. I shouldn't have brought this to you. If I'd thought for thirty seconds, I wouldn't have."

"Why did you?" she asked, sweeping her hair back. Neither her face nor her voice were angry, only oddly intent.

"You got his fangs out of my throat, in the solarium. A little longer, and I would have left the room with a guard on either side. I could see it coming. My own brother sat beside me eating his bloody breakfast while it happened, and afterward behaved as if Pedr had the right idea."

"Idiot," she muttered, but not, it seemed, to him.

"I was so grateful—that I thought of you as my ally, and forgot you were his wife first."

She made a little sound, and laid her head against the back of the lounge, her eyes closed. The lounge shifted itself to her contours. "Your ally," she repeated, as if to feel the shape of the words in her mouth. Then she opened her eyes, turned them to the windows again. "I thought I was a fairy-tale princess. Instead, I'm the wife of a prince. They're not at all the same thing."

This, Niki felt, was over his head. "He still loves you. This is . . . Whatever it is, I think it's something outside him."

Kitty smiled at him, a sad, charming, one-sided smile. "This is going to come as a shock to you. But sometimes that doesn't matter." Her hand moved, stopped in midair halfway between her face and his. On one finger, Pedr's ruby caught the light. The hand dropped and folded in a fist. "Christ. I just want to be happy."

"You should be. Maybe we can still fix it all," he told her. He was helpless to answer the thing in her face that he didn't understand.

"Nobody can fix it. Not anymore." She looked down at her stomach. "Shit."

He took her hand, wrapped both of his around it, and her mouth twisted as if he'd hurt her. He let go, and stood up. "I'm going. Kitty, forget about it. I can get what I need somewhere else."

She laughed.

When he was halfway to the door, she said, "I wonder if the only way to survive in this family is to do what your mother has done. To be so removed from it all that you can look at the people you love as if they were cells on a slide."

Morwenna was his mother, and his mirror, and the device by which he measured much of the world. "Do you think she does?" he said coolly, thinking of the solarium. "I don't."

"I know. That was low of me. I'm sorry."

Which suggested that she'd said it on purpose, which baffled him. "It's all right," he told her.

At the door, he remembered something. "Kitty, do you know where Pedr gets the prescription filled?"

"No." Her voice sounded clogged. "Um. I think I've heard him ask Rhys to get it."

He let himself out without bothering her again.

He went riding. He wanted the exercise, he wanted the air, and most of all, he wanted the chance to be free of the damned

Castle. He hadn't realized that he'd gotten a second wind until it deserted him, which it did as he left Kitty's room. Now he was so tired that he felt as if pieces of him were dying. But there was something frightening about the prospect of going back to his rooms and falling asleep. It didn't feel safe.

The bay gelding was a hunter, used to rough ground and long distances. Niki took advantage of it and went up into the hills. He followed wooded paths where he had to duck low branches, and where the undergrowth closed in and rattled on his boots as he passed. He climbed pathless slopes where the rust-spotted bracken brushed the tall horse's knees, where he rode on the bay's shoulders and over his neck to balance against the angle of ascent. He put his mount at streams and permaplast walls and fallen trees, and the bay jumped them all as if humoring him. By the time he reached the high meadows, Niki had to admit that no matter how many obstacles he threw his heart over, he couldn't throw it out of his body, or his mind out of his head, or the cacophony of voices out of his mind. *"I am the Crown."* *No, you aren't*, Niki said to the memory of that cold, hungry face. *You're the man who wears it. There's a difference.*

"Everything that has gone into you will be like a glass of water poured into the sea." But isn't that what's made me the sort of person who won't leave? Everything that's gone into me?

"I just want to be happy." For that, he found, he had no answer.

And Rhys. What had Rhys said that needed answering? Or, worse, done? Had he filled Pedr's prescription at a pharmacy that didn't exist? Had he sent him to Arcault for something more than a painkiller? Had he really listened as Pedr prepared an accusation of treason against his brother—heard, and not cared?

The end of that thought was sharper than Niki had realized; it was in his heart and the little noise of pain out of his throat before he saw it. The bay flicked an ear backward.

They walked through a rolling field of high grass, thickly dotted with the brown three-pronged blooms of Englishman's Hatrack. The wind was cool, the sun warm, and the air smelled of crushed grasses and the sea. The field was rough with outcrops of rock, and fell away on the far end in stepped cliffs. Beyond them the sea showed, like still gray clouds on the horizon.

Niki pulled the bay up in the lee of a low rock face, where the grass grew short and very green. He'd trained the horse to stand ground-tied; he slid out of the saddle and let the reins fall at his feet, and knew the bay wouldn't wander. Then he went down the slope to the cliff edges, and dropped down in the waving grass.

He'd lied to Kitty. He didn't know how else to get the information he needed without getting his hands on the inhaler, and he couldn't begin to think how he might do that. He thought of Jacob—but why would Jacob have any better luck than Niki? Reg's lead might have to languish unfollowed for a while. *You haven't got a while,* he thought, and shivered, because he didn't know where the thought came from. He lay back and watched clouds go by. At an uncertain point shortly after, he dozed off.

He woke with a start and a rock bruising his shoulder. He had another start when he remembered where he was, and was passionately grateful that he wasn't a restless sleeper. *Three feet to your right, my lad, and you'd have bounced for a long ways.* He shook dry grass out of his hair and tramped up the hill to mount his restless horse.

He approached the Castle from the garden, climbed the steps to the terrace, and found Kitty and Morwenna sitting on it. Kitty got out of her chair and came, smiling, to him.

"You smell like horse," she said, and caught one of his hands in both of hers.

"Funny thing, that."

"Olwen stopped by while you were out. You should call her, at the very least."

"I will," he said, not very convincingly, and thrust both hands in his jacket pockets.

"Just thought you'd like to know."

He nodded and went in through the terrace doors. He took the stairs to the second floor, because they were the first thing he got to, went into his rooms, and locked the door behind him. Then, when he was sure he was alone, he took his right hand out of his pocket and uncurled his fingers from around the hard, cold cylinder of the inhaler.

"Thank you," he whispered, and wished he could have said it to her.

CHAPTER SIX

Do you not hear me calling, white deer with no horns?
I have been changed to a hound with one red ear;
I have been in the Path of Stones and the Wood of Thorns,
For somebody hid hatred and hope and desire and fear
Under my feet that they follow you night and day.
    —W. B. Yeats, "He Mourns for the Change
        That Has Come Upon Him . . ."

He didn't know at first where he was. He was sitting, and stiff, and shouldn't have fallen asleep at all, but that hour in the high meadow was the only sleep he'd had in forty hours. Then he heard the hiss of a breaking bottle seal, and a sardonic voice that said, "Heads up, Aristocrat. You paid enough for 'em, I figure you'd like to hear the results."

Then he realized that his arms were folded on a kitchen table which belonged to the chemist Reg had suggested, and his head was pillowed on them. He raised it and blinked.

The chemist, part of whose name was Marcus, was leaning against a pitted enamel cupboard, drinking from a bottle of beer. ("First name or last?" Niki had asked. Marcus had showed small, irregularly colored teeth, and said, "I thought you public-schoolers all called each other by one name, anyway?" which disposed of the conversation, if not the subject.) Marcus was small and spidery. His long, thin black hair was bound in a braid that fell from the top of his head; the braid was threaded with a faceted gold chain. "You look like shit," Marcus said, as if it gave him pleasure. "Need something to fix you up?"

Niki shook his head. It was hard to drive off the dream-state produced by waking in a strange place at a strange hour; it was the room's smell and dilapidation, the fiberboard shutters on the kitchen windows that sealed out the streetlights, his irritable host. The plastic table was spattered with burn marks. The air in the narrow house had a faint mold-and-acid tang that Niki almost recognized. He didn't really need to; he knew what Marcus did there, and why he was equipped to do the analysis Niki had paid for.

"Well, let's not fart around here, then." Marcus and his beer turned toward the stairs to the cellar. Niki pushed himself out of the chair and followed.

The cellar door, on the kitchen side, looked like molded-panel plastic. On the cellar side, it was a single piece of steel with vault hinges. It swung smoothly shut behind them and latched with oiled finality. The stairs were stone, and steep; Niki wondered if there was another entrance, one more suited to moving things in and out. The room at the bottom was not large. It didn't need to be. One long table with a polished granite top; a heavy-duty lab-calibrated thermal controller; much glassware, in specialized shapes; much stainless steel, likewise; several shelves of brown resizable jars with inventory readouts on them; a collection of analog-to-digital receivers; and on the end of the table, fed by a neat harness of cable from the A-Ds, a custom-built turbokicked 'board with a 50-cm display. In a space perhaps three meters by four meters by three, he was looking at almost half a million Cymric pounds. Lights, venting system, and air cleaners alone—whatever was in the brown jars—no, it didn't bear adding up.

Marcus spun his chair around and sat on it backwards, set his beer on the tabletop, and whacked several keys on the 'board. The big display filled with horizontal strips of color. "And there you have it," he said.

"Is it an analgesic?" Niki asked, watching the colors burn and wobble before his tired eyes.

"Yep." Then Marcus grinned, his underfleshed face made hellish by the light of the display. "Among other things." He hit another key, and the bars of color retreated to half the screen. The other half filled with letters, numbers, notes, and pointers. "Notice the stripes are all the same width? They're all isomers." He tapped the first line with one long, cracked fingernail. "Here's your 'geez. These next two"—he tapped again—"are camo compounds. Carry the flavor and smell signature for the analgesic, and everything else in 'em is dead weight. Inert. Routine analysis would probably only turn up those. But the fun part—ah hah, now we get to the fun part.''

Niki moved closer and squinted at the lines under the fingernail, the fourth color beside the lines.

"This little molecule is modeled partly on THC. Know what that is?'' Niki nodded. Marcus ignored him. "That's the good stuff in cannabis. But this leaves out all the happy things. If I'm right, and I usually am, this is nasty behavior mod. So's this, more or less,'' and Marcus pointed to the next color. "And this. Some of these are related to psychobabblers, stuff they used to test on prisoners in the Hub before the Concorde made 'em stop. We got paranoia here, inconsistent reactions, memory loss, temper tantrums, manic-depressive stuff. But you know what I like best?''

Niki made a small, negative noise.

"This last one. You know what this last one does? If you go off it for more than a couple hours, it gives you headaches. Isn't that a hoot?''

Niki felt the room shift gently. "A hoot,'' he agreed. "I take it this isn't something usually found under a prescription label.''

"Hm-mm. Custom work, this, and very nice. Very professional.'' Light caught the facets in the gold chain, and the flash hurt Niki's eyes. "Not cheap, though. What's the matter with you?''

The room had slipped again, considerably less gently. Niki looked for something to lean on that wouldn't result in broken glass, found the edge of the heavy table, and caught it. His legs failed him gradually, and he was able to slide, not fall, to the floor. He ended propped against a table leg watching the air sparkling before him. No sleep, he realized, and no food except that landmark breakfast in the solarium. And that had been mostly coffee. Marcus was scowling at him as if he were a shattered beaker. Something jabbed him in the arm.

"I said you looked like shit,'' Marcus said. "That ought to be enough to get you out of here without me having to carry you.''

His vision was clearing already. Marcus was good at his trade. "I want a printout,'' Niki said.

Marcus looked at him as if he were a beaker doing a tapdance.

"I know. In your profession, hard copy is bad business practice. But I still want one."

Marcus rolled his eyes and stood up. Niki heard his fingers on the 'board. A minute later a sheet of paper floated into his lap, streaked with color and notations. "Anything else, *burra sahib*?"

"I need the inhaler back. Then help me off your floor and I'll leave."

"Hot damn." Marcus grabbed him under the arms and hoisted him, ungently. Niki creased the paper and tucked it in his coat. Marcus handed him the inhaler, and he pocketed that, too. There was a brush fire spreading through his muscles; in a moment it would reach his legs, and he would be able to walk.

"What was this?" he asked, tapping the sore spot on his arm.

Marcus smiled—genuine malicious delight. "Riptide, my aristocrat. Have fun."

Niki winced. "I'm sure." Marcus was right; Riptide would enable him to get out of the house. What happened to him outside it was no concern of Marcus's.

The color shift alone would have been interesting, but the variations in his depth perception were making him sick. Or something was making him sick. He stopped in the turquoise light of a shop sign to get his bearings, and to hold onto someone's fence until he began to believe in gravity again. The fence felt solid and pleasantly furry.

His hair had dropped into his eyes. He'd brushed it back once already, but he wasn't going to repeat the mistake, not with his bare hand. He considered, dispassionately, falling down and waiting until the Riptide was done with him. But the folded paper in his coat pocket was a presence with an urgent voice. When he thought the gravity might be back, he loosed his grip on the fence and walked cautiously on. His hand, when he looked at it, was scored with deep green marks where the fence rail had pressed. Green? Well, consider the color of his skin. No, better not.

At the end of the block a few mile-feet away, he saw a sign for a public call box, glowing softly purple. It was, he realized, what he'd been looking for, for—some uncertain length of time. Perspective reversed itself between one blink and the next, and he went from feeling sick to being sick. When he was done, he crossed the land bridge to the call box. He couldn't push the

eys; his aim was off, for a start, and their arrangement and the
numbers on them seemed backward. Finally he closed his eyes
and did it by memory and touch, pressed his left wrist to the
scanner and let it read his embed for the call charge.

He didn't open his eyes again until he heard the connect tone,
and the sleep-rough voice saying, "Hello." There was no image
on the screen, which frightened him until he realized that it was
probably two in the morning and nobody would answer with vid
on. "Jacob," he said. "It's Niki."

After a moment, the screen came on. The image stayed bless-
edly two-dimensional. Jacob was knotting a sash around his robe,
and his short hair looked ruffled. "I can't see you," Jacob said.

"Oh, shit. Let me see if I can find the vid switch." Again,
he had to close his eyes and guess. "Better?"

Jacob stared at him. "My," he said at last. "Having fun?"

"Well, no. I'm under the influence of an illegal recreational
drug that's meant to be used only while sitting down."

"I take it you've been standing up. It doesn't seem to keep
you from talking."

"No, talking's fine. I'm not quite able to read, though. Sen-
sory dyslexia, sort of."

"Riptide?" Jacob said quickly.

Niki laughed, though it sounded like a cough. "For shame.
You're not supposed to know these things. Hell of a waste—
under better circumstances, I think I'd like it. Jacob, do you
think you could come fetch me?"

"Where are you?"

"I don't know. But I'm going to get out of the way of the
receiver and let you try to figure it out."

After a minute, Jacob's voice called him back. "You're in
luck. I can see a sign for the street. I'm going to cruise the length
of it until I get to you, so stay where you are, and stay in sight."
He broke the connection. Niki sat on the sidewalk, leaned against
the call box stanchion, and kept his eyes closed.

Jacob had apartments in the Castle—or rather, connected to
it by a roofed and windowed walkway. Half an hour later, Niki
was in them, weak, damp, and flushed from a scalding shower,
wrapped in Jacob's other robe and sunk into one of his library
chairs. He was consuming fish broth and toast, because whenever he stopped doing it, Jacob glared at him. The bitter thing
Jacob had put on his tongue when he'd found him had been
working away at the Riptide. Niki still saw odd colors wherever

the light was strong, and couldn't be sure how far away he was
from what he saw, but that was all that was left of it. Jacob sat
across from him in the other chair, with the printout unfolded
in front of him.

"I told you," Niki said, "that when I found something useful,
I would bring it to you. Is it useful?"

Jacob nodded absently. "This explains a few things," he said,
touching the paper.

"I thought so. But now what do we do?"

He looked up at Niki. The light turned his ginger hair green-
ish, but Niki tried not to mind. "I can't just tell him all this.
Paranoid enough as it is. Did you know he's begun to talk about
infiltrators and offworld spies in high places?"

"Jacob, given that," Niki said, with a gesture at the printout,
"I'm surprised he's not talking about snakes in the air ducts.
But what if he's right?"

Jacob frowned.

"*Someone's* doping him with his analgesic."

"Someone offworld?" Jacob asked. "Who? The Concorde?
The Bear Triangle? Tell me why they would, and I'll listen.
Jesus, it's enough that Rhys is full of offworld expansionism
crap."

Rhys's name hung suddenly between them, like a bubble in
the gloom, only the edges seen.

"I don't think so," Jacob said firmly.

"Neither do I." Niki picked at a rough place in the cloth of
the robe. "But when I asked her, Kitty said she thought she
remembered Rhys filling that prescription for Pedr."

"Pretty vague." Jacob sat quiet for a few moments, his eyes
with the focused-inward look that meant he was matching facts,
incidents, odds. "He wouldn't be my first choice, anyway," he
said at last.

Niki raised an eyebrow; but he hadn't the energy to press the
matter. "What will you do, then?"

Jacob folded the printout. "I'm going to leave the inhaler in
a place where Pedr will think he dropped it—"

"You're going to let him stay on that?"

"How do I get him off it, without telling him what we know,
which he won't believe? But I'm going to stick with him, to make
sure he doesn't do something unfixably stupid. I'm going to
watch everybody who comes near him with a damned suspicious
eye. And I'm going to see that you stay the hell out of it."

"Are you, now?"

"Nik, if whoever's responsible finds out how much you know, you're a dead man."

Niki snorted. "So are you."

"Another reason one of us ought to keep out of the line of fire."

Niki closed his eyes, pillowed his head on the chair back. It would be so nice to let it go, to hand the worry off to Jacob, perhaps to leave Cymru. He felt relaxed now, and clean, and tired. He'd ventured his life, his health, maybe his sanity. Surely he had done his part? "What if there's more information where this came from?" he asked. "What if you can't get at it, and I can?"

"What kind of information?"

"What kind was this?"

Jacob drew a long, irritable breath. "You won't tell me where the original lead came from?"

"I can't. Too many lives on the chain. But it proved out, didn't it?"

Jacob stared at his knees. "No," he said finally. "Stay out of it, Niki. The game sucks, and the odds are lousy."

Niki sighed, and stood up carefully. If he walked slowly, he would be all right. "Can I have my clothes back?" he said.

"Beg your pardon?"

"To get into the Castle from the walkway, I have to go past the guard station. It's going to affect your reputation if I do it dressed like this."

Jacob laughed weakly and went to get Niki's things from the laundry.

When he got back to his rooms, Niki lit the 'board. Message to Andrew, message to the place where he left messages for Reg, about a rendezvous at the Lady de Winter. No harm in pursuing the possibility of an offworld connection, even if Jacob thought it was unlikely. And Jacob would keep an eye on things nearer to home—but two eyes made for better depth perception.

And then, finally, he went to sleep.

Landing Day, that year, arrived like a brick between the shoulder blades: an unpleasant surprise. He knew where he was on the calendar, but he'd lost track of other people's markers on it—holidays, for instance. There would be parties, parades, the streets full of people in period or fanciful costume singing, dancing, drugged, choking the city with a paroxysm of celebration. Curfew was lifted for the night, because it could never have been enforced. And darkness, violence, fear, could run beneath the festival trappings like an underground river. This year Niki wished Landing Day straight to hell.

Landing Day in the Castle had its own undercurrent of darkness. The day was full of public functions, both ceremonial and useful. In earlier years Niki had avoided almost all of them, and so he managed to be out riding when the first official event took place. When he brought his horse back to the stables an hour later, he found Rhys, waiting to escort him to Pedr's study.

At that first event—a dawn ceremony at the worldport—Pedr had made a short and cogent speech about unity in times of change. At the end of it a voice, then another, called Niki's name, until there was enough chanting of ''Harlech! Harlech!'' that some of the chanters had to be removed. Some of them resisted.

The interview in Pedr's study was ugly. Niki, too shaken to do anything else, lost his temper when Pedr lost his. The resolution was unsatisfactory for everyone: Niki would be conspicuous at the Landing Day ball that night. And he would damned well make every observer believe he was having fun.

There was one person in the family he could count on to sympathize with him on the subject of being royal in public. He stalked off to find Morwenna.

She called it her workroom, swearing that there wasn't a facility in all of Cymru fit to be called a lab. It tended to smell of alcohol and yeast, but Niki was still disorientingly reminded, as he looked in, of Marcus's cellar. Morwenna's room wasn't as tidy. There had been a paper slide off one counter, and sheets lay on the floor there like fallen leaves. Dirty environment dishes were piled beside the scrubber, which was full of clean ones that hadn't been put away. Under one of the skylights, what had once been ivy trailed like rusted wrought iron out of its pot. Someone who didn't know her well had given it to her. Niki wondered if she still kept a container of ice cream in the chiller next to the cell cultures.

Morwenna sat at an old oak desk, her feet on the top, her 'board in her lap. Her hair was coiled haphazardly at her neck and secured with a pen that Niki knew she had already looked for and declared lost. There was a teacup beside her. The tea in it was cold, he was sure, but hours cold, or days? She was frowning; two lines, in perfect symmetry, separated one black brow from the other. The sight of her, in what Niki thought of as her natural habitat, made his heart constrict suddenly. He came into the room quietly, and she didn't look up. He'd unloaded the scrubber, put away its contents, and started it cycling on a new load before she said, "Best lab assistant I ever had."

Niki shook his head. "The world's in a sad way, when you have to breed 'em yourself."

Her feet came off the desk, and she thumped the 'board down in their place. "It would seem," she said, measuring her words out with care, "that you have made the news."

"Ah." He turned, placed his hands on the counter, leaned. "I was just getting it firsthand from Pedr and Rhys."

"Happy?"

"No. Was anyone hurt?"

"Not that's been reported."

"Which doesn't mean a God-damned thing."

"So bitter," Morwenna said, and swung her chair around to face him. "What have you been doing, that people shout your name in public?"

"Sticking my oar in," Niki said. The temper raised in Pedr's study caught fire again. "Rescuing maidens. Executing feats of derring-do. Stealing from the fucking rich and giving to the poor. Blowing up Whitehall. If I'd had a grain of sense, I would have done it in disguise."

"Two grains would have kept you from doing it?"

"No. With two grains, all that effort might also have done some good."

Eyes narrowed, lips pressed thin, she regarded him. "Vitriol never used to be one of your outlets. Certainly pouring it over your own head wasn't."

He looked at the floor and tried to marshal reason and dispassion. "Today, in my name, a few people I may not even know created a disturbance. Also in my name, more or less, the Dogs subdued them, with force in some cases. That bothers me."

"Have you always called them Dogs?" Morwenna asked, as if it was a rhetorical question. Niki treated it as one. "Why should it bother you?" she continued. "You didn't ask them to do it. You weren't there to cause it. Why is it your responsibility?"

"Would you mind telling that to Pedr and Rhys?"

"So," Morwenna said, "do you think you could see your way clear to going offworld now?"

Niki raised his head sharply. "What? Why?"

"You're afraid you'll become a rallying point, a locus for radical opinion. What better way to prevent it than by leaving?"

"What better way to make it look as if Pedr has sent me into exile for making trouble? Which would guarantee me a place as martyr for the cause."

She slammed her fist down on the desk. Her teacup jumped and spilled; Niki was frozen, startled. "Why do you care?" she said between her teeth. "If it's time for martyrs, then the people who want them will find them, or make them. They don't need you. God, they don't even need Pedr. There's always an ogre they can use. Don't make it easy for them!"

"Would you do it?" Niki asked intently. "Leave all the history and responsibility, turn your back on it?"

"What responsibility? For an artificial entity with arbitrary borders? For an antique political concept? I have no responsibility here! And neither do you."

"That's not true. Good God, where do I get this? From Father? In the first three years of my life, did he spend all his time whispering accountability into my ear? Or did he pass it on in a chromosome?"

"I can guarantee he didn't," she spat.

"Of course, you're the geneticist, you should know. Was I left in the cradle by fairies, then? Because I begin to think Kitty was right: we're only alike in looks."

"We are exactly alike," Morwenna said. She was standing now, very stiff, white with emotion, and her words came out slow and cold.

"No," he said. Somewhere in his mind or his heart, he regretted every word as he said it. This was not a dispute between a child and his mother. Things could be said here that could never be taken back or forgiven.

"Yes, we are. You said it yourself: I'm the geneticist. I should know."

"What are you talking about?"

"You have no father."

"He died when I was three. You were married to him. Did you forget?"

Morwenna swept up one of the environment dishes from the counter and flung it down. Glass shattered; shards flew like ice across the tile. "That," she pointed at them. "That was your father."

His teeth chattered together. He clenched them.

"There is nothing in you that did not come from me. What wasn't out of my own body was the product of my brain and my skill. You are of me, and me alone. If I owe nothing to this place, then neither do you."

He felt pinned by her eyes, hot and cold at once, fastened on him as if she could burn the impurities out of him with her gaze. And, of course, they were his eyes. It was his face, changed only by gender and age. Gender was so easy to manipulate in the conception of a human being. "I'm too tall," said Niki, casting about to no purpose.

"I've been short all my life," she said with a shrug, as if it was a reasonable question. "It was too late to change it in me." She studied him, up and down, as if for the first time. "I may have gone a little overboard on that. I'm quite satisfied with the rest, though."

The trembling had moved from his jaw, through his shoulders, into his hands. "Jesus Christ. Don't use that tone on me. I'm not something you have a patent on."

"Wrong deity. Hecate rules here." He thought he saw her hand shake, too (Why not? The same muscles, nerves, bone . . .), but he wasn't sure.

"Why did you tell me this now?" he said softly.

She glared at him and turned her head away.

"If you thought you could force me to do as I'm bid and go offworld, then it's backfired on you." He went to the door. Such a short time since he'd come in it, expecting nothing but a little commiseration. The pain caught up with him there, a spasm of emotion that seemed big enough to crack bone and skin (their bone, their skin . . .). He willed himself to work the latch.

"Love would have done it," he found himself saying. The words embarrassed him, and the voice in which he spoke them. There was no sound behind him. He only had to step out the door and close it. "But you didn't try that," he said. Then, by the grace of whatever deity held sway there, he managed to leave the room.

A woman with purple and copper feathers on her head drew her cloak across his face; the world faded for a moment behind a mist of plum-colored gauze. Smell of patchouli mixing with sweat, fireworks, glue, fried food; sound of staccato laughter over shouting, drums, electric strings, bleating horns, thumping and scuffing feet.

There seemed to be more people in the streets than lived in Caernarfon year-round. And it was still daylight—there would be more of them come sundown. Someone bumped into him from behind. He brushed shoulders, hard, with someone else. He slid sideways between dancers' bodies. Someone yelled at him, recognized him, and yelled something else. He changed direction quickly, and lost the voice in the crowd. He was pressed against a wall, along with others, as a red dragon five meters long leaped and jigged down Keir Hardie Street. It had a dead golden lion in its jaws, and another one in each front claw. A woman recognized Niki, blew him a kiss. He dodged away again.

Three people were running a sausage-sandwich business from the second-floor balcony of their flat, almost certainly without a vendor's license. Niki wished he were hungry; he felt like encouraging civil disobedience. Five people were performing rough-and-ready versions of old separatist songs to the music of guitar, synthdrums, and microbass. Tales of Plaid Cymru's perfidy, the Bloody April martyrs, the brave heroes of the WLS. *How long can you hold a grudge?* Niki wondered, because he had to find something to be angry about. *How many years of feeding and grooming and yearly exercising before it dies of old age? We're celebrating Separation and freedom while the nation we made with it rocks on its foundations.* Then the quintet started a song he didn't recognize. In strong harmony that carried over the crowd racket, the words came:

The dogs upon their leashes are hunting door-to-door
For poor and honest Cymric men, their silence to ensure
But when the front door's broken in, there'll be no skulls to
    crack
For Harlech's lads have been there first, and got 'em out the
    back

He stood stupidly, trying to place the lyrics in Welsh history. Then he realized that "dogs" was spelled with a capital "D," and that "Harlech" was him. His objection had been answered. History was a ravenous beast with a mouthful of teeth, and he was looking down its throat. He spun away and pressed blindly through the mob, thinking of a new Bloody April, a new cast of martyrs dying with his name on their lips.

Offworld. Maybe she was right.

It took him twenty minutes to get three more blocks, even walking ruthlessly. At last he reached the corner of Keir Hardie and Powys, the Powys Street Market, and Black's Market Café.

Black's ground floor was fronted with many-paned glass doors. Today they were folded back, opening the café to the street on two sides. It was hard to tell where one ended and the other began. Tables were moved out on the sidewalk, close to the market stalls. Niki threaded through them. It was crowded there; people in streetwear and parade clothes sat and stood, and talked. They were excited, intense, but that mood was always on the customers at Black's. Landing Day only honed it.

He stopped, his hand on the gilded wood frame of one of the folding doors, and felt the noise inside meet the noise from the street. The odors met there, too: coffee and the carbon smell of fax print from the café; burnt caramel, machine oil, and something organic from the market. The latter had reminded him a little of the scent of Morwenna's workroom. Which, of course, had delivered the inner blow once again, and made all his thoughts stagger.

So he was one person's child, and not two. It made no difference. Why should it? Why should he feel as if their relationship had changed, from mother and son to owner and object?

He realized that he had asked her the wrong thing. It didn't matter why she had chosen to tell him now. The question he should have asked, the one he could make no sense of, was *why she had done it*. She had a husband, and a son by the usual methods. What had moved her to *build* another? And once she had, why had she kept it secret? The techniques she would have used were employed all the time, to correct genetic defects in normal and *in vitro* fertilizations. True, it was Simply Not Done; one did not genetically custom-assemble one's offspring all by oneself. But that was not something that would weigh with Morwenna.

Put like that, it seemed a purely intellectual puzzle, about someone else. At least, for now.

The walls of Black's were covered in worn black leather and smoke-darkened crocuswood. The bar was crocuswood as well, amazing in length and ornamentation. A chrome espresso maker took a threatening stance behind it, like the idol of a hostile religion. In every likely spot there were leaflets and posters tacked, announcing meetings and concerts and workshops. Even the concert posters had an air of opposition politics.

Several more people recognized him. But this was Black's; this was Liberty Hall. As he passed, they nodded and went back to their coffee, conversations, books, games. If they leaned across the table and whispered his name, or stared after him, they did it out of his sight and hearing.

Reg was drinking his coffee at the bar, with flagrant disregard for Black's custom and the frowns of fellow patrons. Niki squeezed in next to him, hooked a cup off the stack, and looked hopeful. That got him the attention of the freckled blonde woman prodding the espresso god. "Hallo, Beau," she said, grinning, and pulled a spigot hose from under the counter. Coffee shot, churning, into his cup. "Jesus, Reg, if you'd told me you were meeting your rich handsome friend, I'd've been nicer to you."

Reg snorted. "Where's your revolutionary spirit? I thought you wanted to lop aristocrat heads last week."

"Only the old, fat ones," she told him, with no lessening of the grin. "If I spot a nice-looking one, I'll keep him tied up in me cellar."

Niki passed her money for the coffee. Their good humor scraped against his raw nerves, and it was hard to return it. "I'm not old enough to listen to this," he said. "Come along, Reg, before someone assassinates you for your place at the bar."

Reg led the way toward a table. He was less polite about it than Niki, which meant that Niki was several crowded meters behind when someone bumped hard against his shoulder. Someone else's white jacket suddenly appeared before him. "Excuse me," Niki said, and the owner of the jacket said, "Dominic!" Niki looked from the jacket to the woman's face above it. It was familiar, but out of context—wrong milieu, wrong clothes. There was a firm grip on Niki's upper arm. "You shouldn't stay here," a man's voice said next to his ear, then, louder, "Good God, so it is!"

"I haven't seen you in so long—" she began.

"Come on, let's step outside where there's some air," said the man. The grip shifted, tightened, and the arm lay along his shoulders and pressed him toward the doors.

Niki, with a silent apology to the blonde woman behind the bar, dropped his cup on the man's foot.

It bounced and splashed coffee. The stranger jerked back, swearing; reflex loosened his grip. The woman in the white jacket stepped away, too. Niki saw Reg's face over her shoulder as she backed into him. Reg stumbled and caught the jacket and her arm for support.

"I'm so sorry," Niki said to the man, and brushed at imaginary coffee stains on his coat. Underneath it, he felt the irregular hardness of a weapon. He gave the cloth a last brush, and smiled, and said, quietly, "If you don't leave, I'm going to tell all these people who you are."

Reg and the woman were glowering at each other. The man grunted, caught his partner's eye, and headed for the door. She stood undecided for a moment, looking a little wildly from the man to Niki. Then she hurried after the man.

"She had hardware on her," Reg said calmly, watching her disappear in the street crowd. "And I tried to nick her wallet, but she knew what I was after."

"She's a Crown agent. I've seen her before—she's been assigned to Castle security once or twice."

"Huh. What d'you suppose they wanted in Black's? You?"

"That is a damned good question. They certainly wanted me just now."

"Well, clean up after yourself and come along. We've got people to meet."

He picked up his cup, followed Reg, and thought. There was no reason why he shouldn't be in Black's. Certainly no reason why it should be the duty of agents of the Crown to remove him from it. Unless Pedr had taken a very strange turn, indeed. And to know he was there, someone would have had to follow him.

The question continued to bother him, though he pushed it to the back of his mind. He met the people they'd come to see: a couple who published a much-read alternative artfax. The four of them talked carefully around everything they wanted to say, because all of it required a level of trust and a quantity of shared assumptions that had not yet been built. Niki knew that. Yet he was restless—it took too long, and there was so little time. This was the kind of impatience he would once have expected from Reg. But Reg had developed the nerves of a diplomat in the last weeks.

What the *hell* were two Crown agents doing in Black's? Except for calling him Dominic—a weak spot in their dossier—they'd said nothing to the purpose.

". . . not until the radicalization of the Gorsedd," the artfax woman was saying eagerly. "But the Eisteddfodau were always a political breeding ground." She had slightly protruding blue eyes, and brown hair that fell in them; she would sweep it back and clutch it to the sides of her head with both hands, as if trying to keep her head from flying off. "All those people speaking Welsh, keeping the culture alive by main force, as it were. It's just a hop from the artistic state of the country to the political . . .''

Reg sat with his chin on his hands, apparently rapt, nodding. *Reg, you mealy-mouthed hypocrite. You don't give a flying toss for the continuity of Welsh culture.* Niki wished he could remember the artfax woman's name. Not a common lapse with him. It was a measure of his distraction.

The agents had said damned little at all. Except the man, when he came up behind Niki. And he had said—

You shouldn't stay here.

"Christ," said Reg, "what is it?" The artfax couple looked warily at both of them.

Niki's breath stuck in his throat. "Reg—we've got to get everyone out of here.''

"What?"

He spoke fast, faster than he could organize the words. "One of those agents. He said to me, 'You shouldn't stay here.' They couldn't have been here for me, because they couldn't know I'd be here. But they knew something else was, and it wasn't supposed to get *me*—''

Reg understood him partway through, was out of his chair already. He turned to the rest of the room, cupped his hands around his mouth, and bellowed, "Clear out! Bomb threat! Haul bloody *ass*!''

The artfax couple was confused and frightened; Niki grabbed them and shoved them in the direction of the doors. Other patrons were up and pushing their way out, and Niki could see the warning spreading out of the building, into the market. But there were so many people in the café, so many more clogging the street out front. He turned to look for the blonde woman who'd poured his coffee. If she was backing up the warning, it would help.

She was scrambling over the crocuswood bar, shouting. He took two steps toward her. Then Reg yelled something, grabbed Niki's shoulders, yanked him back. And Niki saw, as Reg had, that it was too late.

Behind the espresso maker, the wall bowed slowly inward. As it cracked with the force of the explosion behind it, Reg flung Niki toward the doors and stepped between him and the bar.

Reg's weight, and pieces of the wall, and the blast kick itself hit him all at once. Across the floor like swept dust, blind and deaf, one hand pinned under his head and the friction taking the skin off his knuckles. That, ridiculously clear: that his knuckles hurt. Then he fetched up against something hard that gave way and fell on him.

He'd been conscious the whole time, he decided. The hard thing was not very heavy, at least. A table? He struggled to his hands and knees and pushed it away.

It was the ruin of one of the market stalls. Black's no longer had many-paned glass doors on two sides. The glass was like sugar dusted over the corner of Keir Hardie and Powys, and the wood frame was in fragments on the pavement, in splinters driven into many soft objects. Some of them were in the street near him, and a few, he heard through his stunned eardrums, were beginning to scream.

He found Reg at the edge of the sidewalk. Enigma thrived in an explosion. Even the most controlled one could produce oddities and marvels of selective destruction. Reg's was that, from the front, he was untouched. From behind it was obvious that his spine and the back of his head had taken the force of the blast, and kept it from his face, his shirt front, and Niki. Niki was afraid to upset that balance by lifting him. But he sat beside him, thinking that Reg would have been pleased. The casket would be open, and he would make a fine, handsome dead hero.

Then he was in the Lady de Winter. He didn't remember any transition, but suddenly he was staring at tiles between his feet and under the base of the chair he sat in, and he recognized them.

"How did I get here?" he asked, wondering if there was anyone to hear him.

"You walked." Jane Wells. He could tell even with his ears ringing.

"I don't remember it."

"No, I thought you wouldn't."

"Reg—"

"I know. You already told me. Or you told anybody in earshot, which happened to be me."

"Oh, Christ," he whispered, and doubled up over his knees. He thought that this time he would lose consciousness, but he didn't.

"Hold still. I'm making sure there isn't any glass in these."

His coat and shirt were off, and she was dabbing at his back. Something pulled at the skin on his forehead. He reached up and found a layer of liquid bandage already hardening there.

"That was making a right mess of you. I'm surprised you didn't get hauled off the street with blood all over your face. Maybe they all thought you were in costume as one of the April Martyrs." She was chattering, talking without hearing herself, but when Niki said, "Don't," she stopped. He wasn't sure what he'd meant.

"I'll give you some of my old man's gear," she said after a bit. "Yours is wrecked." She appeared from behind him, and he lifted his head to watch her progress to the bar. She was pale and disheveled, and the rim of the glass clattered against the spigot when she filled it with whiskey. She drank half in a gulp, and brought the rest to him.

"If they want to make legends," Niki said, "see to it they put him in. That they make him a hero." He spoke in anger, though he knew he wasn't angry at her. "He gave the warning. If anyone got out alive, it was because of him." *I got out alive. Because of him.*

Her face, always so strong and composed, crumpled. She turned her head. This, he remembered, was the woman who'd hoped to put death aside for half an hour. Instead he'd brought her another. He touched her wrist hesitantly. Her fingers twined with his. They stayed like that, while she stood and cried, her face averted, and he wished he could stand up and take her in his arms.

He chose black for the Landing Day ball. Or rather, when he noticed what he'd just put on, he found it was black. It was a close-fitting short tunic and narrow trousers, made of an artificial silk that had no sheen, no reflection to its surface at all. There was gold piping at the seams, barely wider than a thickness of thread. Except for that, he would seem like a man-shaped hole in the festive night. A precise half-inch of white linen showed above the high collar, below the sleeve hems. He was entitled to wear the Harlech badge and gold chain—he would be expected to. He didn't put them on.

He was late. The Great Hall would be packed, all the guests announced, and Pedr and Rhys ready to flay him. They should have canceled it. News of the disaster at Powys Street Market was everywhere; they should have canceled the ball, refused to celebrate when they ought to be mourning. Whose decision had it been to go on with it?

He took the tube down and passed through the family quarters to the Great Hall. The sound dampers were on, and all the talk and music made sense. There were no secrets in the Great Hall with the dampers on. Then, suddenly, there wasn't much talk, either, not in his vicinity. They'd seen him. Inclining of heads, little bows, a subtle shifting, so that his path was clear. One woman—ah, the representative for one of the southern mining districts—spread her dark gray skirts and sank to the floor, as if he were the Prince. Perversity and banked anger made him take her hand, draw her up, and kiss her fingers lightly. He was an idiot. If Pedr had seen it all . . . There was no predicting Pedr anymore.

There was a lot of gray among the brighter-colored formal clothes, he noticed. No one else had quite dared to wear black. But since it wasn't daring on his part, he couldn't take any credit.

An arm twined through his. "Heavens, you look like the Melancholy Dane," said a musical voice attached to it. He looked down to find Olwen's bright head, Olwen's clear eyes, her wide smiling mouth. Her dress was iridescent pink coral. "Are you all right?"

He would have told her the truth a few months ago. "Oh, yes," he said.

"It's nice to see you." She looked uncertainly at his face, at the cut on his temple. That's right, he *was* wearing jewelry. The slight reflection off the liquid bandage would be his badge of office.

He made inconsequential remarks to her for a few minutes, and didn't offer her a dance, which he knew she was waiting for. Eventually she went away, and the hurt in her face fed the reckless anger in him.

Slowly, he moved up the levels of the hall. He was stopped on the stairs and in the galleries. Many of those who stopped him wanted to know if he'd really been in the Powys Street Market, as rumor had it. Yes, he said, and yes, it was a bomb, and no, he wasn't certain who was responsible but he had a few ideas. None of that would make Pedr happy, either. Or Rhys, whose brother (half brother) might have been killed today. He hadn't heard anything from Rhys this evening. The Crown agents would have left Black's, reported that the situation had changed, that Dominic Glyndwr was sitting in a café that was about to be gutted, and what were they supposed to do about it?

Someone had told them: Nothing. Who had they reported to?

On the second gallery, he came face to face with Rhys. His brother met his eyes for a long moment, with no expression at all. Niki hadn't thought Rhys could do that, not with him. Rhys walked past him and was gone. No words exchanged.

On the third gallery, under the crisp, star-studded night sky showing through the polarized ceiling glass, he found Kitty. She wore dark green velvet, as close to mourning, he thought, as growing things came. Her brown hair lay shining on her shoulders.

When she saw him, her face filled up with pain. "I'm sorry," she said, and took his hands. There was as much comfort there as in an embrace. "It's true, then?"

"That I was there? Yes. The friend who was with me died."

"Anyone I know?"

"Oh, no. Not our sort, you see." He winced at his tone. "Sorry. You didn't deserve that. Kitty, don't be nice to me now, or I'll go to pieces."

"I know what you mean," she said, nodding, and even her understanding threatened his self-control. For a moment she seemed about to turn away. Then she stood on tiptoe and kissed him lightly on the chin.

"Very nice," said Pedr, from over Niki's shoulder. Kitty stepped back, eyes widened, lips pressed together.

The anger Niki had felt smoldering in him all evening licked gently upward. "Hullo, Pedr," he said. It should have been a bow, and "Your Highness." Reg's ghost stood at his shoulder, grinning.

"And in public, too," Pedr said, as if Niki hadn't spoken. "Go ahead, neck in front of everyone of any consequence in all of Cymru. If I know about it, I'm sure they've known for months."

"What are you talking about?" Kitty said thinly, her hands pulling at each other.

Pedr turned to Niki, and smiled his breakfast-table smile. "Are you just keeping your options open, or have you decided you want it all?" His voice carried under the dampers. Heads on the crowded galleries turned.

Niki took a long, deep breath, regretting every stupid impulse of the evening. "Pedr, if I understand you, you're wrong. And we don't want to discuss it here."

"What, you mean not in front of witnesses? Nonsense. Make up your mind: Which do you want? My kingdom or my wife?"

Air hissed through Kitty's teeth. "Pedr, you're not—"

"She wants you, anyone can see that. Or maybe you've already had her. There have been opportunities, after all. Your room in the middle of the night. Hers in the middle of the day."

Of course—he was a paranoid. He'd been watching. "Pedr."

Niki's voice came out with a crack of authority that he'd never heard before. "Be quiet."

"So it's the kingdom, then?"

"God damn it, it ought to be! Three hundred people in hospitals or morgues tonight after Powys Street Market, and you're spending the evening slandering Kitty!"

"Don't you *dare* shout at—"

"There were two Crown agents in Black's Café just before the blast. Did you know that? They either knew it was about to happen, or they set it themselves. Has that been passed up through channels? Or were they reporting directly to you? Is that why the afternoon's events don't seem to interest you much?"

Pedr nodded wisely. "Yes, I think we can safely say that you want it all. Which is treason, Dominic."

"You," Niki said, "are mad."

Pedr's big square fist took him in the jaw, and he staggered back. The golden glass railing of the gallery caught him at the small of his back, and he grabbed for it, dizzy and off balance. He blinked, shook his head, looked up. What he saw was Pedr, clear-eyed and pleased; Kitty, her mouth and eyes round with horror and reaching toward Pedr; and Pedr's fist, coming at him once again. "Pedr, no!" he wanted to say, but the blow reached him first. He thrust one hand out, but there was nothing for it to close on. The space between his thumb and forefinger framed Pedr's face, the satisfaction in it as Niki went over the third gallery rail.

The clear night sky receded above him. The deep green floor, he knew, was rising to meet him, though he couldn't see it. He didn't have to. He could feel the distance between it and him, that shrinking volume of air, as if it were a solid thing. In that lucid instant, he thought he could even measure the time before impact. Someone—probably several someones—screamed. Finally he hit. It didn't hurt much, though he couldn't breathe. His head was turned sideways; he could see the expanse of green floor, dotted with feet, go in and out of focus. Jacob's voice: "Stand away, for God's sake! Rhys, call a med team." He was sinking into the surface beneath him. Soon hardly any of him would be visible. The floor grew darker, and darker, and finally turned black.

CHAPTER SEVEN

The blood-dimmed tide is loosed, and everywhere
The ceremony of innocence is drowned. . . .
          —W. B. Yeats, "The Second Coming"

He lay in a glass coffin and watched his breath mist the surface before his face. Outside, people looked in: his mother, his father, Jacob, Rhys, Jane Wells, others. None of them took notice of the fog of his breath. The back of his skull, his spine, all of the back of him, was soft as cotton, so that he settled into himself.

He was inside a dark tube, so narrow he couldn't shift his arms or shrug his shoulders. A drain pipe? A hollow tree? Whose betrayal had trapped him there? Whose words had led him, trusting, to darkness and confinement? The name hovered in the blackness somewhere. If he could only raise one arm and draw it closer, he could read it.

He stood at the window in his sitting room, and the city spilled glittering down the hill before him. Then the thunderclouds came. Where the rain fell, fire coursed the roof lines. He cried out and tried to open the window. Behind him, he heard soft steps across the carpet, felt someone standing close. His hands froze on the window latch. He was afraid to turn. Then slowly, slowly, the window glass bulged toward him, cracked, shattered.

He woke from dreams of confinement to the reality of it. His arms were pinned, but there was light that made his eyes water. Below his chin was a glare of gray-white, as if he were buried to the neck in a warm glacier. A blink, another, and he could see Jacob's face across its surface.

With apparatus that had clearly been dormant for a while, Niki said, "I thought you were going to make sure he didn't do anything unfixably stupid."

Jacob looked abashed, but replied, "You're being fixed."

Niki closed his eyes; it seemed better than arguing. "Where am I broken?"

"Collarbone, in several places. Left arm. Two ribs, also left. An internal lesion or two from those, but they had that fixed in a matter of hours. You're waiting for the bone builders to finish now."

On the smooth surface of the cocoon that held him, over what would be his shoulder, he saw the reflection of moving colored lights. The receiver monitoring the assemblers they'd injected at the break points. "Critters," he croaked. "That's where the dreams came from."

"There's no connection between med assemblers and dreaming."

"We've had this argument. I always have nightmares when I'm on critters. Just because they haven't found a connection doesn't mean there isn't one."

Jacob sighed.

"How long?" Niki said.

Jacob understood him. "Landing Day ball was three days ago." He paused. "Seventy-four hours, actually."

"*Landing* Day," Niki said. "A scrupulous observance." Jacob did not seem to think much of the joke.

Three days. What had happened during them? There was so much that could, and so little he could do about it. "Then it's the middle of the night, Jacob," he added.

"No, it's the end of the night. They said you'd come out from under the knockouts about now, though. Thought you might like to see a friendly face."

"You call that a—"

"Oh, shut up."

"What's to do, then?" Niki asked carefully.

Jacob's chest rose and fell. "It's not good. Too many people saw and heard everything that happened. Jesus, Nik, whoever's responsible for the inhaler trick must have been applauding you.''

''Do you think I was in *control* of things?''

''No. I think you lost your head.''

''He went after Kitty, for God's sake. Kitty! I could probably have let him torture *me* all night.''

''Did I say it was unreasonable to lose your head? But it's been bad for Pedr's credit, except with a few conservatives who are calling you a troublemaker, which appears to be good for yours. By the way, when the hell *did* you become a national hero?''

''That's not funny.''

''It wasn't supposed to be. Kitty's coming out of it pretty clean. Even the people who believe Pedr's little tale are making a tragic figure of her.''

Niki let air out through his teeth. Inside his immobilizing shell, his chest was beginning to ache. ''She shouldn't have to go through this.''

''None of us should. But, my God, it could have been planned. Pedr throws the most popular member of the royal family off the third-floor balcony in front of a few hundred of Cymru's best and brightest.''

''Maybe it was.''

''Planned? I don't think so. How could anyone know what Pedr would do, in that state?'' He shook his head and stood up. ''You should rest. I'm keeping an eye out.''

''Thank you.''

The lights dimmed when Jacob left. After a few minutes, the pleasant, genderless voice of his medistat said softly, ''Lord Harlech, would you like me to administer a pain block?''

His chest had begun to throb, and the medistat was not his to reprogram. ''Yes, please,'' he answered. While he waited for it to take effect, he stared at the dim ceiling. He'd missed Reg's funeral. Jacob couldn't tell him if Jane and Andrew were all right, since he didn't know about them. The things he wanted to ask about Morwenna, Jacob couldn't answer either. And Jacob hadn't mentioned Rhys at all. He wanted out of that cocoon so desperately he might have struggled, if the block hadn't begun to soften the edges of everything.

His nose itched.

Olwen came to visit, cheerful, sparkling like light off water, and certain that Pedr hadn't meant to knock him over the railing.

Niki didn't try to convince her otherwise. It seemed wicked to snuff out innocence when so little of it remained. But he was exhausted when she left.

His other visitor was his mother. The lights stayed low when he was alone in the room, so he wasn't sure how long she'd been just outside the doorway. She was backlit by the corridor lights, but he recognized her silhouette. "Come on in," he told her.

"All right." When the room light came up, he was shocked. Her eyes were dark-circled and feverish, as if all the energy that had once filled her face and body had retreated there, to be mercilessly burned.

"You don't look well," he said.

She shrugged. "May I sit?" she asked, nodding to a chair beside him.

"Of course."

She sat, crossed her ankles, looked over her shoulder, smoothed her sleeves, uncrossed her ankles.

"Mother," he said, in the tone of loving exasperation he'd often used. But the word itself became a presence in the air between them.

After a moment she said, "Do you hate me for it?" as if it were a calculation she had to verify.

"No! Of course I don't. I just . . . don't understand why."

She laughed a little. "Of course. The rest of the human race hates and fears what it doesn't understand. But you—you just don't understand. Maybe I'm wrong. Maybe you *were* left by the fairies."

It was more than her haggard face. He had never heard her talk bitter nonsense. But before he could speak, she went on.

"I see your metamorphosis is complete." She was talking about the shell, which was gone.

"They didn't wake me up until the bones were almost finished. Mother—"

"Then you'll be out soon."

"Tomorrow morning. What's the—"

"Listen to me." She leaned forward, all her life in her eyes again, harsh and intent. "If you . . . if you ever can leave here, go immediately to Dr. Tomas Damion. New Oxford University in the Hub. Unity College. He'll look after you. If you can't reach him, try Genefa Harisal. Though God knows where you'll find her. Galatea, sometimes."

He stared at her. "What's the matter?" he said softly.

"Memorize it, God damn it! Say it back to me."

"Dr. Tomas Damion. Unity College, New Oxford, the Hub. I've read part of one of his papers. Or Genefa Harisal, Galatea. Now tell me why you sound as if you're willing me to them."

She got up. "That's enough. Don't forget it. It's important." And she stalked out of the room like an irritable Ophelia.

Stiffness and confinement made him disinclined to shrug his shoulders, but he made the hand movements, palms up. "Goodbye," he said pleasantly, "I love you, too, see you later." If madness was a virus, he was glad he was in a disinfected room.

Seven days since Landing Day. No one left the Castle without a guard and a reinforced vehicle. Anyone admitted to the Castle went through a security checkpoint, except Pedr, Kitty, Rhys, Morwenna, Jacob, and the head of Security. Niki was patient and polite about the scanning field, because the operators were apologetic and embarrassed and, sometimes, angry.

Parliament was suspended, most of the newsfax were under the gag, broad- and wirecast were limited, with the excuse that, in this Time of Emergency, the government might need their frequencies. Most of that was due to the general strike that was announced the day after Landing Day, the force applied to break it, the rioting that resulted from the force, and the full-scale deployment of the army in response to the riots. The army itself was not pleased; rumor of discipline problems and near-insurrection came up the hill.

He couldn't get to the Lady de Winter, and it galled him. Probably just as well; he might compromise anyone he managed to talk to. He was as sure of the security on his 'board as he could be—so he sent a blind message, by a roundabout path, to a place where Jane would be likely to find it. If she didn't, it would turn to smoke after seven days.

Riding alone was not so difficult to arrange. He told the head groom that he thought the bay was developing a splint, and should be let out to pasture for a while. Then he hid the bay's tack in the cargo bin of a service skid before it was driven out to the fencing maintenance shed and parked there. In addition to ground-tying, he had taught the bay to come when called and stand still on command.

So, seven days after the Unfortunate Accident (lately everything seemed to acquire sardonic capitals in his head), he was out in the hills riding. His bones, knit on the assemblers' needles, were solid and gave him no pain. He had only yellowing bruises at the break sites, and those had been from the injections and the monitoring probes.

The bay was fractious from the change in his routine. He started at birds breaking cover, shied from outcrops he'd passed quietly the week before. It took half again as long to reach the high meadow, and even after the exertion of the climb, the bay wouldn't settle. The tall grass was leaning and tossing like waves in the wind, and he balked at stepping into it. "Come on, you ninny," Niki said, and pressed his heels to the horse's ribs. The bay reared.

Something like a large black fly, but much too fast, hit the horse's neck. And passed through—Niki had a hazy impression of exit wound as the bay screamed and toppled, and a crack echoed from the rocks. He remembered kicking out of his stirrups and falling clear only after he stopped rolling. A fragment of the stone over him chipped away. He heard the crack again. Then silence.

If he stayed where he was, the sniper would simply walk over to him and shoot him. The advantage of being the one who had the gun.

He slid backward, crouched for a moment behind the rock, and sprinted toward the far end of the meadow. A projectile tugged at the back of his riding jacket. He went limp, let his momentum take him over the edge of a one-meter drop, where soft earth had worn away from upthrust, overhanging rock. Niki had known the drop was there. If the sniper didn't, he wouldn't know how deep it was, how much cover it gave. He would have to come and look. Niki rolled under the shallow curve of the stone, felt for a good throwing rock, and waited.

Olwen had complained, that first time in the Lady de Winter, that he didn't seem to believe in his own mortality. She would feel better if she saw him now. He was grateful for the wind, which covered the sound of his harsh breathing.

It also covered the sniper's approach. Niki knew he was above him when the weapon barrel appeared at the top of the ledge. With the sky behind it, it had no depth; it was a thick black line against the light. It moved, sweeping slowly, as if scenting for him. Niki stopped breathing. One step closer; the black line lengthened. Niki stood, picked his target, and threw the rock, almost in one motion.

It hit the sniper in the elbow as it was meant to. Niki vaulted up over the ledge as the gun slid down it and bounced off the rocks a meter below. The sniper—a man in a baggy brown field jacket—jumped after it, and Niki flung himself at the man's shoulders. They hit the ground together, with the sniper on the bottom. They rolled, and Niki stuck to him, in spite of an elbow in the stomach. In his head there was a surface mapped on three axes that was the meadow. The gun was on it, *there*, and they were close to it, getting closer. Niki spared a glance and saw it shining in the grass at the corner of his vision. He kicked out, heard it clatter on distant rocks.

The sniper cursed and hit the side of Niki's head with a fist like a bludgeon. Niki kneed him in the gut and rolled away. He got to his feet, crouching, and found that the other man had done the same. The man's nose was bleeding.

"Your own damn fault," the sniper panted. "Could have been quick—one little bullet and no games. Now it's got to be slow and stupid."

"Why?" Niki asked, desperate to slow him down.

"Because I only got half in advance," the sniper said pleasantly, and leaped at him.

Niki learned immediately, a little late, that he shouldn't let his opponent close with him. The man was strong, very strong. The lesson almost cost him his ribs before he remembered the bloody nose and butted his forehead into the man's face. After that he tried to work with kicks. But the sniper was good with those, too, and good at getting under Niki's guard. A blow to Niki's hip brought him down at last, and another kick, to his head, would have knocked him out if he hadn't rolled aside. As it was, it scrambled his thoughts and brought blood to his mouth. Shadow moved on the grass, and he twisted aside. The heel strike felt like a wrecking ball in the small of his back, even though he rolled with it. But it was not hard enough to break his spine.

It had been meant to. The man in the brown jacket meant to kill him bare-handed, and knew how to do it. Niki lay prone in the grass and watched the man move toward him, frowning, careful. There was a curious distance in his mind, probably helped along by the kick to the head. Everything was happening on that surface mapped in three dimensions. The man in the brown jacket was a moving point of light. He was a stationary one. He felt his position, *felt* it, as if it were part of the pressure of air on his skin. He felt the changing position of his opponent, too, the approach vector. Just like at the gaming consoles.

Niki had very little force left to apply. But Force Majeur was misnamed. The issue was not who used the greatest force, but who made best use of what there was. Such as gravity, and momentum. He was downhill from the man in brown. He stood up.

When the sniper lunged for him, Niki ducked, flung himself forward, hit the man just below the knees. The man fell forward, half over Niki's shoulders. Niki straightened, levering the man the rest of the way, to fall to the ground behind Niki.

But there wasn't any ground behind Niki. At least, not enough for a man falling, prey to gravity and momentum. The slope they fought on was the one where Niki had once caught an hour's sleep, the one that looked to the sea and dropped away in stepped cliffs.

The short burst of the man's scream told him there was more, or less, behind him than he'd thought. The sound of splintering wood, of the meeting of flesh and stone, told him what it was. He lay in the grass for what must have been several minutes, sweating, cold, and gulping air. When he thought he could bear it, he crawled to the edge and looked over.

The trunk of a dead tree thrust sideways from the cliff face; the sniper must have hit that first. He lay in an untidy heap below it, face up, and the shards of broken branches were scattered down the rock face around him. Niki clung to the thatch of grass at the top, panting, waiting for the blankness in his head to fill up again. Then he saw the sniper's hands open and close, scrabble against the rock.

He was over the edge before he remembered that he was exhausted, that riding boots were worse than useless for climbing, that the man might not be as helpless as he looked. The horror of death slow in coming, faced alone, had overpowered his thoughts for that long. By the time he reached the broken tree, his hands were scraped raw, and all those sensible things had occurred to him. He stopped, clinging to the stump. Then the sniper's eyes opened, wild with pain and fear, and met Niki's. He kept climbing down.

The sniper's gaze followed as he approached. The brown field jacket had ripped at one side seam; the shirt under it had torn away, too. The part of the man's torso that showed through was an ugly shape, like a dented metal drum, already streaked beneath the skin with livid red. Internal bleeding—and surely an intact spine didn't bend that way. Niki could never bring help in time, not this far from anything, and the horse dead.

The man's lips parted, and a bubble of blood broke on them. "Good fight, Your Highness," he whispered.

Niki said absently, "I'm not—"

The man smiled, hard and narrow.

Niki stared at him until he realized that the eyes that met his were dead. Then he flung himself at the cliff face without a care for hand- and footholds; he made the climb in a blind lunge that he couldn't remember once he reached the top. At the far edge of the meadow, slow autumn flies had gathered on the bay's face. He passed the dead horse and began to run.

His lungs burned by the time he reached the paddocks, and sweat ran hot and cold down his body. He slid down behind a gatepost and studied the scene.

It looked like peace, or would to anyone who didn't know the Castle's routine. The stables were quiet. No music played to amuse the grooms and pacify the horses. No hooves kicked idly against permaplast. No buckles jingled under the cleaning rag. He couldn't go closer; he couldn't bear to find out if the silence in the stables was that of emptiness, or something else.

He crossed the gardens and watched the Castle from the shelter of the topiary. Quiet. Peaceful. No sign of movement.

No sign of the guard at the doors.

At the entrance to the kitchens and garage, the housecom did not challenge him. He almost offered his embed to the dead plate anyway, out of habit. The door opened for him. If the housecom was down, the doors ought to have been sealed. He paced down the corridor to the kitchen as quietly as he could—his breathing was loud again.

The kitchen was empty. A few indicator lights glowed around the room, from the appliances and coolers. The bread maker's indic was flashing, and risen dough oozed out from under its cover. He left the kitchen and went on.

He heard footsteps at the end of the hall, and ducked into the laundry. They never came close enough for Niki to see who made them. He took the service stairs to the second floor. He slipped through the door at the top, into the family quarters. On the shining hall floor, he found a trail of blood. A few drops at first, then more, smeared and tracked through. It ended around the corner, in front of the down tube doors, where Rhys lay.

Whatever had wounded him at the end of the hall and started the blood trail couldn't be determined now. He'd been shot in front of the tube, with a military issue Wyvern riot gun that its users nicknamed "The Reaper." The dispersal pattern of the sprayed wire was printed across the down tube doors.

Niki knelt beside his brother and closed the blind eyes. He made a surprisingly dignified corpse. Over and over in Niki's head, a memory played: Rhys, a solemn-faced fifteen-year-old, explaining to the gardener that Niki had not ridden his pony through the daffodils; Rhys had done it himself. Niki had always wondered, if Rhys was going to lie anyway, why he hadn't told one that would keep them *both* out of trouble.

The tube lights flickered, and Niki sprang away, ducked inside one of the guest rooms. But whoever it was went past the second floor without stopping.

The door of his own room was broken in; he'd put a touchpad lock on it that didn't speak to the housecom. Very little was disturbed there, though someone had sprayed the 'board on his desk with hot wire. And someone had taken his target pistol. Niki shrugged at the empty case. It wouldn't have been much good against the Wyvern.

He scratched at Kitty's door—he didn't dare call out or knock. There was no answer, but it, like all the other doors, opened. The drapes were drawn across the long windows, and the room was dim.

The Wyvern left no more blood in its victims than a vampire might. He heard the thick carpet sucking at his boots before he saw them, huddled together at the end of the room. The dispersal had caught her face, and the lower half of it was a ruin. Her shining brown hair was incongruous above it, flowers scattered on turned earth.

Pedr lay in front of her, face down. His back was all exit wound. He had tried to defend Kitty with his own body, and The Reaper had taken them both. But something about Pedr's position suggested that he hadn't died immediately. One hand was outflung on the wet carpet. The other arm was folded beside him, palm up near his face. As Niki moved, something shone there.

The heavy gold ring with the seal of Cymru—the signet of the Prince. It was the only thing in that end of the room without blood on it. It gleamed hotly in Pedr's cold palm; Niki, as if ordered to, picked it up. It fit his left ring finger. It had to, now.

At the door of the room, in a sudden delayed reaction, he was very nearly sick. But he bit his tongue, distracted himself with pain, and went on.

How many more people he loved did he have to find here? Jacob, and his mother. Only two. It should be easy.

He found no other bodies in the family's living quarters. The staff was gone. He hoped they'd had enough warning to get away. And if they were dead, none of them seemed to be dead here. He looked into the Great Hall from the second-floor gallery, but he didn't venture into it. There was no cover there.

Morwenna was in her workroom. The smell there now was of alcohol, yeast, and ozone. She sat in her desk chair looking composed and annoyed. In place of the two lines between her brows, there was a small, cauterized hole from a beam weapon.

Rhys's death, Kitty's and Pedr's, had made him horrified and sick. His mother's corpse frightened him. This was a macabre waxwork, a museum display that, if he found the start button, would click and whir and enact a demonstration of gene splicing. And still, it would wear that face that was so like his own. He swallowed fear and bile and closed her eyes, too, but quickly.

The trip to Jacob's apartments was long and potentially dangerous. He heard more footsteps, spent more time in hiding. Never voices, never more than one pair of feet. He could jump their owner—but their owner had the Wyvern, probably. If the security checkpoint outside Jacob's wing was manned, it would be manned with the wrong people. He slipped out of the Castle and used Jacob's outside entrance.

It was quiet here, too—nothing dropped in the middle, but a lamp left on, a video monitor's readout glowing. He could smell food, but the kitchen was clean, and the odor was left over from breakfast. He sat down at last on the library rug, exhausted, hopeless. This was so much like sanctuary—a warm, homelike lie. There was no sanctuary anywhere. He wanted to lie down, to stare at the ceiling until someone came and shot him, or until he thought of something to keep that from happening. But he prodded himself up. He had to search the public rooms. He had to know if Jacob was alive.

He didn't have to go as far as the Great Hall. The security checkpoint down the corridor from Jacob's apartments was deserted—not even bodies, he noted with distant relief. No destruction, no disarray. Just empty. The monitor was intact, and the switching system that operated it. The display showed an empty second-floor corridor. Niki crouched at the switching panel and began to tap the pads.

There were no labels. He could tell what room he'd switched to, but only after he'd done it, and only if he recognized what the video showed. The corridors on any given floor all looked alike. One pad took him, abruptly, to the one where his brother lay. The angle was odd; for a moment he didn't know what he was looking at. Then he did. He slammed at the next pad in the row. Another pad—and he started, and jammed all the sliders on the panel down to zero. There was a person on the screen; it was his footsteps, booming on the audio, that had made Niki zero everything that might be a volume control. Niki froze for long minutes. But no one came to see what the noise was. He found the volume control, bumped it lightly up. The person was a man in army blue. He carried the Wyvern—*a* Wyvern, any-way—at ready. He moved slowly down the corridor (third floor), stopping often in a listening pose, sometimes opening doors cautiously. If Niki knew where the control was, he could zoom to see his badges, his name. He yanked his attention away and pressed more pads.

Fifth pad, third row. It was Pedr's study; and bent urgently over the 'board imbedded in the wide desk was Jacob. Alive.

Niki felt a surge of relief so powerful it drained the strength out of him, brought him near tears. Jacob had, so far, escaped the carnage. If Niki could get to him before the blue-uniformed man did, he might stay that way.

Too late. Niki heard the door of Pedr's study hiss open, and Jacob looked up, dropped his hands into his lap. Unalarmed—but of course, the man was in army uniform. Jacob would not see the threat.

"Report, Lieutenant," Jacob said.

The man in uniform crossed the broad, cold expanse of floor to the desk, onto the video. The Wyvern was under his arm, muzzle-end toward Jacob. It would be an instant's work to bring it up, hit the trigger . . .

"All quiet, sir. No sign of perimeter violation, nobody inside."

Of course not, you bastard. You took care of that. But if he intended to take care of Jacob as well, why this polite charade?

"Thank you, Lieutenant." Had Jacob brought in the army, trying to secure the Castle in the aftermath of the slaughter?

"No sign of Viscount Harlech, though, sir."

But the Wyvern was a military weapon. And this was not the army, but a single uniformed man.

Jacob looked down at his lap. "I'm afraid Lord Harlech is dead. Thank you for your help, Lieutenant." And Jacob's hands came up from under the desk. A thin line of blue-green light leaped from the gray shape in his fist, into the place where the lieutenant's neck met his jaw, out through his hair. The audio was filled with the high-pitched interference of the beam weapon.

He watched the lieutenant fold up, watched Jacob set the pistol down, rise calmly, and roll the dead man into the next room. Then he remembered that he could turn the system off and not have to watch. He did that, and stood braced with both hands on the deactivated controls of the panel until the pain of his scraped palms made him stop.

The name that had floated out of reach in the darkness, that had moved, elusive, before him for months, was Jacob Kelling. Jacob had killed his family, and tormented his country until it flew to bits. Jacob had sat across from him in his library, just down the corridor from where Niki stood now, and accepted the inhaler, the printout, the confidences, the trust.

When Niki was fourteen, Jacob had taught him to play chess.

He laid his face in his hands as if his head were an offering, held in cupped palms. He wished what Jacob had told the nameless lieutenant were true. He wished his horse hadn't reared, that his skull had been there when the shot went by. His life or death changed nothing—except that, living, he had to live through this. But oh, Lord of Annwn, this was hardly trivial.

Well, silly not to suffer through the rest. Niki had been offered to the lord of hell a ridiculous number of times in the past few weeks, and been refused. He was being preserved for some more colorful end, apparently. Cerridwen, overseer of death and re-birth, would stop the wheel where she pleased.

Had Morwenna suspected this? Was that why she wanted him offworld, why she'd said what she had in the hospital? Perhaps he could manage to get off the planet yet. But he thought it might be nice to see to Jacob first.

He went back down the hall to Jacob's rooms. The library yielded a Quickfire auto and several rounds for it. Niki was not particularly careful in opening the locked drawer. It occurred to him, as he broke through the front panel, that Jacob might have something more dangerous than a lock on anything important.

The possibility of getting his head blown off breaking into Jacob's desk roused in him only a vague intellectual interest.

At the checkpoint, he snapped the monitor back on; it told him that Jacob hadn't left Pedr's study. He was still working on the 'board. Niki wondered what could possibly be left for him to do. Hunting for Niki? Making sure that the appearance of his face, his voice, his embed reading, would set off alarms all over the planet? No—he thought Niki was dead. After all, why lie to a man he was about to kill?

But the point was a good one. If the bloodthirsty Fate that held his future wanted him to get off Cymru, his embed had to go. And if he was to die before that . . . well, how did one define "waste of time" when one had nothing pressing to spend time on anyway? Go through the motions and see where they led.

To be without an embed—that, in itself, was a crime, and how would he dig it out of his wrist? But he had heard that sometimes an embed was erased. It happened to power line workers, to technicians troubleshooting 'board nodes. It happened to people found dead with their hands on a power tool and their feet in water. The erasing of his embed took on a sudden sheen in his thoughts.

Niki turned off the monitor system (*Why?* he wondered. *Habit*, he decided.) He found a screwdriver bit in a toolbox under the console, and used it to pry the housing off the monitor. He wasn't especially careful about damaging it, either. Inside, against the back of the display panel, was the plate that distributed the image across its surface. Niki closed his left hand over it.

He was sitting on the floor with his back against the wall. He was fairly sure he'd hit the wall. His whole field of vision was narrowing, as if he were rushing backward in a long tunnel. *Don't faint*, he told himself uselessly, and didn't, quite. His left arm seemed to belong to someone else, but when he finally stood up, it came with him.

Then he began the slow trip back into the Castle's heart. He didn't have to be as careful this time. The man whose footsteps he'd heard was dead.

His breathing was quiet and steady outside the open door of Pedr's study. He pressed against the wall and closed his eyes, re-creating the inside of the room in his mind. The wide desk and the span of floor, daylight from the sloped ceiling falling on the 'board and the chair before it . . . charted in three dimensions, marked with a stationary point of light. He swung around the doorframe, sighted, and fired, while Jacob was still turning to look.

Everything was where he'd remembered, and where he'd guessed. His shot hit Jacob's beam weapon, spun it off the desk in a shower of discharged energy. Jacob winced and lurched backward.

"Stay where you are," Niki said. "Put your hands flat on the desktop and keep them there."

Jacob stared at him, motionless, mouth open.

"Do it!"

Jacob put his hands on the desk. "I take it," he said, his voice unsteady, "that he botched the job."

"Unless you wanted to kill my horse, yes."

Jacob shook his head. "That's difficult. This"—he raised one hand a fraction of an inch, remembered, and put it back down—"was supposed to be the work of a cabal of officers who had learned of Pedr's plan to assassinate you. They were too late to save your life, you see, and their revenge got out of hand."

"It wouldn't have worked."

"Of course it would have," he said irritably. "Every one of the heirs dead, the army trying and executing five of their highest for treason and murder, the yeomanry hating the army and the aristocracy about evenly . . . Or did you think I meant to run the place myself?"

"What *did* you mean to do?"

Jacob glanced down at the 'board sunk into Pedr's desk. "My relief should be here in about thirty-six hours."

For an instant, Niki thought it was a non sequitur. Only for an instant. "Who, Jacob?" he said.

"Concorde Peacekeepers, called in by the acting government—me, according to the Emergency Acts Bill—to restore order. They'll do it so well that Cymru will ask to be placed under Concorde governance."

"How long?"

"I told you, thirty-six—"

"You know what I mean."

Jacob looked into his face without warmth—without any discernible human emotion. "You think I've betrayed you, don't you? I was never yours, or Pedr's. I've been an agent of Central

Worlds Concorde—Special Services—for eleven years. For the last six of those, I've been on assignment on Cymru.''

"Then we meant nothing to you at all," Niki whispered.

"Have you found your mother?" he asked harshly. "Yes?" Morwenna, sitting in her chair, as if stopped in the middle of a conversation. "The beamer's quick and clean and almost painless. And I sent someone else after you.''

Niki felt, somewhere down in the middle of himself, a tremor of hysteria. As if all of this mattered. "You could have killed me at the Landing Day ball. I was lying at your feet. A little push in the right place . . .''

Jacob, by his face, seemed to think this was a reasonable topic of conversation. "I was terrified you'd die without any help from me. I wasn't ready yet. I didn't want a revolution that wasn't under my control.''

"But you didn't mind if I died in Black's.''

"I minded," he said crisply. "But no one would know who was responsible for killing you. That puts a different complexion on it.''

The Quickfire shook in Niki's hand. Jacob's shoulders lifted. "Don't," Niki said. "I don't miss. You know that." *You taught me to shoot, too. Oh, God.* He could almost see the line, cleanly marked, that led down his arms, through the Quickfire, along the barrel, and straight and true to the middle of Jacob's face. He had never before aimed a gun at a human being.

"What are you going to do now?" Jacob asked.

Niki didn't answer him.

"Whatever you do, the Peacekeepers will land. Are you going to be the People's Hero, lead them against the offworlders? How long do you think they'll follow you, into the paths of the beam cannons, and the wildfire, and things that make the Wyvern look like a squirrel gun?''

"We'll never know," Niki said. "Stand up and turn around.''

He made a sharp gesture with the pistol, and Jacob did as he was told. Niki crossed the space between them in two quick strides and clubbed Jacob with the gun. Jacob staggered, sagged against the wall. Niki fired into the 'board (it spat sparks, leaked smoke) and grabbed up the Wyvern that still lay on the floor in front of the desk.

"Sorry," Jacob croaked. "It's a lot harder to knock someone out than it looks in the vids.''

He was slumped on the floor, half sitting, watching Niki. The look on his face was almost pleased.

Niki sighted down the Quickfire at Jacob's head. Jacob stared, unblinking, back. *Assassin*, Niki thought at him. It wasn't enough. *Murderer.* Niki held the pose until his arm began to ache, until the weight of the Quickfire dragged at his mind like an anchor. Then he plunged out the door, sealed it, hammered out the family override code on the lock. Two bolts closed, loudly. He fired the Wyvern until the pad was a jammed ruin, the Wyvern empty.

The city was a series of armed camps that he had to navigate around. Jacob had already spread rumors and truths (bent over that 'board, working, working), and panic had turned the streets into a war zone. He stumbled through it, unrecognized, perhaps unrecognizable. He wondered if Olwen was safe. She belonged to some other world, but she lived in this one even so; Niki hoped that whatever happened next wouldn't happen to her. He longed to go to the Lady de Winter, to Jane Wells, to whatever temporary oblivion might be there. But if he did, trouble would go there, too. He was Cerridwen's to spin; but he would not tempt her with another morsel of human heart.

By the time he reached the worldport, at the edge of Caernarfon, it was twilight. The gate at the end of the field wanted to read his embed. He stared at it stupidly for a moment. Then he jammed his left ring finger against the plate. The signet of the Prince of Cymru spoke, perhaps by means of something built into it. Or perhaps the plate had an optical system, and the ring simply looked like what it was. The gate opened.

There was one ship on the field, a big commercial shuttle glossy under the pad lights. Its registry world was Oasis, an unaligned planet. Niki wondered where it was headed. It didn't matter, but he wondered anyway. A field crew was running the pre-lift check. There should have been more ships. Had they been warned away, sent packing? Or had they seen the madness trickling down from the hill and known what it was?

Jane and Andrew, if they lived out the night, would wonder what had happened to him. No, they would hear Jacob's rumor—that Pedr had had him killed—and believe it.

He was the Prince of Cymru now, and his responsibility was to the nation. His first and last act as ruler would be to leave. River Dyfed into Cystennin Bay into Meridian Ocean: change their names, and they would still be there. When the Peacekeepers landed, there would be no organized resistance; the people would live, and the nation, in whatever altered state, under whatever new name and government, would thrive. Because the nation of Cymru was its people, and nothing else. He worked his way carefully through the long shadows toward the shuttle.

Then a shadow broke, and a man stepped in front of him, weapon raised. He wore police gray, and was not, perhaps, much older than Niki. His fierce expression cracked suddenly, became confusion, and Niki thought he might have known who he was. The Quickfire was still in Niki's hand, forgotten. He dropped it and bolted for the shuttle's ramp. Shots pursued him like loping dogs, from many sides.

Of course. Jacob would have gotten free before this. Jacob, who knew him so well, would guess where Niki had gone.

The ramp would be the worst: they couldn't miss him on the ramp. He would have to count on speed. In the half-light under the shuttle, a man in coveralls looked up, openmouthed. His hair was some light color, thick, and it hid his eyes in a band of shadow. They recognized each other at about the same time. *Good-bye, Andrew*, Niki thought. *Don't, for God's sake, carry on the fight.* And he sprinted up the ramp.

He staggered at the top, flung forward to bang against the edge of the hatchway. His right arm went numb. He hadn't recovered his balance before a gray-haired woman appeared in the hatch, grabbed his coat, and dragged him inside.

"Talk fast," she said, "or you're back out there."

Words had forsaken him. With an effort, he held out his left hand and the signet of Cymru.

She said something that was probably either blasphemous or obscene. "Don't move," she told him, and disappeared into the cockpit.

He did move; he dropped into an acceleration couch. His right shoulder was hot and sore and he felt lightheaded. He couldn't remember why he'd worked so hard to be on this ship. Andrew would probably call it running away. Well, if he wanted to lead a guerrilla war against the Concorde, he was welcome to do it. No, he wasn't.

None of his thoughts seemed to move in a straight line.

The gray-haired woman had come back. Probably the captain, he realized. She sat on the couch next to his. "I'm in a hole. Rule of interplanetary trade: all commercial ships must transport disaster victims and refugees when necessary, to the limits of their capability. You look like a refugee, and that looks like a disaster. But company regs are that I can't take sides in planetary politics. And your jewelry says this is political as hell."

"Scan me," Niki said. So much pointless struggle; he hoped the business with the monitor and the embed hadn't been more of the same.

She used a hand reader, looked up at him sharply. "You're blank."

"Yes," Niki said, "I am." His right arm still wouldn't work; he pulled the ring off his left hand with his teeth. There was a recycler unit in the wall across the cabin. He sighted carefully and tossed. The recycler clattered. "I never miss," he said softly.

The captain stood. "Strap in. We lift in sixty."

There was movement in the cabin—more crew. He hadn't noticed them. He slid back limply in the couch, and his right arm dangled into the aisle. After a moment the faint whine of the engines came up. He also heard a quick patting sound, like a leaking faucet. He rolled his head to one side and looked into the aisle.

Blood was running out of his jacket sleeve and pattering onto the floor. He hadn't stumbled at the top of the ramp; he'd been shot. There was already a little pool on the floor, and his shirt cuff was soaked with it. The last blood of the Glyndwrs, he thought idly. The blood of the last Prince of Cymru. Well, that was reasonable. Cymru had no more use for royal blood. Let it spill out here between the earth and the sky, and be gone, and make no more trouble. Acceleration pressed him into the couch, and sent the pooling blood down the aisle in a little rivulet. He closed his eyes.

"Medtech!" someone was yelling, "Jesus—medtech!" But that was very far away.

‖⋄ HAGGARD

'Because I helped to wind the clock
I come to hear it strike.'
　　　—W. B. Yeats, ''The O'Rahilly''

There's no such thing as information security. Anything that can be stored can be retrieved, whether it's written on electrons, on paper, or on the soft slate of the mind. There are methods, and we've mastered them all. The only security in the world is to make sure that no one wants the information, or suspects its existence. If we know it's there to find, and we have a use for it, it will be ours eventually.

I find myself hesitating over the pronouns. When does the line slip, when does "we" become "they"? Answer: Not yet; and, It always has been. I'll let the pronouns fall where they may. The reader can sort them out.

So this is my secret for only as long as those two things—that they don't know about this file, and that it has no value to them—are true. Assuming they are, even now. Paranoia is its own kind of wisdom, they've taught me. They didn't teach me the fatalism that goes along with that lesson, not exactly. But I learned it at their hands. When they need to know about Niki Falcon, they will eventually look here, and eventually this file will come to light. By that time, I hope, I will want them to have it. *He* certainly won't mind.

Do you see, O my teachers and superior officers? I am a security risk. This is both my flagrant proof of it, and my amends. Do what you want with his name and mine; by now, the now of your reading, I don't think you'll be able to bury them.

I meant to be a journalist, as much as I meant to be anything back in the well-behaved haze of my childhood and adolescence. And I've done that, now. I couldn't have before I met him; there's a difference between a feature article and the output reports of testing machines. Consorting with him made me something more than a finely made piece of laboratory equipment. So if I use those skills, such as they are, to tell about him— Unauthorized Reader, if you don't like it you can take a long jump.

I met Niki Falcon in the OutWell Research Facility at Nexus Landfall on Galatea. He was on the second floor, looking out a glass wall at the rain, at a sky so gray it made the paving seem cheerful, at the long-winged bronze ship soaked and shining outside Assembly B.

No, I want to get that first image just as it was, though it won't mean anything to my Unauthorized Reader. This is for me. So it's not just the sight. I need the context, too. OutFac is a secured area, full of uniforms and lab tunics and passtags on collars. The glass walls are all edged with waist-high railings and signs that say, "DO NOT PASS THIS POINT! Do Not Lean or Stand on Railing." And there he was, impossibly tall and unbearably thin, wearing scuffed black flight pants and a baggy black leather jacket older than he was, his blue-black hair too long, his face hollow and high-boned and undomesticated as a young fox's, with one foot on the forbidden railing and his arms folded across his knee. He was staring hungrily out the window, like that same young fox at the edge of a henyard. He was an outrage.

I was a first-year officer-trainee; I had a blue uniform blouse and a pocket card that beeped politely when I passed checkpoints. I'd been assigned rent-a-cop work for that shift, and hadn't been inside the uniform long enough to know exactly what that work was. I was outraged.

I moved sideways and came up behind him. "You!" I said, as if it were an order in itself. "What are you doing here?"

He lowered his head for a moment. Then he swung his upper body around (his foot stayed on the railing) and smiled at me. He still has that smile. It's the one that comes on him when he sees a delightful irony about to present itself. I thought it was impolite—that and the candid expression. Only gods and crazy people could look so innocent, it seemed to me, and I assumed the most likely choice was true.

"I want to see some ID," I said.

"I'm afraid you can't," he said, his voice polite and pleasant. He had an almost-accent, a way of speaking softly and rounding his vowels. "I don't have any—not the sort you want, anyway."

"What are you doing here? This is a secure area."

"I'm happy for it," he said. That took me several seconds. I blame it on the uniform blouse; it hampers your sense of humor at first. "I'm looking out the window," he told me, as if I was an idiot (which, from this distance, I can see I was). "At that."

He turned one long hand toward the sleeping arrow of bronze outside the assembly building. It was unfinished, waiting for the fitting of its interior. I couldn't blame him. It had the sort of beauty one could reasonably covet. "Well, you can't do it from here," I snapped, "unless you show me some authorization and *take your damned foot off the rail.*"

He did, and turned around. Then he put both hands on the top rail and leaned his hips against it. There was nothing threatening about his height; at least he didn't seem to mean it that way. "I don't think you understand." He nodded toward the glass. "That one's mine."

I'm sure I said something insufferably smart. I'd seen too many vids. But he suffered it with no apparent loss of goodwill, and said, "No, really. They're building it for me." Then his face came a little unfocused, as if he were checking some internal reference, and added, "Or they're building me for it. Take your pick."

You see, I didn't know anything. I should have recognized the ship or, failing that, understood what he'd just said. But I didn't have a brain in my head—it had been replaced entirely with regulations. So I laid a hand threateningly on my billygun holster and told him we were going to the nearest checkpoint. He looked rueful and benign, and went quietly. His movements, I noticed, were stiff and careful.

Of course he went quietly. And when we got to the checkpoint, he grinned at the operator and passed through, to the sound of two polite beeps. The monitor showed, not a passtag of some color hidden in his clothing, but a spot of light in each wrist, and another under his skull.

He was very good about it. Oh, he did raise that one inquiring eyebrow, but he didn't ask out loud if I was satisfied now.

"I'm very sorry," I said, and tried to sound like it. "I didn't know—"

He shook his head. "I'm the new one. Hardly anyone recognizes me yet." He frowned and stretched his back, slowly, as if it hurt him. "In fact, I just got out of Install last night." And he slid the jacket cuffs back and showed me the insides of his wrists.

The little slide-away covers of artificial flesh would be effectively invisible when he was healed. Now they were lighter-colored rectangles surrounded by reddened, slightly puffy skin. "Do they itch?" I asked, feeling stupefied.

"No, but the rest of me feels as if I've been jumped on repeatedly. I should sit down. Do you want some coffee?"

I thought of sitting, in uniform, across a commissary table from this half-wild creature, where anyone might see me. I thought about what they'd think when they found out the creature was the new gestalt pilot. "I'm on duty," I said finally, since that, as usual, made it unnecessary to think at all.

"Doing what? Keeping people from leaning on the railings?"

"No—yes—and other things, security work—"

"You already told me this is a secure building. It'll stay that way for half an hour. Come on."

That was when—that hour, that very moment—I began the other half of my training, the half that brought me to now, to here, to this place. But if I'd known then, when would I have had time to think about it? Even walking stiff and sore, he set a good pace. At the sliding gate in sublevel four that opened onto the Bullet platform, he informed the officer in charge that he was making an emergency trip to the city, and that I had been assigned as security for him. ("No, it's not on the duty logs yet—Harisal just went to cut the orders three minutes ago. It's an *emergency*, damn it!"). The points of light on the monitor and the authority in his voice put us in the first car. (He winced when he leaned back in the seat, but only said cheerfully, "A secure building.")

So it was the little Portuguese café on Drexler where I sat with the half-wild creature. And people stared, not at him, but at my blue uniform blouse, while we drank coffee strong enough to kill my intestinal flora, and ate wedges of sweet bread with butter.

He made me talk about myself. I can't explain why that was so extraordinary—no, I can, but I don't plan to take the time here. I can only say that it was. I told him about my career in the Service, such as it was then, and about University, and about my father—how, after all, could I talk about the first two without explaining about the third? He decided to make a project of me then, I know. He has always seemed to know where he was needed, and I'm sure that, at first, that was the connection between us. When I had said enough, he thrust the last piece of bread into my hand, paid the bill, and dragged me out into the street.

When I got back to OutFac, it was four hours later. My shift was over. I'd been on a tour of half the street markets in the city. I'd had a dragon painted on my face and a spray of eyes-of-heaven stuck in my lapel. I'd heard, and danced to, a six-piece Cajae band and a street-corner pianist. And I stepped out on the Bullet platform with a sack of papayas, a rainbow kite, a tin whistle I could already play three tunes on, a pen that wrote in six colors and upside down, and a blue ceramic mug with a homely face on it. Anyone who cares to may find the last three in, or on, my desk. That afternoon, for the first time in my adult life, I'd had fun.

The duty roster showed me as assigned outside the facility for the last four and a half hours of my shift. The duty files were as secure as the rest of OutFac. I had neglected my responsibility; in return, obviously, he had remembered his.

For the next week, his path seemed to cross mine all the time. Whenever it did, he had a book to lend me, or a disc I ought to listen to, or a nonsensical scheme he wanted help with. I didn't realize then that I was going through my days looking forward to each of those crossings.

At the end of the week, he arrived at my station—the chart room; I can remember him against a background of changing monitors—and asked, "When are you off duty?" The question was unlike him, and he asked it gravely. I told him. "Meet me in the commissary then?" he said, and I agreed.

I had forgotten, you see, the second stage of *his* training. He sat pale and composed in the sunny end of the commissary, waiting for me, staring out the window wall at the sunken garden. And so I saw him before he saw me; I saw him unguarded, all his heart in his face, as it had been when he looked out at his ship. At that worst time in both our lives, I fell firmly and irrevocably in love with him, though I knew as much about love then as I did about fun.

"My conversion starts tomorrow," he said when I sat down.

There's no suspense in that now. Of course he survived it. But he couldn't know then, and I couldn't know, and my emotions were already rubbed raw—they'd changed state between the commissary door and the chair, after all. He hadn't yet made me human enough to cry in front of anybody. So, in the middle of his second sentence, I stood up and walked out.

Conversion lasts twenty-five days. For twenty-five days the assemblers, the critters, are loosed upon the nerves, the guts, the veins, to eat away the undesirable parts and replace them with the marvelous, alien structures they have been designed to build. They link them all to the wrist and spinal cord ports already in place, and are monitored from those ports. They prepare their host body for its new addiction, and construct the mechanisms it will use to manipulate the drug. When they are done, the first dose is administered. Then, finally, if that has been survived, if the body has made all the adjustments it can stand to make in twenty-five days, the biotechs wake its owner up.

Nobody thinks to release progress reports during the process. For twenty-five days I walked in the city, watching street-corner bands, drinking strong coffee, and retreating to lavatory stalls when my eyes began to burn. In a hundred-foot elm in a park I lost the kite, and afterward went out of my way to avoid that street and the sight of it, vivid and beyond my reach, trembling in the branches.

Then one morning I came into the commissary—and there he was. Same table, though the light was weak and gray. Both his hands were clasped around his cup, and his head was bent, his eyes closed. He looked like a fasting saint. "Niki," I said—an invocation. He lifted his head. His eyes were huge in his pared-down face, the eyes of a man who has been living with nightmares—which, of course, he had been.

Then he smiled at me, and the life in that smile drove away all the nightmares and the hollows. When I reached him I was crying.

I don't want to write any more.

CHAPTER EIGHT

Once out of nature I shall never take
My bodily form from any natural thing,
But such a form as Grecian goldsmiths make
Of hammered gold and gold enamelling
To keep a drowsy Emperor awake;
Or set upon a golden bough to sing
To lords and ladies of Byzantium
Of what is passed, or passing, or to come.
    —W. B. Yeats, "Sailing to Byzantium"

Hair clung to the sweat on Chrysander Harris's forehead. His fingers remained arched and tense over the keyboard, still reaching for the last urgent chord that echoed in him. His hands ached; his muscles were pricked with pins of fatigue. He looked up at the engineer's box, blinked to focus on it.

"Is it right?" His voice was thick and felt like someone else's.

"That's your call, isn't it?" Vere pulled off her glasses and scrubbed her face with her palms. "We got the levels, though. Come fly the sucker."

"Kill the field, will you?" An instant later, Chrysander could hear the faint sounds of the room. He stepped away from the keyboard and stumbled. A few too many takes, perhaps—but overwork was part of working. Vere snapped, "Chrysander? You all right?"

"Just stiff. And tired."

"Come sit down."

Chrysander climbed the short flight of stairs to the box, closed the door behind him, and dropped into a chair near the main board. Vere frowned, opened her mouth.

"No, Vere. Just fly it, all right?"

"All right." Vere turned sharply away and clicked things.

Chrysander tucked his feet up under him as the talking drum spoke, spoke again, then rolled the rhythm out in front of the opening chord. He leaned his head back and closed his eyes.

It was an uneasy progression in E, uneasy because it never really resolved. It was proud and brittle, brilliant as some great city on the night before its fall. It was built on a percussive helix that was forever one beat short of completion. His left hand had supplied a deep-voiced theme that wove through the song like a black fog through night streets. His right had spangled it with melody, bright as jewels or the souls of martyrs. But the fog thickened, and the shine of the jewels became the glare of artificial light. The melody picked up again in the mid-ranges, but it was pierced and circled with harsh sounds: they might have been metal on stone, crackling distortion, wind across the neck of a bottle. The climax pulled the whole song to bits, like centrifugal force. In its ruins wandered a thread of folk song in a different key, and the hollow sound of broken buildings.

Silence finally pulled him back to the sound booth. It was not what he'd heard in his head. The effect fell short, as always. But Vere wouldn't know what it was supposed to sound like, and neither would anyone else. That would drive him crazy someday, if anything did.

"Did you like it?" Chrysander said.

"Yes," said the engineer.

"Why?"

"You're a cruel bastard," muttered Vere. But Chrysander continued to watch her. "Because it sounds like a really ugly story told in a really beautiful way."

"Ah," said Chrysander. It didn't sound like what was in his head. But the idea seemed to have come across.

"What does 'ah' mean in this context?"

"Probably that I don't want you to know what I'm thinking."

Vere turned away and tapped buttons. "Are we done? Christ, I hope we're done."

Chrysander unfolded his legs and stretched them out before him. "We're done."

"You know, I love to engineer for you. You call up and say you're on FourCorners for a little while, you've got a couple of sketch tracks you want down, just a tune or two, and Vere, can you spare a few hours? I wind up in here from dawn to dinner, no breaks, no slack time, and not a frivolous word spoken. What the hell do you do when you're *working*?''

"When I'm working, I drink engineers down like glasses of water. I'm sorry, Vere. It's an attitude I have, I suppose. It doesn't mean anything."

"Bullshit. It means you don't recognize that we're all flesh and blood. Including you."

"Vere," Chrysander said, "shut up and save the take."

"And stay out of your face, I know. I already saved it. Where d'you want it sent?"

"One to my drop, and one to Talliver's. He thinks I go insane at the full moon and dump all my files."

Vere watched the status lights flicker. "He'd be worried about you now." Her hands moved swiftly on the panel.

"He gets ten percent to peddle my flesh. I don't pay him to shrink my head." Chrysander smiled, but his shoulders were tight.

"And I'm being paid to push buttons."

"Yes," Chrysander said softly. "You are."

Vere pushed herself away from the board. "You're a cold sonofabitch, d'you know that? But some of us are still crazy enough to care if you live or die." She went to the door. "Cut the box lights when you go."

"Vere." She stopped in the door. He wanted to say he was sorry; he almost did. Instead he asked, "What do you know about gestalt pilots?"

She looked over her shoulder and frowned. "Not much, except that they beat musicians for Live Fast and Die Young. Why?"

"Just wondering. I've never met one."

"There *is* only one, anymore. I forget his name."

Chrysander shrugged. "That's all."

"Oh, shit—I was going to tell you before. There's a woman who's been around asking about you. How long are you here for, what are you working on. She says she's local media, but she's not. Thought you'd want to know."

"I do. Thank you." Though he didn't need to hear it from Vere. He'd known she was there—she was always there, lately. Certainly since he arrived on FourCorners. He settled his head against the chair back. "I've been expecting her."

"Shall I tell her anything next time?"

"No. She'll have all the answers by then."

A moment later he heard Vere close the door. The lights went out down on the studio floor.

First there was the voice, unaccompanied, riveting. The first notes stopped all motion in the bar: the bartender, a woman with black-and-white printed hair, forgot to fill the glass she held; drinkers forgot to drain theirs; gamers froze over their chosen diversions. Niki Falcon held an empty mug, and couldn't be bothered to remember what it was for.

The voice overlaid itself, as if reflected in mirrors. The instrument that spoke tentatively behind it was like, and unlike, Irish pipes. Heads turned to the vid grid at the end of the room.

Dust and smoke seemed to pull together over it, and glow gold, until they became a still, half-kneeling figure. He looked up as he sang, as if he'd noticed he wasn't alone. Everyone who watched would have sworn he stared only at them. His face was just within the parameters of human beauty; were it any closer to perfect, it would cease to be human.

He lifted one arm with dreadful slowness, reached toward them. As he did, the image warmed with color. His hair was like honey and wheatstraw, his face and throat and arms tan as coffee rich with cream, and his eyes were the impossible gold of clear amber, or the fearsome yellow of tigers'.

"Implants," someone near Niki muttered.

"Shut up," said someone else.

Niki settled his back more comfortably against the pillar. He hadn't seen this one before.

There was no background, except what the singer seemed to sketch with his body. His motion suggested a vast, flat landscape, and a powerful gravity that he pulled against. With perfect grace, he conveyed a tangled, trammeled state that allowed for no grace at all, that threatened to make his body only a knot of contracted muscle. Some instrument provided a rhythmic, low-end harmony, almost too low to hear, but with a razor edge on each note rarely heard from a bass line. The deep notes pulled the singer down, the percussion hammered him. But his voice rose above them and his hand reached up as if to follow it.

Niki felt his own arm tense to rise, and pressed his elbows against his ribs. Around the room, other hands stretched toward the ceiling. He did that, this singer: he seduced his audience, consumed and compelled them. The vid might have been recorded months ago, but the singer's magic was new every time. He was a restless spirit, and all the room was the medium whose body he possessed for the length of the song. Niki wondered what the effect of seeing him live would be.

With a burst of power, the golden figure stood, and the once-empty background filled with multicolored chaos. He stepped, gestured, and where his hands and feet passed, order was imposed. A city square sprang up around him in marble and polished brass, hazy with its own light. It was built at some cost—the bright head was thrown back, the white teeth bared; muscles were knotted in jaw and neck and arms. He stretched upward, as if the existence of the sky itself depended on his sweat. And he was shining with sweat. His stillness was the greatest exertion of all—it would break soon, flare into gorgeous motion. But it did not. The shine of sweat had turned to the shine of a polished surface, so slowly that no one could have said when. And the motionless pose would never break. The singer was a statue of clouded amber in the city square he'd made, the dance stopped, the voice silent. The beauty of the statue was a bittersweet memorial to the beauty that had been destroyed in its creation.

One long, slow note from the pipes hung in the air, and passed away.

Niki couldn't remember having noticed the words, but now his head was filled with poetry that he knew were the lyrics to the song. The words, the music, and the images wove into one another and couldn't be pulled apart, any more than a limb could survive off the tree. The singer had been called inimitable, and it was true. No one else could be Chrysander Harris. No one else could do what he did, or even determine how it was he did it.

The room sighed, rustled, and stretched. Another vid brought the grid to life, but it was background noise. The unquiet ghost had let them all go.

Niki stepped away from the pillar and rolled his shoulders. The dream/nightmare of the vid was a mist he walked out of as he moved toward the poolcube. There was a woman at the vector pad, wearing a close-fitting gray hood and a gray satin halfmask on the left side of her face. The right side was marked with tension. In the glass block before her the balls—silver, gold, copper, pewter, metallic blue—spun and shot. Copper disappeared in the black vortex at the heart of the second quadrant. Pewter was devoured by the lower nova. Blue and red struck and rebounded, plunged into pools of light in quads four and one. When the opposing force in the world of the glass cube finally stopped the balls, there were three left.

The hooded woman clenched her fists at the cube. "Blood-sucking traitors!" she told the balls, but cheerfully.

"Yo, now," said a voice from the other side of the glass. "Accept the fate as it comes, sister. It's no good to rail at it."

The woman snorted. "If you lose to me, d'you mind if I spout that hooey at you?" She stood up from the pad and stretched.

The other speaker came around the cube, smiling. His hair was apple-red, except where artificial strands of silver sparkled. His suit was silver, too, elaborately ornamented at shoulders, elbows, wrists, and knees. "Why should I mind? I always take good advice."

She grimaced and headed for the bar.

As she passed Niki, he said, "As a matter of fact, it was a very good shot."

She looked surprised and pleased. "Thank you. Won't be good enough to ground Talbot, though."

"He's a hot boy?"

"*The* local hot boy, I think." She shook her head. At this distance, Niki could see the little lines around her mouth and right eye. "I shouldn't have taken the hook. I mean, spec out that damn suit of his. Talbot's in it for the loot."

"Well, all of us are in *something* for the loot."

"Speak for yourself, Legs. My motives are pure as hundred-credit smoke."

Niki grinned and turned away to set down his empty mug. And cursed, very softly, as the bottom of it rattled on the table. His hand was shaking.

"Something wrong?" the hooded woman asked.

"No," he said softly, "nothing that won't be fixed." He tucked his hands into his back pockets. *Two hours to the next dose,* he thought. *Here comes the end of the world. A little late for warnings, body of mine . . .*

He held his hand out before him. The trembling had stopped. He shrugged and moved toward the poolcube to watch Talbot.

He'd taken the hooded woman's place at the pad. He sat as if meditating on the balls as they racked. Niki fixed their arrangement in his mind, the points at which the colored metals touched, the distances between them.

When they were a shining multihued molecule in the center

of the cube, Talbot laced his hands together and flexed his fingers. "Single-shot, brothers and sisters," he declared, in the carrying voice of an actor. He tapped the pad, and a light burned at the top of the cube, to show that the shot limiter was on.

"Clean 'em out, Tally," said a man in a featureless, iridescent green leather mask. He slapped the redheaded man on the shoulder.

"As the fates will," Talbot intoned. "But don't spoil my aim." Several spectators around the cube laughed. Niki wondered if it was an in-joke.

Talbot's hands hovered for a long moment over the pad; then they came down, typed vectors in a single fluid motion. As the rack burst, Niki let out a breath and triggered the drug in his blood.

The world went sharp and slow. Niki felt his breathing quicken, his pulse chatter in his wrists, and he clutched the back of a chair, fighting the sense of sudden motion. The action in the cube became a web of angles and prospective angles. Calculations sang across his brain.

He was flying alone through a mental night bright with stars. His senses were full of a glimmering pattern of objects moving in space, force against ideal force, embroidered with probabilities drawn like ghosts made of fire.

Reality duplicated the ideal he'd envisioned. The balls in the cube followed the courses he'd imagined for them, like shadow filling up a line of light. Red would go to fourth quadrant pocket. Silver to the upper nova, where it would become argent vapor, gone. Gold to the down one. Purple would take the force of the collision with gold, transfer it to copper, send copper spinning toward quad two. Black to quad one. But copper would lose impulse just before it reached its quadrant; and green, purple, and pewter would slow and stop . . . just . . . there. Niki took his next breath and shut off the bright inhuman visions. It was a beautiful pattern; after such magic, it was anticlimactic to watch mere metal go through the same motions. But he did.

And it didn't. The moving net of steel inside glass skewed, as if something too heavy for it was caught in it. The purple ball missed its proper course and leaned toward quadrant four. Pewter curved in an unlikely arc toward the up hotspot.

A handsome face, long brown hair, a blood-colored coat, seen through a glass sphere full of lightning.

The disorientation was almost physical. This glass was flat, and the man with the long brown hair had been dead for ten years. He closed his eyes, but the illusion was already gone.

There were enough spectators to make a satisfying rumble of approval as purple and pewter were swallowed up. Only the copper ball and the green one remained in the cube of glass. The man in the green mask touched his fingertips to the leather over his lips. "Prettier than any girl in this town," he declared. The onlookers laughed. A blond man in a worn Concorde surface force coverall handed Talbot a full glass.

"You're not thinking of trying it, are you?" said the hooded woman, from over Niki's shoulder.

"He's cheating," Niki said.

"That's nuts. How the hell could you know? And how could he cheat? There's no way to twist that thing."

"I'll be damned," Niki muttered. "Yes, there is." He stepped up to the poolcube. "Looks like fun," he said.

Talbot looked up. "You want to tickle the vectors, long brother?"

"No, I think not. I'm not dressed for it."

A flicker of alarm crossed Talbot's face. "No dress code here."

"Really?" Niki smiled gently. Talbot's forehead tightened, an arrested frown. "Then slide your chair back for me, will you?"

"Why?"

"Indulge me."

Talbot rose, protesting loudly, from the console. Niki pulled a little iron FourCorners penny from his pocket, aimed, and flipped.

"That trick's so old it must have been carved on the Rosetta Stone," Niki said into the silence that followed. "I've never seen it used on a poolcube before. But all you need to know is the layout of the controller field under the cube, so you can position the magnet."

The iron penny hung, damningly, from the tree-of-life appli-que over Talbot's left knee.

Talbot's voice cut like an axe through the rising babble of the crowd and killed it. "What's your name, brother?"

"Niki Falcon."

There was no reason why it should mean anything to him. Niki had never been one of the celebrated ones. He'd come along too late, when even the romance of dying young had palled on the fax and the public. But Talbot frowned, then gaped. "Falcon?"

Here it comes. Niki nodded, and closed his eyes against a surge of weariness and anger. It wasn't worth it—had never really been worth the effort. The world was not a better place because he'd caught this man cheating at the poolcube. But he'd done it; now he had to wade through the results.

"You're the plug-fucker." Talbot's voice was dangerously soft.

The base of Niki's skull itched. "You'll understand, perhaps, if I object to that."

Talbot stared. "You . . ." He turned suddenly, toward the door.

"The stake?" Niki called. His voice was unexpectedly loud in the silence, and he gritted his teeth. What chivalrous impulse was it that had made him challenge this Black Knight at this bridge? He wished it would go away.

Talbot stopped, looked back at him. "You think I should pay the sister?" He nodded toward the woman in gray, who'd stepped forward to the cube, and said to her, "How much do you pay him, sister? Or maybe you belong to him, hey? Some girls have nasty tastes like that."

"Accept the fate as it comes, *brother*," she said, grinning ferociously. "Cough up."

"Yo, come on, let's see it!" someone else hooted.

Talbot walked up to the table. "All right," he said softly, "I'll pay up." He put his hand in his belt pouch, and Niki felt tension in his shoulders, his legs. The hand came out full of chips. Niki shivered, and the tension eased. Talbot counted them deliberately and let them fall one by one to the table. He met Niki's eyes and showed his teeth. "It's all my joy, plug-fucker. Michel, Gorham, let's leave. The place stinks of wire." The man in the army coverall and the one in the green leather mask followed Talbot when he turned and left.

Niki leaned his head back and exhaled at the ceiling. He'd tried to put all his anger in the breath and let it out that way. Either it was a technique suitable only for little angers, or his heart wasn't in it. The spectators began to drift away.

"Can I buy you a drink," the hooded woman asked, "or would that screw your nonprofit status?"

They sat at the bar, where the willowisp lights hung from nothing and conjured columns of smoke, polished wood, and patrons from out of the gloom. She'd pushed her hood back, and her hair was pale and short as velvet. She ran her palm over the nap of it now and then, as if to test the texture. She wore a roughly polished bit of turquoise in one earlobe. Her name was Maris, he learned, and she flew lifter boats in-atmosphere for a mining consortium.

"You really are a gestalt pilot?" she asked.

His fingers tightened around his beer mug. "I really am."

"Is it fun?"

He looked at her. "What an odd question."

"I don't mean to be rude—"

"No—it's all right. No one's ever asked before, is all. I suppose it is."

"That's an odd answer." She tilted her head to one side, and the shadow of her nose streaked the masked half of her face. She would think the effect was ugly, he decided.

He drank some beer. "Like most things, it has its drawbacks. And its pleasures. I don't get drunk, for instance."

"Is that a drawback or a pleasure?"

"I haven't decided," he said.

He'd hoped she would laugh, but she didn't. She looked down, pushed her glass through a puddle on the bar and back. "There's weird stories about gestalters . . ."

Niki felt anger spring up in him again. "No, we do not screw the hardware."

She flushed. "I didn't think you did."

"Oh," he said. He looked at his beer, picked it up, took a gulp, set it down. "I'm sorry. If you'll forgive me, I promise not to make a fool of myself again."

She shook her head. "That's a lot to promise."

"You're right," he said when he stopped laughing. "I give up. Ask questions."

"What's it like, when you're plugged in? When you're flying?"

She hadn't, at least, asked what the Cheat felt like. "It's . . . There's no interface. You *are* the ship. Beyond that—either it was different for all of us, or we could never agree on a description for it."

"When you caught Talbot cheating. Was that gestalting?"

"I wasn't plugged in."

She smiled and looked away. "You're pretty slippery."

He wondered if his smile was as sad as he suddenly felt. "I'm sorry. It's a habit."

"You're entitled. . . ." she said, and finished the sentence with a turn of her hand.

"No, it's all right." He rubbed the inside of one wrist with his thumb. "I have access to the drug all the time. Which means that when I want to, I can think fast. And I'm good with numbers, spatial relationships, things like that."

"Well, I'm glad you were here. He wouldn't have bought for the loser, that's sure. What the hell brings a world-class wing to FourCorners?"

"Pharmaceuticals. Critters, for the Marad Abyad."

She froze in the middle of running her hand over the tips of her hair, stared at him. "Heaving Jesus. You brought the hunter virus in. Didn't you?"

Niki nodded cautiously.

She sprang up. "I've got to go."

"What's wrong?"

"Maybe nothing, now. My sweetie and four of my friends are on that contam unit. D'you know if they've used it yet?"

"They were breaking it into doses in my hold."

"Jesus." She was already past him, yanking her hood up, when she stopped. "Will you be okay? Talbot and Company might hold a grudge—"

"They almost certainly hold a grudge," he replied, grateful for the change of subject. "But I can manage."

"Right. Well, thank you." She made another lunge, then stopped again, spun around, took his face in both her hands, and kissed him on the mouth. "I mean it," she said. Then she dashed through the dim-lit room. The door leaked sunset as she slipped through it.

Niki sat very still for what seemed a long time before remembering his beer and drinking some. He felt as if he'd stolen her gratitude. It was a job, that was all. He'd been paid a lot to do it. His cargo might as easily have been guns, except that guns didn't usually have to travel so fast, or at such expense.

Enough, enough. He was still bitter about the poolcube and Talbot. If he wanted to avoid too many more consequences of that game, he ought to leave now. He might be able to dodge Talbot and Associates. He might at least be able to face them by daylight.

"Excuse me. Niki Falcon?" said a voice behind him. A wonderful voice, full of silver and velvet and smoke, resonant, powerful even when soft. It made Niki choke on his beer.

What stood at his shoulder, glowing in the willowisp, might be a deity from a mythology he didn't know. It had a man's body, small and slender, in a buff-colored tunic with full sleeves and buff-colored close-fitting leggings. A hooded coat hung from one shoulder. The head was a cat's, gilt and snarling, polished silver lips curling back from crystal fangs. The eyes were burning topaz set deep in the skull.

"Hello," said the mask, which it was.

"Oh. Yes, that's me. Hello." Niki couldn't remember sounding so stupid in all his life.

"He took it badly."

"What? Who?"

"The one who was cheating."

"That," said Niki, "might be the understatement of the week."

"I was watching the game. Your name came up just in time to save me the trouble of asking for you."

"That's . . . nice." The Mask continued to stare at him. Niki returned the stare, and the Mask finally took the conversational ball back.

"I've a commission for you."

That, at last, was something he could react to, something familiar. "Ah. Let's find a table, and talk fast. I have an appointment with destiny." The Mask, with exquisite unconcern, turned and headed for a corner.

Niki followed the fantastic figure to a table. A willowisp hurried up after them, settled above the table, and began to brighten. The Mask flicked his hand, and the light dimmed a little.

Niki collapsed into a chair and set his beer down. "Who gave you my name?"

"Laura Brass told me where I might find you." Light gleamed in one of the artificial eyes.

"You're a friend of Laura's?" With the possible exception of Niki, Laura did not have friends.

"No. She turned the job down and sent me to you."

Niki raised both eyebrows. "Anything Laura won't do, I certainly won't."

"Moral scruples?" The voice behind the mask was faintly mocking.

"Cowardice." Niki smiled.

"For a coward, you faced that red-haired man rather well."

"Even cowards can be stupid. Why won't Laura do your job?"

The stranger's fingers tapped softly on the table. "Brass didn't say she wouldn't; she said she couldn't. And that you could. And it's not illegal."

"No?"

"Not . . . exactly."

"I'd love to know what constitutes 'not exactly illegal.' "

"Brass also said it was a challenge that might appeal to you."

"Who else have you tried?"

"No one will take it." Some quality of the voice suggested that this was not hyperbole. The stranger's elbows rested on the table. The fingers folded together; the gilded chin settled on them. "Either they can't, or they won't."

Niki shook his head. "You must be offering less than the going rate."

"Seven yellow binary sapphires, perfect, around four carats."

"What in the name of God," Niki said slowly, "do you want done?"

"I want you to take me to Lamia."

It meant nothing to him. "Which is . . . ?"

There was a long inhalation from behind the mask. "My homeworld."

The two words vibrated with something that made Niki think of hills vivid with autumn, of a city that cascaded down a hill, of ranks of red dragon banners . . . He bit the inside of his mouth to stop the progression of thoughts. "Go on," he said harshly.

"There's . . . trouble there. I need—" The stranger's hands opened, the tan, slender fingers spread and pleaded. "I need to be there."

No, Niki thought, *no. Shut up.* But he had tried, once, to explain the same need to a stranger in the back room of a bar, when he wanted her help. The memory of that was what he wanted to silence, and couldn't. He shivered and closed his eyes.

"Is there something wrong?"

"No. What do you want me for?"

"Lamia is under Silence."

No communication out. No navigation beacons. No ships allowed to lift. And a fleet standing out of atmosphere to enforce it. Silence was the Concorde's ultimate quarantine, imposed to prevent the spread of cancer of the body politic. It was a way to contain a situation already deemed hopeless. Let the planet burn, but keep the flames away from the next on the route. It hadn't been used, to Niki's knowledge, since the Credit Rebellion eight years ago. "Why?" he asked.

"If I knew, I might not have to go back. Can you do it?" The Mask spread his hands, palms up, above the table. Beautiful hands. Very strong hands.

Niki yanked his attention back to the man's words. "Break Silence? Maybe. But I'm not going to."

The Mask leaned forward sharply, hands flat on the tabletop. "I may be able to help where no one else can. I may be able to save lives." The magnificent voice pounded Niki with desperation, and something else that struck very deep, that raised a need to strike back. "Doesn't that weigh with you? Will you live with those lives on your conscience?"

"Yes. They'll be good company for the ones I already have."

"What can I do to—"

"Nothing. Nothing you can do will change my mind. I can get you, unseen, past the fleet. I assume that's what you really want?"

The Mask was stiff and silent, but Niki recognized a sort of angry assent.

"I doubt that anyone else in the world could. But even I can do it only because they're not expecting anyone to land. Once I was down, I'd never be able to leave."

"If I succeed, the Silence will be lifted."

Niki laughed. He'd tried not to, but there was no help for it. "I'm sure it will. If you succeed. Until then, breaking Silence is one of the Concorde's few capital crimes. If they catch me, they kill me. Nothing you've told me makes it worth that."

The stranger's hands closed around the edge of the table, white with the force of the grip. "There is a world at stake," he said.

"Once," Niki said carefully, "I said, and believed, what you've been saying. I was wrong. You may be, too. Prove to me that you're not, and I'll think about it."

The stranger stood, with the slow grace of well-trained strength. "I'm not giving this up. I'll talk to you again."

Before Niki thought of a caustic reply, the stranger turned and stalked away. The willowisp trembled wildly for a moment as their combined heat traces split, and Niki's shadow leaped across the tabletop.

His beer was warm. He stared into the glass for ten minutes or so, looking at his reflection. *There is a world at stake.* But how, if Lamia was under Silence, could the Mask be sure of that? Niki shook his head and walked out.

There were no private vehicles allowed in the limits of the city. The consolation was the magtube, which went everywhere. There was a station only four streets from the bar. Niki had expected an ambush, if it happened, along those four streets. When he reached the station, when the meter had painted a click stripe on his thumb and the gate had let him through, he relaxed a little. He took the lift to the tube levels. When the door opened, and he saw the man in the faded Concorde coverall, he realized he'd been an idiot.

They blocked him from the tubes, forcing him away from the well-traveled parts of the station. He was on Talbot's home ground, and Talbot had used the advantage well, laid a good trap with only three men. It was a shame, Niki thought—all that potential expended on brutal street games.

They caught up with him in a maintenance corridor that ended in a locked door and a metal ladder with a locked hatch above it. Well, no need to make it easy for them. By the time they had him down, the man in the coverall was curled up against the wall, whimpering.

Talbot and the man in the green mask dragged Niki to the ladder. He made that difficult for them, too, until Talbot kicked him in the jaw. That gave them time to lash his wrists to one of the upper rungs. Then Talbot broke something under his nose that burned when he breathed it in, brought every nerve in his body relentlessly awake. He flung his head back in reflex, and it banged hard against the ladder.

"Plug-fucker," said Talbot, "you took the bread from our mouths."

"Did I?"

"Yo. But we can afford to be generous." He paused. When Niki didn't respond, he slapped Niki's face just hard enough to sting. "Ask me about that."

"I'm asking."

Talbot slapped him harder. "Not good enough. Ask."

"I don't . . . remember what I'm asking about."

Talbot broke another ampoule. "There, feel better, brother? Oh, wrongo—you're no brother. You're no human. We forgive you because you got us a job."

"Tally," the man in the green mask said. He sounded as if

he'd been punched in the mouth. Niki remembered doing it. "Fuck this all. Let's have his money and lift."

"Neh. Got the fear on you, Gorham?"

"I got me on the Short List, you little piss. That's good enough."

"Then what's to lose? Why go to the stone box for spare change?"

The argument had given Niki a little breathing time. But Talbot hadn't lost his place. He turned back to Niki. "You see, plug-fucker, someone fears you will do a thing they don't want done. Our job is to warn you from this error. A memorable warning."

"I wish you wouldn't," Niki said politely, and kicked him.

After Talbot recovered, he made Gorham tie Niki's ankles to the ladder as well. Then he twined his fingers in Niki's hair and swung his fist. Niki tasted blood. *Maybe I'll pass out soon,* he thought. But Talbot seemed to have an inexhaustible supply of ampoules to break. After one of them, Talbot chose to tell him what he was being warned against. By then he hardly cared.

They'd broken the overhead lamps in the corridor before they left. So when he opened the one eye that would, and found a wash of dim light over his face, he knew someone else must be there.

"Don't move yet," he was told, by a voice like smoke and silver. He almost recognized it—twice over, though he wasn't sure what he meant by that. He was no longer hanging; he felt the floor under him. Couldn't feel his hands, though, and he wondered where they were. He disobeyed the wonderful voice and turned his head a little.

The gilded cat's face hung at an odd angle before him, and an arm seemed to be protruding from one of its ears. No, the mask was unfastened and hanging on its owner's chest. His gaze traveled upward to the real face.

The lighting was bizarre, cast by a pocket lamp lying on the floor. But by it he could see that the face was just within the parameters of human beauty. It seemed as if it must have been carved; it was too cleanly made, too perfect, to have happened by chance. The lips were thin, and yet not harsh. The brows, which were slightly darker than the honey-colored hair, arched over one-of-a-kind golden eyes. They reflected the light a little, like a cat's.

Niki began to laugh, weakly and with some pain.

"I told you not to move. I think you've broken a rib."

"I didn't break it. Someone else did. Are you really who you look like?"

Chrysander Harris frowned down at him. "I suppose it would be cruel to let you think you were delirious."

"Probably am anyway."

Harris moved out of his line of sight, but his voice went on. "I'm very sorry. I could have prevented this, I think, if I'd only paid attention. They obviously weren't done with you when they left the bar. But by the time I remembered that, and followed you . . ."

Niki wished he'd stop saying things that made him laugh. "How old are you?"

There was a pause. "I beg your pardon?"

"I used to take credit for everything that happened. I was nineteen, though."

"I'm twenty-eight," Harris said irritably. Niki couldn't honestly blame him.

He now knew where his hands were; Harris was pounding the circulation back into them. "This *is*—ow—your fault. Ow. Sort of." He dragged air into his aching lungs. "They were hired to warn me away from you. From taking your commission. Isn't that funny?"

At that, Harris let his hands alone. He said something, obscenity or invocation, in a language Niki didn't know. "I'm so sorry," he whispered. "I didn't know she would— I didn't know."

" 'S all right. They did your work for you."

"What? I don't want—"

"Your proof. Someone's scared to death you'll get to Lamia." His muscles were threatening him with something. In another minute, he'd figure out what it was. "So you may be as important as you think you are."

"I don't understand."

"I'm accepting your commission. Besides, they made me mad." He laughed, and the sudden spasm in his back strangled it.

"What is it?" Harris's fingers dug into his shoulder.

"What time is it?"

"2400. No, 2430."

"Ah, Christ." He was two hours over the limit. His nervous

system was about to crash. "I need my dose. Empty my pockets, will you? You're looking for a needle tab."

He felt Harris searching the ruins of his jacket. "Someone already emptied them."

"Oh, no. Oh, Talbot, you *bastard*." Talbot had known his name. He would know enough about gestalt pilots to know what the needle tab was. Niki hoped, viciously, that Talbot would try the thing.

Another spasm—Harris's strong hands pinned him down. "I've got to get to my ship," Niki gasped.

They rode the magtube, under the eyes of a few frightened late-night travelers. Niki could imagine it: the snarling gold cat-mask creature, and the tattered, bloody madman it dragged into the compartment. Harris was silent the whole way.

There was mist in the air, and the field seemed full of luminous gauze. The *Gerfalcon* was silent and sparkling with the condensation on its bronze-colored plates. Niki managed to hold his hand to the lock long enough for it to recognize him. Harris dragged him through the hatch when it hissed open and let him down onto the friction flooring.

"Slot near the door," Niki hissed through his teeth. "Bring me what's there."

Harris came back with a needle tab and put it in his hand. Niki slapped the point through his shirt to the vein in his armpit. He was ready for the convulsion, which didn't make it any more bearable. When it was over, he lay flat on the floor, panting. Harris sat and said nothing.

"I'm sorry," Niki said at last, "to subject you to that. It's not the usual treatment for customers."

"You're a junkie," Harris said. His voice was flat on the archaic word.

Niki wanted to raise himself on an elbow. Just now, that was beyond him. "I am a gestalt pilot," he said, with more anger than he could control. "I have a rebuilt nervous system, an unrecognizable metabolism, a connect port on each wrist and a port in the back of my skull, and an addiction to the drug that makes it all work. That's what a gestalt pilot *is*. Don't call me names for being what you've paid me to be."

Harris stared. Niki wasn't sure when he'd taken the mask off, but it was off now. His golden hair was disheveled, his golden eyes were wide. "I'm sorry."

Niki turned back to study the ceiling. "So am I. I also don't subject customers to fits of temper. Let's forget the whole stinking thing.''

''Will you be all right?'' The wonderful voice shook a little. Niki wondered if he'd scared him. It was unlikely.

''Yes, thank you. I will. I'll have lift clearance by tomorrow night—call it 2300. Be here half an hour before that, if you can.''

Harris nodded and rose. ''Can I get out the way we came in?''

''Yes. It'll lock behind you.''

Niki could feel Harris's steps through the floor, heard the hatch open. Then he was alone. Soon he would have to get up and begin to repair the damage, but for now, there was no more discomfort in lying on the floor than in lying anywhere else. A few more hours on that ladder, without the drug, and he'd have been dead. He wondered what it would have been like. Would the spasms have brought him awake before he died?

Death was going to quit circling one of these days and nail him. In the meantime, the waiting was starting to get to him. The few tears that got out of his eyes burned in the cuts on his face.

CHAPTER NINE

What matter though numb nightmare ride on top,
And blood and mire the sensitive body stain?
What matter? Heave no sigh, let no tear drop,
A greater, more gracious time has gone. . . .
                    —W. B. Yeats, "The Gyres"

Vere had left, no more in charity with Chrysander than when
they'd stopped work yesterday. It didn't matter; they'd gotten
another take recorded. It shouldn't matter. And Niki Falcon was
now in Chrysander's employ, committed to going to Lamia.
Surely Vere's state of mind was dwarfed by that.

It was, Chrysander found. But not in a way he'd expected.

He sat motionless, trying to find a still point in his mind, in
the island of light lifted above darkness, the engineer's box in
the darkened studio. There was no still point, only specks of
light, notes of melody, desperate thoughts spiraling with blurring speed.

He could turn his thoughts into a line of music. But nothing
made law of the chaos; the best of his songs only recorded,
defined, focused the confusion until it was sharp enough to stab
with. He had filled the hearts of his songs with longing, fury,
reaching out, and it wasn't enough. The execution didn't match
the idea. They didn't resolve.

Still, better to transmute it all into music. The alternative was
to kill someone. He'd get a lot of relief out of it, Chrysander

thought, if only he could decide who, besides himself, was the right victim.

He'd hunted through the passageways of the magtube station, cursing his carelessness, knowing that if he had lost Niki Falcon, he had lost the game. That had been an abstraction. When his light fell on the man hanging from the ladder, nothing was abstract anymore. Blood washed away abstraction. And Falcon had accepted the commission. Which shamed Chrysander most of all.

Across the dark studio, the door opened. Silhouetted in it was a figure in a long coat.

The box lights went out, and Chrysander cursed, remembering the master panel by the studio door. The green indicators on the control board glowed on the planes of his eye sockets, the underside of his nose, his jaw; the resulting corpse-face stared back at him in a stuttering reflection on the double glass of the window.

He considered his pulse until it steadied, took a long breath, and opened the channel between the box and the studio.

"Chrysander Harris?" The voice was a woman's, low, with the crisp diction of the Hub.

"Here." His reflection seemed to say it, a green ghost painted on the glass between them. "What can I do for you?"

"I'm Jhari Sabayan, cultural attaché for Central Worlds Concorde's embassy here. I would . . ."

"Yes, Lieutenant Sabayan. I'm sure you would."

"Well," she said at last. "I didn't think I was so well known." But she didn't sound surprised.

"You've been fastened to me like a tick for three weeks. Did you think I wouldn't know it?"

She stirred. "I've come to ask if you're ready to consider our offer."

"I told your people I'd let them know at year end."

"That's sixty-five days from now. A lot can happen."

Chrysander shrugged. "You could have me kidnapped, for instance."

"I suppose we could. I know we'd rather not."

"Or you could keep me from making a living. Seizure of the new recordings, a ban on concerts . . ."

She sighed. "Thus making ourselves look like monsters in the eyes of the world. Chrysander, we want you to come to us willingly. In return, we can give you anything. Anything. We have the resources.''

She paused, but Chrysander said nothing.

''My favorite of your songs is 'Street of Stars'—the image of the stars reflected in the muddy water in the road. It's a recurring theme in your work, that perfect beauty is unreachable, that we can only pursue a blurred reflection in a fouled mirror.''

''How poetic. Did you read that somewhere?'' But he was chilled.

''What would you do with the power to change what you see? To help, where now you can only observe? We can give you the chance to use your ability with the scope it deserves. That you deserve.''

''I'm not for sale, Lieutenant.''

''Let us in, Chrysander. If you help us, we'll work for you. Help us, and we can do things for you, for Lamia.''

He laughed. ''Tell me, Lieutenant. What's happening on Lamia?''

She didn't move, but he could hear the tightness in her voice. ''I wouldn't know. That sector is outside my authority.''

''I think you'd better go, Lieutenant.''

''Harris . . .''

''Now, Lieutenant.'' Softly, slide the first word down to the note that carries the tattoo of the last three syllables, driving it all with the diaphragm. The pitch and cadence of I Mean This.

The hem of the long coat swirled slightly. ''All right. But this time you'll have to stay where I can see you. On FourCorners.''

''I don't—''

''You're going to a party tonight at Green Columns. Niki Falcon's ship, the *Gerfalcon*, is cleared for lift at 2300. If you're wise, you'll still be drinking Aurelia Yarretic's liquor at 24.''

His hands closed tight over the edge of the mixing console. ''Don't you have to accuse me of a crime to hold me?''

She had turned to go, but at this she paused in the door and looked back. The edge of her face was backlit from the hall lights beyond.

''Tell me, Chrysander,'' she said softly, ''have you committed any lately?'' She closed the door behind her.

Gyre: a spiral upward, outward. Turn it back on itself, and the slow beating of great wings works against desire, dropping, twisting ever more tightly toward the hard, cold earth. . . .

"Crow." She caresses the side of his face, her nails shivering his nerves. Her wrist, inside, is blue webbing in alabaster, traced by moonlight through the long window. "But that's not your name."

"No." He feels a smile coming on, and lets it happen. He has been careful with them lately. He lifts a curl of her dark red hair from her shoulder and watches it circle, like a band of wine-colored ribbon, around his finger. An afterthought: "It's Niki." His lips move against her stroking fingers, ending with a kiss. She has given him something pleasant, dropped into a drink in the bar downstairs. It has warmed and shrunk the world. Now she is the center of it, and he will suspend all logic for her.

"Niki. I like that. I like you. What's your last name?"

His lips stop. "I haven't got one."

She laughs, low and hoarse, and he feels it shiver along his ribs, across his belly, down over his thighs. Something very pleasant in the drink.

" 'I haven't got one.' Be honest now, Niki." She strokes her finger around the sharp line of his jaw.

He looks into her face, so close he can see the down on her cheeks and the striations of pale color in the irises of her eyes. "I'm sorry. I can't tell you."

She laughs again. He wants to trace the shape of her mouth with his fingertip. "Oh, a Man of Mystery," she says, and her words are more breath than voice. "Niki, Niki." She draws him closer. Her lips flutter over his throat and her hair sweeps across his face, smelling like sweet herbs burning. Her hand is at the small of his back, pressing him against her, and he sinks his face deeper into her hair. Her back muscles move firm and strong beneath his hands.

"Niki. Sweet, sweet Niki. Do you want me?" she whispers, kissing the hollow of his throat. Her fingers on his back spread wide and low. Desire freezes his mouth and constricts his throat, and he can barely force out a "yes." Hair like red twilight in his eyes and mouth, its scent in his breathing filling his lungs and rushing down down into his heart—

Muscles writhe in her back. A line of pain bright and sharp as an edge of broken glass draws itself across his stomach.

Wine-red, but not in ribbons. On his shirt. On the front of her white dress. On his hands, now, from the reflexive clutch. Blood trickles between his fingers from the slash of wound that *had appeared like a thing misplaced in time and space. Shock is a gag in his mouth.*

"I'm sorry, Niki. I shouldn't have surprised you like that. But if I'd told you what I wanted to do, you wouldn't have come up with me, would you?" She smiles at him. Wine-red on her dress, her hand, the knife. A little thin one. She could have had it hidden anywhere.

He shakes his head, slowly, and backs away. She follows, smiling.

The door is somewhere behind him. He turns his head; the knife flashes and licks one of his ribs, shaking a little animal cry from him. She is between him and the door now, laughing throaty and warm.

"Come to me, Niki."

She has his name in her mouth, above the knife bright with moonlight. This small world is all the world there is, and she is all the logic in it. He hears a sob and knows it's his own. She reaches lazily out with both hands and he twists, only to catch the full extension of her arm in a shallow gash across his chest.

"Oh, baby, come here. Come here, Niki, and let me make it feel good."

He shakes his head. He has backed up to the long window, and the glass presses cold on his back. She smiles and moves toward him, one hand already reaching to cup his cheek.

Her arms close around him. His fingers tangle in her hair and yank down, drawing her head back, back, to show her throat to him. The herb smoke of her hair is in his nostrils, the taste of—

The impact of the knife in his side snaps his head back. But the blood that fills his mouth is not his.

He staggers backward, still entangled with her. Breaking glass, and falling, blinded by night and dark red hair. The stinking water hits him like a hammer. Somehow there is a gravel beach under him. He doesn't remember when he let go of her, or whether he swam. The salt water burns where her knife cut him, and he is too weak even to vomit against the taste of her in his mouth.

Spiraling upward and out, springing from the soiled earth into a sky of light and pain . . .

He was alone. That wasn't right; hadn't there been someone else with him? His sides hurt, and his stomach. That was right. But why did his face hurt so?

"Name of the Goddess. Niki?" It was the wrong voice. The eye that wasn't swollen shut snapped open.

The face that blocked his view of the ceiling of his cabin had the color and sheen of brown silk. It was printed over one broad, high cheekbone with a blackwork tattoo fine as engraving, an abstract patterned curl. The eyes set in the face were black and almond-shaped. The whole vision was topped with an asymmetrical cloud of black hair stranded with copper. He tried to open his mouth, but his lips would only part on one side. "Laura," he said with a dry tongue. "What are you doing in my bedroom?"

The words must have been clear enough, because Laura Brass said, "It's not the first time, sugar. Niki, who did this?"

He frowned, which hurt, and opened half his mouth again. "No. I don't want you to kill them for me."

"Well, it's not as if *you* can kill them, in this condition. I hope you gave a good account of yourself, at least. How the hell did they manage not to break your nose?"

"They liked it. It melted their stony hearts."

"You're such an ass. I bet you drove them to this." Her movements provided counterpoint for her voice; she was dissolving the bandages on his face and examining the mess underneath. "I have to go get my gear. Some of this is real work. Don't go out shopping or anything, okay?"

When she came back, she turned his cabin into a surgery. But he saw very little of it. She put a mask over his nose, and he inhaled the smell of orange peels and dry grass. Then he opened his eyes—both of them. He'd been having nightmares.

"You do great anaesthetic," he said. "Thank you. I feel much better." He turned his head and found her, folded neatly up in a chair she must have dragged in from the galley. She wore a sleeveless jumpsuit of black silk, thin and crisp as a handkerchief, and her feet were bare.

"You know my creed. You should be able to cure 'em at least as well as you kill 'em."

"Did you *have* to use the critters?"

"Of course not, dear. You could have sutures and scars and a two-week recovery, instead."

"I must look a treat."

"You look like something I once got out of my Galleymaster when three hives died. Speaking of scars, where in the name of the Goddess did you come by yours? I never had a chance to see them *all* before.''

He folded his arms over his stomach and looked at the ceiling. "It took a long time. Do you want the whole list?"

"Now you're annoyed. I would be, too, I guess. But Goddess, Niki, did you make a fetish of it? Scar tissue is medieval."

"If you can't afford the critters, or you're too far away from a place that has them, you get scar tissue. Both cases apply." He closed his eyes. "I don't want to talk about this."

Laura sniffed. "Sure. I rebuild your stupid face, and the only payment I get is 'I don't want to talk.' "

"Laura—" No, she deserved more than silence. "I had no money, no identity, I was nineteen years old, and the Concorde wanted to know where I was. I did . . . the sorts of things one does."

Her head went down, and he couldn't see her face. Copper strands shone like jewelry in the smoke-cloud of her hair. "I'm sorry, Nik. I'm one nosy bitch. Must be why I pick locks." She stood up and smoothed her jumpsuit. "Do you think you could eat?"

He thought about it. "I suppose I'd better."

"Niki." There was menace in her voice. "When did you last eat?"

"Mmm. Lunch?"

"You mean lunch *yesterday*?"

"I suppose it was."

"Was there breakfast yesterday?"

"Nnnooooo."

"You stupid *fuck*. What's your dose now?"

"I was a little busy most of yesterday, remember."

"What's your dose?"

"Ten mikes for maintenance. Thirty for the Cheat."

"Maintenance how often?"

He would have to answer her. She wouldn't let him dodge this. "Six hours."

Her face went blank. "Oh, Niki."

"Well, you knew it would get to that eventually."

"So. Not much longer." She stared unfocused at the wall above his feet.

"No," he said, very softly, "not much longer. That, too, is bound to happen eventually." He looked at her, studying her strong, hard, angry features. "You know, when I went into conversion I didn't care whether they'd perfected the process. I didn't care about living, and this way I'd be a pilot for a few years. I'd always wanted to be.

"And it worked. And I started to care about living, and myself, and other people. The last five years have been worth dying for."

Her head turned; she stared at him as blankly as she had stared at the wall. "Oh, shut up," she said.

"Yes, ma'am."

"You have a tremendous black eye. Do you know how stupid you look, talking bullshit with a black eye?" He knew she didn't want an answer. She jammed her fingers into her hair and tugged it. "Shit. Well, I'd better go do something about food if you're going to be out of here by 2300."

He pulled himself up on one elbow. "Who says I am?"

"Field controller's log. You put in for lift clearance last night."

"Christ, Laura, you're not supposed to access that."

"I'm not supposed to access the inside of the *Gerfalcon*, either. But if I hadn't, you wouldn't be ready to go at 2300."

"Busybody. Did you break my lock?"

She looked affronted. "Of course I didn't. What do you take me for?"

"A law unto yourself, dear heart."

She made a rude noise and moved for the door.

"Thank you, Laura," he said.

A single, sharp bell sounded all around them, and they both jumped. "Why don't you turn that thing off?" Laura asked.

"Because no one ever calls me," he said, and sat up in the bunk. He was weak, as well as stiff and sore. Laura was right, he needed to eat. He opened the 'board in the wall, turned the outgoing video off, and tapped the "accept" pad.

"Niki Falcon?"

The voice came first, rich and startling even in simulation. Then the spots of color snapped across the panel, and the image bloomed from them, tan and gold against a background of irregularly-colored shadow. Beside him, Laura gulped air.

"Hullo, Chrysander Harris," Niki said, to answer the question he knew was on her tongue.

"I'm not getting vid," Chrysander Harris said. The golden eyes were wide, the beautiful face full of uncertainty.

"Laura Brass says I look like something even she wouldn't eat. I turned it off."

"Oh." The face moved very slightly, as if with some contained emotion. "Are you all right?"

"Close enough."

Harris's shoulders drew forward a little. He might have been cold. He was wearing jacquard satin and velvet, Niki noticed suddenly: evening clothes.

"I need some help," Harris said.

"All right."

Laura settled back into the chair without looking away from the panel.

Harris's hands rose, dropped out of sight again. "I'm at a party, a sort of reception."

"Where?"

"Green Columns. Outside of town. It's—"

"Aurelia Yarretic's little shack. Go on."

"I don't think I can get out of here by 2300. Not by myself."

"You what?"

Harris closed his eyes and took a deep, visible breath. "I'm under Concorde surveillance. I can't walk out of here. I've tried."

Niki felt the drug lying ready in him like adrenaline, waiting to be triggered at need. Not yet, not yet . . . "How many people are covering you?"

"About half the staff has been replaced by Concorde agents. Maybe ten. Jhari Sabayan is here pretending she's a guest. She's . . ."

Niki was cold, and his mind had emptied abruptly. "I know what she is." He stared at the image on the panel; though it was blank on that end, Harris stared back, almost meeting his eyes.

"Can you get me out?" Harris said finally. He hadn't moved, but suddenly his face, his voice, even his shoulders seemed to plead, until Niki was dizzy with it.

He gritted his teeth. "Sorry," he said, trying for as much cheerful callousness as he could, "I've had enough fun on this job. I'm not going to wade in there and let the Concorde take a few more pieces out of me. If you're not here at 2300, the bird flies without you."

Niki watched the color drain out of the exquisite features. He cursed in Welsh, too softly to carry.

Harris looked down, then swiftly up, his face hard and distant. He said, his voice harsh, "And if I double what I first offered you to do it?"

"That's fourteen stones," Niki said weakly. The math wasn't difficult, but the concept was so shocking that he felt it ought to be clarified.

Harris nodded.

"Good God." Niki rubbed cautiously at the bridge of his nose. "No, no. It won't do. If I'm dead, I can't spend 'em anyway."

"You mean that."

"Absolutely."

Harris's expression was cold. "All right, then. Thank you anyway." The panel went to black.

Niki turned to Laura. "What time is it?"

"That was— He was the one in the mask?" she said, wide-eyed.

"Yes, he was. What time is it?"

"And you took him on?"

"Laura, the time!"

"2100-something. I didn't really thing you'd—"

"Two hours. Or less. Ye gods."

"Niki, you're not going to go in there for him?"

"Of course I am."

"You didn't tell him that."

"Don't be silly—Jhari must have an ear on every line. Why should I let her know? Can you get me a floor plan of that place? I was there once, but it was two years ago."

"Niki—he doesn't know you're coming."

"No, I suppose not. The idiot. If he'll just keep from doing something stupid before I get there . . ." Niki sat up, carefully. "Oh, I feel like hell."

"I don't work miracles. Forget it, Niki. Leave him there. What you told him just now was the smartest thing I've ever heard you say."

Niki looked sadly up at her.

"Goddess give me strength," she muttered, helping him out of the bunk.

He padded over to one of the lockers, clicked it open, and ran his fingers over hanging fabric. He reached soft black and stopped, unclipped it, pulled it out. "There." He tossed it on the rumpled bunk.

Laura stared at the folds of black velvet. "You're going in the front door."

"And handing my hat and cane to the butler. Jhari Sabayan won't expect that much gall even from me."

"The gall she'll expect," Laura said, examining the fitted tunic. "It's the good taste that'll throw her off. I've got some painkillers I can give you, but they'll slow down your access to the trigger."

"Mmm. Can't do it, then. I need to be able to turn the drug on fast."

"What are you going to do about the black eye?"

Niki pulled on the black velvet pants. He grinned up at her. "Trust me."

"The day it snows purple. I promise."

Chrysander's pulse laid down a beat, too quick, and the leaves of the trees below played percussion in the night wind. Cool, damp air rushed into his lungs and was trapped there. He felt caught in a fever dream, a dark fantasy of uncontrolled speed and blind falling. He clung to the balcony rail.

Across the slope of the lawn, through the trees, on the edge of the city—the *Gerfalcon* sat on the field, waiting to be towed to a ramp. A few kilometers. He would be able to see it lift from where he stood. Such an artistic, ironic failure ought to be celebrated; maybe he should fetch a bottle of champagne to toast the flight.

No. He hadn't failed yet. *Despair is a traitor within your walls*—one of his teachers had said that, or some irritating thing like it. He couldn't remember the context: music or martial arts or some other area of talent or potential talent. All of his education seemed, on reflection, to have been about attack and defense. He took long, slow breaths, and forced his tension to dissipate like a built-up charge.

The light-curtain in the balcony doorway sizzled behind him. He swung around. Sparks showered over a woman-shaped darkness paused between the party's warm clamor and the threatening night. He recognized the outline, and turned his back to the door.

"There's such a thing as too much drama," he said when she didn't step out. "Or have you forgotten your entrance line?"

"They never let me see a script," said Jhari Sabayan. A soft sound on the paving marked her steps. "Nice night."

"There's a storm coming."

"I like storms."

She was at the railing, not close to him, watching the tossing treetops. Moonlight leached color out of her shoulder-length brown hair, and paled her clear skin like frost.

"I don't want to go on fighting with you," she said. "I respect you. I admire you."

"Stop it, Lieutenant."

The corner of her mouth quirked. "Call me Jhari if you like."

"I don't like."

She shrugged. "Call me what you will, then. But we don't have to go on as jailer and captive."

He laughed, and saw her wince. "Then the next move is yours, Lieutenant. I've given it my best shot, and that's still what we are."

They stood for a while, pretending to listen to the wind. "Falcon was right, Chrysander," she said. "He can't get you out. He won't try it."

"You were listening."

"My people have been on every call in or out."

"Our hostess must love that."

"She doesn't know. Her secretary is one of mine."

There was nothing to say. He thought of the blinded panel in Aurelia Yarretic's library; the cheerful voice with its softened vowels burned in his memory like lye. *The bird flies without you.* If it did—no, there would be no living with the consequences.

"He's not coming, Chrysander," Sabayan was saying. "He's not a fool. Nothing's going to stop him from leaving."

Chrysander shook his head, but it was reflex.

"You've got only one friend left. Me. And we may as well be friends, Chrysander, because you've never had a lover stay as close to you as I'm going to."

She was a meter away, but suddenly Chrysander had to step back, and back again, and still he could hear the closing of the trap.

"No." He modulated his words for her. "I'll break my own neck first. *No.*" He felt grim pleasure as her hand went blindly out to the railing.

"Don't turn that shit on me!" she hissed, her face twisted with fury.

"What's the matter?" he asked, baring his teeth at her. "Too much scope for my ability? You've built the cage, Lieutenant. But you haven't got me in it yet.'' He turned his back on her, because he knew it would make her angry. The light-curtain tingled sparks against his face as he left her behind on the balcony.

Perhaps he'd been wrong. He should have accepted her offer, and made the condition of his cooperation Lamia's freedom. Lift the Silence, give Lamia gifts, and the Concorde could have him. But he couldn't be certain of the Concorde, Lamia, himself. If tonight the *Gerfalcon* left him behind, maybe then he would see what he was worth to the Concorde.

The salon was an enormous room—there were perhaps a hundred and fifty guests in it, and still it was only comfortably full. The floor was rose-colored stone, the walls were white, and the ceiling beams were carved and painted to look like the peeled trunks of slender trees. He could smell smoke and scent and wine, but only what little the air cleaners hadn't drawn away. A refreshment tray found him, and he looked longingly at the champagne. But he gestured it away. He needed to be sober.

''I could find you something else,'' said an alto voice at his back.

He turned to find his hostess there. ''Hello, Aurelia.''

She was attractive, but not in a way that moved him. Her slenderness seemed more the product of nerves than nature. Her eyes rarely settled on his face, and her hands never settled at all. She could talk easily on any subject and turn it deftly into a discussion of herself. Any other time, he would enjoy watching her try to maneuver him toward the bedroom.

''If there's something you'd rather drink . . . ?'' she said.

''No, thank you.''

''You're bored, aren't you?'' she managed to sound contrite and conspiratorial at once. ''I should have taken you to see the stables after all. But there's no escape for the hostess. Forgive me?''

The proposed trip to the stables had almost worked. That had been right after he'd called Niki Falcon, after he'd come out of the library sick and angry and cold. He'd made it to the entrance hall with Aurelia on his arm. Then the butler had met them there and said, apologetically, that a crisis in the kitchen required Madame's attention. When Aurelia was gone, the butler had told him, in the same tone, that Chrysander would be more comfortable with the other guests. There was nothing apologetic in the butler's face. Chrysander had considered violence, looked again at the butler, and given it up temporarily.

"Of course I forgive you." *I don't suppose you have a cache of weapons in the house,* he imagined asking her. That would have damped the conspiratorial expression.

Aurelia Yarretic's secretary appeared in the double doors to the entryway. "Dominique Corbeau, Viscount Rose," he announced. Chrysander noticed the secretary's excellent voice, and was annoyed.

The Viscount moved with slow grace, as if walking underwater. He was very tall and slim, and showed fit middle age: a thick white streak marked his black hair at each temple, and his dark-tanned face was scored deeply around the mouth and the one visible eye. Over the other, he wore a black patch edged in gold. Another man might have looked funereal in a tunic and pants of such unrelenting black; the Viscount looked only elegant. A fire-carnelian blazed at his throat as if too hot to touch, and a ceremonial sword hung at his hip, barely moving as he descended the short flight of stairs.

Chrysander watched the nearest guests knot around him, lured by the title and the tasteful evidence of wealth. *A hostage,* he thought, delighted. *Now, which of us will prove more valuable to Jhari Sabayan?*

He watched the Viscount's long brown hands move languidly as he flirted with a blonde woman in a half mask of silver feathers. The man's heavy black moustache gave a piratical cast to his single-corner smile.

"Who is he?" Chrysander asked his hostess.

For a moment Aurelia looked blank. It was very like Aurelia to forget who she'd invited, he thought with disgust. "Planetary title," she said, fluttering one hand. "You know, the kind privateers and freetraders seem to get. Rich as hell, though." Chrysander suspected that she'd made the whole thing up on the spot.

"Always nice to know money. Can you introduce me?"

She smiled. "Stay right here. I'll bring him to you."

She crossed the room and cut deftly through the group around the newcomer. Chrysander watched the Viscount greet her. He kissed her hand, and it seemed flattering, intimate, and not at all extraordinary. Aurelia clearly loved it. She twined her arm through his and led him over. "My lord," she cooed, "I'd like to introduce you to Chrysander Harris. Chrysander, this is the Viscount—''

"Please, Aurelia," the Viscount said quickly. Chrysander was disappointed; he would have loved to see if Aurelia could remember the title. "You'll let me be Dominique here, surely?" He turned to Chrysander. "Pleased to make your acquaintance. I'm a great admirer of your work." And he extended his hand.

Under the faint overlay of the Viscount's accent, Chrysander heard soft vowels, a certain music of inflection. He stared into the gray eye, and it widened, cautioning him. He stammered something polite and shook the offered hand. Gently.

"I believe we have a friend in common," the Viscount said, visible eye sleepy once again. "She . . . asked about you." In his tone, his expression, there was a wealth of delicacy. Aurelia looked tantalized.

"Someone I know?" she asked.

"I think not. Not in your circle at all, my dear."

Aurelia took that as a compliment, as she was meant to.

"May I kidnap your talented guest for a few minutes?" the Viscount asked her. "I know I may rely on *your* discretion, but if we were overheard . . ." He finished with a weary sigh.

"Certainly, my lord. Use my study." She used the conspiratorial look again. "It's quite private."

"Thank you. If I might impose . . ." he said to Chrysander, who nodded. A long, thin, brown hand settled on his shoulder, turned him, nudged him lightly.

Once out of the room, they moved more quickly. Chrysander began, "The study's down he—" before his companion grabbed his wrist and pulled him through a door.

"What—"

"Shh."

It was a bathroom. Chrysander watched him thumb the switch for the ultrasonic shower, and heard the mechanism start up.

"What's the matter? Weren't you expecting me?" Niki Falcon grinned.

"You said—no, I—" Then reaction swept over him, and he covered his face. "Dominique Corbeau, Viscount Rose. Poor Aurelia—played like a piano!"

"And I bet she *still* won't remember my name. Not even the Dominique."

"Oh, God, the eyepatch, and the odd smile . . ."

"Well, I've got a black eye and a fat lip."

Chrysander suppressed an appalling desire to laugh aloud. "Why's the shower on?"

"Confuses Ears. Old spy story trick. You didn't recognize me?"

"Not 'til you spoke."

"Good. Then maybe no one else did, and there's a chance of getting out intact."

The door swung open, and Aurelia Yarretic's secretary stepped in, the cutter gun in his hand aimed at Niki's middle.

"Whoever you are, don't move. Keep—"

The secretary's attention was on Niki's hands—until Chrysander's driving fingertips pointed out his mistake and doubled him over. Niki ducked sideways. The beam from the cutter gun shattered the plastic shower enclosure as the secretary staggered back against the wall. "The gun—" said Niki. The secretary had held onto it, was struggling to raise it. Chrysander kicked, and the weapon sailed up and into the smashed shower.

"Get out!" Niki yelled, and they dived out the bathroom door, sliding, as the ultrasonics set off the gun's charge and exploded it. Shrapnel whistled past. Shouting welled up at the end of the hall.

Niki led through a confusion of identical passages, some stairs up, and others down. One door led to the second-floor gallery of a library with no apparent access to the first floor; Niki swung unhesitatingly over the gallery railing, hung from it for an instant, and dropped to the floor below. Chrysander shrugged, and followed.

"You do know where we are?" Chrysander said finally, catching up to him.

"Yes. These are the private rooms, which we're not supposed to know our way around." He was breathing hard, and pale under his makeup. Chrysander suspected that the drop had been a bad idea. "I just hope *they* don't know where we are."

They rounded the corner and faced a semicircle of terrace, walled only with the slight blurring of an insect screen—and with five men and women in the livery of Aurelia's household in an irregular curve.

"I've got to stop saying these things," he heard Niki mutter.

Only two of them armed, Chrysander thought, but he was dismayed. *I should have tried the butler, after all.*

"Hold that pose," one called out, a strongly-built man with

a Concorde military beam pistol. "Harris, move to your left, away from the ringer, there. Or we'll put holes in both of you."

"Grab me!" Chrysander whispered. "And stay behind me. They want me alive."

Niki clamped an arm around him, pinned him to his chest. "Go ahead," he said pleasantly to the half circle of agents. His heartbeat hammered against Chrysander's spine.

"When I tell you, swing me toward the blonde woman," Chrysander murmured. If they could take out the ones with weapons quickly . . . "Then drop, fast. Now!"

His knuckle strike crushed the woman's windpipe almost before she saw him. Niki's swing had been wonderfully fast. He spun, kicked, drove the breastbone of the next man into his lungs. Then he saw a horrible thing.

Niki Falcon had not dropped to the ground to avoid the fire that would center on him. He had drawn the dress sword at his side and leveled it in a neat, short, useless lunge. Chrysander wondered why he hadn't heard the beamer's purr—

But the beamer was on the pavement. Its owner and the two agents next to him were folding helplessly after it, sobbing, retching. Chrysander felt a whisper of nausea, incipient loss of balance, a graying of vision, brush past him. Nausea, vertigo, blindness— A Vertigen? In the sword?

Niki rose from the lunge to a perfect fencer's salute. The three agents he'd dropped were too sick to notice. The two Chrysander had dropped were too dead. "Out of charge," Niki said, tugging off his eyepatch. The fake moustache was already gone. "You can't store much in a sword-hilt."

It *was* a black eye. "Then we'd better—down!"

Niki dropped as if he had no bones, and rolled when he landed. The man in the garden with the autorifle filled the space he'd occupied with projectiles. Chrysander was watching Niki, saw the arm with the sword move before the head turned to look. The bright blade arced with supernatural accuracy to end, quivering, in the rifleman's breast.

"Well, I'm impressed," Chrysander quavered, breaking a moment's silence.

Jhari Sabayan stepped onto the terrace. Her hands were empty, and her green gown, billowing in the rising wind, had no place to hide a gun. "Niki," she said, and her voice was full of things in conflict: rage, pain, shock, amusement. It was a rich and terrible combination.

Niki was still crouched on the floor, halfway to his feet. She might have been the medusa, so still he was at the sight of her. But he didn't seem afraid. "Hello, Jhari," he said at last. Another, different, combination of conflicts. Chrysander moved toward her. If he killed her quickly, they might still get away before any more reinforcements appeared.

"Don't," Niki snapped. "There's a pavilion at the south end of the lawn. Make for it. I'll be right behind you."

Chrysander's gaze moved from one to the other. "When we get out of this," he said, "some things need explaining."

"Go."

He passed Jhari Sabayan, but she paid him no attention. Her empty hands stayed at her sides, and her eyes were on Niki.

As Chrysander stepped off the terrace, he heard Sabayan say, "Don't take him, Niki. Whatever this is, it's too big."

"I have to." Niki's voice was ragged and soft.

"I don't want to end up killing you over this."

"You won't. You'll have someone else do it."

Then Chrysander was too far away to hear them.

Rain spattered his shoulders by the time he reached the pavilion. He saw it spidery-pale in the dark, revealed one moment, then obscured by the tossing of the ornamental trees around it. He heard a thump ahead of him. He crouched and peered into the night, feeling his pupils flare fully open.

Niki came up behind him, and Chrysander motioned him down. "Something there," he whispered.

"Mine," Niki said, and went forward.

A moment later, he led two horses out of the trees. "I stole them from Aurelia's stables. Which no one knows why she keeps, since she can't ride."

"Neither can I," said Chrysander.

"You'll learn."

"I've seen *pictures* of horses," Chrysander said.

"Don't quibble. There's no time." Niki nodded at the quieter of the two animals. "You straddle him, and hang on with your knees and both hands. Don't worry about steering, he'll follow mine."

"This is a terrible idea."

"What, shall we take the magtube and let them pick us up at the next station? Left foot in the stirrup. Okay, one, two, three."

He was astride. He didn't like the fluid feeling of the horse beneath him, but he could balance. "There must be a better—"

"Come on."

His horse did follow Niki's. He nearly fell when they leaped forward, but he crouched in the saddle and found his center immediately. *It's fighting stance,* he realized. *Stay low, stay flexible, and nothing can move you.* His muscles had recognized it before his mind.

Their mounts' hooves made what seemed to Chrysander a huge racket on the residential streets, a hard-surfaced percussion in a rhythm he didn't understand. The rain began to come down hard and cold, and Niki slowed his horse a little.

The walls around them were older now, enclosing warehouses and wholesalers. One weary little saloon with a corner door sent bubbles of green light bouncing up the front of its building at irregular intervals. Niki's mount seemed inclined to object to the sight.

This isn't right, Chrysander thought. *Sabayan isn't going to give me up so easily.*

Niki's horse reared, neighing, skidding on the pavement. "Harris, pull up!" Niki yelled. But Chrysander's mount plunged forward, eager to pass its stable-mate.

He felt something terrible in the way the horse lurched under him, the motion of a dancer who has put a foot irretrievably wrong. He leaped clear and landed hard in the street on his side. The horse crashed to the pavement, screaming. A second look told Chrysander that all its legs weren't attached. He turned his head away to keep from being sick.

"Police! Don't move, either of you!"

Chrysander looked up. There were three of them, probably Concorde. *We might be able to fight past them.* But Niki's Vertigen was planted in someone's chest a few miles away, and Chrysander was tired, so tired. His horse still struggled, though shock was beginning to blunt its efforts. Someone ought to kill it. He got to his feet slowly.

"And get off that God-damned animal!"

"Make me, you bastard!" Niki's voice behind him, full of rage and wildness—he turned.

They might have sprung out of an old tale, the dark figure on the dark, rearing horse. Niki's teeth were bared, his eyes reflecting green light. One of the agents fired, and Niki charged.

Gestalt pilots know all about aim, Chrysander thought, as the horse plunged toward him, looking very large.

Niki's arm caught him across the chest and yanked him off

his feet. Chrysander clung to it, flung his other arm over the saddle. "Good. Hold tight," said Niki, and Chrysander's stomach dropped as the horse seemed to take flight.

It wasn't until they'd come down on the other side that he saw what they'd flown over. A hotwire shimmered knee-high, almost invisible, across the width of the street. The remains of Chrysander's horse made a dark heap on the pavement behind them. He remembered the animal's movement and life between his knees.

When they were far enough away, Niki stopped the horse. "Here, swing up behind me," he said, and Chrysander did. These streets were populated; people in bright, cheap clothes passed them quickly, looking startled.

"How much farther?" Chrysander asked.

"Close. If Laura's all right, we lift in fifteen minutes."

"Niki?"

"Mmm?" Niki looked over his shoulder at him.

It was hard to say, to meet the gray eyes when he said it. He looked down. He had only to wield the talent, the Voice, to drive his words deep into this man's heart and honor. "Don't let them stop me. Promise me that."

After what seemed a long time, Niki said, "You don't have to do that."

Chrysander started. "Do what?" he managed to ask.

"Whatever that is you're doing. And if they want to stop you, they have to stop me." Niki urged the horse into a canter.

"Thank you," Chrysander whispered, and wondered what it was he was riding toward.

CHAPTER TEN

What is it but nightfall?
No, no, not night but death;
Was it needless death after all?
—W. B. Yeats, "Easter, 1916"

No guard stood watch at the field gate; they plunged through
it unchallenged with, Niki thought ruefully, a fine disregard for
the mare's footing. The untended gate must have been Laura
Brass's work. Niki was glad she'd taken care of it, and didn't
want to know how.

He pulled up at the base of the launch ramp that cradled the
Gerfalcon. Laura stepped out of the shadow there and took the
reins. That was a formality. The mare trembled under him, head
low. If it weren't for the rain, there would be lather on her. She
would be sure to founder; that would be another sacrifice for the
evening's work.

Harris let go of Niki's waist and slid to the ground. "Go on
in," Niki said. Harris cast a swift glance at Laura, nodded, and
ran lightly across the wet tarmalon to the ship.

"Did you get my lift time moved up?" Niki asked Laura as
he slid out of the saddle.

"Yep. You've got five minutes 'til the line goes hot."

"*Five?*"

"Don't worry. I started your drive clearing fifteen minutes ago." Laura looked smug.

"I'm going to change the lock."

"Heartwarming confidence in technology." She caught his chin suddenly and frowned. "How are you?"

"After an action-packed rescue and a thrilling ride across town? *Terrible*, Laura, but it can't be helped."

He shouted at the mare, swatted at her, and she shied for the gate. "You're ready if I need you?" he asked. Laura nodded. "Remember, get in, do as much as you can, and get out. Don't stick around for a second try, no matter what happens."

"You gonna talk, or you gonna leave?" she said, her voice rough.

The heavy rain glittered in her hair without flattening it, and gleamed on her face and arms. Niki kissed her on the mouth. "Thank you, dear heart. For everything. In advance."

"You're a pain in the ass. Beat it."

Harris was waiting inside the *Gerfalcon*'s hatch. "What do I do?" he said. His golden eyes were wide, the pupils expanded like an alert cat's.

"Go find the bunk and strap yourself in. We have about three minutes before we wing up."

"But—"

"I can take care of everything. One of my sterling virtues. *Go*."

Niki swung himself into the control cell and locked the door. In the couch, with the harness closed around him, he reached for the needle tab that waited in its case, balanced it on his middle finger. With his other hand, he found the vein that pounded in his throat. He pressed the tab against it and the point bit in. He'd never gotten used to that pain. His fingers touched the lump of bone at the base of his skull, and he parted his wet hair away from the socket underneath it. It was cold.

He slid the spot of plastic flesh back from each wrist, exposing the pinhole ports there. He reached down the armrests to the gauntlets and curved his hands into them. Shadow messages came up his arms from his wrists and muttered in his mind. He settled his head back, closed the connection between the ship and himself, and triggered.

The conversion drug was only an unfortunate side effect. His real addiction, his need and joy and exaltation, was the white-light leap of the gestalt. A wash of heat coursed his skin like a high fever. He tasted copper on his tongue. He felt his blinded eyes close, felt a harsh breath leave his parted lips as if it were his soul fleeing his body. Then flesh faded away as he caught up with his ship.

He was steel now, and ceramic, resin, plastic, glass. He stretched his great limbs, sent a ripple of information down his many-branched spine to check its travel. His mind spread like a penetrating gas into space and time and stored knowledge. His eyes filtered the field lights, saw the stars, his skin, his guts and heart and brain. His heart was a furnace of rebellion against natural law, his brain a metropolis of living machines.

The gestalt allowed him to savor, unhurried, the paradox of his being.

The himself-that-was-clock showed ninety seconds to lift. A gulf of time. Contact with the ramp felt like talons around a perch, secure, easy to let go. But something was wrong in his sky. He turned a fragment of his attention outward.

A Bayonet fighter hung in the night above him. The field controller's computer was sending an insistent warning to clear the exit corridor, but the fighter held its position in silence.

Five seconds. His comlink opened on the hailing bands, and his simulated voice said, "Get him out of my way, Jhari."

One second. Zero. The ramp line went hot as he dug into it, and he leaped toward the sky.

Jhari Sabayan spoke in his receivers. "He has orders to force you down any way he can, Niki. And there are more fighters scrambling. Land now, and you won't risk your ship. I only want Ha—"

Interference mauled her words as Laura Brass's ship thundered upward after him.

"My, lot of traffic for this hour," Niki observed.

Jhari's voice, blank with anger: "You son of a bitch."

Laura Brass roared on the link, "Get your ass out of my way or I blow it off!" She sounded pleased.

"She will, you know," Niki added. "*Mercy of the Goddess* is armed."

Jhari swore again. "*Goddess*, I'll remember your registration."

"Don't bother, lawgirl. I'll change it."

With several eyes, he watched the Bayonet veer across his bow, fire, and miss. He increased thrust.

Laura fired, and bits of plastic spattered the air from off the fighter's flank. "His starboard gun's out," Laura called. "Shall I scrap him?"

"Are you sure you're a vegetarian? Get out of here."

"If you insist. You'll be in touch?"

"Scat!"

Laura veered out and away. The Bayonet stayed on Niki's tail, but only the portside gun traced his path. The fighter was quick, but not quick enough to negate the advantage of the gestalt. He could dodge that single gun.

He was almost far enough out for the Cheat. The fighter shifted to starboard behind him. Niki did, too, and another shot missed him. The fighter dropped low and rolled away, giving up; they were nearly to the smaller ship's altitude limit. Niki turned his mind to the Cheat, and began to fold the necessary numbers.

He shrieked as a ripping pain drove down his right side. No, the side of the ship— *Where is he, God damn*—

It was a second Bayonet. He should have watched; Jhari had told him that there were more. This one pushed its altitude, climbed and rolled as if fuel lines never choked and resins never turned fragile in the cold. The bite it had taken blazed in his own skin, and left him a quarter blind. It was still close, hunting another shot. Too close—*no, close enough*, Niki decided savagely. *Come ride with me, you bastard.* He grabbed at coordinates, turned the world inside-out.

Pure-spectrum color shattered around him. His every nerve fiber was a gallery of singing angels. He lay weightless in snow, burning in solid stone. He had broken the rules of space and time, Cheated the universe of its geometry, and for a fragment of an instant knew its true name. Then it was over. He was alone in the dark, hollow with spent bloodlust.

The damage to the *Gerfalcon* was a burning furrow cut through his body. After a struggle, he managed to raise his head and break connection with the ship. His senses reverted with a snap to his own flesh; the sudden switch nauseated him. He had a pounding headache.

There was no point in replaying those last moments in his head. But he did it anyway. The other pilot had been close at Cheatpoint, well within its globe of bent geometry. The Bayonet hadn't the advantage of the *Gerfalcon*'s drive and Niki's guidance; it and its pilot would have come apart and been distributed at random through space-time. Not an accident. In fury and pain, he'd crumbled a ship and a life in his hand, and scattered the dust.

I should have let Laura stay. She'd have let him fight back.

He unfastened the harness, slid sideways off the couch, and staggered to the door. When it opened, he saw the galley in the underwater gloom of the emergency lights, and Chrysander Harris waiting.

"What happened?" said Harris.

Niki leaned against the doorframe and breathed deeply. "Never," he said softly, "unstrap until I tell you to. Never. You were lucky this time. The next time I might have to sponge you off a wall."

Harris's eyes narrowed. "This is not my first trip out."

"It is with me. And I'm used to cargo that stays where I put it."

One of Harris's eyebrows lifted a fraction. "Ah, I'm a parcel."

"I don't want to look at you right now."

"I see," he said, crisp and cold. He turned and disappeared into the cabin.

Niki watched him go, thinking, *I should apologize for that. I should tell him I just killed somebody. I'm not myself, excuse me please.* He closed his eyes. *But I'm too tired.* He dragged himself back to the couch, fell into it, and sank into a doze full of serrated dreams.

Full moon. She stands at the window in almost-silhouette, light glossing the skin of her shoulder and hip. Her ruffled hair, usually brown, is no color at all in this light. He can't tell if she's looking out, or at him.

"Niki, I have to—" It's the pause that makes his insides knot. Such innocent words, such a brutal pause. He wants to get out of bed, to go to her and put his arms around her, but he is afraid to move. If he holds still, time may follow suit, and she will never finish.

She turns to face him. Brave Jhari. Even in the dark, she's trying to meet his eyes. Or perhaps there's light on his face; he could tell by looking down, but that would mean looking away from her, and he can't do it.

"I have to leave you," she says.

He knew it; he still feels as if something fell on him. "Tell me why," he says softly.

Her hands come up—to her face? "Don't . . ." Her voice is stronger. "You know why. Can't we kiss and part friends and skip the agony?"

"A few months ago, we could have."

"The captain was right," she says bitterly. "Basic is a shitty time to have an affair."

He is stung, though he knows better. "Is that what we are? An affair?"

"Yes," Jhari says at last, but the pause gives her away.

He draws his knees up and props his chin on them. "You haven't answered my first question."

"God damn you!" Her teeth are clenched; he can hear it. She is across the room in a few steps, and she grabs him by the shoulders and shakes him once, very hard. The strength in her hands is frightening. Then she twists away.

He slips out of bed, comes up behind her, puts his arms around her. "I'm sorry," he murmurs.

"Oh, God. Oh, Nik—I'm splitting down the middle. The conditioning pulls me one way, and you pull the other. It's going to pull me to pieces. If I don't leave you. I have to, Nik."

She is warm and soft and smooth against him, human and suddenly, for all her strength, fragile. He strokes her back over and over, knowing it may be the last time he ever touches her skin. He rubs his cheek against her hair. "Do you have to, Jhari?" he whispers. "Do you have to let them do this to you?"

He feels her stiffen. It's the conditioning, he tells himself desperately, as he's done countless times in the last few weeks.

She steps away, and her head tilts in slow deliberation. "What's this, compared to what you're letting them do to you?"

Niki woke up with a start and a sense of loss so fresh it still bled. After so many years—there she was. He'd dreamed of her because he'd just seen her, under harrowing conditions. That was all. But he felt like an atheist who'd discovered that he had been sleepwalking to church.

They'd avoided each other with no great effort for a long time. Jhari's business was dark and secret things, and his was honest trade, in the light. Why, when he finally involved himself in something questionable, had she appeared immediately?

Such a bare-faced dream, no more than a replay of memory. Something in that bothered him, but his mind was still too fuzzy to chase it down. And much too fuzzy to deal with the damage lights on the console.

The alternative was to go out and face his passenger. That was almost enough to make him run the damage report. He sighed and rubbed his face, then opened the control cell door.

He found Harris sitting in the galley, doing nothing with perfect self-possession. The satin and velvet he wore was torn and marked with water and dirt.

Niki sat down across from him. "I've killed two people today," he said finally. "One of those killings was certainly not self-defense. The other probably was. But it turns my gut, and I keep trying to blame it all on you. That's . . . why I said what I did."

Harris shrugged. "It is my fault, isn't it? You killed them in my service, at my need."

Niki sat, and blinked. The feudal expression of it shook him. "I told you, you've got to stop taking responsibility for everything."

"You look terrible," Harris said after a moment.

"What?"

"The black eye, what's left of your makeup job . . ."

"Oh." Niki looked into the polished chrome front plate of the Galleymaster. His eye was purple and yellow; brown paint, smeared by rain and abuse, mottled his face and the black velvet of his tunic. "Charming."

"What was the second one?"

"The second . . . ?"

"Person you killed."

"Oh." Niki told him about the Bayonet pilot.

Harris shrugged. "He asked for it."

"No, he didn't *ask* for it," Niki said, exasperated. "He knew I was unarmed, and he wasn't shooting to kill."

"So he's honorless, and stupid."

"Stupid?"

Harris leaned back and looked at him patiently. "Stay your hand, or strike to kill. Half measures leave walking enemies."

"Are you a vegetarian, too?"

"I beg your pardon?"

"Never mind. You've got questions, I suppose. Can you wait for the answers 'til I've washed?"

Harris nodded. "I realized a few hours ago that we probably had all the time in the world."

"I don't think it's that bad. Be right back."

In the head, he stripped and cleaned up as well as he could. The black velvet went into the recycler. The stubble he decided to leave; it made him look like the convict he would probably be, if he lived through this. How did Harris manage to look perfectly respectable in the ruins of his evening clothes? He pulled on a long black robe and went back to the galley.

There was enough power, even on emergency, to run the Galleymaster. He tapped in code, then dropped back into his chair. "Now," he said to Harris, "for the expository lump. You want to start?"

Harris shook his head. "Always save the best for last. It's good showmanship. How do you come to be on first-name basis with Jhari Sabayan?"

Niki had expected that one. "We were lovers." He saw Harris's eyes narrow, and added, "Years ago. We've been sidestepping each other ever since."

Harris's beautiful face seemed more than ever like carved stone. "And what did you mean when you said, back in the city, that I didn't have to 'do that'?"

"I meant what I said."

"I didn't have to do *what*?"

Niki rubbed between his eyebrows. The headache was coming back. "I don't know what it was. That was the third time you'd used it on me. It didn't take, whatever it was."

Harris swung his chair aside and stared moodily into a corner.

Niki sighed. "Well, that point goes to me, more or less." He got up, snapped the Galleymaster open, and dispensed the results into cups and plates. He set one of each in front of Harris. "No one here will mind if you talk with your mouth full."

Harris's lips twitched. "What is it?" he said, nodding at the plate.

"Coffee. And Stuff. Don't worry, it tastes good."

"It looks like scrambled eggs."

"Everything that comes out of one of those looks like scrambled eggs. Stop trying to change the subject."

"Sorry."

"What were you using on me? Trying to use."

Harris shrugged and took a bite. He did not, in fact, talk with his mouth full. "All right," he said. "I suppose it would have come up eventually. It's a long story," he added, and looked up hopefully.

"I like long stories." *Besides, I need the rest.* Laura had been right to worry about him; he could run on the impulse of the drug alone for a long time, but when it let him down, he'd go down like a falling star.

"Lamia has a higher-than-normal Rhine-Soal index. That's not that odd—other worlds have turned up with a bias toward it. But on Lamia natural resources are a little short, so we develop every one we have."

Niki raised his eyebrows. "If Lamia was producing real, useful telepaths, you couldn't possibly have kept it secret. Could you?"

"No. No real telepaths. Though not for lack of trying. But it has produced me."

"And you are . . ."

Harris opened his mouth, closed it, and looked suddenly embarrassed. "We're not sure. I don't do it entirely on a conscious level. But it's a telepathic suggestion reinforced with the right set of sounds. Or vice versa—sound has a lot of psychological impact." He waved his hands over his plate. "I'm sorry. That's awfully tenuous."

Niki propped his chin in one hand and stared across the table. Harris looked younger and somewhat less perfect when he wasn't being self-possessed. Niki wondered if he was being manipulated now. It didn't feel like it; but then, perhaps Harris had only now gotten his range. "Tenuous. Is this a dependable thing, this ability?"

"No. It changes with distance, with how well I know the person—with an audience, for instance, I get only generalized effects. And how receptive the person is. I've had it not work." Harris frowned. "But you're the first one to be able to tell I was using it, who didn't already know about it."

Niki eyed his plate. "If I don't finish this, will you promise not to tell Laura?"

Harris looked puzzled.

"Oh, never mind." He took another forkful of Stuff. "Does it have something to do with why you're on the run?"

Harris was a good actor, but Niki didn't think that expression, that combination of surprise, wariness, and unfocused anger, could be produced consciously. "The Concorde wants to recruit me. They think it would be a useful thing to have."

"Even," Niki went on, "if it's not dependable?"

"They think it can be improved on."

"Ah," Niki said. "Then I take it the research on Lamia was not a joint effort with the Concorde. Now, does that have anything to do with why the Concorde is moving in on Lamia?"

Wide, wary golden eyes met his. "Maybe. But a Silence? There must be more to this than a limited telepathic by-product."

Chrysander Harris said nothing at all.

Niki stood up and cleared the plates. Then he leaned against the wall, folded his arms, and studied Harris gravely. "Here we are, east of the sun and west of the moon—did you know that? We're parked between two points in real space. If the drive fails right now, it's Welcome to the Singularity Zone."

"We can't be," Harris said, startled. "You can't sit in Cheat-space."

"Ordinary Cheatships can't. But this one has a gestalt pilot. Now, this may be the last time in our lives when we're completely safe. Do you suppose you could take the time to tell me the goddamn *truth* now?"

Harris's chin came up. "I haven't lied to you."

"Have it your way. But if so, I'd suggest traveling in the opposite direction. The way you're going about it, if it all goes smash, they get the research and the prototype both."

"And if I ran, then what?" Harris asked. "Run for the rest of my life? You can't do that, not really."

"Nonsense. Plenty of people have." *Shut up, Niki, you idiot.*

"Lamia is my home. If it dies . . ." He shrugged elegantly. "My place is still there."

"May I be rude?"

Harris's look was not encouraging.

"Horse shit," Niki said anyway.

"You don't know what this is like," Harris told him kindly.

Niki stopped then, left that statement unchallenged; if not out of good sense, then because his voice might fail him. "I'm going to go shoot up and see about getting us out of here," he said finally.

Back on the couch in the control cell, Niki shook his head. *At this rate, I'm going to pour out the whole sorry tale, just to keep him from reliving my life. And it probably wouldn't work anyway.* He settled back and made contact.

This time he knew to keep his flesh and blood out of the connection; the damage didn't transfer to his body. He swept the ports as if he moved through a room walled with doors, some of which opened on light, and some on darkness. He had expected to find the unresponsive optics on his starboard flank. He had even been prepared for the dim flickering where the rear starboard power grid had been. But the drive control system was

showing failure lights in places—that was bad. He could limp
the *Gerfalcon* along with any of the other damage, but if he
couldn't fix the drive control, Harris was right. They would have
all the time in the world, until they left it.

He summoned displays of hardware status. One of the power
branches pulsed yellow, running from the damaged grid. But it
didn't feed drive control. He magnified the display, and magnified it again. There were no other down lights.

He shifted into the operating system for the living quarters,
and found the intercom that, in a one-man ship, he'd rarely used.
He patched it to his voice simulation, and said to the galley,
"Excuse me."

After a long pause, he heard, "That's . . . creepy." Even trans-
lated into ones and zeroes, it was the voice of Chrysander Harris.

"I almost used your first name. Then I realized it was a
household word, and I felt funny."

"Please do use it. You don't sound quite like you."

"I'm digital. I just called to tell you that I'm going to be working
for a while. Make yourself at home, and don't start to worry inside
of a couple hours."

"I can write you a better voice. Is there a 'board somewhere?"

"In the cabin, at the head of the bunk."

"How does it look, so far?"

"Too soon to tell. 'Bye."

Drive control was an interlocking pattern of live-, firm-, and
fluidware. It was engineering, intuition, and madness, built to
regulate a force that dwelt only uneasily in the universe. Wan-
dering through the drive control system was like riding a bicycle
with a crate of nitroglycerin under one arm: it required a little
concentration. It didn't seem too much to ask of himself.

He slid down into levels of his ship-self where the minute
workings hid the pattern of the whole, where there was no sense
of system or subroutine. Here there was only on or off. He was
an impulse passed from molecule to molecule in the hives. There
were a few dead spots there. Assemblers were already filling the
holes, repairing the fabric of the ship's thought. It was Niki's
business to find the thing that had made the damage, and keep
it from happening again.

He let himself be pulled around drive control by its own operation, changing state when he had to. Nothing was down. It
was running smoothly and by its own eccentric logic. No anom-

aly to account for the hive damage. Unless it was an intermittent failure . . .

Just as he realized his mistake and the size of it, the anomaly found him.

He was suffocating. The feeling was the same, of sucking in vast gulps of nothing. The panic was the same. He was literally senseless, unconnected, alone with his self-awareness. Then even that began to shrink, like a video image when the power fails.

The power grid. But drive control doesn't run off starboard rear— Power harness drawn in fire on the back of his brain. A branch from starboard fore, that crossed beneath the line of damage on the *Gerfalcon's* skin. Not broken, but scorched, undependable, cutting in and out. Cutting his throat. Other cable ran nearby, so close— Light-years away. Nothing between him and life but a bit of insulation, or the arrangement of wire at a junction. His conscious mind was barely a spark when he reached out, like the last effort of a dying man, toward a stream of electrons and life.

The darkness around him began to run and streak. *Something's opened up. Wider. Where's it coming from? Never mind. Get out. Look from outside.*

He pulled back hard all the way to his body, and found it sweat-drenched, shaking, panting. He was losing his mind. Shouldn't he have guessed he had a power flutter? Judgment, he remembered, was one of the first things to go. *I don't want to die. Not anymore.*

He called up the self-test. Now that he knew what he was looking for . . . yes, there, the line that fed drive control. It was dead now, light blue on the display.

But drive control was running. He flipped to the nearest junction point, magnified the display. And magnified it again, and again.

The line that had supplied the drive control system—didn't, anymore. Drive control took power now from the next line over, one that ought to power the cargo bay lights and didn't, anymore. The switches at the junction that shunted the power had been tripped.

Niki stared at the display for a long time, then shut it down. The ghost of the image seemed to hang on the screen, showing a pair of switches—*hardware*—that had changed state.

Now when, Niki asked himself, *did I learn to do that?*

CHAPTER ELEVEN

... When I was young,
I had not given a penny for a song
Did not the poet sing it with such airs
That one believed he had a sword upstairs. . . .
— W. B. Yeats, "All Things Can Tempt Me"

The Cheat was accomplished without fanfare, and with a fluid smoothness Chrysander had never felt before. It wasn't the not-quite-painful moment—being two people in one place and one person in two places—that even the best passenger liners gave him. This was like water running off a ledge, a simple, inevitable movement on one axis. Never mind that the axis was imaginary. He wondered why there was a difference. Wasn't the Cheat just a mathematical problem, to be solved or not solved, not subject to improvements?

He heard and felt the in-system thrusters fire and fall silent again. "Where are we?" Chrysander asked the ceiling above the bunk.

"Coming up on an el station around Breakneck," said the ceiling, with Niki's voice. "We need a repair or two."

No atmosphere entry, then; he wondered what that would be like in the *Gerfalcon*. He'd find out eventually, if nothing went wrong. The thought gave him surprisingly little satisfaction. "Do I have to stay tied down here?"

"I'm sorry, but there's no place else to put you." Yes, the

voice was much more like Niki's. It sounded genuinely apologetic.

"The control room?"

"There's no place to sit and nothing to see. The whole approach is happening in my head. No, you'll have to come to terms with your boredom."

Chrysander sighed.

"And *stay strapped in*, or I'll have Laura cut your nose off and feed it to you."

"Why Laura?"

"She's better at that sort of thing than I am."

"And she calls her ship *Mercy of the Goddess*?"

"Well, you have to remember which goddess."

"Which?"

"Kali," said Niki, with sepulchral relish.

"Oh. How much longer?"

"I've got a bay assignment—call it fifteen minutes. Can you stand it?"

"I suppose I'd better."

"Courage, child." The ceiling took on the silence that meant Niki was no longer there.

It had never occurred to Chrysander that the man he was bringing back would be good company. Or even that he'd be a human being at all, someone who would be increasingly hard to lie to.

He was having an attack of conscience, he admitted at last. He was not used to it, and he didn't like it. He was beginning to suspect that the best way to enlist Niki's aid was to ask for it. He could call out to him, and Niki's voice would answer. Then Chrysander would say—what? That Chrysander's arrival on Lamia meant nothing, and Niki Falcon's, everything? What more information could he offer, when little more than that had been offered to *him*? Niki Falcon was a likely key in a possible lock. And as with any key, nobody was going to ask if he wanted to be turned.

Chrysander would have wagered money that Niki would help, if asked. But he couldn't wager Lamia.

A moment later the room gave a lurch. "Sloppy," he said.

"Sloppy?" said Niki's voice, in cheerful outrage. "Come and bloody do it yourself, if you're so smart."

"Can I get out of the bunk now?"

"I suppose."

Chrysander gave himself another pat for the voice simulation.

All it lacked was that hint of something in the vowels. He sprang off the bunk, slid open the cabin door, and stuck his head out. "Where's your accent from?" he called.

Niki stopped halfway through the control cell door. The simulated voice wasn't subject to the weariness that showed in his face. It might have been the light, but his cheeks seemed hollower and his eyes darker-shadowed than they had only hours ago. "I don't have an accent."

"Yes, you do."

He shook his head. "It's a little of this and that, I suppose."

"But where are you from?"

"No place you've ever been. Now haul it out of there. I want to get dressed." Niki gave him a long, fierce look. Then, for no reason Chrysander could tell, his gaze dropped. "I could probably tell you. All the issues involved are dead, even if the people aren't. But the name wouldn't mean anything to you, and that'd make me feel rotten." He glanced up, almost smiling. "D'you mind?"

Chrysander shook his head, and stepped out of the way.

When the cabin door thumped closed, Chrysander sighed. He hadn't been prepared for this. It should have been as simple as hiring a car. Of course, his cloak-and-dagger experience was limited. Why should he ask Niki where he was from? Why should he care if he didn't answer?

Just a key in a lock. *And so am I*, Chrysander thought suddenly. *A particularly attractive and versatile sort of skeleton key.* Anything he had an aptitude for, all his life, had been fed and honed. It was the way anyone on Lamia was raised; as he'd told Niki, they were short of natural resources. *Have we all been brought up to be tools and weapons and working prototypes?*

That thought, and all the companions that came on its coattails, spun in his head, unanswerable. Was it a pastime among spies, to analyze their childhoods? He had a mind full of static. Maybe he needed exercise.

He did his stretches quickly, and began the slow exercises— opening gate, shield, stalking cat. He tried to fill them with power, but what he achieved felt more like tension. *What did Lamia get out of teaching me to fight?* he thought. It shook him out of his form, and he had to start again. At this rate, he'd be a ruin by the time he reached home.

There was a sound at the outside hatch. Then the inside hatch door opened and Laura Brass flung herself through it. He found himself in defensive stance with his back to Niki's cabin. He questioned his instincts, but he didn't override them.

"Where is he?" Laura snapped. There was something of defense and attack in the way she stood, too. Bravo for his instincts. Niki was right; cutting off noses could well be in this woman's line.

Chrysander drew himself up, more graceful than he needed to be. "Getting dressed," he said, and with a nod, moved aside. At home, in context, that could be called insulting. Here, too; Laura's eyes narrowed. *Have I gone crazy? I can't afford this.*

Laura hammered at the cabin door. It opened on Niki, in a loose white shirt and dark blue leggings. "You're all right," she said, and wrapped her arms around him.

"Ooof. 'Til you got hold of me." But Niki smiled down at her, and kissed the top of her head. Then he held her away. "And when are you going to learn to use the doorbell?"

"There's a furrow down your starboard side that ought to have its own atmosphere. And you're late. Fuck the doorbell."

Chrysander noted that Niki had not been precisely honest about the damage.

"Anxiety," said Niki, "does not excuse a lapse of manners."

"Dung. It was Sabayan's little tagalong, wasn't it?"

Niki sighed. "One of them."

"You should have let me kill him."

"It's taken care of." Niki's lips pressed together.

"Oh. Well, he deserved it," Laura said cheerfully.

Niki met Chrysander's eyes. "So I've been told."

Chrysander stepped forward and inclined his head to Laura. "Nice to see you again." A perfectly innocuous thing to say, if it hadn't been said so very politely.

"I'm sure it is," said Laura, matching his tone. She turned back to Niki. "Has he been a nuisance?"

"Laura!"

"I have, I think," Chrysander answered. "But my host is much too polite to say so."

"Poor Niki," said Laura.

Niki leaned against the wall and covered his eyes. "You two," he said, "are more fun than I can bear."

To Chrysander's surprise, Laura laughed. "Can't take me anywhere, can you? Come to dinner," she said.

"You're forgiven," Niki said promptly, and gestured at Chrysander. "What about him?"

"Him, too. I should behave better," Laura said to Chrysander. Her smile was dazzling. "It was only worry."

Oh? thought Chrysander, but he smiled back.

Niki looked curiously at them both, but said only, "I've got repairs to commission. Dinner at 20?"

Laura nodded.

Chrysander looked down at his stained silk shirt. "I suppose I'd better do something about this."

Niki looked at Laura. "Should we let him off the hook?"

"Neh," Laura said, with a wicked pleasure that Chrysander didn't understand. "No exceptions."

"We dress for dinner," Niki said at last, with a sort of apologetic amusement.

"You what?"

"Dress. Semiformal." Niki nodded solemnly. Laura was obviously trying not to laugh.

Chrysander rolled his eyes.

To his surprise, the el station was pleasant, though only a native could love the way the horizon curled up and around, instead of down and away. Prefab buildings mingled with fanciful shot-foam ones, all painted with trompe l'oeil and murals. The natives, after a first startled stare of recognition, ignored him.

In the nearest town center, Chrysander found lunch, a few changes of clothes, a bathhouse, and an Entropic 700 with expandable keyboard and a voice library he'd helped develop. He felt provisioned.

After lunch, he walked to the outside of town and found a low hill that sprouted the town's water tank. The metal tank itself was walled in with more shot-foam, shaped and painted to look like a ruined brick tower. Stalks of heartflower and blades of grass were painted around the base as if growing there. Chrysander laughed when he discovered the cartoon drop of dew on a flower petal.

He sat down on one of the tower footings and began to customize the Entropic. A child, dark as Laura Brass, wandered up; then another, a little girl with large brown eyes. When there were six of them, he gave it up and played "Forward View." The children (there were now ten or so) sat quiet when he was done, staring, openmouthed. Chrysander decided this was applause, and tried "The Belt Miner Girl." That got them to laugh and sing along.

He finished with "High-Water Line."

But every storm that rakes the waves,
And every wave that lifts us,
Is a span of time between me and mine
While she watches and waits at the high-water line.

They've probably never seen a storm, he realized, feeling foolish. *Or an ocean.* Not even as much sea as on Lamia, where the
water was cruel with salt, but kind in buoyancy, and warm . . .
He faltered the last chord, and shook his head. Then he smiled
up at the children.

"Shoo," he said softly. They straggled away. He closed the
Entropic and walked slowly down the hill back to the *Gerfalcon.*

He was glad he'd taken the "dress for dinner" warning seriously when he saw Niki. The close-fitting dark red doublet and
trousers he wore made him a prince from an ancient folk song.
Most of which are tragic, Chrysander recalled, frowning.

He pulled on his own clothes (a snug black jacket, pants to
match, and a gray silk shirt and neckcloth), combed his fingers
through his hair, and stepped back into the gallery. Niki looked
him up and down, and nodded.

"Laura will be pleased," he said. "Not that she'll tell you
so, of course. Come on."

They left the *Gerfalcon* and walked down the docking tube to
the central rotary. Niki waved to a man sitting in the glass-
walled monitor room, who waved back.

"I think I'm nervous," Chrysander said.

"Don't be. For all that we dress for it, there's really not much
that's formal about Laura's dinner parties. Except the food, of
course."

But this had nothing to do with knowing which fork to use.
Especially since he knew which fork to use. It wasn't stage fright,
either, but the focused anxiety he felt in a fight. He breathed
deeper, stretched his spine a little.

Niki led the way down another tube to another hatch, a dark
blue one. He thumbed a black glass square on the door. "And
if she starts to claw you," Niki said, "I'll chase her off."

"Hah," said Chrysander, to hide his surprise. The hatch slid
open.

Laura Brass stood in the opening, queenly and tall. Her calf-
length tunic was some weightless fabric that answered every

movement and breath of air with an animallike stirring. Deep plum in shadow, it showed a tracery of golden peonies in light. She wore skin-fitted leggings underneath in the same plum color. Her hair was bound back from her forehead with an abstract twist of gold wire. She bowed, and the tunic whispered like an expectant audience.

"Be welcome in my home and keep its peace," said Laura Brass.

Niki bowed in answer, low and with the heels of both hands touched to the forehead. Chrysander recognized it for what it was just as Laura looked measuringly at him.

Chrysander, too, bent deeply at the waist and showed that he trusted his host enough to look away from her, and touched his hands to his forehead to show that he held no weapons. When he straightened up, he saw the quirk at the corner of Laura's mouth. He could feel an answering one on his own lips.

"You do me honor," Laura said to both of them, but her eyes remained longest on Chrysander.

"No more than your due," Niki said. It didn't sound like a ritual response.

Laura smiled then, and no longer seemed forbidding. "That's why I like to invite you to dinner."

"So you'll have someone to play up to you?"

"I *was* going to say, 'Because you're so flattering and courtly,' but I've changed my mind."

Laura led the way into *Mercy of the Goddess*, and Chrysander looked around him, amazed. Laura must have noticed; she said, "Oh, I don't run her like this. I only pull out the knickknacks when I'm in port."

It was a profound change from the spare and functional fittings of the *Gerfalcon*. The living area was one large, low-ceilinged central room, divided only by groups of furniture and by the hydroponics tubes. The latter ran everywhere, and flung up walls and curtains of foliage. The largest area was marked out by a figured carpet in pale colors. There were low ivory cushion-stools on it, arranged around a short-legged, honey-colored table with a brazier built in. Where the light came from, Chrysander couldn't be sure. But little copper pierced-work lamps hid under leaves and hung from branches, looking like lighted houses seen from far away.

Niki sank down onto a cushion, and Laura waved Chrysander

to another. He sat with his legs crossed. "It's beautiful," he said at last, since he felt the need to say something.

"The *Goddess* is a much bigger ship than the *Gerfalcon*," Niki said by way of explanation. "If I shared Laura's passion for stuff, I wouldn't have any mass allowance for cargo."

"*Stuff?*" Laura was returning from a nearby alcove, carrying a tray. "Just where do you want your soup, boy?"

"It's very nice stuff," Niki said hastily.

"Better," said Laura. She knelt beside the table, then set the tray down. Chrysander saw that the soup in the green glass bowls was undisturbed by Laura's motion. He wondered if he could have done as well.

"You eat the water lily first," Laura said.

And there was what appeared to be a miniature water lily blooming on the soup. Chrysander picked up his chopsticks, hesitated over the lily, and looked up. Niki was watching him, one eyebrow raised, grinning. Chrysander ate the lily. It was some fragile, milk-white vegetable, cut to shape; it disappeared into sharp sweetness after a single crunch.

Niki gathered up the leaf that still floated on his soup with a quick twist of his chopsticks. "Did you have any trouble getting away?" he asked Laura.

"At FourCorners? No. They were worried about you. But Sabayan won't like knowing you have a war bird on your team."

"It's good for her. Especially since she's not going to see you again."

"We will not argue at the table," said Laura.

Niki grinned. "Nor anywhere else."

"We'll see about that."

"Good God," Chrysander interrupted, looking down into his soup. He dipped in with his chopsticks and brought out a fish. Like the water lily, it was carved from some vegetable, this one a golden yellow, and exquisitely detailed with fins, scales, and pouting fishy mouth. The whole thing was no longer than the first joint of his finger. "I can't eat this," he answered Laura's inquiring look. "It's too . . . I mean, I can't just *eat* it."

Laura looked pleased. "That's what it's for."

"But it's . . ."

"Thank you."

Chrysander sighed over the fish once more, and ate it. It had been marinated in something, and tasted wonderful. So did the rest of its companions in the bowl, all carved to represent a variety of sea dwellers.

There were filled, thin-skinned dumplings cooked over the brazier and served with a peppery sauce, and crisp, lacy-looking noodles in sesame paste. These were followed by scallops grilled with three kinds of subtly flavored peppers, and tender greens in a spicy dressing. Laura poured thin ceramic cups full of white wine, and kept them full.

Chrysander held up a scallop and turned to Laura. "I thought Niki said you're a vegetarian."

"Have you ever seen a live scallop?" she asked.

"No."

"Looks exactly like a dead one. It's hard to regret the passing of a mollusk."

"And people?"

"I never eat 'em. You don't know where they've been."

He smiled. "You know what I mean."

Laura shrugged. "Depends on the people. At least the clam doesn't ask for it."

"Laura," Niki said gently.

"I know, I know. Every man's death diminishes you."

"Well, it does."

"I bet you felt bad about that shit in the Bayonet, too."

"Yes, I did." Niki's smile was sad.

Chrysander remembered, with a stab of guilt, how Niki's face had looked that first time the control cell door had opened onto the dim galley. Why could he remember it so well now, yet not have noticed it then and behaved differently? Or had he noticed then, and not cared, because he thought he was looking at a useful tool, not a man?

"You're an idiot," Laura was saying sorrowfully to Niki. "And people like him"—she nodded at Chrysander—"and me have to look out for you."

"What do you mean, like me?" Chrysander said. Too quickly?

Laura Brass's gaze was measuring. "How many of yours have you regretted?"

"How many of my what?" he asked, feeling as if there was blood under his fingernails.

"Oh, yeah. I forgot," Laura said. "You're just a musician, aren't you?"

He glanced at Niki. Niki's eyes were on his food, but Chrysander could have sworn he was trying not to smile.

By dessert, he was almost comfortable again. He suspected that Laura had had a little too much wine. If he was lucky, she would have forgotten the conversation tomorrow. He hoped the wine had nothing to do with his own relaxation. Laura was telling pilot stories, and he was laughing.

Then, "What is it?" Laura said sharply to Niki.

Niki was sitting very still, his spoon halfway to the plate. After an instant, the blank look cleared from his face. The expression that replaced it disappeared almost immediately; Chrysander wasn't really sure he'd seen it. But for that moment, it had looked like fright.

"Niki?" said Laura.

Niki shook his head. "Sorry. I think I'm falling asleep on my feet."

Laura leaned back, and her eyes narrowed a little. "Anything I can do?"

"No, I'm fine. But I think I'll go back and sack out. As usual, dear heart, you're a terrific host."

She laughed, and rose from the cushions. "Sure you don't need me to carry you back?"

"Such cheek." He frowned. "What day is it?"

"Twenty-ninth of Wisdom."

Niki looked at the floor and smiled. "I'll be damned. I missed my anniversary."

"Oh," said Laura. She went to Niki and put her arms around him. "Happy belated anniversary," she said, but her voice cracked.

Niki laughed and kissed her. Laura was tall, but he still had to lean down. "Thank you. Now I hold the record."

"What about Caitlin Wyn?"

"She's in the deepfreeze. I think she's disqualified."

"Well, I guess you can make the rules."

"Exactly. Absolute power. Thank you again for dinner." He pointed at Chrysander. "Finish my almond curd," he ordered. "And whatever she tells you, don't believe it."

When the hatch had closed behind him, Laura leaned against it for a moment, her back to Chrysander.

Chrysander said, "What *about* Caitlin Wyn?"

Laura turned. "He told you not to believe anything I said." She seemed to be trying to read his face. Not knowing what she wanted to find, Chrysander put nothing there.

"Caitlin Wyn," Laura said at last, "was the next-to-last gestalt pilot. She's the only other one who isn't dead. She couldn't face the downhill slide, and had herself put in suspension. The fiction was that she could be revived if anyone ever found a 'cure.' ''

''The downhill slide?'' Chrysander repeated stupidly.

Her eyes widened, then narrowed. ''You don't know anything about gestalt pilots, do you?''

The temptation to reply rudely was almost irresistible. He only shrugged.

''The viable working life of a gestalt pilot, after conversion, is four and a half to five years. Then the lights go out. One way or another.''

''I don't understand.'' *And you're not trying to make it easy for me.*

She came and knelt on a cushion across from him, leaned her elbows on the table, and smiled. ''They die,'' she said.

Some appalling misunderstanding was at work. Surely. ''Of what?'' he asked, from a rusty throat.

''Of being what they are. The gestalt is the first man-made degenerative disease.''

He had drunk too much wine. He couldn't hide his reaction. His hands knotted around the thin porcelain cup, and Laura, with exaggerated solicitude and strong brown fingers, took it away from him. ''Who would do such a . . . And *why*?''

''Oh, if it had worked, it would have been profitable as hell. As it was, all the victims—pardon, *subjects*—earned out their indenture in less than two years. But the process was damned picky about who it worked on. And, ultimately, you don't get maximum profit margin out of five years of operation.''

''And the anniversary?'' But he thought he already knew.

''Yesterday was his fifth.''

''Longer than anyone else.'' Why couldn't he change the subject?

''The next longest stopped a week short. That was Martin Spinelle—Spin. He didn't mess around; he parked his bird, walked back of a maintenance shed, put a grenade in his mouth, and blew his head off.''

Chrysander stared. Laura refilled the wine cups, as if they were talking about—anything, except Niki Falcon. Her face was remote and calm as her goddess's.

''What happened to . . . the other pilots?''

''There were some accidents, stupid mistakes—that probably weren't mistakes at all. The rest of 'em committed suicide and didn't care who knew it.''

Chrysander stopped himself before he said, *Niki wouldn't do that.* "Why?" he said at last.

Laura folded her hands. "A lot of pain, in the later stages; the body requires so much of the drug that it's in withdrawal all the time. And because it cranks up the metabolism, the victim's undernourished—can't eat enough to make up for the calories burned. Something happens to the memory, too. I'm not sure what—it's not amnesia. Can you imagine having a mind like that, and knowing that it's breaking down?"

"No. I can't."

"He talks about it, sometimes . . ." Laura shrugged. "They made the gestalt pilots one by one," she continued. "Each time, they thought they could beat the time bomb. That this time, the conversion would be complete, and the subject would be stable over a normal lifetime. Niki was the twelfth."

The relentless irony in her voice made Chrysander want to flinch away. "They'd failed eleven times?"

"No, no, only seven. There were four of 'em still alive, who they only *thought* would die. But with Niki, they were sure they had it. His initial physical specs, apparently, were the closest to ideal of any pilot-candidate ever. Then his metabolism began to run hot." Laura played with her spoon.

"He told you all this?"

"Some of it. The rest is a matter of record, for anyone who gives enough of a damn to look." Her attention was still on the spoon, but her voice told him that she thought he ought to have given a damn.

Chrysander said softly, "You're very close to him."

Laura raised her head, and her face was fierce and proud. "The last time I had someone I called a friend, I was ten years old." Then she rose and took the dessert dishes to the galley. The plum-colored tunic sounded like wind through dead leaves.

"I'm sorry," Chrysander said to her back, and inlaid his voice with all the charm he had, the little bit of *her* that he knew. She looked over her shoulder at him. "I shouldn't have pried. But it upsets me, too."

A smile played around her lips. He wasn't sure if it was the feral one, or something safer. "Nothing you did—as far as I know, anyway."

Feral and friendly both. That seemed to be the essence of Laura Brass. "You can sit down again. It's safe."

She threw back her head and laughed. "Is it, now? For both of us? Well, let's move to someplace comfortable. Coffee?"

He shook his head. Laura led the way through the greenery to a smaller alcove. All the colors here were green—the deep carpet, the low couch and strewn cushions. The air carried the smoky sweetness of incense.

Laura dropped onto the couch and stretched out, which left Chrysander to sit among the cushions at her feet. She produced a tortoise-shell box from somewhere (he should have been able to notice where), took out a thin brown cigarette. "Want one?"

"No, thank you."

"They're bad for your wind." She cracked the igniter, and smoke and spices joined the incense. Then she fixed him with a cat-look. "Which is very important for a *musician*."

He returned the look. "Yes. It is."

"So," she said, and stretched, and breathed smoke out. "As I was saying, Niki is my friend. I care about him. I would also follow him into hell." She turned her head and held him with her eyes, wide and black in a dangerous face. "So when you lead him into hell, remember that. I'll be right behind you."

"What makes you think I'm leading him anywhere near hell?" Chrysander asked, lips stiff with lying.

"I'll start with the little gunfight above FourCorners. And backtrack to whatever trouble he might have had getting you out of your soirée."

She didn't mention the business in the tunnels of the magtube station. Perhaps Niki hadn't connected it for her. But Chrysander thought of it. She was right, about everything. And if she wanted, she could ruin his plan as thoroughly as Jhari Sabayan and a hundred Concorde gunships could.

"You don't just need the ride," she went on after another pull on the cigarette. "There's a bad smell following you around. Why should a musician want something as dangerous as breaking Silence?"

"If I'm dangerous, surely it's his problem?"

She showed her teeth. "But I'll make it mine. Bring him out of it alive, Golden Boy. Or I'll show you the error of your ways."

They stared at each other for what seemed a long time. She was half reclining on the couch, as beautiful and dangerous as a panther on a tree limb. With an effort, Chrysander reminded himself to look harmless.

He laughed a little, weakly, and raked both hands through his hair. "I suppose I can't refuse to look after him. I mean, if he dies, I'm in trouble, aren't I?"

Laura's chin came up. "Self-interest," she said coldly. She ground her cigarette out in an enameled brass dish on the floor. "The great motivator. Why didn't I think of that?"

"I'm sorry," Chrysander said. "I didn't mean it the way it sounded."

After a moment, he felt her hand on his, where it lay on the cushions. Her index finger traced over the knuckles and tendons. He let her lift it, turn it over; she probed his palm, and he knew she was feeling the hard muscles beneath the skin.

"Musician's hands?" Her words were mocking.

"Yes." There was a tightness in his chest and gut that kept him from saying any more, and he kept his eyes on her hands.

"Strong?"

I'm in trouble. He closed his fingers around hers and tightened his grip. "Yes." Their eyes met.

She smiled and fired a knuckle strike at his throat. The blow grazed his ear painfully—then he realized that his forearm hurt, too, and knew that she'd missed because he'd blocked her.

"Uh-huh," she murmured. "I suppose you learned that playing the flute." He didn't answer.

She slid off the couch and onto the cushions next to him, smooth as an animal. "When I was fifteen, I got drafted," she said, as if changing the subject. "I spent three years as a grunt on Anvil. After a few months, I learned to recognize a civilian. And you aren't one." She absently rubbed her free wrist against her side. Ah, of course—his block.

"I'm sorry if I hurt you," he said.

Laura looked into his face. "Oh, if you hurt me, I'll let you know."

An almost-shiver ran through him, like a jolt of current. Her left hand lay on the carpet next to his; he lifted it, stroked her fingers with his thumb. It occurred to him, hazily, that it could be a dangerous thing to do. But he did it anyway.

Her eyes widened, and she turned her head aside. "I think I've had too much wine."

"So have I," said Chrysander. The light caught in all the copper flecks in her hair, and reflected off her skin as off polished dark wood. He lifted her hand and kissed the palm, lightly but slow. He could think of ways she could cripple him, from where she was, in seconds, and wondered if she knew them, too. When he raised his head, her hand followed, fingertips to his chin, his mouth, then the length of it curved around his cheek and jaw. Laura's lips parted, as if she might speak, and her eyes were in shadow. He leaned forward and met her mouth with his.

Chrysander felt a building tension so strong it was almost sickness. Her hands were tangled in his hair, as if she were prepared, but unwilling, to pull him away. Beneath his hands she was lean and hard, warm and smooth.

Then her grip tightened in his hair, and she drew his head back, his lips away from hers. And held it there. He could see only the light-washed ceiling; if he'd needed to, he couldn't have swallowed. With her breath warm on his throat, he felt a surge of fear. He curled his hands lightly around her rib cage just under her breasts and pressed his thumbs between them, against the fragile projection of cartilage at the end of the breastbone.

She laughed, and her lips closed warm and moist on his throat. Air hissed past his teeth. She kissed her way from his jaw to his collar, then freed a hand from his hair and pushed back his jacket, pulled his neckcloth open. He shivered.

"Cold?" she whispered.

His mouth formed "no," but made no sound.

As her hand opened his shirt, her mouth followed it down his chest. When she released her grip on his head, he pressed his face into the dark cloud of her hair.

Her hands slid over the hard muscles of his abdomen, and she looked up, smiling wickedly. "And these?"

Chrysander knew what she meant. "All the diaphragm exercise."

"Liar," and she lowered her head and nipped him on the stomach.

He hissed and grabbed her face in both hands. "Gently," he breathed.

"Then be good."

His heartbeat seemed to have taken him over. "I will be," he said. He closed his hands over her shoulders and pressed her backward, until she lay against the cushions and he loomed over her.

She smiled. "Just remember. If anything happens to Niki Falcon, I'll kill you."

She could, too. He sank down into her arms.

Dominic Emrys Ieuan Glyndwr, Viscount Harlech, Prince of Cymru in exile. Of course he told me. As he said when he did it, I would only dig it up eventually, somewhere else. "Dig it up" are my words, not his. I'm as tenacious as a scent hound, galloping after my chosen spoor, clawing at the moldering earth until I bring something ripe to light. I'm one of the best hounds Central Worlds Concorde ever had on a leash, and if I'd gotten a whiff of mystery in my nose, I would have pursued him like the red-eared dogs of his own mythology.

He robbed you of that himself, Unauthorized Reader. He knew us both too well to leave such a fascinating trail. When he gave me his name and his past, like a handful of dandelions, he made me believe that they were no more valuable than that.

Damn it. No, I don't think that. Or only part of me thinks that, the weasel part that *they* nurtured, *they they they*. The rest of me knows that Niki Falcon gave his past to me because he wanted me to have it. And what that says about what Niki Falcon thought of me, I can't write down or say. The weasel part won't believe it, and the other part recognizes that if it's true, I'm a worse betrayer than even the weasel can manage.

The walls they made in me are broken, if only in this one place. The things behind them are pale and twisted from the dark and the confinement, like dandelions caught under fallen debris.

I thought I could tell this neatly, in order. It can't be done. Not by me.

Do you think it's contemptible that I fell in love in a week? I thought so, sometimes, especially in the hardening months of Basic, after I left him. I called myself pitiful—this is how they cut us off even from our own pasts. Later I was only embarrassed, thinking, "How silly, how childish, how little you knew about adult relationships." That last is perfectly true. I'd never been in love—I'd never had affection, in fact, that wasn't diligently earned, carefully measured and doled out. I'd lived surrounded by other "young men and women" (God forbid we should be called "children") who'd received about the same. And they, too, were busy earning their handfuls of affection, with test scores, with athletic records, with all the measurables that came in reach. We were all too busy shouldering each other aside to seek comfort from one another.

Then Niki landed on the bare branch of my spirit and made the whole spindly tree shake. Magical birds that speak with the voices of men, and bring messages from far kingdoms: most mythologies have them. But I had no mythology at all—and no, no experience of love. What could I do, in the face of someone who dealt in unmeasurables, who refused all tests in bursts of laughter, who competed as water competes: by parting, going around, sliding over?

I couldn't compete with him, anyway. I had none of the prerequisites for gestalt piloting, and if I had, I still wouldn't have matched his uncanny sensitivity to space, to movement, to time. He could glance at a moving target, look away, and still hit it, dead-on, several seconds later. If he had to dodge something, he never dodged farther than necessary. Do you know that trick you can play on someone, when you come up behind them on their left and tap their right shoulder, so that they'll look behind them on their right and not see you? Niki always looked to the side you were standing on. *Always.*

Spin almost hated him sometimes. Spin understood competition the way I did, and once Niki was fully fledged, he confounded his peers (and Dr. Ms. Harisal, for that matter) with that talent for knowing where things were, and had been, and would be. But Spin, too, loved Niki in his way, a way that makes me think the rock loves the river that flows around it.

I'm avoiding my subject. Mine, not yours, Unauthorized Reader, and screw you, anyway.

I fell in love with Niki Falcon because he gave me affection like the sun gave me light. He didn't even wait to see if I accepted it. That shocked and frightened me: such wasteful use of such a limited resource! I learned better. Once I did, I should have gone on, grown up, loved again deeper and better for having learned my lesson. Right? Well, I did. But I no more outgrew Niki Falcon than I could outfly him.

First year officer training is spent in learning to follow orders and observe regulations, and in convincing your superiors that you have the potential for anything more. To that end, you take tests. I was starting my second year, and had been eight months in Niki's company, when the results came back.

Out of a class of 526, only seven had the qualifications, and I was one of them. I was invited to apply for Entry Training for the elite. For Special Services.

I was ecstatic. I was drunk with it. I still was when I told Niki. And he heard me with the same face he'd worn in the commissary the morning after his conversion, the face of a man who'd had too many nightmares. He asked my pardon, very polite and quiet, and left the room for maybe half an hour.

I was surprised; I was miserable, my happiness blighted; and then, of course, I was angry. How dare he do this—cut through my joy as if through the stem of a plant? Was he jealous that now I, too, would be part of an exclusive company?

There—that's what I'm ashamed of. Not of falling in love with Niki Falcon on a week's acquaintance, but of believing, after eight months' acquaintance, that he could think that way.

Basic was the ruin of us. He knew it would be, but he fought against it harder than I did. Every time the training stripped away a chunk of my past, a belief we shared, a soft piece of my humanity, he would appear at the end of the day and hand it back, keep handing it back until I took it. Love weakened and frayed under such treatment. Or some part of love did, some smaller, comfortable part. But it was my spirit that was under siege, and to preserve me, Niki sacrificed comfort. I couldn't.

Basic won me away because it was just like my childhood: accomplishment brought acceptance.

I know why I got the assignment to keep the pressure on Chrysander Harris. I've been SpecServe for too many years to be ignorant of how it works. Though I was never told it (naturally not; I said I know how SpecServe works), someone, my superiors or someone over them, suspected that this job might ultimately lead to Niki Falcon. And I know more about him than almost anyone alive. Knowledge, to SpecServe, is a cold thing, a tool, an instrument of power. They think it's synonymous with "information." If they were right, I would be the perfect person for this assignment. But maybe there's something in Niki Falcon that changes the nature of information.

No, I didn't dig up every buried fact about him, not the way I might have. But I set my hound nose to his backtrail once, and lied to myself about it—it was cathartic, I'd transform him into just another case, I'd find out things that would embarrass him if he knew I had them.

As backtrails go, it's hellish, crossed and recrossed, broken by water and air and vacuum, obscured by the darkness of illegality and the sheer meanness of many of the events. If it is mysterious, it's not an inviting sort of mystery. But I learned some things—acquired some information, if you will. I'll give you a little of it here, because it applies to the matter at hand, after the oblique fashion of fables. The rest can die with me, made insignificant and irretrievable with one stroke.

He was first reborn after the figurative death of Dominic Glyndwr, and that incarnation was street smoke on the Underside of sweet and glittering Emerald City. Maybe that one died, too, and the next incarnation; or maybe he changed his name every time someone asked him what it was. But some five years after Dominic Glyndwr, there was a young and clever man named Giovanni della Rosa. He gained the trust and confidence of many powerful people—none of whom knew he had any connection to all the others. He learned where their money came from (which called for trust, indeed, since all of it was ill-gotten), and where it went. When he'd learned enough, he sat down in front of a 'board in a tiny room in back of a storefront produce wholesaler and went to work.

For twenty minutes, Giovanni della Rosa was the richest living thing in Hejira sector. At the end of that twenty minutes, the wealth had been dispersed, almost untraceably: disease control centers, schools, small businesses, and God-only-knows were suddenly neatly in the black.

Several hours later, employees of the former owners of all that wealth found Giovanni della Rosa in that little back room. He'd hidden the trail of the money, but had left his own trail untouched. He'd remained at the spot where it led, when he could have disappeared into dark places or bright ones as quickly and easily as he'd made the money disappear. So the employees found the little room, and took the only valuable thing they could find in it as recompense.

That's the story that comes to light when a good hound sets to digging. But I'm more than good. I found the hospital where a nameless young man was dragged from the edge of death, all the holes where life had run out of him filled in and smoothed over; where like archaeologists the medtechs reconstructed his looks from what remained of them. It all cost a great deal. But then, rebirth ought to.

This time, it won't be the death of records and identity. It will be the death of the body. Enough rebirth. The lessons are learned, the lives are changed out of all recognition, in a path as long and wide as a field of stars. Let it be Nirvana at last. If there are any more debts, the souls that remain will pay them. I'm volunteering mine.

CHAPTER TWELVE

It must be that the terror in their eyes
Is memory or foreknowledge of the hour
When all is fed with light and heaven is bare.
—W. B. Yeats, "The Phases of the Moon"

Niki leaned against the closed hatch of the *Mercy of the Goddess* and wished he had some night air to breathe. This time he'd been awake—no chance to brush off what had happened as a vivid dream.

He had remembered Morwenna, eighteen years ago, on the sand below the beach house. She wore loose white trousers and a gray blouse, and her black hair was short and tangled. They had been playing keep-away with a remotefloat; Niki had won seven bouts out of ten, and they were both laughing and breathless.

"Look!" she'd cried.

Four gulls sailed up from the sea in perfect formation, a white chevron row against the glowing blue of the sky. They reminded him of the pattern of the quilt on his bed. He smiled at Morwenna, and knew that she, too, had thought of the quilt. He felt suddenly happy and secure in a way that threatened to overflow him.

Then he was sitting at Laura's table, his spoon in midair, wrenched out of time, sick with sudden knowledge.

The memory playback had started.

Laura had reminded him of Caitlin, not knowing how cruelly appropriate that was. It was Caitlin who'd asked him to meet her at The Three Laws, who'd walked up with that look of blank terror and despair and said, "It's started—"

No. He was afraid to think about anything in the past, to try to remember in detail, for fear his memories would take him over. Caitlin's had. She'd told him that her brain skipped wildly from past to present, as if her brain was a vid deck always slipping out of record and into playback. No mental discipline would stave it off entirely; no effort of concentration would hold, would last.

When he'd dreamed of the red-haired woman and of Jhari, they hadn't been dreams at all. They had been memory replayed, perfect and entire, by an electrochemical command he hadn't given. With a little caution, perhaps he could stave off the worst of it for a while. He had to. If it happened in the middle of the Cheat, it would probably be the end of him, and the end of Chrysander, as well.

Maybe I should tell him to find himself a new chauffeur.

He set off down the tubeway to the rotary. It was curiosity that urged him to continue on with Chrysander, he told himself. Lamia was under Silence, and the Concorde was in hot pursuit of its most illustrious son. The reason for the latter seemed straightforward enough; but Niki had a profound distrust of coincidence. As for Chrysander's desire to break the Silence—there was no reason for that at all. He'd seen Chrysander dispatch several people with quite unmusicianly efficiency, and had appreciated Laura's less-than-subtle hints over dinner, even while he'd been amused at Chrysander's reaction to them. No, clearly there was rather more to Chrysander's story than had yet surfaced.

He was all the way to the rotary before he admitted, *And I'm getting to like the supercilious little maniac.*

When he reached the rotary, Niki drummed his fingers on the glass door of the dock control booth. The big man inside nodded and jabbed a switch on the panel before him, and the door parted in the middle.

"Older but wiser yet?" the man at the panel said gruffly as Niki stepped in.

"No, Uri," Niki grinned. "Give up on me?"

"Nah, not yet. Bastards might unplug you. Then I'll give up."

"Retirement holds no terrors for me." Niki dropped into the other chair.

"Somebody tried to pension you off early, from the looks of your repair order."

"Just offered me some vacation time. And you're a nosy old coot."

Uri wasn't finished. "From listening at the cosmic keyhole, I understand the Concorde wants a word with you."

Niki raised his eyebrows. "Heavens, I'm a celebrity."

Uri scratched his temples, where the hair was sand-white. A display changed and rotated, showed a maintenance creeper on the outside surface of the el. A row of colored dots flashed at the bottom of the display. Uri slid his thumb across a section of touchpad, a smooth, thoughtless gesture. The dots went out. "Not the kind of trouble you usually go in for," he said finally. "I thought you and the Concorde had yourselves a polite divorce."

"True. Maybe it's the drug. D'you suppose it's given me a split personality?"

"Kolya, I'll give you a split lip if you don't put some corners on it."

Niki studied the hunch of Uri's wide back over the status lights and monitors. He said quietly, "Then maybe we shouldn't talk about me."

Uri spun in his chair and slammed one great fist on the console. Niki jumped.

"You goddamn stupid sonofabitch!" Uri roared, his flat features red with it. "You trying to get snuffed? Is that it? You figure you'll go out like Spin and Fe-Seung and Brady and WhatsHergoddamnName? When did you start doing that kind of thinking?"

"Newis," Niki said quietly.

"What?"

"That was WhatsHergoddamnName. Linni Newis."

Uri grunted and turned back to the board, where he did angry things with the touchpads. After a moment he said, "Newis was a friend of yours."

"Yeah. And Spin. Brady and Fe-Seung were before my time."

"They weren't bad."

"Not bad? Fe-Seung did the Grand End-to-End in two bounces."

"That's bullshit. He never did that."

"He didn't? Uri, we're talking one of the great foundations of the gestalting mythos here."

Uri shrugged. With shoulders the size of Uri's, it became a sweeping gesture. "Bullshit. Might have shifted up his cargo. He liked the credit vouchers too much for that."

Niki grinned. "You've shattered my youthful illusions."

Uri sounded the snort that passed, with him, for laughter. "Yeah." But the laughter didn't last. "Is that why? Is it getting you, being the last?"

"Uri, I've been the last for a while now."

"Then why? I've known you for what, three, four goddamn years? I don't know if you ever did anything before that got you shot at, but I'm pretty sure I never heard of you getting hit."

"I'm carrying some . . . *contested* cargo. But I won't claim I didn't know the job was dangerous."

Uri swung his chair round again, and glowered at Niki from under his eyebrows. "Was that your cargo walked up the tubeway with you? That looked a whole damn lot like Chrysander Harris?"

Niki folded his hands over his knees. "You saw someone with me? Hmm. I don't remember."

"Kolya . . ." But Uri stopped there, and turned away to answer a light on his monitor. He shook his head as he did it. "Well, whatever you want to do with it, I guess it's yours, eh?"

"Whether I want it or not. No, Uri," he said, to answer a sideways look, "that was a joke. So get back to work—I have to go check my mail." He opened the door.

"Hey."

"Mmm?"

"Be careful, shithead."

"Sweet-talkin' guy," Niki said, and shut the door behind him.

Laura's dinner was fast turning into lead in his stomach. He should have known that the Concorde would issue a pickup order for him. Part of the consequences of taking Chrysander Harris off FourCorners. But he couldn't shake the feeling that something was closing on him, like a hand curling into a fist.

He came out into the borderlands, neither docks nor town, in the half light that passed for nighttime in an el station. The architecture here might best be described as Salvage Revival; it lacked the wit and effort of the buildings in town. Tonight, it was the perfect setting for his mood. One block in, he found what he wanted: a sign above a door that read, "Private Accesses—Secure." The last half of the sign flickered with a weak and irregular pulse. He went in.

The front room was small—there was just room for the counter and its console, three metal-and-hard-plastic chairs, and the space to walk between them to the back room. It was also badly lit and needed paint. The woman behind the counter was slow to look up, and when she did, Niki decided that she was probably more girl than woman. Her makeup was thick and a little unsteady. "Yeah?" she said.

"Terminal open?" said Niki.

"This hour? Yeah." She stood up and crossed to him as if she were trying to make time pass. "Gimme your plate."

"No plate," Niki said. "Cash."

She scowled and screwed up her lips. "Y'pay in advance then, five hours."

"My child," Niki said, smiling, "I could have the Worlds University library downloaded in ten. And so could you. One."

She looked him up and down, made a spitting noise, then held out her hand. He dropped the money into it. "Number Two," she said. When he'd passed through the connecting door, she added, "Pisser." He tried not to laugh.

The first terminal was down, but the other two, old ones with plasma displays, were warm. He took Number Three and tickled in his code. If she was monitoring from the front room, it would have taken her that long to realize he'd used the other machine, and she would have missed his access string.

The wait was just long enough to make him nervous. Then words faded into view:

YOU ARE TRESPASSING IN A
HUB ADMINISTRATIVE AREA

and:

SECURITY PROTOCOLS ACTIVATED
YOU HAVE THIRTY SECONDS TO LOG OFF

"Yes, yes," Niki muttered, "take your bloody time about it."

Finally the screen cleared, and filled up again with:

```
******WELCOME TO CIGFRAN
ANY NEUTRAL INPUT FOR GUIDE
      OR GIVE COMMAND NOW
```

And at the bottom of the display,

```
                              YOU HAVE MAIL
```

So he called it up. There was the repair bill for the work he'd just had done on the *Gerfalcon*, three articles, which he shunted off to a buffer on the *Gerfalcon* for later reading, and—

No salutation or sender's ID, only the time and date.

HIS NAME WAS L'CHAI HOTAKH. HE WAS 19 YEARS OLD. THOUGHT YOU'D WANT TO KNOW—OR MAYBE YOU DON'T, ANYMORE. I HAVE TO TAKE THE NEWS TO HIS PARENTS. HARDEST PART WILL BE EXPLAINING WHY THERE'S NO BODY.

YOU WERE A HERO OF HIS.

Bitch, he thought fiercely, wildly. *Jhari, you steel-plated bitch.* It folded him up over the touchpad, and hurt in his gut like drug withdrawal. Now the pilot in the sky over FourCorners had a name and age, and parents. He dropped his head forward, and his forehead banged against the screen. He let it rest there. She knew where his heart was, because he'd shared it with her. This was why he'd stepped wide around her for the past few years, because she could do this to him. But he hadn't really thought she would.

Or perhaps she was genuinely horrified, as he had been, that he had killed a man who wouldn't have killed him.

He was crying, he realized: for the dead man, for himself, and for no damn good reason that he could see.

The glass is cool and hard against his forehead. Beyond it, below him, the landing flats are floodlit, and ground crews and vehicles crisscross the tarmalon like panicky fleas on gray satin.

"What?" he says, and wonders why there doesn't seem to be any air in his lungs.

"I said, Linni's dead. What, are you fucking deaf?"

"Spin, shut your head." This in a woman's voice (Caitlin's?). *"He hears. Nik, I'm sorry. She screwed up, came out of the Cheat too close in. She popped the drive trying to correct."*

Was she in atmosphere? Did she burn? She hated fires. No, if she'd been that close, the paradox effect from the Cheat would have turned the whole field into landfill. "No," he says. *No, what? What is he talking about? Does he think they're lying to him?*

Someone touches his arm. He shrugs away. "Fuck you, then," Spin says.

The tarmalon is probably cooler and, from 'way up here, harder than the window glass. He presses both hands against the pane, then pulls them back and drives his fists into the glass with all his strength. The noise is like thunder and lightning. He does it again.

Someone grabs his arms above the elbows, and he arches away, trying to break free; the grip holds. He throws himself backward and the grip is gone. He whirls and strikes at those who surround him. His wrists are caught. A blow lands hard across his jaw, and he's falling, falling, but not far enough.

The blue friction flooring is under his nose. Spin's arm circles his chest and pulls him gently upright, holds him there. Caitlin crouches and touches his face, looking for damage.

"I'm sorry, Nik," Spin says softly, "I'm sorry."

The transit from memory to now was sudden and vertiginous. Niki clutched the table. *Linni's dead,* he told himself, *long dead, never mind that it just happened all over again. Breathe deep.*

The cursor's blinking seemed to chide him, to draw his eyes to the monitor and say Read This Again. He cleared the display instead.

He couldn't blame Jhari for sending the message. Oh, of course he did; bitterly, and with a feeling of betrayal as strong as it was stupid. She was doing her job. She was not the person he'd loved—would love, if only she still existed. She was Concorde Special Services, and they'd honed and hardened her until she played to win and had no thought of ex-loves. No, he couldn't blame Jhari.

But he'd be damned if he'd let her get clean away with it.

He cleared his mail buffer, and addressed a message to her.

CWNET2524//T8IO
SABAYAN//MoX1E

"Um . . . is there a story behind that ID number?"
She laughs, with her head tossed back and the laugh lines . . .
Stop it.

TOO BAD ABOUT YOUR WING-BOY, DEAR. TOO BAD
ABOUT MY CARGO, TOO—TOTAL LOSS IN THE AIRSTRIKE.
REMAINS ARE NO USE TO ME. YOU?

She'll tear her hair. Not that Jhari would quite believe it. But
she'd have to check it out, which would be hard, and report it
to her superiors as an unsubstantiated rumor, which would be
harder. And if there was any mercy in the universe, it might
slow her down.

Niki shut down the terminal with thirty minutes elapsed. He
felt a creeping sensation of time running out. He wanted to be
back in the *Gerfalcon*, to drug up, to get done with all this.

And then he remembered that he would never be done with
all this. He would deliver Chrysander Harris to Lamia. If he was
supernaturally lucky, he might get off the planet. Then he could
start dodging the Concorde, which would pursue him the rest of
his life. That wouldn't be long, admittedly, but it was all the
time he had. Perhaps his predecessors had had the right idea.

He got up, feeling shaky and scared, and pushed through the
door into the front room.

"No farther," said a man's voice. Its owner stood with shoulders propped against the closed front door. He had brown hair
cut short and at an angle, light-colored eyes, and a Sabre cutter
gun in his left hand which hummed at Niki with gentle insistence.

"Is this a stickup?" said Niki, trying not to sound as if his
mouth was dry.

"No. Sherry, you recognize him?" the man asked the girl at
the desk. The pale eyes never left Niki's.

"I don't know." There was an edge of fear in her voice. "I
missed his incode, so I couldn't—"

Did one thing right, Niki thought, while the man said, not
unkindly, "Shut up." Then to Niki, "Who are you?"

"Dominique Corbeau."

"Touch it in," said the man.

Niki could see the girl at the corner of his vision, curled over the touchpad. "Just regular stuff, Trace," she said at last. "He's not anybody."

Very true. Dominique Corbeau was the electronic outline of a person, a long-ago present from a friend. Niki had supplied the name himself. He'd never expected to use him for anything but an in-joke, and here he was in his second incarnation already.

Trace looked him over, and Niki, less obviously, did the same to him. Though he was tall, Niki was a head taller; but the snug, flexible coverall and vest the man wore made a discreet show of the power in his arms, chest, and legs.

Then, of course, there was the cutter gun.

"Turn around," said Trace. Niki raised his eyebrows. "Do it. Face the wall." Niki did. "Arms up, hands on the wall." Trace searched him one-handed. The hum of the cutter, so close, seemed to vibrate in Niki's blood.

And suddenly the searching hand raised the hair off Niki's collar and exposed the socket.

"Okay," Trace said. "Turn around. Sherry. Get into the L.E. 'base. Now put this in as I give it to you." Niki turned as Trace rattled out a series of characters.

A pause, then Sherry said, "Holy shit."

Niki cast a slanting look at her screen. The graphic was of his face. It rotated, and the photographic representation became a drawing of the back of his head, with the socket highlighted.

"Trace, I don't know what th—"

"Read the caption to me."

She did. It was harder to understand out loud, but Niki could imagine how it looked on the display. "Falcon. Niki, Nik. H-2.03 m. W-77.1k. Complec: 2g, hr. black, e. gray. No facial marks. Gestalt socket, back of head, base of skull. Arm: unkn. Bounty class: A.10."

Trace smiled and nodded at Niki. "Now, you see, you are somebody. Like magic, how that works. And you're a new listing."

Niki swallowed. "A new listing."

"A new bounty listing is top money—no creds paid out as reward for information, and whoever wants you still has that nice hungry edge on. Now you, Falcon, you're an A.10. That means I have a choice. I can bring you in warm or cold. I'd rather it was warm, but I don't lose money if it's not. Sav?"

It was not just a pickup order. It was a bounty. *By love and by honor, Jhari, you didn't ask for me dead or alive?* But she had warned him, back on FourCorners. . . .

"So, you see, if you behave yourself, you get to live," Trace said.

Niki had never heard of a bounty hunter who, when given the option of bringing in his quarry peaceably dead with no penalty, would turn it down. He didn't think he'd just met one, either. That Trace preferred not to kill him in quite such cold blood as this—that he could believe. Once out on the dark street, and especially if he tried to bolt . . .

"How did you happen to find me?" asked Niki. It was hard to study the room, plan any motion, with Trace watching him so fixedly.

"This is a quiet little place. I like to cross-check the new listings with the docking bay registers. Then I'll keep an eye out, around the dock access. See if anybody's visiting that I recognize."

"Ah." He probably should have expected that, too. "Well, I'll try not to be any trouble."

"Good for you. Let's take a walk."

Niki turned toward the door, laid his hands on the back of the nearest chair, and triggered the drug.

It wasn't really that everything around him seemed to slow. Trace's expression changed in normal time; but Niki's mind and body had left time behind. So when the chair slammed into Trace's midsection, he still wore the broad smile with which he'd said, "Let's take a walk." The cutter gun scored a smoking track in the ceiling as it flew. Sherry screamed, and Niki had to hear it for an inordinately long time.

Niki lunged toward the door, but a hand came out of the confusion of Trace and chair (Trace had been still for so *perceived* long that Niki had thought he was unconscious) and caught his ankle. Niki went down hard, his vision shorting for a second in a shower of sparks. Trace was on top of him before it cleared. His hands closed on Niki's throat, lifted, slammed his head against the floor again. The drug quit. More sparks. Then through the blurring that followed, Niki saw Trace pull his fist back. He snapped his head aside, and Trace's fist hit the floor.

Niki rolled away and to his feet, and kicked Trace in the kidneys. Then he grabbed the chair and swung it down on his head.

The drug was shut down, but adrenaline had taken its place.

His own ragged breathing was the only sound in the room. He gathered up the cutter gun and staggered upright.

Sherry's eyes and mouth were enormous. He pinned her to the wall by her throat, where she went limp as old cloth.

"If your God-damned boyfriend ever comes to—" He had to stop for breath. His voice was rough, and it hurt to talk. And his teeth wouldn't unclench.

"Don'thurtmepleasedon'thurt—"

"Quiet," he said, and shook her. "If he comes to, you tell him . . ." There wasn't anything to tell him. The girl was white under her paint, tears trailing down. He felt sick, and it wasn't from the drug or the adrenaline.

"I'll tell him anything you want, please, don't hurt me—" She was talking almost as fast as he would under the drug. He let go of her, and she slid down the wall into a heap on the floor, sobbing and begging.

He stumbled out the door, into the dark street. After a few blocks he noticed he was holding the cutter, and dropped it.

When the *Gerfalcon*'s hatch chime sounded, many hours later, Niki was sitting in the darkened galley, watching the reflection of the digital clock in the surface of a very cold cup of coffee. "It's open," he said, which was the voice code for the lock. The hatch slid.

"Hello?" said the beautiful voice.

"Galley."

He was only a dark shape in darkness. Niki watched him come in, sit down.

"I could have been anybody," Chrysander said at last.

"No. I programmed the door. It wouldn't have rung for anyone else."

"Not even Laura Brass?"

"If I had thought I could get away with it," Niki answered, "it wouldn't even have rung for you." Niki lifted the cup, sipped, and was reminded, as he'd been repeatedly for an hour, that the coffee was cold. He set the cup back down.

There was another, longer, silence. Niki noticed that the irises of Chrysander's eyes were faintly luminous, thin gold rings now in the dark. "Is . . . there something wrong?" Chrysander said.

Niki thought about that, then said, "I think so."

"Is it something I need to know about?"

The phrasing and tone were so careful, so gentle, that Niki's voice failed him for a moment. Then he remembered that that was Chrysander Harris's gift, the ability to drive a wedge of himself into someone else's psyche. It made it easier for Niki to hold himself together. "Did you tell anyone you were going to Lamia?"

"No."

"The Concorde—" (it wouldn't do to say *Jhari*, for fear it wouldn't come out in a decent fashion) "—has almost certainly figured it out by now. They'll be waiting for you. You should know that." Niki raised the cup again, but remembered this time before he sipped.

"There's something else, isn't there?" said Chrysander.

"I don't think . . . I think you shouldn't . . ." Niki licked his lips and started again. "I can't take you there."

After a moment, Chrysander got up and began to pace. Niki wished the lights were on, then was glad they weren't.

"Lost your nerve?" came the voice thick with its cruel magic, like a lash, like claws, and in the struggle to keep from clawing back, Niki flung the cup against a wall.

"Don't do that," he said softly, and this time Chrysander didn't ask him what he meant by "that."

Instead, Chrysander said, "I'm sorry."

"Would you go into a building if someone told you there was a bomb in it that might go off at any time?"

"If there was something inside that I had to have."

"Then you're an idiot. Once we leave here, you're in my hands. And I may well kill you long before the Concorde gets a chance."

"I don't understand."

"I'm deteriorating. I'm unsafe. The more pressure they put on us, the sooner I'll burn out." *There, and there, and now, God-damn you, leave.*

"Can I turn on some lights?" Chrysander said, his voice small.

"No."

"Cover your eyes." The light by the Galleymaster came up low, and Niki squinted. "I told you to cover your eyes," Chrysander said. He came back to the table and sat down. He looked elegantly disheveled, his golden hair rumpled, shirt unfastened at the neck. His black jacket was draped over the back of his chair. "You look terrible," he said.

Niki sighed and closed his eyes. "You know, that's the second time you've said that to me. These high standards of yours."

Chrysander didn't laugh. "I'll make some more coffee."

"You're avoiding the issue," Niki called after him, eyes still closed. He felt empty, boneless, as if he could pour like water out of the chair and onto the floor and be picked up only with a sponge.

Galleymaster noises. The click of cups on the table. Then Chrysander's hand on his shoulder, and his voice. "Hey, don't fall asleep there. Are you all right?"

Niki opened his eyes to find Chrysander frowning over him. He shivered, shook his head, and straightened up.

"Do you need . . . anything?"

A tab, he means, Niki realized. "No." He leaned both elbows on the table, held his head up with both hands, and inhaled coffee vapor in the hope that it would give him enough strength to lift the cup. "Now, tell me that you'll get out of here before I turn us into frozen hamburger somewhere out"—he gestured vaguely with his chin—"there."

Chrysander looked sadly at him across the table. "I won't. I'm sorry."

"Even if I say 'please'?"

"I have to do this. It's the only way. I'm sorry." He looked miserable.

Niki shrugged. "You're an idiot." The smell of coffee wasn't working. He let his head slide down to the tabletop.

"Probably," Chrysander said bitterly, somewhere above his head.

A blank period, length uncertain, followed. Niki was then aware, fuzzily, of being lifted and carried, lowered onto something that might have been his bunk. It crossed his mind to protest; he'd intended to sleep in the acceleration couch in the control cell. But the thought only crossed and wouldn't stay. He fell profoundly unconscious.

CHAPTER THIRTEEN

The innocent and the beautiful
Have no enemy but time;
Arise and bid me strike a match
And strike another till time catch;
Should the conflagration climb,
Run till all the sages know.
—W. B. Yeats, "In Memory of Eva
  Gore-Booth and Con Markiewicz"

It was snowing on Bellmaker's World, great weighted flakes
that fell like rain and cloaked civilization until it was unrecognizable. At least, Chrysander assumed they did; Niki assured
him that this was civilization. He hunched in his borrowed too-
long coat and shivered, and pulled the collar up high against the
wind and the whiteness. All his worldly goods—three changes
of clothes and the Entropic—felt heavy in the bag that hung from
his shoulder. The *Gerfalcon* was at the port, somewhere behind
them, all its shining surfaces safe inside a rented hangar. One
of the binary sapphires had paid for it. "I didn't mean them to
cover expenses, too," Chrysander had said. He had known, but
couldn't say aloud, that the stone bought the *Gerfalcon* safe har-
bor for the next three decades. *Providing for his loved ones,*
Chrysander thought, sickened by his own humor. *But how will
we leave here if we don't fly?*

He had no idea why they were there. Niki had said something
about a legacy, when he woke from that frightening, unbreakable
sleep. He'd looked drawn and exhausted, and Chrysander had
come nearer to losing his nerve than ever. He'd seen death hap-

pen between one breath and the next—he'd brought it that way, clean and fast and honorably. But to watch death accumulate with each inhalation—it was an abominable thing. *A man-made degenerative disease.* But nothing Chrysander did, or didn't, would save Niki Falcon's life.

"Here," Niki said. He stood tall and dark and straight in the street in front of Chrysander, studying the snow-caked front of a block of buildings. Chrysander squinted miserably through the snow and wondered if Niki was as comfortable as he seemed. Was he from a place this cold? Did his augmented metabolism make him feel warm here? Or had he slipped into that trancelike state that came on him now and then, when his voice and face seemed to be transmitted from another room?

"Yes, I know," Niki added patiently. "The sooner we do what we have to do, the sooner you'll be out of the weather." He guided Chrysander toward the buildings. It was probably not an accident that he blocked some of the wind, too.

The door hissed shut behind them and sealed out the weather, and the snow clotted on their coats began to melt and steam. Chrysander brushed water away from his eyes and found himself in a grocery store—groceries and other things. There was a desultory-looking rack of clothing in one corner, a few tools on one wall, some hover parts and less identifiable machined objects stacked on the floor, and a shelf unit of liquor flasks and beer bags. Everything seemed dusty, but it might have been the steam.

Niki stepped up to the cluttered counter (candy, smokes, a rack of old and overpriced music discs, a pile of dog-eared print-out), and Chrysander noticed that there was someone behind it. The man was probably not as old as he looked; the lines in his face were tired-old, angry-old, old with self-abuse.

"Asher Spinelle?" Niki said. He was polite, as always. But Chrysander missed anything else in his speech, either warmth or coolness. He was as impersonal as the voice of an oracle. Chrysander moved closer, checked, unobtrusively, his freedom of movement.

"Yeah."

"My name is Niki Falcon."

The not-old man looked up at that, a flying, venomous stare. "What do you want?"

"I've come for the legacy."

"I don't know what you're talking about."

"Yes, you do. Mr. Spinelle, it's not any good to you."

"It's no good to anybody. And I've had the expense of storing it. Did you think of that?" In spite of the venom in his look, his words were passionless. He might have rehearsed this conversation over and over, alone, until there was nothing left of it but sounds without meanings.

"Yes," Niki said. "I did think of it." His hand went out. A faint "tick" on the surface of the counter—when he pulled back, another of the golden binaries lay there, like a drop of heat from the sun. The man turned white.

"Blood money," he said, his lips barely moving.

"Not from me. You know that. May I have the instructions?"

The fight, the venom, the spirit, had drained out of the man behind the counter. He bent down as if it hurt him, stood again with a flat leather packet in his hand, and gave it to Niki.

"Thank you," Niki said. His voice warmed a little—with pity, Chrysander thought—and he added, "It's over now. You'll never see any of us again."

"I know," said the old man. And now he *was* old. More things than death could happen between one breath and the next. Chrysander wondered what had happened here, before his eyes.

They were back out in the snow before Chrysander was ready for it. He moaned when it slapped him in the eyes.

"Not much longer, honest. This way."

Chrysander hid his face in his collar and didn't look up again until he bumped into Niki, who was opening another door. This one let them into a great echoing space—a hangar again, he saw, but this time it must be attached to an airfield, not the spaceport. There were six hopcraft neatly ranked on the cement floor. Niki rented one. He was cheerful and pleasant, but Chrysander thought he was working at it.

In the cockpit, Niki opened the leather packet. Chrysander couldn't read the contents, not without craning his neck, but it was a handwritten sheet of paper. After his first look at it, Niki closed his eyes.

"Are you all right?" Chrysander asked.

"Yes," Niki replied, more breath than voice. He looked again at the sheet of paper, slid it back in the leather case, and taxied the hopcraft out into the snow.

They went straight up, nose first, quickly. Chrysander felt his heart pressure-weld itself to his lungs, and his lungs to the back of his rib cage. Then they broke the cloud layer. Niki half stood the hopper on its right wing and it turned like a hawk.

"Well," Chrysander said, when he could. They were level and fast above the clouds; he couldn't have said what compass point they were traveling toward. "Is this legacy perishable?"

"No, but we are."

"Mmm. Easily bruised, too, keep in mind. Should I ask what was going on back there in the store?"

There was no reason why Niki should keep his attention fixed forward, but he did. "I assume Laura filled you in on every grubby fact about gestalt pilots?" He said it as if the issue was distasteful.

"No. She told me what she thought I ought to know about you, to make sure I didn't get you killed. Give her credit for it."

"Did she mention Martin Spinelle?"

The conversation was distorted in his memory by wine; it came back to him in pieces floating to the surface. Then: *He parked his bird, put a grenade in his mouth, and blew his head off.* "Oh," Chrysander said. "I'm sorry."

"Why?"

"It's just . . . Never mind. Go on." So many apologies he needed to make. He remembered, regretfully, failing to offer one to Vere, back on FourCorners. What would she make of this vulnerable, uncertain, floundering Chrysander Harris? He could explain to her: it was like the action of the sea. The stone of him, his strength and certainties, his vanities, his insulation from the world, were being worn away by this contact with Niki Falcon. When this was done, would he be stone at all, or would he be something else? If he lived, of course. It would be amusing if he became the sort of person who didn't like Chrysander Harris's music.

"The man in the store was Spin's father," said Niki. "The legacy is from Spin."

They flew on in silence after that, and the thick cloud tops unrolled below. When they dropped through at last, the terrain beneath them was low hills, bleak and barren and eroded into sullen submission. It was a cold sort of place, but there was no snow. "What are we looking for?" Chrysander asked.

"Nothing. We've found it." With a gut-wrenching maneuver, Niki brought the hopper down. Just before they touched, Chrysander recognized a landing strip in the smoothed wide stretch

of brown grass before them. From above, it had seemed like
natural valley floor.

Chrysander cracked the hatch. It *was* cold, but the hills kept
the wind off. He swung down off the wing and waited for Niki
to leave the cockpit. There was nothing around them but the
hills, and dry brush, and a tiny metal outbuilding, buckling with
its own weight, rusted to the color of the earth around it. Several
of the roof seams had popped, and the sheet metal shrugged a
little in the wind. What had this been, here in the heart of nothing?

Niki finally slid out of the cockpit, and stood leaning against
a landing strut, his forehead pillowed on the back of one hand.

"What is it?"

"Nothing. Just a—" Then he raised his head, and smiled
wryly. "I ache, rather. It will go away." He picked up the bag
at his feet and walked toward the metal building.

Chrysander missed the meaning of it at first, because it was
said in a burst of that elusive accent, and because the words
were so ordinary. But Laura Brass had told him what he needed
to know. It was an ache; and it would go away, after enough
time, after it had gotten worse. Chrysander stood frozen by the
hopper. There was no action he could take, nothing he could
say, no notes that he could add or remove to make music out of
pointless chaos. He trudged after Niki Falcon.

Niki was rummaging in the dry brush that climbed one steep-
sided hill face, past the metal shed. "That's got it," he said.
"Help me with this thing, will you?"

The thing was a stainless-steel handle, sunk into the hillside
next to a lock plate. Chrysander pulled, Niki pushed, and what
had once been the side of a hill became folds of rigid plastic
that mimicked brush and red-brown dirt. It opened as smoothly
as if some ancient shaman had raised his arms and said the
words.

But it was not a tomb they had opened. The bunker was huge,
much too large to see all at once. It was more than half underground; a long ramp began at their feet and sank into the cavern.
Breaking the door seal had brought the lights to life. It was not
a tomb. Its contents were not dead, but sleeping.

The wings, folded, were longer than the *Gerfalcon*'s when
deployed. The surface was unmarked black that reflected no
light. On the nose, the wings, the tail, were the telltale ridges
of gun housings. It was as beautiful as the Angel of Death.

With a sudden stirring of horror, Chrysander looked back at the rusting metal shed. It was stove in on one side, as if, he had thought, crumbling with its own weight. But a controlled explosion could have done the same thing.

"Yes," Niki said behind him, with a crack in his voice, "that's the place." Chrysander turned and found he couldn't say anything. Niki continued, "It's hard enough to have your son commit suicide. But Spin said his good-byes out here. And not to his father." Niki rubbed his gloved hands over his face. "I'm going in. Will you come along?"

It sounded like a request for backup. "What do you expect to find?"

"Oh, no—nothing dangerous. Not from Spin. I just . . . well, if I fall over, someone ought to catch me, is all."

Chrysander still didn't understand. But he thought he should have, and there was something shameful in admitting otherwise. He shrugged and followed when Niki went down the ramp.

The black ship was so much larger than the *Gerfalcon* that he couldn't estimate it properly. Twice as large? More? Niki knew, perhaps, but Chrysander didn't ask. They stood outside the hatch, but Niki made no move to open it. A thing like this, so beautiful and powerful—if it fell into one's hands, it would be reasonable to gloat over it, even a little. But in Niki's face, there was only sadness, and resignation.

"Spin flew like a madman until he'd made enough to sell his ship out and have this one built," Niki said. It was the measured voice of someone talking into a recorder. "I don't know why he wanted a gunship. I don't know if the damned guns have ever been fired. But they'll work. Spin would have made sure of it."

"If it's been sitting for a while, it'll need a checkout. It'll take us days."

Niki shook his head and pointed. Chrysander saw what the ship had dwarfed: the supply, cleaning, and recycling lines and equipment. The black ship sat at the center of a web of them, and the web clicked and vibrated with power from heaven-knew-where, with the carrying-out of orders programmed—how many years ago? One pair of hands carefully, lovingly, fastening each connector. Calling up the diagnostic and the scheduler, making sure all was safe for the black bird's long sleep. The same hands, sealing the hill face shut. The hands that set the grenade. There was passion and care and commitment in this bunker. How terrible *was* the last stage of a gestalt pilot's disintegration, that passion and care and commitment couldn't outweigh it?

Niki laid his palm on the hatch plate. The hatch slid open in answer, silent and smooth. Nothing waited inside it but clean, polished surfaces. Niki stepped over the threshold.

It was an excellent artificial voice, even by Chrysander's standards. It was low-pitched and rough, and came from one wall at ear level. " 'Bout time, Nik," it said. And then, softer, "Thanks for coming." Then Chrysander heard a faint hiss, and silence.

Niki leaned against the wall, his face averted. Chrysander found himself disliking Martin Spinelle, which did not even compare to the pot calling the kettle black.

"He shouldn't have done that," Chrysander said after a moment.

"No, it was the right thing to do." Niki straightened up, wearing something that was almost a smile. "If he hadn't, I'd be waiting for it all the way to Lamia. Now it's over with."

"He might have left something else."

"Spin hated long good-byes. That's what the grenade was for."

Niki disconnected the black bird from its lifelines, brought it awake, taxied it up the ramp, and sent the hopper home on auto. Chrysander had nothing to do. He crouched in the brush on a hillside, his bag at his feet. He listened to the windbroken silence, and imagined it filled with an explosion, echoing off the hills, falling away into quiet again. Every death, he realized suddenly, must have its own sound. He couldn't remember hearing any of them; but this one, that he had never heard, wouldn't leave him alone. *Every man's death diminishes*—many things. All the neatly integrated parts of himself were undergoing continental drift.

The bird waited at the end of the valley runway. The bunker was sealed again, invisible. Chrysander mounted to the hatch, and was stopped in the opening by Niki's disembodied voice. "Breathe deep. This is your last free air before Lamia." Unspoken, but present, was the other half of the thought: that if Niki failed, they wouldn't breathe the air of Lamia, either.

Chrysander took his breath, and turned his back on Bellmaker's World.

"Come on forward," said Niki's voice from the cabin walls. It sounded like him, but politely pleasant and detached. Chrysander didn't know if he should blame the ship's voice synthesis or not. They were in the air, Chrysander knew; but how far into it, there was no way to know. The black ship had no observation ports. He didn't think they'd Cheated yet. He unfastened his acceleration harness and headed for the beak end of the bird.

The running lights in the corridors were purple-blue: very restful, as long as you didn't look down at the skin on your hands. Chrysander felt his night vision working, his irises pulled wide. The lighting would give you an advantage, if you needed to step prepared into planetary darkness. But if someone came down the corridors with a hand lamp to shine in your eyes . . . Had Martin Spinelle been the sort of person who thought that way? Did Niki think that way? Chrysander suspected he ought to be able to answer that by now. Continental drift. Well, he was supposed to bring Niki Falcon to Lamia. Nowhere was it stated that he was supposed to understand him by the time he did.

There were other doors along the corridor. He should have investigated them, learned the threats, the weapons, the lay of the land. An unwillingness to pry kept him from it. Once that wouldn't have weighed with him, against the demands of self-preservation. Once.

"This way," said the detached voice, at the end of the passage. In faith or resignation—Chrysander couldn't say which—he obeyed.

The door slid open and he stepped through before he saw what surrounded him. By the time he did, the door was closed, and he was left to deal with his panic where he stood.

Where he stood was a moving platform in space. He knew there was a floor; it was there, under his feet. Besides, it was unbroken black. But what should have been ceiling and walls was the sky—the stars and the night between them with no atmosphere to strip the brutal clarity and closeness from the sight. Then he realized he was breathing.

Not windows—a simulation? Over the entire surface of the control cell? But why not? This was a ship designed, at great expense, for a gestalt pilot. And gestalt pilots had no use for readouts and function pads and status lights, all the things that usually filled the control cell surfaces. This must have been Martin Spinelle's idea of a beautiful room. Chrysander felt like some burrowing animal forced to sit exposed on a hilltop.

In the center of the room was a block of polished black, waist-high and two meters long. It reflected the moving stars in smears and flashes, and the changing patterns seemed always about to reflect something else, something that wasn't there. Niki Falcon lay on top of it.

He looked like a carved figure on the lid of a tomb. His eyes were closed; his hair fell back from his forehead and was lost against the black surface under him. His hands were at his sides, and only the restraining clasps around his wrists indicated that they could ever move from there. Only the contoured and padded surface of the black slab indicated that the burden on it was able to feel discomfort still. In the strange light of the too-close stars, color was dulled and distorted. It was impossible to tell if blood moved under his skin.

"Oh," said the voice around him. The figure on the plinth didn't move. "The stars. I'm sorry. I can probably find the shut-down for the display, or change it. . . ."

"No. It's all right." The words bounced off the fabric of space, all wrong for the apparent size of the room, unpleasant. "It just takes some getting used to." And so did the sight of a gestalt pilot at work. Chrysander wished suddenly that the control cell was off limits to him. "Does everything do what it's supposed to do?"

"Nicely, so far. I'm running a bastard combination of my ops and Spin's, depending on what subsystem I'm paying attention to. I feel like Alice after she ate the cake, though. As if I have to send mail to my ankles."

Chrysander missed the reference, but thought he understood the gist. "You haven't tried the Cheat yet."

"No, but I'm not worried about it. It's realspace systems I want to have perfect. Once we drop into realspace near Lamia, all the fun starts, and I'll need to know where my hands and feet are."

"Do you need help with anything?"

He felt stupid when the words came out, but Niki replied, "Have you ever operated a lasergun array?"

There it was: offered to him slantwise and half-visible, but still, the opportunity to speak the truth. Perhaps exposure under the stars had weakened him; or the action of the sea had worn away the last of his stony convictions. Chrysander tucked his hands in his armpits, drew a breath, exhaled all his reservations with it. "Yes," he said. "A few times. On atmosphere boats rigged for hit-and-run engagements with Concorde packet ships. You see—this has been going on for a long time, on Lamia.''

Chrysander had expected a bit of silence after that, but he'd forgotten that Niki Falcon's mind ran a lot faster than his did. Always had, apparently. "Off and on for almost ten years. I know. Even the Concorde doesn't Silence a developing situation. It's a last resort. Besides, what do you think a netbase is for, if not to scrounge a little history on one's current assignment?''

Chrysander sank slowly, until he sat cross-legged on the floor. Of course. None of his efforts to manipulate Niki had worked. So the lowest level, the "trust me" that he used almost unconsciously when talking to people, hadn't worked, either. Niki Falcon might be the only person in the universe who would have double-checked the facts. "How much do you know?''

"There was a major research project on Lamia, Concorde-funded and secured to hell and gone. Lots of money spent, high military clearances required. The Concorde shut it down over a decade ago, and classified it until light couldn't get out. I can't find out who was working on it, let alone what it was intended to do.

"But the researchers didn't quit when they were told to, did they? That was the first dispute. They went underground. Now, were they doing a little community outreach? Is that why Lamia stood so hard against joining the Concorde?''

"There's a very strong 'Says who?' reflex among Lamians,'' Chrysander explained, a little embarrassed. Oh, yes,—Niki Falcon would make all the connections. "As far as they were concerned, the Concorde was trying to regulate scientific and technological development. Planetary law says that on a non-aligned world that power belongs only to the planet. By that time, too, all the remaining project members had become Lamian citizens.''

"A matter of *zeitgeist*, then. And I don't suppose the Credit Rebellion hurt, either. The Concorde, of course, figured their security was blown to hell and gone once the team refused to shut down. Now, explain to me why the heat has gone so high in the last year.''

The disembodied voice and motionless figure on the slab were ruining his ability to judge his words. It was like talking to a ghost. After all, Chrysander half-reasoned, Niki looked dead, and if he was dead, what harm was there in telling all of it? "It's the other side of the same coin. The Concorde now wants all the data produced since they tried to shut the project down. A policy shift somewhere. . . .'' Chrysander shrugged. "But all *that* data is of economic and military value to Lamia. Or at least, that's what they say.''

"I suppose that will have to do. Why are we on our way to Lamia?''

Chrysander clenched his fists on his knees. "We're not. *You* are.''

"Ah.'' Damn Niki Falcon, couldn't he at least pretend surprise? Or was the gestalt and the voice synthesis washing the inflection out of his words?

"My instructions were to find you and bring you back with me. I don't know what for. Honestly, I don't know.''

"I believe you. Then you didn't, in fact, ask every available pilot before you asked me?''

"Of course I did,'' Chrysander sighed. "In case you had checked. But between the way I described the job and the voice I did it in, there was very little chance anyone would have taken it. Laura Brass is probably still wondering why she referred me to you.''

That did produce a moment of silence. "Do you ever regret manipulating people?'' Niki asked from that cool distance.

"Yes!'' He took a quick, deep breath; the next words sounded almost calm. "I do. But sometimes it's better than the alternatives.'' Was that true? It had been once.

"Like, say, having someone beaten?''

Chrysander's muscles had all locked in panic. The bowl of stars, which he'd almost gotten used to, threatened him again. He longed to deny it, to claim ignorance, to indulge in a paroxysm of cowardice. But he'd abandoned all his high-minded excuses for lying. "The Voice didn't work on you. I was running out of time. And I believed, then, that it was right.'' His words were breathy, cracked, and uncontrolled. He felt as if his spine was too proud to go on holding his head up.

"It wasn't like Jhari, you see,'' Niki said. "Too risky, too inefficient, and too good a chance that it wouldn't accomplish what she wanted.''

Chrysander stumbled to his feet. All his joints were wooden. "I should leave now,'' he said, and as he did, realized that he couldn't find the door to the passageway unless Niki opened it.

"Sit down or stand, as you like, but we're not done yet. You have no idea why I'm wanted on Lamia?''

"I know that there's a connection between gestalt pilots and Lamia." Chrysander wanted to pace, but the room was too bizarre. He stood where he was. "The research that produced the gestalt program was derived from the original project on Lamia, the one the Concorde tried to shut down."

"Was it?" Niki asked. The synthesis didn't wash that out. He was startled.

"Yes, it was. Dr. Genefa Harisal, the head of gestalt research . . . ?"

"Oh, yes." Niki sounded amused. "I knew her."

"She was part of the original Lamia staff, though I don't think she was very high up. Have you ever heard of Dr. Tomas Damion? My whole name is Chrysander Harris Damion—I'm his son. He was co-head of the original project team."

There was a noise from Niki—from his body, not from the air. It sounded like choking, or a parody of laughter. His eyes were open and vacant.

"Oh, God," he whispered roughly. "The last loop in a cyclical life."

"What?" Chrysander said.

Niki turned his head, and his eyes focused on Chrysander as if with difficulty. "Does the name Morwenna Glyndwr-Jones mean anything to you?"

"Yes. She was the other head of the team."

It was definitely laughter, of a horrible sort.

CHAPTER FOURTEEN

Others because you did not keep
That deep-sworn vow have been friends of mine;
Yet always when I look death in the face,
When I clamber to the heights of sleep,
Or when I grow excited with wine,
Suddenly I meet your face.
— W. B. Yeats, "A Deep-Sworn Vow"

Cheat, and Cheat, and Cheat again. Chrysander felt the axis slip each time it happened, as if the course of his life had shifted slightly, as if the future had just changed. Once Niki had decided he could stitch realspace with the black ship, he parted it over and over, in no predictable pattern. Chrysander imagined the ship appearing on scanning hardware like a vision in the desert, long enough for anyone who saw it to know it was unidentifiable. If the Concorde waited to receive them at Lamia, they waited for the *Gerfalcon*, whose capabilities were known. It would be an eagle that burst out of Cheatspace, invisible against the black sky, long in beak and talon.

Though it would not be called an eagle. Niki had told him, his steady, simulated voice amused, that Spin had left one last, oblique greeting. The name of the ship, in all of its current records, was the *Falconer*.

Chrysander heard him from the isolation of the laser array headset. He sat half-reclined in a room the size of a clothing locker, the next one down from the control cell. "I don't understand this," he said, as the simulation of realspace around them flared into life over his eyes.

"Well, frankly, I don't trust myself to push those buttons when I ought to. It's your fight, you can shoot to kill over it."

"No, I meant, why is this here? Why a second control station for weapons in a made-to-order gestalt ship? Equipped with a headset, instead of a plug?"

"Cheat up," Niki warned, and a moment later, Chrysander felt the slide. The headset flung a fistful of luminous confetti at his eyes, and he closed them before he could master the reflex. "It's a damned good question," Niki went on. He didn't sound as if it bothered him. "I can run Weapons from here, so he didn't mean to make them exclusively a manual function. And Spin was territorial as a tiger; the thought of him with a co-wing . . . Here we are, the engineering drawings."

It was all vaguely unreal, Chrysander decided, the conversation of one ghost to another. But then, this was Cheatspace. East of the sun and west of the moon, he'd said, and in their present relationship to the tangible, measurable world, they *were* ghosts.

"Lord of Annwn," Niki said indecipherably, "it was put in just before he parked her. He thought I'd want it. But who did he think I'd put—" And for a moment that must have been very long to Niki Falcon, there was silence. "Oh, Spin. If you hadn't already blown your head off, I'd do it for you."

"Is this something I should know about?" Chrysander asked, and was surprised to feel no irritation at all. Ghosts were, perhaps, unflappable.

"No, thank God."

There was silence in the air around him after that. He made another pass over the laser controls, rolled his mind lightly around the view the targeting headset gave him. It was Niki's own view, 360 degrees of it all the time. But his brain wouldn't let him take it all in at once; anything outside his usual field of vision felt like peripheral vision, unless he paid attention to it. Did Niki see all of it at once? Was that one of the restrictions that had been lifted from him when he became a gestalt pilot?

Under Chrysander's hands were the touchpads that fired the laser arrays. He tested the reach from one to the other, stretched his hands in what he suddenly realized were finger exercises for keyed instruments. The pads were sequenced and grouped; belly guns were a suspended third chord, spine were an inverted major triad, starboard wing clippers were a minor seventh, and the port ones were an inverted minor. Or at least, the relative finger reach was the same. *I should write a song for them,* he thought. *Ballad for Falconer's Guns. But only if they save our lives.*

Niki claimed to be—and so must be—the son of Morwenna Glyndwr-Jones, the bioengineer who had co-headed the first research done on Lamia, thirty-some years ago. The subject of that research, Chrysander didn't know. But split into two parts, it had become the Concorde's gestalt project, and Lamia's attempt to harness its latent mental talents. Niki Falcon was the end result of the first; Chrysander was the best accomplishment of the second. And the nexus from which both paths spun out seemed to be Morwenna Glyndwr-Jones. Or was he diagramming that wrong?

Niki's disembodied voice broke into his thoughts, and Chrysander felt a quick, foolish guilt, as if he'd been caught prying. "I feel required to say this, and you'll feel required to ignore it when the time comes, but let's get all the requirements out of the way. Don't fire those things if you don't have to, all right?"

"All right," said Chrysander, who was prepared to comply. He wondered, though, if "have to" was a distinction that would occur to him in a fight.

"Okay," Niki said, on a sigh. "Battle stations, then. The real thing. Going down."

Chrysander began the breathing, and had his focus on the third exhale. It gathered in a tight ball of heat, like a sun under his ribs. The confetti ripped past his ears, reconstituted itself—

Realspace was full of Lamia, the grasping hand of its gravity, the mass of it laid out as background in the targeting display. *So close!* thought Chrysander, dismayed. There were no tall structures there to be threatened by the shock wave. But it would alert everyone, *everyone,* that a ship had made a wide, wild crack in realspace.

And why not? Speed was the point, not secrecy. Lamia knew they were coming.

They plunged planetward as if the *Falconer* might be driven like a wedge into Lamia's crust. Chrysander felt, distantly, a knot of fear. Accidents, stupid mistakes that probably weren't mistakes at all. The grenade. And Niki Falcon telling him to go before he killed them both. Chrysander's fingers were dry and cool on the fire controls. Waiting for the downbeat.

Over Lamia's horizon, two yellow arrows in a hunter's arc. Two hostile ships on the targeting display. They spat fire, poison, death. Chrysander felt the black bird twist; the display spun as if he wore the wings himself, and the world swung under his naked eyes. Another yellow hunter rose from the eastern continent. They would pinch the *Falconer* between them like a thumb and fingers. Black wings strained and slammed against inertia, and one yellow ship hung neatly pinned in the sights of his belly laser. He played a suspended third, stitched it with thin red thread, and it fell.

Two more yellow ships dropped down from above. The spine guns reached red fingers toward them at his command. Arpeggio in a major key, but the death song missed its audience; the ships above him leaned away, out, back.

Another ship-marker appeared at planet's edge, painted with yellow light. Then he heard Niki's indrawn live breath, and the ship changed from yellow to green. Green. Friendly craft.

"Laura," Niki whispered.

She wouldn't have had to land; she could have appeared in space, claimed a breakdown, and lain in repair orbit until the shock wave and her scanners told her they were here. But how had Laura Brass known they were coming to Lamia? Oh, God, why not—everyone else seemed to. He used to be so good at keeping secrets.

Chrysander was out of the comlink. If there was any communication between Laura and Niki, he didn't hear it. But *Mercy of the Goddess* reached out, and a long catclaw scratch of red crossed his vision and lashed one of the ships above them. Its drive chamber imploded. The *Falconer* slid down like falling light, between laser bursts from the ship above, between the two ships below. Chrysander cut one open with the belly guns.

They would be in atmosphere soon, where the lasers would burn air before they reached their targets. If the attacking ships followed them down . . . Did they have projectiles? Niki would have to forgive him for one more thing. He couldn't let them live.

Niki was threading a path through laser fire, as if flying between trees. Earning his pay. He was right; only someone who could put time on a leash could get them through this. Only a gestalt pilot.

With a cold spike of terror, he realized what that meant. He pulled the spine gun into line.

Too late. Above him, *Mercy of the Goddess* lay pinned under the belly lasers of one enemy ship. *Falconer* itself cut off her line of retreat. Niki heeled away, Chrysander aimed—

Red lines intersected with green ship even as Chrysander slammed his fingers down on the formation. *Mercy of the Goddess* imploded before his eyes, then flung itself outward in bits, each fragment following its particular vector.

So when you lead him into hell, she'd said, *remember that. I'll be right behind you.* Chrysander's fingers turned her killer into dust.

No voice came to him from the control cell. But the black bird hurtled relentlessly at the last yellow ship, maneuvered Chrysander a perfect shot. He took it, and they were alone.

Into atmosphere, down, down, until the air was thick and sullen with golden dust. "Give me a landing spot," Niki said.

Chrysander peered into the display, distinguished one mile of churning sand from another. "There," he said, and watched his chosen area rise breathtakingly fast beneath him. Watched, and realized what had just happened, and kept it to himself. When their motion stopped, he swung the targeting headset away, rolled off the couch, and opened the door to the control cell.

Its walls were black now. Light came from a thin white band around the ceiling. Niki had risen from the black slab and was leaning against it, head down, eyes closed. *It must drain him,* Chrysander realized; there was more there than grief. But when Niki's head came up, his eyes were wide and burning from inside, and his face was pale, dry as chalk. He flung his black hair back with a jerk.

"What now?" he demanded. "It's your show."

No mention of the dead ships, or of her. Something wrong. "You're not well," Chrysander said.

"I'm on drugs," Niki replied, as if the precision of each word, its spacing from the next one, was crucial. "Let's get this done."

"I need a port for the Entropic and a thincast band to send the output."

Niki raised his eyebrows. "There's a port in here. Bring it," was all he said.

Chrysander dragged his bag out of a locker in the corridor and brought it back to the control cell. Niki was pacing when he came back. At intervals one of his hands would reach out, tap quickly on something. He looked like a man moved by high fever. The port was on the side of the black slab, open. Chrysander plugged in the keyboard, set the voices, then checked and double-checked them until his teeth ground together. If the waveforms came out wrong, he and Niki would, at best, be abandoned in the maelstrom of sand.

He played his four measures, watched the thincast echo back on the Entropic's display. It would be cutting now through the storm outside, identification and query. He sat on the control cell floor and watched the display go flat, heard only the sound of Niki's steps and the intermittent tapping of his fingers.

Then four more measures spoke out of the Entropic. Identification and answer. Chrysander let his breath out and unplugged the Entropic. "That was our roadmap," Chrysander said in answer to Niki's look.

Niki seemed to have as much trouble with the sand as Chrysander had had with the snow on Bellmaker's World. He flung one long hand over his eyes against the wailing, grating wind, and stumbled in the grip of the drifts. Chrysander caught his elbow, steadied him, wished he could block the wind as Niki had for him. But they hadn't far to walk in it, and it would hide the *Falconer* from air and surface scanners. He found the hatch cover, wedged between and sheltered by two upthrust rocks, and when he yanked it open, there was the row of pressed-resin rungs, descending into gloom. He sent Niki down them first, and dogged the hatch after himself. Sand sifted out of the hatch rim, hissing in the loud silence.

Four meters in, the tile lights in the wall registered their motion and ignited. After that, they climbed down in that fragile golden haze, like dreamlight. Niki slipped once, and hung for a moment below Chrysander's feet, as if to get his breath back.

"Are you all right?" said Chrysander.

Niki tipped his head back, showed that white face full of artificial, febrile energy. "No. This is hell," he said. "Nor am I out of it. Yet."

At the bottom was a broad hall, and the sound of a vehicle coming toward them. Chrysander pushed Niki back against the darkest wall, then flattened himself out beside him. A skidder platform came into sight, sand-pitted, the engine hissing as if in need of a cleanout. Cross-legged at the controls, like a sorcerer on a flying carpet, was a woman in a khaki surfacesuit, the hood down. Her hair was vivid auburn, voluminous with curls and static.

"Faelle," Chrysander called, stepping out from the wall.

The skidder dropped with a thump, and Faelle launched herself at him.

"Ooof," said Chrysander.

"Will of *God*, we were worried," she declared. Then she stepped back, began to brush sand out of the folds of his clothing. "That was some damned dogfight. Then I lost you on the scans, and by the time your tune came in, I was sure it must be an impostor—did you bring him?"

"If I hadn't," Chrysander said, "there wouldn't have been a dogfight. Niki Falcon, Faelle Ryzal."

Niki, who had come forward as they talked, nodded to her.

"This is him, ey?" She squinted at Niki. "You look shitty."

"Thank you," Niki said, perfectly polite. Chrysander was abruptly, disorientingly reminded of himself and Laura Brass facing off in the *Gerfalcon*.

"But if you can fly like that," Faelle said, clearly deciding it on the spot, "you must be okay. Chrys, we're going to have trouble. The Concs are rattling like hot gas, up top. And security's breached on a couple of the tunnel sections between here and there."

"We can't travel surface. We're not equipped. It's the tunnels or nothing."

"Yeah. Just so you know." Faelle looked doubtfully at both of them, and shrugged. "Hop on."

The skidder was fast and nimble, and Faelle used it that way. Chrysander wrapped one leg around a tiedown on the platform and kept a grip on their bags. Niki looked more as if he were holding himself together than on, with both hands. Chrysander thought his teeth might be clenched. "How much longer before you come down?" Chrysander muttered to him.

"Unfortunately, never." Niki's face was empty of any particular expression. "This is the last resort, to run full-time on the drug. A friend of mine did it for three weeks. It seems to cut down on the memory playback, but it doesn't do shit for pain."

"I can find you something for the pain."

Niki shook his head. "Can't use both at once—they just blunt each other."

"Do you . . . did you bring enough with you?"

"My entire stock is in that bag."

"You didn't leave any on—"

"Chrysander. I'm not going to have to worry about getting off Lamia." He seemed to regret that sentence as soon as he'd said it. He stared forward over Faelle's shoulder as if he were seeing visions, after all.

They'd gone hellbent through the tunnels for an hour before Faelle slowed down, touched a finger to her lips. Burned areas marked the walls, and the tile lights were damaged in many places. Faelle took them down what Chrysander knew were detours. Sometimes she stopped in a dark end tunnel, listening.

After one of those stops, she moved forward slowly to the intersection of a passage, and made to take the right-hand fork. Niki touched her shoulder and shook his head. Faelle looked back at him, scowling, but he didn't seem to see her. He pointed left.

"Go ahead," Chrysander whispered. "He's Got It."

The scowl was turned on him for a moment; then it changed. Her widened eyes went back to Niki.

Chrysander nodded left, and Faelle turned.

"Got what?" Niki murmured at last, when talking didn't seem so risky.

"You asked me for a landing spot," Chrysander told him. "I said, 'There,' and you set down in it. But you couldn't have known which 'there' I meant. Not from what I said, or did."

"Which might just mean that *you've* got it."

"I do," Chrysander said. "But not that kind."

Niki shook his head irritably, as if the whole notion were a biting fly. But now and then he suggested a turn to Faelle, and she took it without hesitation.

At last they came back into safe territory, and tunnels that Chrysander knew well. They were under the original settlement warren, now. The speed of the skidder made red froth of Faelle's hair. "Your father told me to send you straight to him," she said over her shoulder to Chrysander.

"And Niki?" Chrysander asked her.

"Him, too. Nobody's telling anybody anything, these days— which is a good trick, with all of us eight to a room. What's he supposed to do?"

Niki looked at her back, then turned to Chrysander, wearing a derisive half smile. "Good question."

"I don't know. No one tells me anything, either," Chrysander said, and hoped that would shut both of them up. "What do you mean, eight to a room?"

"Well, that's an average. It got too hard to secure the outlying warrens, so everybody moved into First."

Everybody? Chrysander found it unimaginable.

Faelle took a brisk corner, and three outsuited figures jumped back against the wall, out of her way. "The Concs have been doing lots of containment, but nothing much like attack for weeks. Hope your arrival doesn't change their tactics." She sounded as if she was grinning. "I thought we ought to use the time for hit-and-runs. We'd have their balls in a month if we did. They'd break discipline like crazy for a shot at us, then—wham! But no, the Twelve are Working On It, so we have to sit and stare at the walls. Assholes."

In other words, the remaining population of Lamia was under siege in First Warren. He was surprised Faelle couldn't hear it herself, in what she'd said. Or she did, and saw no point in admitting it. There would be water; they had always had to fight the planet for that, anyway, and they'd learned the tactics. And there would be power, since the planet and its sun gave that away so freely. But food and ammunition . . . "Faelle," Chrysander said, surprised at himself, "be quiet."

"I didn't mean your father, Chrys, I meant all Twelve. They're different when they're a committee. It's like mob psychology."

"Faelle . . ."

She looked over her shoulder again and made a disgusted sound, but said nothing more.

There was a work crew where they stopped, six people loading shock-proof canisters on another skidder. All six carried beam rifles. Three of them he recognized; they nodded at Chrysander, and there was wary relief in the gesture. He couldn't remember their names, but he nodded back. Their eyes moved often to Niki, he saw. He couldn't read their expressions when they did.

Up another, shorter, row of rungs, and they were in the warren levels.

"Chrys," said Faelle, "I'm gone. I have to go sit monitor. Is there anything else you need?" She sent a swift look at Niki, who was not paying attention. Highly un-Niki-like.

"No, we're fine. Later, I hope."

She nodded, and loped down the hall. Through the crowds.

He'd thought it was unimaginable, and he'd been right. He would never have envisioned this. The passage was clogged with people, and only some of them were on their feet, moving. The rest were camped along the walls.

There seemed to be a rigid structure to it. Families lived on blankets or tarps, laid out end to end, that broke only for corridor intersections and doors. There seemed to be some allowance made for family size—larger blankets—but the edge of each rectangle of cloth appeared to be as inviolate as house walls. Children played frantic, aimless games among the pedestrians, but none of them ran across a blanket.

The hall smelled of cooking and babies and damp cloth. No smoke; the Council would have banned smoking as soon as it became clear that First Warren's ventilation would not cope with so many bodies. Some families had snapstoves on metal plates; Chrysander wondered what the others did.

He stretched, trying to wring the tension out of his shoulders. Before him, mostly hidden by the crowd, was the bright, larger-than-life bazaar mural that the Kearn brothers had painted, full of visual puns and caricatures of their friends. Chrysander's younger self was in it, doing a bad job of juggling oranges. To the right of the mural were the double pressure doors that led to the Testing Center, where he'd been bored as a child and challenged as an adult, where he'd learned the difference between Got It and Not Got It. Blankets edged up to the doors on both sides. Six corridor branches down on the left was Helena Bucket's, where he and his friends had learned about alcohol consumption, and he had played four nights a week for six months, when he was eighteen. He wondered if people were sleeping on the floor there.

I'm home. The phrase brought him bitter amusement.

Niki had his bag over his shoulder, his hands in his pockets, and his eyes fixed fiercely on the middle distances, as if conducting an argument in his head.

"This is it," Chrysander said. "This is First Warren, where I grew up. Though not precisely the way it was then. Come on." Chrysander led the way, to the right, toward BioEng and his father.

"Is it all sandstorm up top?" Niki asked as they threaded the crowds.

Chrysander remembered that he'd done his research, and probably knew better already, but he didn't say so. The question was a useful distraction, which might have been why Niki had asked. "No, but it's all pretty harsh. Enough arable land on this continent to support the colony, which is topped out at fifty thousand. With synthesis and imports, we do all right. And we're doing oasis-chain reclamation, but that takes lifetimes before it affects the climate."

"What's your place in it all?"

"I'm one of our exports, I guess."

"What do you mean?"

Chrysander struggled with the explanation; it reminded him of his conversation with himself, about keys and weapons and tools. "I bring in money. I think half the computing power in the Testing Center was bought with my last three recordings. I also gather information, try to influence people when we need it, and do whatever errands I'm suited for. Like collecting you. A sort of covert operations lobbyist."

"Mmm. Happy with that?"

"Not exactly." Another half-dozen steps later, he added, "No."

They stopped to let a convoy of skidders go past, and when they'd gone, Niki stayed leaning against the door they'd backed into. His mouth was tight with pain, but his eyes were calm and steady. "Chrysander," he said, "if you know anything else that I should know . . ." He frowned and closed his eyes. "It feels wrong. It feels all wrong. There's nothing here for a gestalt pilot to *do*, Chrysander, so why am I *here*?"

The thin voice, somehow younger, shook Chrysander. "I've told you all of it that I know. The connection has to be the original project that your mother worked on. But I don't know what it is."

"We can only find out by walking into it, I guess." Niki pushed himself roughly away from the door. "So let's walk."

BioEng's double doors were painted pink and blue, which Chrysander had always thought was a stupid joke raised to the level of tradition. He pushed the blue one open with his shoulder and stepped through with Niki right behind him, as if this were a vid and they were a pair of heroes in the villain's lair. He was home, and the feeling wouldn't go away.

Everyone knew Chrysander by name here, and used it. Their faces blurred before him; he found he was paying attention to nothing in particular, his awareness moving lightly over the whole room.

Work went on, as it always did, even when the fighting got bad. It was more intense now. Staff from outlying warrens were trying to share table space and equipment with the residents, and the noise level was startling. Someone was rotating a DNA helix on one of the big screens, using the cursor to point at a segment, and arguing with someone else about why it was there. Someone else was rigging video probes over a sample tray. The room was large and bright and had, at great expense and, sometimes, risk, everything a lab should have. But it was still crowded, still thick with nerves.

These were the keepers of Lamia's family bible. Chrysander's data was stored here, he knew: his mother's gene specs, his father's, the modifications made to his own genetic material, and every apparent or suspected result of it all. The yellow eyes, for instance. His father sometimes used them as proof that human genetics was still a black box, that no matter how much you refined the input, the output could still surprise you.

Niki looked bleak and ill. "So odd, to think of her here. Bloody odd." He shook his head, rubbed his eyes. "Sorry. These little psychological shocks build character."

"What happened to her?"

"She was murdered. Along with the rest of my family."

Saying "I'm sorry" seemed like a bad idea to Chrysander. "Let's walk."

His father had an office with a pull-down bed in it, at the end of the lab. Chrysander tapped the call plate.

"Who is it?" His father's voice, hoarse from too little sleep. It was such a familiar sound that Chrysander's answer stuck for an instant in his throat, his wariness caught like wind-carried debris against an obstacle.

"Chrysander. And Niki Falcon."

A moment of silence. "Thank God," said his father. "Come in."

His father stood behind his worktable, smiling, and Chrysander smiled, too, came forward and touched his hand. But his father's gaze moved past him, fixed on a point above and behind Chrysander's head, and the smile fell off his face suddenly, leaving it blank. To that point, he said, "You're very like her."

"The resemblance was even better," replied Niki Falcon, in a voice Chrysander had never heard him use. "But the face got broke and I had to buy a new one. They hammered out the dents, but it was just never the same."

Niki came forward, two swinging strides, and dropped into the other chair. "Of *course* I'm like her. She built me out of her spare parts, for God's sake. Or didn't you know that?" Then Niki covered his face with both hands and shivered. "I'm sorry," he said through his fingers. "That was inexcusable. Chrysander will tell you I'm not myself right now."

Who, me? Chrysander thought wildly. The currents were there in the room, easy to read: resentment, animosity, pain from Niki; alarm from his father, fear, even, and something in his face like guilt. But reading wasn't understanding. He felt as if he were required to swim through air. Then he heard the words properly. *She built me out of her spare parts.* The diagram he'd made, of paths and their intersections, began to rearrange itself.

"I did know," said his father. He looked older than Chrysander remembered. His gold-and-white hair was dulled, his skin freckled and slack. And no, he hadn't been sleeping much, from the look of his eyes. "I was the only one who knew, I think. Morwenna was always damned secretive with her data."

That brought a staggered sort of laughter from Niki. "I think you could say that. Do you happen to know *why* she did it?"

Chrysander's father stared at Niki. "Will of God, she didn't tell you? That's a little much."

Niki said nothing; he only watched, like a man waiting to hear sentence passed on himself.

"You were part of the project. We had a falling-out over it, actually. She became convinced as we went along that we weren't going to get results unless we worked from scratch. That it wasn't enough to help natural mutations along—we had to do the sculpting and sorting, take total control over the process. She used her own chromosomes for the work, grew the embryo, and implanted it in herself."

Niki's hands were folded tightly in his lap, knuckles showing red on white fingers.

"It was rotten methodology. No controls, no hope of unbiased observation and measurement—I told her so. She left then. I think she would have come back, but the Concorde shut down the project and confiscated what they thought were all the records. I had copies of mine, of course. And Morwenna had you. The Concorde didn't know about that."

Chrysander found he was watching his father as if he were a hostile stranger. Such a hard, self-centered way to tell the story, as if Niki Falcon had no part in it himself.

"She told me to go to you." Niki's face was composed, his eyes focused on the far wall, his breathing admirably regular. A strenuous effort, Chrysander realized. "When I finally could, I found out I was too late. The New Oxford laboratories were burned, and, as far as they knew, so were you. Cold trail. I found Genefa Harisal eventually, but it took five rather hard years.''

His father frowned, folded his arms on the desktop. ''Sorry. I didn't know. The cold trail was meant for the Concorde, so that I could come back here with my material and work in secret.''

''Did you know she was dead?''

''Morwenna? Not for a long time.''

''It wouldn't have made a difference,'' Niki said in a constricted voice.

Chrysander stepped forward, laid a hand on Niki's shoulder. ''I was planning on making introductions, but at this point, it would be silly. Do we have to do this now? We've been going flat out for hours.''

It was Niki who looked up at him and said apologetically, ''I don't know how long I have.''

The flesh burning away from inside, the body burning itself to keep going, fever-coloring in the skin stretched over the cheekbones that seemed to have thrust upward overnight, like the earth slipping at fault lines. He was running on willpower, emotion, and his damned drug. If they stopped the momentum, they might stop him, too.

Chrysander let his hand drop to his side, and said to his father, ''Tell him what you want of him.''

The guilt came back. Only for an instant, but Chrysander saw it, and was afraid. He saw his father suddenly as a stranger, as Dr. Tomas Damion, as Niki must see him. ''The Concorde,'' Chrysander said, and wondered where the words were coming from. ''The Concorde wants the data.''

His father's head came up. ''Only the old material. Only the original project.''

''And its experimental animal. What did they pay for him?''

''Chrysander . . .'' Niki said softly.

''What did they pay?'' The Voice was a whip out of his throat.

''Three Gaea Units in orbit, enough to control the climate on both continents. Recognition of our independence from the Concorde. Is that enough, by your exacting standards?'' The cold, righteous anger with which lesser beings than his father hid shame and guilt. And here it was on his father's face.

''Independence? If we depend on the Concorde for our *climate*? You should have stuck to genetics,'' Chrysander spat.

"The agreement's been made. There's a Concorde representative en route right now, empowered to deal with the Council of Twelve."

"Jhari," Niki said. " 'Empowered' on the fly, I'll bet, and baffled as hell." He sounded almost amused. "She has a terrible temper when she's been baffled."

Laura Brass died for this, Chrysander thought. "How was this deal made? When I was here last, there was no communication between Lamia and the Concorde. As a matter of policy."

"We've been hard-pressed since you left. The Silence has cut us off. We're going to starve in another few months. Morale is bad. A diplomatic courier from the Bear Triangle did the negotiating for us, and we're damned lucky he could."

"What courier?"

"He was stranded here by the Silence. With a diplomatic clearance, he could initiate contact with the Concorde. They sure as hell weren't listening to us anymore."

Chrysander raked his hair back with both hands and stared at his father. "You can't do this. What are they going to *do* with him? Have they even told you that?"

"They're going to collect the rest of the data and wrap up the original project."

"What does that mean?"

"Chrysander, what does it matter to you? It will save us! You brought him here, you're done with it."

"Exactly. I brought him here."

"I'll be in charge of the work myself. Don't you trust me to know what's right?"

"No," Chrysander said.

"History's repeating itself," said Niki. He had one elbow on the chair arm, and the fingers of that hand propped up his forehead. He looked resigned, and perhaps even amused.

"Well," Chrysander asked brightly, "d'you think you're worth thirty pieces of silver?"

Behind his hand, Niki grinned. "Nah. You got a deal." Chrysander's father looked from one to the other of them in confusion. Chrysander gave him a bland smile.

The call plate triple-clicked. "Hello?" said his father.

"Have they arrived?"

Niki's head came up.

"Yes, they're right here. Come in."

The door slid open. The man who stepped in was medium height, with short graying hair that had once been a sort of red-sand color. Chrysander recognized the strength in his shoulders and hands and slender body, the iron-hard place somewhere behind his polite and pleasant expression. "This is the courier I told you about," said his father. "My son, Chrysan—"

Niki rose slowly from the chair. Even the flush of fever had left his face, and his eyes, fixed on the man in the doorway, were wide and wild. The stresses pulling at his features made him look, not older, as Chrysander would have expected, but younger, more vulnerable.

Then his eyes closed, as if he didn't expect to open them again. "Some people's lives go on," he said, in a conversational tone horribly at odds with his face. "Mine just seems to come around again. Hello, Jacob."

"Hello, Dominic," said the man in the door.

I think there are only so many changes that can be wrought on an individual in any set period. Once that number is exceeded, rigidity sets in. Or unreasonable flexibility. Even now, I'm not sure which one I'm suffering from. Am I planting my feet, or being swept, will-less, by the power of the people around me? Chrysander Harris, brilliant and devious, swinging between cool asceticism and the explosive energy of spontaneous combustion, and all of it under precise control. Jacob Ridgeway, with the patience of a glacier and the long vision that goes with it, in his own way as out of synch with time as a gestalt pilot. And Niki Falcon, the perfect catalyst, who sticks to everything he touches, and by that means acts on all of us even when he's not there. Who, even helpless and dying and hardly aware, is altering what we are, and all the work of our hands.

At a point in objective space halfway to Lamia, in pursuit of Chrysander Harris and Niki Falcon, and as angry as I've ever been in my life, I became a fully accredited Planetary Governor. If you think that's part of the usual antiroutine of a Special Services agent, you may think again. No, pardon me; you already know the facts. You need the context.

I'd lost them. Twice. With a deep and abiding admiration, I hated Niki Falcon. Every time I dredged up another bit of knowledge about him, formed it into a hunch, and followed it, I learned I'd been right, but too slowly. At the Breakneck el station, I found Uri Daal, who said nothing, and a bounty hunter in traction, who said a lot, to no purpose. On Bellmaker's World I found the *Gerfalcon*, and Asher Spinelle (and suddenly understood Spin better than I had when he was alive), and an empty underground hangar. There was nothing left but to follow my quarry, like some dimwitted flatfoot policeman in an old video, to Lamia.

My orders were to put pressure on Chrysander Harris, and to know where he was at every moment. I now know that order was meant to get Niki Falcon to Lamia as quickly as possible, and to make sure SpecServe knew when he got there. Oh, Special Services is a byzantine thing, full of contradictory thoughts and crossed paths, and we of little faith believe, in the hours before dawn, that there is no single controlling intelligence over it all. Only factions that rarely speak, and share no common goals.

Then, suddenly, the security-sealed burst came in, and I was a different player, for a different faction, acting a different part. I was to go to Lamia, carrying codes that would cause the ground and air forces stationed there to believe I was what I said I was, and to do whatever I told them to do. Someone in SpecServe, I'm sure, particularly liked that. We have no connection and no authority with Concorde regular forces, at their insistence. But I had the codes and the cover and the title, and all three would hold up under scrutiny. I was to collaborate with the Special Services agent already in place on the mission, on Lamia.

Was I pleased? Of course I wasn't. What agent? What mission? That, at least, was answered, and I learned that everything I'd done until then was, in the accomplishment of my new assignment, counterproductive. Lamia was to be pacified from within, its cooperation bought with this and that, and the gestalt pilot program was to be wrapped up, the experimental records completed, the files closed and sealed. Since the only gestalt pilot left was Niki Falcon, there he was, self-delivered and ready for study.

The gestalt pilot program?

It smelled of Damage Control, containment, and of other things that I didn't want to be involved in. It smelled of a level of deceit unparalleled in even my experience of Special Services. But no one was asking me. I was expected immediately if not sooner by Jacob Anton Ridgeway, SpecServe 2.

You should know, if you don't already, that everyone level 4 and below believes that all the Spec 2's are crazy. You should also know that I've never met a Spec 2 who gave me cause to doubt it.

I met Jacob Ridgeway in what had become his room in First Warren on Lamia. His exalted position got him a room to himself—as did mine.

Most underground architecture shares certain features, some of them foolish. Ceiling height, for instance: with all of *down* to use, and with the efficiencies of earth-sheltered heating and cooling, why are underground structures always squat? But Lamia was full of vaulting and arches, remarkably free of the assumptions about space that come from building free-standing things out in the air. Ridgeway's room had a ceiling like the inside of a center-pole tent with the pole missing, almost four meters high. The light came mostly from a wall covered in white paper painted with a scene of cranes on a lakeshore.

He lived a monk's life, from the looks of it. True, his cover would limit the number of things he would have brought with him, but even for the quarters of a man caught out unexpectedly by Silence, the room was bare. And ruthlessly ordered.

He greeted me by my new title. Straight-faced, too. But you don't hit a Spec 2 without an introduction. "Pleased to meet you, and what the *fuck* is going on here?" I said.

"You got your orders?"

"Of course I got my orders. Which were in direct conflict with my last set. I thought maybe I'd get here and have it happen again."

He looked bland. "Did you join Special Services for stability?"

"In a way, yes." There was a mock-wicker chair in one corner. I was a Planetary Governor now. I could certainly sit down when I felt like it. So I did.

He sat cross-legged on the backless couch, and made a formal pose of it. I put his age at a little over forty years, and decided they'd been full of excessive wear and tear. Both guesses have since been verified. He told me what we were doing on Lamia, or as much of it as he wanted to tell me then, and I have heard more emotion in the narrators of eduvids.

Someone in the thin air of the highest echelons had noticed, finally, that the gestalt pilot research was unfinished. That it was unfinished because none of the subjects had the decency to remain alive until the gestalt killed them. And that the research traced its lineage to Lamia, which was strategic and useful and which refused to lie down as it ought. By the logic that thin air produces, the plot was concocted, and all its witless pieces moved into place.

Results expected: Lamia will belong to the Concorde in all but name, and Niki Falcon will be constrained to live out his life under the close observation of a battery of testing devices and Dr. Tomas Damion.

No logic can account for that. I don't understand. I am—we are—missing a piece. There's that odor of Damage Control, the feeling that all of this has to be done quickly, and with the knowledge of as few people as possible. We're all balanced on the edge of a disaster, but no one will tell us if it's earthquake or flood. Jacob Ridgeway knows. And Dr. Tomas Damion knows, too, or would if he'd let himself think about it.

"So," I said, "let's see if I have it all. What the Concorde really wants is to have Niki Falcon on Lamia, being dissected"—Ridgeway frowned—"by Damion. So I was assigned to make sure that Chrysander Harris had as much trouble as possible accomplishing that very thing. Makes perfect sense."

Then he *really* frowned. "Don't be thick. If Harris hadn't been under pressure, he wouldn't have been willing to act with so little information. He would have asked questions. And we would have lost Falcon. You know what was going on."

"Yes, I do. Some idiot piece of SpecServe, present company certainly excepted, maintained such textbook security on the operation that all the other idiot pieces ended up stepping on it. And idiot piece number one, when it needs some political advantage over all the others, will cite this mess to prove what a gaggle of incompetents the others are."

Ridgeway laid his hands on his knees and looked austere. Prime Spec 2. "The Lamian government has to believe that they brought Niki Falcon here all by themselves. They're buying their improvements with an innocent man's life, and as long as they know it, and know that we know it, too, we've got power over them."

"I like my explanation better. But even it doesn't account for what's gone on here in the last few hours."

"What do you mean?"

"If you wanted him here," I snapped, "why the hell were you shooting at him?"

Ridgeway looked as if I were someone else's graduate student who had failed to live up to expectations. "The Lamians would have spotted a setup immediately if he'd come in unchallenged. Besides, he was never in danger."

"Enlighten me."

"First, it wasn't me shooting at him. I can't order regular forces to do anything, you know that. And a Bear Triangle courier sure as hell can't. But I've got the codes for the regular forces command net. An adjustment of the duty rotation, to make sure that none of the first-string pilots are on shift . . ." Ridgeway shrugged.

"My God. Haven't you ever heard of the lucky shot?"

He looked pleased, I swear he did. "That's why I made sure he had armed backup."

"What?"

"The second ship." I must have looked blank, or not blank enough. "You've got holes in your information. I leaked Falcon's destination to a woman named Laura Brass. She arrived right on schedule and ran interference for him."

Laura Brass. Niki's crazy friend. *Mercy of the Goddess*, and FourCorners, and an elegant, offhand bit of wingwork. "Where is she?"

Ridgeway looked disgusted. "All over the western continent," he said. The obligatory punchline to a joke he thought I ought to know. Niki's crazy friend, a better friend to him than I'd been, was dead.

"Let me see Niki Falcon," I said to Ridgeway.

"Why?"

"Because I've never seen a sacrificial chicken before. What harm can it do?"

Ridgeway folded his hands and watched his thumbs rub together. "You have a connection with him, don't you?"

"None of your business."

"I'm mission head on this. It is my business. I know you're good and reliable. But Niki Falcon has an incredible talent for screwing up what he comes in contact with, and because you're here, I assume he's come in contact with you. I'll trust you more if I know what that contact was.'' He has cold eyes, does Jacob Ridgeway, though I'd bet he can hide it well. ''If I tell you what my connection is, will you tell me yours?''

I showed him my teeth. ''You can't buy trust.''

''Of course you can. You just can't buy it with money. We do it all the time, or we'd never get anything done. Do you know about Dominic Glyndwr?''

I nodded, because I didn't think I should do more.

''I was the agent-in-place on Cymru.''

Maybe that's the beginning of it, really; when I began the slide from dependable agent to security risk. I'd known it was Special Services. Niki had told me that. But I was sitting across the room from the man who had killed Niki's first incarnation, and there was nothing in his face to say that he thought he shouldn't have done it. The muscles in my fingers seemed to be run by little AI servos that were thinking about strangling him.

''The operation,'' he continued, ''took years to set up, and three months to fall apart. I made a series of mistakes, all of them having to do with Niki. Culminating in letting him get away alive. Worse, he was seen getting away alive. The population loves a prince in exile. Cymru never did settle down enough to reassure the Concorde, and the whole transit path project had to be moved to one of the other planets in the system. It was,'' he finished, with a flash of almost-humor, ''a setback for my career.

''Now,'' he said, ''what about you?''

''I was fucking him for a year,'' I said, because I was damned if I'd use a word like *lovers* where Jacob Ridgeway could hear it. ''I haven't any setbacks to make up for. May I see him now?''

Eventually, he let me.

Niki was housed rather differently. It had been a hospital room, I think, and technically still was; but anything that wasn't strictly necessary had been removed, and the door was locked. There were white walls, and a white cot, and a walled-off corner with a white door behind which, I assume, were the banalities of life. There weren't any possessions in this room, either, because someone had taken them away.

He'd been pacing the small space. I could tell from the way he was standing when the door opened and I came through it, and they locked it behind me.

I'd seen him at Green Columns, at Aurelia Yarretic's wretched party, and that was the first time in three years that I'd been in the same room with him. He'd been disguised with black velvet and paint, moustache and eyepatch. And that was still Niki, but this—this was *Niki*, and the sudden proximity to him hit me like a stone in the chest. He wore a loose white shirt, very clean, and black flight pants. He had a shadow of beard, and his blue-black hair was in disorder, as if he'd been raking his hands through it. His high-boned face was so pale and pared away he might as well have been dead already, but for the eyes. I can't describe them, or won't, maybe. But to have them fixed on me, full of what was inside him, when I came in that door, made me want to whistle up my weasel self and hide behind it.

And the son of a bitch smiled at me.

"You can sit on the bed if you want," he said. "I'm not using it right now." No, he wasn't being snide. I swear it was the same expression, the same tone of voice, in which he'd once asked me to go for coffee.

He was pacing again, graceless and compulsive. I sat on the smooth white bed and said, "You're making me tired."

"Sorry." He stopped, leaned against the wall. His fingers drummed on it; he rolled his head on his neck, stretched his spine, tapped his foot. Then he pushed away from the wall. "I can't help it, I'm afraid. I've got a nice fresh thirty mikes in me that just came on line, and if I stand still, I'll start screaming."

I knew what that meant. But I couldn't think of anything to say about it, except, "Oh."

"It won't happen again. Chrysander slipped me this tab, but I haven't any others on me. And I have a nasty feeling that they're going to take me off the stuff."

"You have Spin's ship, don't you?" Yes, I was changing the subject. "I was too late to catch you on Bellmaker's."

Mild surprise pooled in his expression. "You *are* good. I didn't think you'd know about that. Spin was thinking about you, toward the end."

"Me?"

"Oh, yes. He made some modifications to the bird before he hid it, thinking I'd have a use for them. He added a headset and couch for weapons control."

Weasel-twist. I kept it from speaking. "We were through long before Spin died."

"Spin could be unwarrantedly hopeful about anyone's future but his own. Speaking of unwarranted things, what did you have in mind when you left me that bit of mail?"

I dug my nails into my palms—I suppose because I knew I deserved it. "I sent it from FourCorners," I said hollowly. "From the port. I was upset."

"So was I," he said, very softly.

"I knew that. About five minutes after I sent it. I'm sorry."

"You know about Laura, I suppose. I seem to be leaving a trail behind me lately. Does it make you wonder who's next?"

He was talking too much, and at first I thought it was just the drug. Then he propped one hand against the wall and turned away from me, but not before I saw a little of his face.

I leaped up and pulled him around by one shoulder. It was all painted there: arched eyebrows straight and pinched in toward the thin, high bridge of the nose; eyes shut, the lashes black ink curves against the ink-wash shadows under them; lips alternately open for air and drawn tightly closed against the pain.

"What can I do?" I demanded.

"Nothing." He opened his eyes. "It's only sometimes. I can manage for a while yet. But I can live for longer than I can manage."

"They're going to make sure of it," I said.

"I know. Jhari, find out why. Something to do with the original project."

"The gestalt program—"

"No. The research done here, before that. Damion worked on it. What was it? That's the piece I'm missing." He no longer breathed as if there were a weight on his chest. "The Concorde slammed the lid on it, as if they were afraid of it. We've got to know."

We. I'm not sure I noticed that at the time. "How does that research connect with you?"

He laughed thickly and told me.

Then he tossed the hair out of his eyes. His face was ablaze with the drug again, as if, when the pain ebbed, there was no place for the energy to go. "Find out, Jhari. If I leave this room, it'll be in a box. You're the only one who can find out why."

I stood with my mouth and head full of words, all of them unsuited to the time and place. Then he stretched out one shaking hand and touched the side of my face. I couldn't draw breath to say anything, anyway. And I couldn't bring myself to do even as much as he'd done. He turned, paced to the opposite wall, and stayed there until I left the room. No, I didn't say anything about Laura Brass. What earthly good would it have done to tell him what Ridgeway had told me?

So I left him leaning against the wall of his white tomb, and went first to find Chrysander Harris.

He was under what passes for house arrest—well, protective custody—in the warrens. I had to ask his permission before I could come in, and I tried to decide, from his tone of voice on the call plate, whether he intended to let me leave in one piece.

He'd been pacing, too, but he had a little more room to do it in. The space was full of things he could use to kill me, if he wanted to. I've never been under many illusions regarding Chrysander Harris. He's a man with two vocations: musician and warrior. Not hobbies, either of them; he could never have achieved what he has if they weren't balanced, twined, mated in his hands and head.

Music is numerical, analytical, spatial—leave inspiration out of it for now. So is the gestalt. But fighting, numerical? And the synthesis ability Chrysander Harris has, the voice—what part of him does that come from? Numerical, analytical, spatial? Or something else, which would make my speculations nonsense.

Well, there I was, and his expression and the set of his body made me feel remarkably breakable. His was not the face of someone who knew it would be stupid to kill me.

"If either your government or the Concorde forces here find out I'm a Special Services agent, whatever's left of me will be shipped home in an urn," I told him.

He blinked those appalling golden eyes. "Shall I call them both?"

"Up to you. That's my security deposit, as it were. Use it against me if you decide I deserve it."

"Oh, you deserve it," he said, with a voiceful of quiet music.

"Do I? Maybe I deserve it for letting you deliver him to Ridgeway and your father."

He drew a quick, hard breath and sat down. "Nicely done. I would have had to use my voice trick to get that effect." He wasn't done with me, though. "Did you ever really want to recruit me for Special Services?"

"Of course. But no one expected you to agree. My job was to put pressure on you and keep it there, to make sure that, whatever you'd been sent to do, you did it quickly, sloppily, and where we could see you."

"Did you succeed?"

"Not exactly. When you latched on to Niki Falcon, the people running my end of the operation didn't know what it meant. Based on my report from FourCorners, they panicked and put out a bounty on Niki." Harris looked startled. I shrugged. "They were afraid they would lose you. The people at Ridgeway's end of the operation hadn't passed on that they wanted Niki, too."

"You weren't part of this charade from the beginning?"

"Not directly, no. SpecServe can't draw a straight line."

Harris laced his fingers together and rested his chin on them. "You must love your work," he said sweetly. "Then the Twelve didn't get this idea all by themselves?"

"Afraid not. Though Ridgeway wants 'em to think they did. I suppose they didn't tell you what they wanted Niki for?"

He shook his head. "You make a hole in the Silence, you poke a message out. There isn't room for a very big one." Then he slammed his fingers through his hair, an abrupt and uncalculated gesture. "No," he said gruffly. "That sounds like an excuse. No, I didn't know, and I didn't have the sense to keep from doing it until I *did* know. That was wrong."

I looked at his bent golden head and thought wildly, *Niki's been here.*

"SpecServe's little internal intrigues aren't usually this bad. I think someone's trying to keep something so secret they can't even tell it to the rest of the secret-keepers." I stopped to catch my breath, and added, "I've just come from seeing him."

Harris raised his head. "Niki? Is he still—"

"Alive? Conscious? In one piece? Confined? Lit up like Hub Palace? Yes. Why are you locked in here?"

"Because if I wasn't, he wouldn't be confined anymore. I'd have him back on that ship and gone in an hour."

"It *is* protective custody, then. You'd both get killed. Even he couldn't get out of the well now." And I explained about the second-string pilots, and Laura Brass.

Harris looked so sick that for the first time I almost liked him. "What have you come to me for?" he asked finally. "Or are you just making sure I know everything, so I can feel as bad as possible?"

"I came to ask you what the original research on Lamia was supposed to do."

Harris, God damn him, laughed. "Go ahead. I don't know."

"All right, I can't expect you to trust me. If your damned

voice trick worked both ways, you could tell I was honest by the way I sounded."

He glowered up at me. "It doesn't matter if I trust you or not. I really don't know. Ask my father."

"Assuming I could without smoking my cover, would he tell me?"

"No."

"Would he tell you?" I asked. Harris shook his head. "Is there anyplace else I can find it out?"

He sat quiet for so long that I thought he was simply refusing to answer. Then he raised his head, frowning. "There must be other people here who worked on it. But I don't know who. And they might not have been told what they were working on."

"Right," I sighed. "Government work. I'll bet you any amount of money Jacob Ridgeway knows. For what good that will do me." I'm not much familiar with despair. I haven't had the right kind of life. But when I feel it, it makes me snappish. "I can't save Niki's life," I said, "because at this point, no one can. But I am going to line up the facts and make them jump through hoops because *he asked me to*. This is your last chance to contribute."

Another long silence, during which neither of us moved. "Niki's mother," Chrysander said, his rich voice rather vague, continuing as if he hadn't heard me. "And my father. And the late Genefa Harisal, who headed the gestalt pilot research. No, she doesn't matter. My father said . . . they argued, and she didn't think it was enough to help natural mutations . . . Oh." He looked up at me, his yellow eyes huge. "How old is Niki?"

"Twenty . . . nine?"

"Huh. Can you get me out of here?"

I thought about it. A little abuse of my cover, and I could do it—no. Ridgeway would think it was odd, and what he thought was odd, he would squash. "I don't think so."

"Damn it. You'll have to do it, then. Can you get into the BioEng lab?"

Without trying it, I didn't know. I shrugged.

"If you can," Chrysander said, "use this." And he gave me a string of words that I realized was a hypermap. "That will get you into my file, in the BioEngineering base."

I didn't thank him before I left, because I didn't know if what he gave me was useful. Besides, I was used to the focused, calculating Chrysander Harris; this person, who made intuitive leaps and forgot to explain them, was someone else. Or was it the same calculating soul behind a well-made façade? If so, I have no idea why he gave me anything, useful or not. Unless his misbegotten trick does work both ways.

I'm exhausted. I'm slightly crazed from lack of sleep. I'm in possession of what may be the facts. If I'm right, then what I've written for you, Unauthorized Reader, will be a history of one of your most impressive failures, when I'm done. If I'm wrong—then I'm sorry, Niki, and Chrysander, too.

The technique that enabled me to follow Niki Falcon from FourCorners to Lamia got me the missing piece. Synthesis, layering—a mental path like a spiraling cone. The mind comes back to an established fact, but always with another layer of context added, a broadening of its meaning. Up and out.

Chrysander was right; there was one other person who knew *all* about the original research, besides Jacob Ridgeway and Tomas Damion: Morwenna Glyndwr-Jones. Dead, you say? Oh, yes. But she kept her notes, remember, and added to them, refining her data and her experimental apparatus in the process.

For nineteen years.

And I know more about Niki Falcon than any other living person, save one. That one is Ridgeway, of course. But I think I've negated even his advantage.

Synthesis. Combine Chrysander's own records, of his testing and training, with what the Concorde knows about Lamia's breeding program. The Rhine-Soal index measures potential for telepathy, clairvoyance, psychokinesis. Lamia sought to develop that potential just as it would any other resource, and its efforts were based on something that Damion and Glyndwr-Jones had been studying in the local gene pool.

Combine those with the gestalt research and procedures. The gestalt is a highly refined interface between the human nervous system and the nearly-living mechanism of a ship's computer, making communication possible in a way that is only partly physical. That, in its turn, makes it possible to manipulate the Cheat in ways that the unassisted computer can't. The computer must move in stop-look-leap, stop-look-leap lurching movements. The pilot-computer gestalt flings itself into the unspace of the Cheat with the economy and grace of a hawk and lands lightly, leaves and arrives in what seems a single action. But to become a gestalt pilot, a person must have certain characteristics, physical and mental. They aren't part of the gestalt modifications, but they are essential to its success.

Combine those with Niki Falcon. He must have become a gestalt pilot, not by coincidence, but because it was the closest thing to what he'd been bred and shaped to be. It called to him because all its parameters must have fit the outline of him. And Niki Falcon understands movement through space, over time. When fastened to and in communication with his ship, he is the ultimate expression of the gestalt.

Back reference to the gestalt. Remember I said that it facilitates things for the computer, not the human.

So I made my hunch. I took it to Chrysander Harris, who wouldn't believe it, but who couldn't tell me it was impossible. Now I'm taking it to Niki. However he may have perceived the time, it's been three objective days since I visited him in that white room. If pain and memory run wild has left enough of him, I'll put his future in his hands.

I know him better than anyone else. I think I know what he'll choose.

CHAPTER FIFTEEN

Let the new faces play what tricks they will
In the old rooms; night can outbalance day,
Our shadows rove the garden gravel still,
The living seem more shadowy than they.
    —W. B. Yeats, "The New Faces"

"What are you doing here?" he says without air—but this voice requires none, and traverses the space that has none. It is a question that begs to be a denial; it wants to become "You are not here," and to be true when it does.

"Riding shotgun for you, stupid," she replies.

"But how did you know where—"

"Sweet boy, I can access anything. We've had this conversation."

His awareness spreads out, a flung net without holes. In that net hostile ships swim, unaware that he has made his cast. He does not "see" them; what he uses is not an analog for eyesight. He feels them all over his skin, feels their position, their distance from him, the rate at which that changes and in what direction. A strong feeling, stronger than it has ever been, a pain in his mind like the withdrawal pain in his meat-body, when he is wholly in it.

"Don't, Laura. Go away."

"Too late," she says, perfectly cheerful. She's right, of course.

Her guns cut and kill, spilling the inside of a Concorde ship into the vacuum. The spot where he felt it on his skin is cool and still now.

He drops like a slicing knife between two red lines of laser fire. They are part of the net and he is part of them. The fisherman and the fish, all connected. His own lasers fire, from somewhere under his diaphragm, and the counter-lines connect him with the ship they hit. Lines and ship dissipate, devoured, out of the net.

"Nice shot," says Laura.

"Chrysander," he tells her. "Go, Laura, please. I've already seen six killing shots at you that they didn't happen to take. The luck is running out."

"There's no place to go, Nik." Not cheerful, this time, but not sad, either. "Ever hear of all those funny religions on Terra that sent honor guards with their dead into the afterlife? I have served you, Kali. . . ."

He has 360-degree vision, multiple awareness, the speed necessary to use them. "Laura, zero-up!" he cries.

She does not have the vision, the awareness, the speed. His warning is no use at all. Touch of red light. Slow falling-inward of her ship, slow in his eye-time; then out, out, each piece catching sharp sunlight, the whole sparkling like a handful of glitter tossed, a round expanding flower of desolation.

Time, for him, is on a leash. He has time, between the desire to scream and the impulse that will work his throat, to realize the futility of it. She cannot hear or answer. Instead he stoops on his prey and lets Chrysander work the talons that break its back.

There was no difference between the old memories and the new ones; they all came out bright as new-cut metal. And out, and out. Between one blink and the next, they came, and Niki could not be sure which he would open his eyes to, present time or waking dream-past.

This time he blinked, and focused on a smooth, shining tube of glass. It stood in a rack on the taboret beside the examining bed. As he looked at it, a longing rose up in him, under intense pressure. He'd forgotten it, how it felt; he'd been without it almost since he'd entered the gestalt program. But here it was again, roused like one of his memories by the sight of the glass and the pain that etched deep, complex patterns on him outside and in.

If he could summon the strength, he could reach out, take hold of the tube, crack it like an egg on the side of the taboret. With its broken edge he could draw one or two firm, swift lines, through the patterns of pain and despair. It would feed the vampire thing in his heart whose hunger hurt worse than withdrawal.

He wanted to die, and he no longer had the strength to make it happen.

Strength and speed—for he was not alone in the room, and they wanted to keep him alive. "Will of God," said one of them irritably. Faded blond hair, sagging features, frightened blue eyes: Damion, rising from the monitor station that tried to interpret Niki to him. "Another irruption. None of this is coherent. There's nothing I can get out of these waveforms. Maybe if I'd been able to start months ago—"

"I'm sorry," a voice he recognized said mildly. "I wish you could have." Jacob.

"If I could get my hands on some of the drug he's been modified for . . . See, here, this spike? The clipped one, at the ending of the recording? His endorphins are clipping that activity in self-defense. But the drug would raise their threshold."

"To allow for what?" Jacob asked. "What's the activity?"

"How should I know? If I can't get the drug, I can only guess."

"Ah," Jacob said.

Damion came to the side of the examining cot and stared down as if Niki were blind, or unconscious. "You don't want this to work, do you?" he said to Jacob. "You don't even care about the rest of the gestalt figures. You just want it wrapped up so you can take it home."

"There's more to this than what I want. Unfortunately. So I can't shoot a big hole in your patient's brain right now, because it would show up clear as air in all of your data and test records. And the people I report to would want to know why I terminated their project before it had run its course."

"If they want useful data on the gestalt research, why won't you let me do anything more constructive than watch him die? They won't get anything more out of this"—Damion's hands flourished toward the monitor—"than I can!"

"If they were here, I'm sure they'd agree. But they're not, I am, and I have a much better idea of what we're in danger of than they would. Or than you do."

Damion looked mutinous. Of course; his wisdom had just been doubted. "I believe I know what we're dealing with."

"Of course," Jacob said. "And you'd be delighted to risk unleashing it on all of us, just to see if it would work. No. You're going to watch him die, and compose me a nice little report I can take back and close all the files with."

The blue eyes flicked toward Jacob, saying as clearly as a pointing finger and a scream where the fear in them came from. "Who do you work for, really?" said Damion, with ill-advised belligerence. "Army intelligence?"

"Better you shouldn't know. Then you won't be tempted to mention it. And I won't have to threaten your son to keep you quiet."

Chrysander was alive, then. Good. (Though why he should be other than alive wasn't clear.) If they would only say something about Jhari, Niki would feel better.

But he blinked, and opened his eyes on the past again.

Sometimes Niki moved into a parody of sleep, when his body simply shut down in the face of pain and exhaustion. The blackouts never lasted long, but they were as close as he came to zero brain activity, and when they faded, he always felt a little stronger. After one of them, his vision cleared to show him Jacob, sitting beside the cot.

What Niki had for laughter was an articulate exhale. It drew Jacob's attention to his face. "Here we are again," Niki whispered, "and it's not even Landing Day."

"You were right," said Jacob. "I should have killed you that night in the Great Hall." It sounded ridiculously like an apology.

"I thought it would have ruined your plan."

"It was ruined anyway. You know that, don't you?"

"A little. What I could find out from a distance. I'd learned my lesson about not following the news, you see."

Jacob lifted one shoulder. "You were a great revolutionary leader. Trust me."

Niki looked at the gently curved ceiling and recalled, with the decent inaccuracy of normal memory, Andrew Fisher standing in the shadow of the offworld shuttle's landing struts. "I left to prevent that very thing from happening. Too much blood and fire to no good purpose, I thought."

"There was some," Jacob said.

"But was it to no purpose?"

At last, grudgingly, he said, "No. We finally gave up. And it's still Cymru, with almost everything that means. Including the warts."

"People do tend to prefer their own warts to others'."

"Don't you want to know about Olwen?"

"I already do. Emigrated to Glorianna and married a banker."

"You *did* follow the news."

But Andrew Fisher and Jane Wells hadn't been newsworthy. He would never know what had happened to them. Niki closed his eyes, hoping for another scrap of oblivion. But whatever perversion of circadian rhythm his body had settled on was in its upswing, and all he got was a sudden, vicious cramp in his shoulder. When it faded, Jacob was still there.

"Where's Damion?" Niki panted.

"Sleeping."

"I'm glad someone is. Jacob—"

"No," Jacob said quietly. "You want me to behave as a friend would. I did that ten years ago. If I hadn't, neither of us would be here now."

"Jacob, please. I heard what Damion said. No one is going to get any useful data out of this anyway. This is pointless torture. I didn't think you did that."

A knot of muscle snapped into relief in his jaw. "Well, now I do," he said. He turned and left the little white room.

It comes to him, slowly, that he is about to be followed. Strange, to put it like that, but true. His vector is about to cross two others, which will be matched with his. If he stops and turns around now, it will not happen. But this is the direction he wants to go. And besides, it is such a strange thing to feel.

He goes on, through narrow, wet streets. The houses here, in bright laminates, lean toward each other over the pavement and sometimes flow together at their second stories, like self-grafting plants. He walks under the tunnel of one of these, past a door painted with religious symbols, between floating lamps like water lilies head-down.

The two vectors have joined his. He feels them on his skin, mass in motion. He begins to feel the points, somewhere ahead, where they might all intersect. He adjusts his speed to make for the best one.

He is light-headed and feverish, but perhaps it's only that he's unused to the drug. Perhaps he'll be this way for the rest of his life. He's had a great deal of alcohol, in celebration of the fact that it can no longer do anything to him. But is that true?

Where things are—he's always been able to tell that. But this is hypersensitivity, more like seeing the future than using his senses. It is almost too strong to bear comfortably.

At his chosen point, the vectors meet. They walk past him, where he presses back in a hollow in the base of the Peace statue. For an instant he wonders, dizzily, how they can go by and not know it, not be aware of the shape that his mass cuts in the fabric of the universe. Theirs are solid as carvings he runs his hands over.

By the time they realize he is no longer in front of them, he has stepped from the niche. They turn. One of them gets his heel in the stomach. The other nicks his wrist with a snapknife, painfully, over the bone. The knuckles of his other hand meet the face, break cartilege.

He is gone, down another street; the Peace plaza is the emptying basin for twelve of them, some little more than service paths between the houses. One of the reasons he chose it. He is six blocks away and alone before he realizes that the almost painful hypersensitivity is gone. But his skin prickles, his throat hurts, and his head aches. So it is a fever, after all.

He wonders if he will remember to mention the whole business to Jhari.

Her eyes were bloodshot and blue-shadowed underneath, and her lips were chapped. Too much attention paid to some bit of classwork that fascinated her, too little attention to sleep and food and putting her head out-of-doors now and then. He would have to carry her off somewhere for dinner—

Then he felt the cold sweat on his skin, the consuming pain in his guts, a sensation as if his bones were white phosphor and someone had touched off the fuse for them. The transition was too sudden to bear, but he was so weak he couldn't scream properly. He made a thin, windy noise that trembled in his throat.

Jhari lurched forward, cupped one hand around his cheek. The touch was excess information down the nerve paths, part of the ongoing overload, and he shivered. But he didn't wince, and so she didn't know she was hurting him, because he didn't want her to.

And she was still there. She should be gone with the memory. Or, depending on the memory, not there yet. This must be real-time. He said her name. From her face, he thought it hurt her as much as her hand hurt him.

In a sudden attack of lucidity, he thought, *Our entire love story in microcosm.*

He wanted to talk to her—no pressing subjects, just talk, comfort between friends—but he was too weak, and there was nothing, really, to say. Certainly nothing about love, which, like her hand and his voice, would give pain when comfort was meant.

She leaned over him. The white-shining ceiling made a cloud of light out of her hair.

"Kill me," he whispered.

Her face folded in on itself, as if radiating cracks from the center. "You should know—I have to tell you—" Then she shook her head; her hair fanned out and across her face. "Oh, Christ, maybe I don't. Maybe you already told me what I needed to know." She grabbed his hand, uncurled the clenched fingers, and rolled them closed around something small. "I got it from Chrysander," she said. "It's a thirty." She stepped back.

He nodded. "Good. Go, now. Hurry."

She understood; she had to be far away when it happened. She stopped almost on the edge of his vision, and seemed about to say something painful. But she shook her head again, and flew out the door.

He had, of course, no time sense. He struggled against that, trying to make his internal clock function one last time. He had to give her a chance to get away. Under his fingers, the thirty mike needle tab rolled and rolled. He was careful not to squeeze it too hard. Not yet.

There wasn't enough of him left to take the blow the tab would deliver. The convulsion would tear his muscles from their bindings. The dam-breaking force of it would burst his heart. The surge of activity would fry his nervous system. It was going to be a very unpleasant death, but it was the only one in his hand.

One last time he rolled the tab, to place it properly in his fingers. Then he turned his wrist and drove it into his thigh.

The attenuated seconds dropped, slowly, like thick liquid from a spoon. Then he felt the oncoming tide. Just before his body clamped down on itself and burned, he heard the frantic beeping from the monitors that kept watch over him. Too late. The examining cot, responding to its programming, tried to extrude restraints. Too late. Jacob would not be pleased.

All sensation was overload, but dropped at last to silence.

CHAPTER SIXTEEN

For wisdom is the property of the dead,
A something incompatible with life; and power,
Like everything that has the stain of blood,
A property of the living; but no stain
Can come upon the visage of the moon
When it has looked in glory from a cloud.
                    —W. B. Yeats, "Blood and the Moon"

All events happen in space, over time. And the medium in which they occur—space and time—is part of the events themselves. If the events are witnessed, they are recorded in memory, which is itself subject to space and time. If the past is recalled, does it become part of the fabric of the present? If the present results from things done and words spoken years before, is it part of the past? Is time—past, present, and future—air at three temperatures, stirring, molecules bumping against one another until they are indistinguishable? Or is time a windless sky, with a gradation of light and temperature from top to bottom?

And if an event, like a long-winged hawk, spirals upward into the thin cold air, and closes its wings, and dives, the wind of its passage a whistling scream along each feather shaft— Now what is time, now that the space it occupies has been disturbed?

In the corridors of the biomed research facility in the Medical Center on Lamia, several delicately worded messages are repeated and repeated on every call plate speaker. Two people understand them: Jacob Ridgeway and Tomas Damion. They are aware, suddenly, that the spiral climb is over and the dive begun, even as they begin to run toward the small white room.

Jhari Sabayan hears the messages, but does not know they are part of the passage of the hawk until the door of her little hostel room crashes open. Jacob Ridgeway fills the doorframe with rage. "Bitch," he says. "You mad, stupid bitch."

"Excuse me?"

"You did it, didn't you? Where did you get the drug?"

Her shoulders sink, relaxed, and the settled calm of martyrs falls on her face. "I can't imagine it matters, now. Yes, I did it. Are you going to break me for it?"

"Yes," says Ridgeway, hissing.

Facilities for imprisoning people are scarce on Lamia, but civilized. Small, clean, secure chambers—not so different from the hospital rooms. But locking Jhari Sabayan in one is fraught with difficulty. She is either a Concorde diplomatic representative or the Planetary Governor, depending on which faction is describing her, and Jacob Ridgeway is not entitled to throw either identity in a cell.

He manages it, in the end, by stealing both of them from her. He gives her the name and cell of a madwoman; where the madwoman is, Jhari is afraid to wonder. She stands in the center of the bare little room, her strong mind empty and numb. Waiting, out of habit, for an event that has already occurred.

Chrysander Harris feels the air move around him, in its confusion of temperatures. He does not realize what it is, or even that he feels it. But the tension in his body, the wariness, the waiting in his mind, are all echoes of the falling of the hawk.

Then his father comes in, wearing a face he has never seen on his father, on anyone: incomprehension, fear, profound horror. He has come to Chrysander, but does not seem entirely aware of him. He sits on the edge of a cloth-covered bench, his fingers clasping and unclasping between his knees, his eyes fixed on the invisible motion of air before him.

"What is it?" Chrysander asks.

"You brought him here," his father snaps.

The subject, now, is clear. "Yes, I did. You told me to."

"It's that bastard's fault! It's Ridgeway who insisted I let him die. I would have helped him!"

Chrysander stares at his father's distorted face, hears the rising, breaking voice, and the words it says. A slow cold begins to rise in him; slow, because it is too deep to move quickly.

"He was in pain, for Christ's sake. I'm a doctor. . . ." The whine changes to a wail. "They'll blame me. Everyone will blame me. He . . . he . . . Oh, God. Oh, almighty God—" And Chrysander's father begins to cry, great cracking terrified sobs.

Chrysander looks down on the faded blond head, and remembers Jhari Sabayan's ridiculous hunch with the fierce, angry yearning of a child for a fairy tale he wants to be true. He hears, as if from a distance, the whistling shriek of air over feathers.

Jacob Ridgeway, long-sighted in both space and time, leans over a well-shielded 'board, entering an order. It is to the officer in charge of Concorde regular forces on Lamia. It begins with all the proper authorization codes, properly entered, and ends with Jhari Sabayan's name and illusory title. The words in between are a masterpiece of tone: restrained and yet moving.

The Lamians, out of courage or madness, have made a plague. There can be no pacification of Lamia, no peaceful coexistence with its citizens. Anyone, invader or negotiator, enemy or ally, who enters the warrens will become a victim and a carrier of a long-lived, fast-acting disease that ruptures the walls of human cells. Containment—swift and complete containment and destruction—is the only alternative. The Planetary Governor regrets the necessity of so many deaths, hers included, but when weighed against the possible death of humanity . . . Jhari Sabayan will be a hero for centuries.

He stores the message when it is finished. He is not ready to transmit the order yet. His own survival must be looked to; Special Services will need more than this myth he is leaving for history. Now he must, unnoticed, steal from the warren's closed ecology the things he will need to live alone on Lamia.

His stomach turns over unpleasantly, a nervous reaction. He has never been subject to nerves. The worst disasters in his career have only brought out his best work: actions, solutions. Even now, he is moving the solutions into place. There is no reason for nerves.

Long-sighted though he is, he cannot see the trajectory of the hawk. He knows it is there. Nerves are the only possible response.

The politely worded messages on the call plates happened at sunset. That night passed, and the next, along with the days attached to them. Dr. Damion lived in his office and saw no one, sometimes did not even answer calls at his door. The courier from the Bear Triangle was much in evidence, helpful when he could be to the Twelve (Eleven, without Damion), if a little distracted. Chrysander Harris was hospitalized with, it was rumored, a breakdown. No one was allowed to see him even if he'd wanted it. The gestalt pilot, who would have been their bargaining piece with the Concorde, was dead, and the Concorde representative was nowhere to be found.

And the air and ground forces of the Concorde kept the warrens under siege.

Chrysander woke quickly and clearheaded, but couldn't tell what had broken his sleep. There was the faintest dim edge of light at the junction of floor and walls: night light. The clock in the head of the hospital cot told him the day had just turned.

He lay still for a little while, breathing evenly, listening. Nothing. He slid off the cot and landed knees bent, arms up for a block. Still nothing.

The room lights were controlled from the stat station at the end of the hall. He had to do his searching in the dark—and he did it carefully. There were so many dangerous things one could hide in a hospital room, and Jacob Ridgeway was a clever man. But when he found the thing, it was so familiar, so inoffensive, that he almost didn't realize it hadn't been there all along.

It was the bag he'd carried, slung over his shoulder, on Bellmaker's World. Its edges were silvered by the floor lights, and he could see the jutting corner of the Entropic pressing against the inside of the bag.

It made him think of blowing snow, the inside of the black ship, and Niki Falcon. That brought on a familiar rush of emotion that, once again, made him want to break something. He wasn't quite desperate enough to resort to the only appropriate thing in reach. After all, as his father had so kindly reminded him, it was Chrysander who'd brought Niki Falcon to Lamia.

He felt for the top seal of the bag, and found a scrap of paper on it. A piece of lab toweling, from the feel. He laid it on the floor, near the wall, where the faint glow of the night light would fall on it, and saw a crisscross of lines in ink that at first made no sense to him.

He gave the paper a quarter-turn . . . and realized it was a very swiftly drawn diagram of part of the warren, a slice of spiderwebbed radials. A spot at a point along one line of ink, a spot at another. If one of the radials was the hall his room was on—and, yes, that dot would correspond to where his room lay in the hall—then the other dot would be *there*. The location had no significance for him, but he could find it. There were six numbers under the diagram. Chrysander memorized them, tore up the scrap of towel, and stuffed it in the lavatory disposal to vaporize.

Someone had made a cursory search of the room he'd been staying in, and put a few useful items in the bag. The Entropic, of course. A dark gray-green coverall, which he put on; they'd taken his clothes when they'd locked him in here, on his father's orders. (Which had come, originally, from Ridgeway.) A set of willowleaf knives, five of them, in a chest sheath. He put that on, too, against his skin under the coverall. A polarizing outcap and hinged visor—that he left in the bag.

Now, what was he meant to do with these things? And who had left them? Ridgeway, baiting a trap? Surely there were better ways to get rid of him. Did his father intend him to restore the family honor? Too late. Jhari Sabayan? No, the trickle of rumor he had access to said she had disappeared. Chrysander suspected that Ridgeway had done his professional worst there, too.

Well, he was no use to anyone with the door locked. And the door, like the room light, was controlled at the stat station. He tried it anyway. It opened.

He found out what the cap was for the first time he had to pass a corridor guardpost. It hid his bright hair, shadowed his bright eyes, especially when he touched one hand to the visor in greeting. His other hand scratched idly at his chest, near the opening in the front of the coverall, an inch from the hilt of the first knife. The guard nodded at him, without recognition. Chrysander went on, through the crowded, sleeping halls, toward the marked spot on the towel diagram.

The guard was not someone he knew. But imagining her with one of the little knives in her throat, or her eye, affected him as if she had been. At that astonishing dinner on board *Mercy of the Goddess*, Laura Brass had teased Niki Falcon about being diminished by the deaths of others. Chrysander wanted suddenly to be at that table again, to explain the feeling to Laura, to see Niki surprised and amused at the source of the confirmation of his ideals. Laura and Niki. One after the other, they were both dead; and did those responsible feel diminished? Chrysander certainly did, and he was one of them.

He recognized the area when he reached it—the cells. There were five to a side in the corridor. The mark had been on the east side of the line, past the middle but not at the very end. Chrysander went to the fourth door in the east wall, pressed the memorized six numbers on the door lockpad. The latch clicked.

The person who rose from the edge of the bunk, startled, fully dressed, and holding a light-duty beamer trained on his chest, was Jhari Sabayan.

"I take it," Chrysander said, "this isn't your plan."

She blinked. "Then I take it it's not yours, either."

"You knew I was coming?"

"I knew someone was." She lowered the beamer. "I woke up about fifteen minutes ago and found Lucille, here, on my pillow, with this stuffed in the trigger guard." She handed Chrysander another scrap of toweling.

This was a larger slice of the warren, but he found the spot that marked the cell. The other spot, then, was . . . "The Netcenter," Chrysander said aloud, rubbing the toweling between his fingers.

Jhari nodded once. "I knew it was a map, but I don't know enough about the warren to read it. And my door was locked. Translation: wait for native guide."

"My door wasn't. And my map led here."

"So we're supposed to go together." She glanced at the charge indic on the beamer and tucked it in her trouser pocket.

Chrysander stared at her, and said at last, "Aren't you even a little curious about why? And on whose orders?"

She raised her eyebrows, and it occurred to Chrysander for the first time that something might have been *done* to her. Her perfect calm did not seem sane.

He shrugged and followed her out of the cell. It was as good as any other direction.

Jacob Anton Ridgeway stepped into his rooms, sealed the door behind him, and prodded the wall panel to bring the lights from night level to full. It didn't work.

He stood stiff against the door for a long moment, as if listening, or trying to adjust to the darkness, or possibly (though not likely) grappling with fear. The paralysis broke in one smooth movement; body turning, right hand coming up, the thin turquoise streak of beamer shot bisecting the air. Silence.

Then, very clear in the dark room: "Jacob Ridgeway."

Jacob fired again, straight at the sound.

"If you recognize my voice, you know that isn't going to work."

Jacob was breathing unnecessarily hard. "It will if I'm quick."

"You knew about the original research. You saw the last recordings off the monitor. And you saw the examining bed. You're lying to yourself."

Jacob turned suddenly, yanked at the door seals. Nothing happened. He fired the beamer at the latch and realized his mistake in the faint blue-green light it cast on the mechanism as it fused it. "Goddamn. Goddamn it." He sliced lines of pale light again and again across the darkness.

"If you hit me now, how will you get out of this room?"

"I'm never getting out anyway. You might as well kill me."

"I'd rather have you alive."

Jacob shook his head.

"What are you afraid of?"

"SpecServe is afraid of the possibility that an uncontrollable entity will be set loose."

"And you?"

Jacob said, his voice low and hoarse, "I'm afraid it will come for me."

"And do what?"

"You don't dare let me live," Jacob said wisely. "Because I *do* know. The monitor record, with the unclipped spike and the flatline. The examining bed, with the restraints all fastened down over nothing. The locked door on the empty room. You don't dare leave me alive to talk."

Laughter, genuine if a little hysterical. "Oh, Christ, Jacob. If no one can shoot fast enough to hit me, why should I care how many people know?"

Jacob Ridgeway stood very still, just as he had when he first came through the door. Then, with another single swift movement, he thrust the beamer in his mouth and triggered it.

Sometimes no amount of speed is enough. Sometimes even the lightning reactions of a gestalt pilot cannot beat an event to its conclusion in space and time. Sometimes disbelief, shock, horror, give the event a head start.

So Niki Falcon found himself on the other side of the room, staring down at the body prone at his feet. The neat cauterized hole through the back of the skull showed through the short ginger-and-gray hair. "Why?" he whispered. The air was full of ozone stink and perfectly silent.

For a few seconds he braced himself, trembling, against the wall. Then he cupped his hands over his face, gathered himself together. His senses spread outward, brushing minutely over his chosen cross section of space and time until they found the bit of it he wanted.

Then he Cheated.

The Silence had reduced Netcenter's functions to the automated ones, particularly in the middle of the night. There was one drowsy tech in the outer chamber waiting in vain for her expertise to be called on. Chrysander wasn't sure what sort of orders anyone might have regarding himself or Jhari Sabayan. But they would certainly never get farther than this without identifying themselves as *somebody*. So he peeled off the outcap.

"Good grief," the tech said mildly.

Jhari Sabayan, to Chrysander's surprise, said, "Is there anyone else here? We're expecting to meet someone."

We are? Chrysander thought. He studied her face and voice for clues; but her face was calm, and her voice was even and carrying and full of authority. Her hand was in her pocket, with the beamer.

"No," the tech said, looking back and forth from the person she recognized to the one she didn't. "I've been on for four hours, and you're the first live things I've seen."

Jhari shivered a little, and rubbed at her face. "It has to be—" she muttered.

Behind the tech, the door to the inner chamber, the routing room, clicked and slid open. Chrysander noticed Jhari's first reaction, and the tech's, only peripherally. He was too involved in his own.

"I thought you were dead," he said, unimaginatively, to Niki Falcon. He was aware, all in a rush, of rising hope, and of an unexpected sheer joy that had nothing to do with any practical concern.

Jhari Sabayan, at Chrysander's side, did not move at all for a long moment. Then she stepped forward, her face full of something like fear, and put her hand, the one that had been in her pocket, on Niki Falcon's chest. His two thin hands came up and covered it; he bent his head, closed his eyes. Jhari's expression was no longer fearful, though Chrysander couldn't tell what it was—pain and relief were mixed in it. He thought he ought to be somewhere else.

"So did I," said Jhari. "After a while."

"How the hell did you get in there?" wailed the tech. "And who are you?"

Niki's eyes opened. "Oh. Sorry," he said. His voice cracked a little, as if he hadn't used it much. "Explanations and reunions later. Jhari, Chrysander—come in, quick." They did, and he sealed the door behind them.

In the clean, indirect light of the routing room, Chrysander studied Niki Falcon. He was still gaunt and pale, and seemed profoundly weary. But he looked like a man whose fever had broken, and the smoking, burning edge, which had been only partly a product of the drug, was gone from his face and body and voice.

"These are yours, then?" Chrysander asked, holding the second map.

"From a time when life was simpler. About fifteen minutes ago. That was when Jacob Ridgeway changed games on us," Niki said. "Read this."

Jhari took the piece of printout he offered, and Chrysander read over her shoulder. And sucked in his breath. It was an order to the Concorde commanding officer, from Jhari Sabayan as Planetary Governor, to destroy the warrens. Jhari crumpled it. What Chrysander had really wanted, all those times he needed to break something, was Ridgeway. Nearly fifty thousand people crammed into First Warren.

"Ridgeway sent this fifteen minutes ago?" Jhari asked.

Niki nodded. "Will they do it?"

"If he sent the proper codes with it, hell, yes. And he wouldn't have bothered to send it if he didn't have the codes."

"Do you know how long we might still have?"

"It's not an order they would have been prepared for. They'll have to pull out the squads they've got in the near tunnel sections, scramble some air support, maybe—oh, lord. They'll have a couple of drain cleaners with them, I'll bet you anything. They'll fly a bomber over and drop those on us."

"Drain cleaners?" Chrysander asked.

Niki said, "Bomb with multiple shaped charges in isolated chambers. It blows its way through obstructions as it gets to them. How long, Jhari?"

"Maybe thirty minutes from when they got the message."

Niki thrust his fingers through his hair. "I had Jacob snared a few minutes ago—he must have just sent that. When he realized he couldn't get away from me, he killed himself."

"He what?" said Chrysander, outraged, then realized that Jhari had said it, too. Revenge wouldn't call back that order, but he wanted it just the same.

Niki said, "I couldn't figure out why. But this must have been it. He must have been afraid I'd pry the codes out of him."

Jhari looked up sharply. "If they're any good to you, *I* have the codes."

"What do you mean, if they're any good to me?"

"Anything that's already in the air will be off line. Keeps the enemy from tapping into the autofunctions and taking control of the equipment."

"But ground forces?"

"I can try to get through, tell them to back off. I *am* supposed to be the Planetary Governor."

Niki turned and leaned on a countertop, his back to the room. The fingers of one hand drummed lightly on the plastic. Chrysander slid into a chair in front of the local message console and lit it up.

"What are you doing?" said Jhari.

"Getting everybody evacuated to the bottom levels, I hope. Without a panic, if I'm lucky."

She would have asked him more. But Niki spun away from the countertop, his eyes wide. "Jhari, enter your codes. Then see if you can get their tactical system to tell me what they've put in the air, and where it is."

Jhari frowned, but didn't waste any time over it. The main net 'board was already lit; she dropped string after string into it, and the display screen pattern unraveled into black each time she did. After several precious minutes, it came to life with moving graphics. The ship was a red outline over the topography of Lamia; its coordinates ran next to it in blue, changing steadily. "Big one," Jhari croaked. "A bomber, by the specs. That'll be it."

Niki hunched over the screen, watched the numbers shift past. "Only one so far?" he asked, still watching. Jhari nodded. "That's what I want, then. Jhari, see if you can countermand that order with the surface troops."

Jhari had already started jabbing at the console; Chrysander had to ask the obvious question himself. "What are you going to do?"

Niki looked up a little from the display. The moving ship and its changing coordinates were reflected in one eye. With the ghost of a smile, he said, "I'm going to hijack a bomber."

Then he straightened up, took two steps back from the 'board, and disappeared.

"Come *on*," said Jhari to the screen in front of her. "So it's a state of emergency. Answer your fucking *calls*."

"You were right," Chrysander said, stunned. "He teleports." He stared at the space that, until moments ago, had had Niki in it. He felt a sudden foolish resentment: how dare such an amazing thing happen, at a moment when he had no time to stand amazed?

Jhari was entering commands furiously on the 'board. "God, I hope I can get voice link," she muttered. Then, to him, "It was the only possibility that connected everything. The Cheat, the gestalt, Lamia's PK index, what Niki's good at . . . Come on, you pig, give me queue priority."

"But where is he?"

Jhari turned to the monitor, tapped the red graphic of the Concorde bomber with a fingernail. "Right there," she said, and her voice made Chrysander's scalp prickle.

It all seemed to take years. He opened the wide-voice channels and began to talk. He'd told Niki that he could get only generalized effects, using the Voice on an audience. Now he had to reach an audience from a distance, demand from them speed and self-control, and know that if he got hesitation or panic instead, some of them could die.

But this was no audience of strangers. He thought of Faelle, bloodthirsty and carefree. His father, hiding in his office. The tech in the front room, the guard in the corridor. They were all of Lamia, all of the warrens, and because of that, he knew them. He sang his words for them, finding the part of him that was theirs and giving it back, binding them to each other before he asked anything of them. Binding himself to them. His mouth got dry, his throat got sore, and still he spoke, or sang. He lost track of what he was saying. The words weren't important—only what he did with them. His coverall was icy with sweat.

Behind him he could hear Jhari Sabayan: "I'll *tell* you where it came from—your Bear Triangle courier was SpecServe! I don't know what those weasels get out of having us blow each other up, but the sonofabitch had our codes, and forged my signature character! No, God damn it, *there is no plague!*"

He faltered at last, and fell silent. He had done everything he could, except sit white-knuckled at the console, wondering how many were left on the upper levels, if they were about to be hit from above, if, in spite of it all, there'd been a panic, and the Concorde's work was partly done. So he did that, too. Niki had removed himself from the routing room perhaps ten minutes ago.

Over his shoulder, he heard a thick, strangling noise from Jhari Sabayan.

On the display in front of her, a narrow-petaled red flower bloomed in time-lapse. Then he recognized the surface beneath it—Lamia's topography—and the color and design of the graphic. And the numbers next to the blossom, now frozen and flashing yellow. A second explosion painted red radials where the Concorde bomber had been. A third.

"I was right," Jhari said, her voice high and tight. "That was our drain cleaner."

He stood next to her, his hand on her shoulder, his mind pulled apart by thoughts that couldn't remain side by side. An agony of relief—it didn't matter, now, how many people had not reached the relative protection of the low tunnels. There would be no bomb. And simple agony. He'd come back from the dead.

"He wasn't on it," Chrysander realized, and said.

"What?"

"There's no reason why he should have still been on that bomber when it blew."

Jhari held still for a moment. Then she leaned forward and clutched her hair with both hands. "Oh, Jesus. Jesus," she gasped. "I'm an idiot. But it's not something you get used to right away . . . Jesus, Nik."

They sat silent for a moment. Then Jhari used the Concorde forces' tactical system to check on their surface troop movement. None—or rather, withdrawal. She'd stopped them. She used the tactical to hitchhike onto the main Concorde command net. (Explaining to Chrysander as she went. He thought she was talking a little too fast, a little too much.) As Planetary Governor and Concorde diplomatic representative, she declared Lamia to be nonhostile, not particularly useful to the Concorde as a possession, entering into diplomatic relations, and unworthy of Silence. She got on the voice link again, made sure that as many high-ranking people as possible among the Concorde regular forces knew that the saboteur had been a Special Services agent with codes SpecServe was forbidden to have. "I'm gonna break those weasels," she said softly, unsteadily, when she'd snuffed the link.

And still, theirs was the only movement in the room.

"Where is he?" she said at last, and there was so much laid bare in her expression that Chrysander had to turn away. There was no reason why Niki Falcon had to have been part of that red blossom of death. Chrysander had seen him alive when he was supposed to be dead, and assumed that all was well, that Niki Falcon's nightmares were done. Still, he hadn't come back.

Jhari rose, paced to the door, returned. Then, "No," she whispered. "Oh, no." And she bolted back toward the door to the front room.

Chrysander ran as well as he did anything else. But he couldn't catch up to her, not until she paused for him in the corridor outside BioEng. It was empty. "For God's sake," she snapped. "Have you given an all-clear? Do you think all those people like sitting in the sub-basement waiting for the ceiling to fall on them?"

"Where are you going?"

"Forget where I'm going. You've got other responsibilities. Stay here and take care of them." Then her expression softened, just a little, and she caught one of his hands, squeezed it clumsily. "If I come back, I'll tell you where I went, okay?"

It was not enough; but he could tell it was all she'd give him. He stepped back. "Good luck," he said, and realized he meant it. Then he walked quickly away, back toward Netcenter and the local console. Before he rounded the corner, he looked back. She was nowhere in sight.

When he came in the front room, he noticed the tech was gone. Of course—she was somewhere in the lower levels. He got on the box and declared an all-clear. If he sounded weary, it didn't matter this time.

He looked for the shoulder bag that held the Entropic. There it was, where he'd dropped it. Hadn't he flung the outcap on top? He didn't see it now. He slid the strap of the bag over his shoulder. Then he hesitated. He had to go somewhere, and he didn't want to start out until he was sure of the destination. Not a spatial "where." He had been a key, a weapon, a tool, and willing; but he wasn't that anymore. He could be replaced—

somewhere in the warren, even now, were others who would also be willing.

Perfect quiet in Netcenter; one of the strangest of juxtapositions. Jhari Sabayan's messages and orders would already be cracking the surface of the Silence, beginning the process that would bring this room back to life. And then what?

You've got other responsibilities. Stay here and take care of them. He wondered where his father was, and what he thought was going on. Was Faelle down in the tunnels, unable to shoot something and chafing over it?

A desire to shoot things, as a method of problem-solving, seemed to have become part of the Lamian character. Chrysander knew it; it was, or had been, anyway, part of his. If the whole culture were to lose its taste for it, what then? Shooting things did not create oases in the barren lands, after all.

The Voice also created no oases. But it could transform other barren places, wake a dormant seed or two. Lamia still had a need for someone who could sing or speak and be listened to, by people who had the power to bring water into dry places. And by the people who had need of that water, but were too foolish or proud or divided to admit it.

He stretched, savoring the freedom of movement.

I don't know why it begins with me in the rented hopper on Bellmaker's, leaning windward, starting the slow spiral down toward that smooth, straight bit of turf in those red-and-white hills. But it does. Not in the front chamber of Netcenter on Lamia, when for the first time in all those years I felt his heart beating under my hand. Not even on Lamia's surface, with sand snake-hissing against the snapped-down faceplate of Chrysander's hat, when through a grinding golden fog of sandstorm, I saw the black bird of prey that was Spin's ship—he hadn't lifted yet, I wasn't too late. Certainly not anywhere or when in the unmeasurable spaces between Lamia and Bellmaker's World, with the black ship's silent corridors wrapped in dim purplish-blue light, silence like the lid of a stone coffin that I lifted through sheer bloody-minded endurance.

No, I do know why my hopper descent over Bellmaker's roughlands is the beginning. Because, as I made my approach, I saw the straight, thin black line of him against the mottling of snow and brown grass and rust-red rock. He'd set me down at the port to get a hopper and meet him in that valley. He could have escaped me, one way or another, before I came down through the overcast. But he was there, and waiting. So that's the beginning of the new timeline.

I jumped down from the cockpit and crunched across the snow and frozen grass. The hillside was already sealed closed; the next fall of snow would hide the tracks that led to it. He stood, collar up, shoulders hunched, hands in his pockets, staring off at the tops of the hills. His hair tangled and whipped in the wind, across his face and in his eyes.

"You're sure of this?" I asked.

He nodded. "For now. Until I figure out what I'm doing. It'll still be here if I change my mind." Then his eyes dropped, focused on me. "Spin was right, you'd be a great gunner. But I don't have anything to shoot at." Very slowly, a smile moved his lips, like a gradual thaw.

His metabolism was stabilizing; his conversion had, this time, really occurred, and all the parts of him, born and made, were settling toward a balance of power. The color and texture of his skin showed it, the clarity of his eyes, the steadiness of his hands. It was too soon to know if he still needed the drug. But given time, he would, perhaps, even gain a little weight.

"Well, I've been a Planetary Governor without a planet. I suppose I can be a gunner without portfolio."

"Jhari," he said, and stopped. He walked a few steps away and stopped that, too. "I don't know what I am," he said at last, "or what I'm going to do, or what I'm *able* to do. I seem to have reached a point at which I have only future, and no past to base it on. I'm not . . ." He looked over his shoulder at me, rather wildly. "If you asked me questions right now, I'm honestly not sure where the answers would come from."

"Oh, talk sense," I said, and saw him start and blink. "What you're working up to saying is that I should go away, because you don't know if staying would be good for me."

He looked unexpectedly young, and a little silly, staring at me. "Yes, but it sounds terrible if you put it that way."

"Too bad. Listen to me, you self-absorbed ass. What point do you think *I'm* at? I'm out of a job. Out of a career, actually, because the Concorde isn't going to pay me to clean toilets once everything I've done comes out. I'm a full-featured adult, capable of making up my own mind and taking my own risks. If I want to run off with you, I'm entitled. If I discover, later, that it's not what I want, I can leave. The only question you have to answer—and you can ask it yourself—is whether *you* want to run off with *me*."

Hearts don't really stop in suspenseful moments. The reverse, in fact, is true: you can hear it, banging away in your chest, making giant seashell noises in your ears. However the suspense ends, it's always a relief to your circulatory system.

"Yes," he said, in a voice so small the wind almost got it before I did. "I would like very much to run off with you."

I reached out my hand, and he reached out his. But it was too damn cold on that piece of Bellmaker's World to stand there for long.

"Let's go get the *Gerfalcon* out of mothballs," he said, smiling.

"Shall I drive?" I asked.

"Hell, no. I'm too good a resource to waste."

ADDITION TO LASTFILE
T23 91

A minute ago, he arrived, in his inimitable fashion, on the second-floor deck behind me, naked, wet, smelling of seawater and sun. There's something that happens, in the air or in my head, a moment before he manifests himself that tells me he's coming. I wonder if it was always there, or if I've changed, too.

"You're dripping on my shoulder," I told him.

"Good. Come on down. We'll scare the fish."

His hair, like rivulets of black water, slid across my ear. "I should finish this. Mahde wants to run it next week as the lead."

"And *Yesterday's News* wants an analysis of Kerneghian's statement on pacifism."

"Damn! I thought you wanted me to come swimming. Why didn't you tell me this before?"

He looked charmingly vacant, surprised. "They haven't told you yet?"

I took his wet head in both hands and kissed him on the mouth. "You're hell to live with."

He smiled. "I told you I would be. But you do get a jump on your deadlines this way. Come swimming."

"In a minute."

"Promise?"

"Promise."

And he was gone.

I stashed my article, and called this up, because it occurred to me that it wasn't finished. It's been over a year since the preceding section, and perspective has been sneaking up on me.

It's almost a shame I no longer believe in my Unauthorized Reader. He was the perfect excuse, and to talk about Niki, still, I seem to need an excuse. Whatever the reason for it then, now I'm just selfish. This knowledge, these events, this *life*, is all mine.

Three months ago, on Lamia, Caitlin Wyn was brought out of suspension. It was a very close thing, several times; but the modifications they made, based on Tomas Damion's studies of Niki, held up. She's still alive, and still improving. Damion (who may yet become a rudimentary human being) is sounding almost optimistic.

Me? Niki says I'm doing more for the future of humanity than he's ever likely to do; the power of a free press and all that.

Chrysander Harris makes his own legends. If he wants them immortalized in prose, he can hire someone. But I don't believe he thinks about that. I got a present from him for my last birthday, a disk with a handwritten label. The piece, an instrumental, is called "Ballad for Falconer's Guns." There was a note with it, with a little cartoon of a piano shooting laser beams. He and I have the only copies recorded.

And there's Niki, who teleports. You say teleporting isn't enough by itself, that knowing he teleports doesn't tell you about him, that it's what one *does* with teleportation that matters? Quite right.

Which is exactly why teleporting, or not teleporting, isn't important, except to people like Jacob Ridgeway and Morwenna Glyndwr-Jones. It isn't complete in itself—and all the important things in the world are.

What is important is that Niki Falcon has left a trail behind him, of changed lives, reexamined beliefs, rediscovered knowledge. Chrysander Harris, Tomas Damion, me. Martin Spinelle and Laura Brass. And more people, living and dead—in Cymru, Emerald City, FourCorners, *anywhere*—whom I've never met, never will meet, who came close to him and were changed.

Niki Falcon; who he is, what he does, what he thinks and says: this is complete in itself. Yet it's not inert, but reactive. It's replicated infinitely, from a single point—him—spiraling outward and upward in time and space with each life that comes in contact with his. I'm a point on that spiral, one of the people he's touched and changed. I'm also a potential starting point for another spiral.

By this method he—and all of us—change the world, and are changed, and live forever in motion. Death doesn't even slow the spiral's climb.

Still, here's this file. It, too, should be complete in itself. So, Unauthorized Reader, whatever and whoever you are or were or weren't, though you, too, are now part of it, to live and grow and change forever—this is the end of the story.

-30-

ENDFILE

About the Author

(Number Two in a Series)

Emma Bull was born in 1954 in Torrance, California. Her earliest memory is of looking over the backyard fence, watching the neighbor mow his lawn. Since the Bull family left California when Emma was, at most, two years old, she can't have been tall enough to do any such thing. But this dubious memory has contributed to her fondness for watching somebody else mow the lawn.

She is the author of *War for the Oaks* and co-editor (with her husband, Will Shetterly) of the Liavek anthologies. She performs with Cats Laughing, a psychedelic rock, blues, and loud folk band. Her three requirements for a good writing atmosphere are coffee, cookies, and something exciting on the stereo; she recommends Peter Gabriel's ''Here Comes the Flood'' as the score for the ending of this book.